MOTHER MAY I?

There I was, face to face with a woman, no more than five feet tall, who was wearing the all too familiar—and yet oh so flattering—spiffy brown uniform of the Manhattan meter maid.

Her stubby arms were crossed over her chest and she kept her head cocked to the right as she watched me emerge from the car. Maybe she had never seen a human being like me before, but the ___ ___ ___ ___ that I was, inde___ ___ ___ ___ her mouth was ___ ___ ___ ___ teeth poked out ju___ ___ ___ sat crooked on h___ ___ ___ of black hair looked like they were trying to escape from under her chapeau.

I was mesmerized. Not only had I never seen a person who looked like the embodiment of the word ''befuddled,'' but I had never in my life seen a woman with so much facial hair. I tried not to stare at her upper lip but it was impossible.

''What are you doing?'' she asked, scrunching up her face. She scratched at her lower lip with her two teeth tines.

An honest answer would have been breaking and entering, but I smiled and tried to look stupid.

''What do you mean, officer?''

———————

''Fast-talking, funny, and smart,
Sydney Sloane is one lady who can think
on her feet and knock you off yours.''
David Morrell, author of
Double Image and *Extreme Denial*

Other Sydney Sloane Mysteries by
Randye Lordon
from Avon Books

FATHER FORGIVE ME

MOTHER MAY I

a sydney sloane mystery

RANDYE LORDON

AVON BOOKS NEW YORK

AVON BOOKS
A division of
The Hearst Corporation
1350 Avenue of the Americas
New York, New York 10019

First Avon Books Printing: April 1998

AVON TRADEMARK REG. U.S. PAT. OFF. AND IN OTHER COUNTRIES, MARCA REGISTRADA, HECHO EN U.S.A.

Printed in the U.S.A.

WCD   10 9 8 7 6 5 4 3 2 1

For the Immediates.
Selaine, Jay, Allen, Marla.
Zelda & Harry
Buddy, Ruth, Wendy, Larry, Candy.

You have all touched my heart, my soul,
my funny bone, and my rage.
Thank you.

Acknowledgments

For their kindness and invaluable assistance, I would like to thank Kris Graue at Lincoln Controls, Inc.; Ed Silverman at The Jewish Home & Hospital for the Aged in Manhattan; Dr. Blake Kerr of Wainscott, New York; Kelly McCoy; William and Arlene McCoy; Officer Stacey Rabinowitz; and Cheryl Pottberg.

I would also like to thank the following friends for their support, wisdom, humor, and, why even guidance: SW, Cyndi Raftus, Elizabeth, Jennie and Peter, Mr. Lennny (a Pearl among men), Neal, Karen Chester, Lee and Arlene Shelley, and Ms. Brooklyn herself, Sarah Segal.

Charlotte . . . thank you for doing what you do so well and doing it for me. Cynthia . . . again, and again, and again. Bettina . . . many thanks.

Last, but not least, I would like to thank Annemarie and Tess, who laughed at all the funny parts.

One

My last client, ninety-two-year-old Selma Onder-donk, proved to me that a person can get through two world wars and several personal tragedies, and still retain her own teeth. This is, for me, a most comforting thought.

I met Selma through her brother, Enoch Zarlin. Enoch is a strikingly handsome eighty-five-year-old retired investment banker who is also my eighty-one-year-old Aunt Minnie's "main squeeze," as she likes to say. In October he hired me and my business partner, Max Cabe, on behalf of his sister, Selma.

Max and I are private investigators. We've had our business, CSI, for over twelve years now, and though we've helped friends in the past, this was unusual all the way around. To start with, I'd never had a ninety-two-year-old client before. It shouldn't make a difference, but it did. Maybe her age made her endearing or vulnerable, but there was something deeply compelling about Selma Onderdonk. Perhaps she reminded me of my mother. I know I thought about Mom whenever I saw Selma, but the two were not really alike at all. My mother was tall; Selma is petite; Mom was full-blooded and fiery, whereas Selma is fair and contemplative. Who knows what the connection was? Sometimes you just connect, even if you don't understand it until much later. As far as the outcome, well, I normally feel good about *something* when we close a case, but it's almost

1

two weeks after the fact, and I'm still confused about what, exactly, it is that I feel.

It all started on a fine autumn morning. I was awakened too early by a lustful pigeon who was cooing loudly under my bedroom window. By the time I threw a balled-up pair of socks at the licentious old coot, I was wide-awake and annoying my partner, Leslie, who for some reason wasn't bothered by the impassioned pleas of the lecherous bird. I don't like pigeons, I never have, and when they mate they are particularly irritating. Not wanting to start the day in an advanced state of vexation, I glanced at the clock and knew I was sure to get a solo lane in the pool at the local health club, which I did. As a matter of fact until the very end of my workout I had the whole pool to myself, which in this overcrowded city is bliss. After four thousand yards, I showered and arrived at my office earlier than usual, where I found my Aunt Minnie's boyfriend waiting for me.

"Enoch? What are you doing here?" I asked, genuinely surprised when I found him sitting on the stairs in front of our third-floor office, bent over the *Wall Street Journal*.

He jumped at the sound of my voice. "Sydney, my dear . . ." He held out his hand and warmly clasped mine. "You startled me."

"Sorry about that." I offered him a hand up.

"Thank you." He was over six feet tall and handled his height with elegance and grace.

"Were you coming to see me?" I asked, nodding to the door behind him, which was stenciled Cabe-Sloane Investigations.

"Whatever gave you that idea?" He pushed a strand of white hair out of his eyes. When he smiled, his eyes positively sparkled.

"Hey, they don't call me a hotshot detective for nothing. Come on in. I'll buy you a cup of coffee." As I rooted around in my bag looking for my keys, I wondered what had brought Enoch to my office. Not only had he never been there before, but at 8:30 in the morning, it wasn't even

2

office hours for most businesses. The only thing I could think of was that he wanted to ask for Minnie's hand in marriage. They had been a couple for close to two years now, and it was no secret that he was crazy about her. Aunt Minnie married; just the thought of it made me smile.

"Beautiful day, huh?" I said to fill the gap.

"Yes, truly, there is nothing quite so splendid as the month of October. Especially in New York City."

I unlocked the main office door and led Enoch through the door on the right, which leads to my office. "Coffee?" I asked as we entered the sun-filled room.

"No thank you. I've had my morning fix, but please feel free to have some if you like." Mine is the corner office, and Enoch walked to the windows, that face east and look out onto Broadway. "Quite a view you have here. You must spend hours watching life filter past your window."

"Well, on the rare occasion when I do have time to watch life filter by, I only get anxious, because it means I'm not working."

"The work will always be there, my dear. You mustn't ever castigate yourself for taking a moment to breathe. Breathing is good."

"So I hear." I hung my jacket on the coat rack and told Enoch over my shoulder, "I tell you, though, I'm more drawn to the way the sunlight plays in here."

Enoch turned and studied the spacious room. "Yes, I see what you mean." He rested his hands on his hips as he took in my home away from home. Aunt Minnie calls Enoch *Easy* (which is actually based on his initials, E.Z.), but she says that it suits him, and, of course, she's right. Watching him standing there I could actually envision him as a young man, deliberate and decidedly comfortable with himself. Finally he declared, "I like your office, my dear. It truly seems to reflect you in that it's easy on the eye, comfortable, and yet not *so* relaxed as to be unprofessional."

I grinned at the handsome gentleman standing in the sunlight. "Now I know what Minnie sees in you, Enoch."

"Oh yes? What's that?" He straightened his tie and craned his neck.

"You're a good bullshitter."

"Nonsense, everything I've told you is sincere . . . heart-felt, you could say." His smile revealed a set of extraordinarily white teeth, which I assumed—at this point in his life—were a damned fine investment.

"Mmhm. So, what brings you here? I don't think you've ever been to my office before."

"No, I haven't. And I wish I could say I was here for pleasure, but the fact is, I want to hire you." With his back to the sun, momentarily blinding me, I couldn't tell if he was serious or pulling my leg.

"To . . ." I asked cautiously.

"To investigate a murder."

He could have bowled me over with a feather.

Murder? Enoch? The two didn't seem to fit. I talk to my Aunt Minnie every day, and she never mentioned a word of this.

"Why don't we sit down?" I suggested as I sank into my desk chair.

"Fine." Enoch walked the length of the room and sat on a peach-colored director's chair facing my desk. He crossed one long leg over the other and rubbed his forehead with his hand.

"Are you all right?" I asked.

"I'm just tired. It's been a difficult week. Do you know my sister?" He squinted.

"I know you have one, but we've never met." The week before, Minnie had told me that Enoch's grand-niece, Jessica, had committed suicide. Leslie, the woman I love and live with, had sent Enoch a condolence card on our behalf. "Is this about Jessica?"

Enoch took a deep breath and glanced at his watch. "Do you have time for this?"

"I always have time for you, Enoch."

He splayed open his hands in a helpless gesture and

looked almost pained. "As silly as it might sound, coming from an old man like me, Selma's my big sister, Sydney. She's also my last sibling—my last immediate family member, for that matter—and my best friend as far back as I can remember. She called me late last night, very upset. The stress from having lost Jessica has been overwhelming for her, and, naturally, at her age, this has concerned me." Enoch proceeded to give me Selma's entire family history, including details of her happy marriage to Günter Onderdonk and the tragic death of their only child, Margot. Selma raised her granddaughter, Jessica, after Margot died in a car accident.

Jessica had been found in the garage of her Brooklyn home with the car motor running, an apparent suicide.

"It turns out that it wasn't." Enoch cleared his throat.

"Wasn't a suicide?" I asked.

"That's right. Jessica didn't kill herself. She was murdered." Enoch wrapped his tapering fingers around the arms of the chair and kneaded the wood.

"How do you know?"

"I guess the police were suspicious right from the start. There was no suicide note, and her husband—who's a physician, and a diabetic—had left his office early that day and refused to account for his whereabouts. He has several hours unaccounted for. When an autopsy was performed, they discovered that she had been injected with insulin. There was also traces of chloral hydrate."

"And so, naturally, hubby automatically becomes suspect number one." I finished the scenario for him.

"That's correct. However, Selma's convinced Michael didn't do it. That's why she was calling. She wants *me* to do something to help him."

"Do you know Michael?"

"Sure I do. He's a nice boy."

"A nice boy capable of murder?" I asked.

He pursed his lips.

"What?" I questioned his body language.

5

"This is breaking Selma's heart. You have to understand that she loves that boy as if he were her own. I don't know what he is or isn't capable of, but Selma's convinced he didn't do it. Personally, it disturbs me that he won't tell anyone where he was when Jessica died, or that he refused legal counsel at first. But it doesn't matter what *I* think, I told Sel I'd help her. She just lost her granddaughter. She doesn't want to lose a boy who is like her own flesh and blood." He put his hand into his jacket pocket and withdrew a checkbook. "Ergo, I want to hire you and Max to find out what happened to my grandniece."

I held up my hand and waved him away. "Put your checkbook back in your pocket," I scolded him.

"Oh no, my dear, this is business. Friendship is one thing, and business another. I came to you for your professional help, not for a favor from a friend. Am I making myself clear?"

"But this is precisely what friends are for, Enoch."

"Sydney, I suggest you don't waste our time haggling over money. I will pay the going rate, plain and simple." He opened the checkbook and pulled a pen from his breast pocket. "To whom do I make it out and for what amount?"

I took a deep breath and exhaled. I knew there was no use in even trying to talk sense into the man. "Cabe-Sloane Investigations." I told him as I opened the top left drawer and pulled out a standard contract. I explained the terms of the contract as he filled out the check. Enoch grunted and nodded at the appropriate places, but I knew he didn't hear a word I said. Since he'd made a fortune as an investment banker, it surprised me that Enoch didn't pay more attention to money. Although my parents' estates have left me comfortable enough to never have to work another day if I don't want to, I can't fathom not looking at a price tag or the right side of the menu, but that's me.

We both signed on the dotted line, and Enoch gave me all the information I needed to start the investigation, including Selma's address and the name of the officer in

Brooklyn Heights who was handling the case. As I was walking him to the door, my partner, Max, came racing into the outer office like the Mad Hatter in *Alice's Adventures in Wonderland*. He stopped short when he saw Enoch.

"Enoch!" Max, who is a ruggedly handsome, middle-aged man, hugged Enoch warmly. "Good to see you. What the hell are you doing here?"

"Mr. Zarlin is a new client." I perched myself on our secretary's desk and idly pondered where she might be. It was now almost ten, which made her nearly an hour late for work.

"Really?" Max stepped back a foot. "For what? Why?"

Enoch glanced at his wristwatch and apologized. "I'm afraid Sydney will have to fill you in, Max. I'm already late for my writing class."

"Writing class?" we asked in unison. "I thought you were taking Yoga classes," I added.

"I am. However, I made the mistake once of telling your aunt that I'd always wanted to write fiction. Next thing I knew I was signed up for a class." He chuckled like a schoolboy, which, technically, he was. "Between you and me, I've fallen head over heels in love with my teacher, but I think her nose ring could present a problem, if not physically, symbolically. I shudder to think of what it might mean. Anyway, I'm off. Let me know what you find, Sydney."

When he was gone, Max started a pot of coffee, which we took into his office. A dart-riddled photograph was pinned to his dart board. "Who's that?" I asked before he got started.

"Byron De La Beckwith. He's the one who shot Medgar Evers in sixty-three. They finally found the arrogant putz guilty of murder." Max has no patience for white supremacists, any kind of bigotry or zealotry.

I sank into the loveseat and explained what I had learned from Enoch. Jessica Callahan's death had been made to look like a suicide, but as there was no note, no history of depression, and no accounting for her husband's whereabouts for close to three hours on the day of her death, the DA had decided to request an autopsy. The autopsy revealed that the cause of death was carbon monoxide poisoning, which was what they had expected, given that she had been found in her garage with the car running for what they determined to be at least an hour, probably longer. What they hadn't anticipated was an elevated level of insulin in her system, elevated enough to cause even more suspicion. The medical examiner found the track from the injection, but no paraphernalia. No syringe, no nothing. That, combined with the fact that her husband refused to cooperate with the police, was enough for the DA's office to think they had a case against him. Dr. Michael Callahan had been arrested and arraigned, and had probably been released on bail this very morning.

"You going to start with him?" Max asked when I had finished.

"Actually, if Callahan's released today, my guess is he'll be easier to talk to a little later, after he's had a chance to wash jail off. I thought I'd start with Selma."

"Good idea. You want me to go with you to meet her?"

"No. But if I need some backup with the ninety-two-year-old, I'll give you a call."

"You're so very amusing."

"Why, some folks would even call it droll. Okay, I'm out of here. I'll be back in a little while."

Just outside our building, en route to the subway, I bumped into our secretary, Kerry Norman. She was wearing a paisley cowboy hat, a lime-green leather motorcycle jacket with fringe, and shoes that resembled fat black pontoons. She was also hanging on the arm of a man who could melt dry ice with his eyes. Patrick was Kerry's latest boyfriend, and a man prone to unforgivable taste in clothing. Before the two of them met, Kerry dressed like any other aspiring actress in New York City, alternating between basic black from head to toe or the layered look. However, when she met Patrick, a self-proclaimed Soho artist, her style changed drastically. Whereas her clothing statement before had screamed *Artîste*, it now read *Nightmare of Color on Flotation Devices*.

Kerry shrieked when she saw me. "Sydney! You must hate me I'm so late for work!"

"Kerry, how could I hate you? You wear such entertaining clothes." I gave Patrick a kiss and chided him, "It's all your fault, you know."

"I brought a note for her tardiness." He flirted shamelessly, never once letting go of Kerry.

"Not her lateness, Pat, her fashion sense. She used to have some, now it's gone and I hold you entirely responsible."

"Cool," he said, the way only a groovy, laid-back, now-and-happening artist could.

The sun reflected off Kerry's jacket, temporarily blinding me, but bringing me back to the moment. "You planning to visit the office today?" I asked in passing.

"Do I have a choice?" She squeezed Patrick's right arm.

"Sure you do." I smiled and sidestepped them. "You could quit, in which case we could replace you with someone who actually wants to be a secretary. Wow, imagine that."

"Hardy-har-har." Kerry pulled Patrick in the direction of CSI.

I proceeded to the subway and considered how I had initially thought that Enoch wanted Minnie's hand in marriage. I would have preferred the marriage concept over a murder investigation, but that's life, isn't it? Just a big old roller coaster ride. Roller coasters . . . I could feel the subway train pulling into the station under my feet. I bolted down the steps two at a time and made it into a subway car just as the doors were beginning to close.

Two

The Treelane Nursing Home is in Greenwich Village, about a block and a half away from the Hudson River, on a street where there are no trees and no lane. It is a wide, deserted street that had once been a factory road. Years earlier, two of the larger factory buildings had been converted into luxury co-ops, but both buildings were still unoccupied. Sharing the block with the Treelane was a small deli, a trendy new Italian coffee house, two bars, and a shop that sold—among other things—leather whips, harnesses, enormous rubber appendages, and red lace bras—just the sort of paraphernalia I imagined the nursing home residents needed.

At the front door, I buzzed to be admitted. A huge cardboard jack-o'-lantern with crepe-paper legs was taped to the inside of the smudged glass door. Very festive. Once inside, however, I realized that Jack had been a decoy. It was a dull place, neither dirty nor clean, warm nor cold. The entrance was overwhelmingly beige. Even the coffee tables—which were actually simulated oak—felt beige.

There were three wheelchairs parked at the far end of the lobby. Two were beige and empty with sagging leather seats. The third was blue and occupied. Its dozing driver, who looked like a female Jimmy Durante, jerked to when the door slammed loudly behind me. She let out a yelp and looked confused as she grabbed the arms of her chair and bent forward. A young woman with an unfortunate hairdo was positioned behind a pass-through that, from my vantage point, made her look like a fortune-teller in Coney Island.

"It's all right, Isabelle." the fortune-teller called out. "It was just the door."

"Floor?" Isabelle squinted at me from the wheelchair and then looked at the floor with great intensity. "What's wrong with the floor?" she asked, clearly miffed at having been awakened from her nap.

I shrugged and smiled dumbly.

Isabelle stared at me as if I had two heads. Before looking away, she declared loudly that I was "stupid," then quickly lost interest in both me and the floor.

I walked up to the fortune-teller and was nearly bowled over by the scent of her perfume. This woman was definitely combustible.

"You can't take Isabelle personally," she said goodnaturedly as she methodically removed staples from a stack of papers.

"Okay, I won't." It was the weirdest thing; this woman didn't seem affected in the least by her scent, and yet my eyes were practically burning out of their sockets.

"How can I help you?"

Position, squeeze, remove. Position, squeeze, remove. She was piling up a neat stack of staples.

"I'm here to see one of your residents, Selma Onderdonk."

She nodded without taking her eyes off the task at hand. "And you are . . ."

"A family friend."

"Okay. First thing you have to do is sign in." Still without removing her eyes from her job, she motioned with her head to a ledger on the counter. "Then I'll give you—"

"Oh my God, they'll let anybody in this joint!" A familiar laugh followed the friendly insult, and when I looked up to see who it was aimed at, I was floored. Coming out of the elevator was Naomi Lewis. I hadn't seen her since high school graduation when we shared a joint in the locker room and she confided that she was going off to join the Peace Corps. The two of us hooted with laughter and fell into each other's arms, squealing with delight. Naomi was amazing; aside from the straitlaced outfit and an extra twenty pounds, she looked absolutely the same.

"I can't believe you're here." Her smile was irrepressible. "You look fabulous. I hate you."

"*You* should talk, you look exactly the same."

"You big liar. I've gained a whole other person here. What are you, crazy? But I am happy," she added before I could argue. "Fat, happy, sassy, and in love." She flattened her hand to her chest and rolled her brown eyes skyward.

"New love?" I asked as she led us to a beige sofa.

"Honey, the only *new* thing in my life is my lipstick. Nah, my love is old, but solid, you know?"

I nodded, like a learned old sage. "So what are you doing here?" I asked.

"Being boss," she said with an exaggerated New York accent.

"You?"

"I know." Her face lit up. "Only *senile* people would hire me to be boss. It's great."

"Go on."

"Seriously, I really am the boss." She held out her hands for me to look at her, as if her outfit was proof enough. Sneakers, nylons, business suit, briefcase, knapsack.

"God, remember your stupid polka-dot sneakers?" I asked fondly.

"Remember? Hell, I still have 'em. I keep promising my daughter if she plays her cards right I'll give her all my old clothes and she can open a retro shop. Cool, huh? We've lived long enough to be retro."

"You have a daughter?"

"Two. You?"

"No kids."

"Okay. The last I heard about you was from Debbie Martini. She said that you were a cop and living in Brooklyn with a woman."

"That was a long time ago. You still see Debbie?"

"I haven't seen her in years. From what I've heard, though, she left the fire department and opened a bed-and-breakfast with her sister someplace you don't want to be, like Utah or Arizona. So, is it true, after Jimmy Ryan you turned to girls?"

I grinned. "Jimmy Ryan. You never forget anything, do you? I haven't thought about him in years. I wonder where he is."

"My first guess would be jail. Either that or the Marines. You always had bad taste in boys. It's probably a good thing you're a lesbian. You're still a lesbian, aren't you?"

"Oh yeah. I'm still gay. Men are too messy."

"Please, don't I know it. So? Stability? Same gal?"

"Stability, yes. Same gal, no. Get this, though, I moved back into my parents old apartment on West End."

"Oh my God, I *loved* that apartment! Rent stabilized?"

"Rent controlled." Which meant it was even cheaper.

"Figures. And we bought a place at the height of the market. Still a cop?"

"No, I left the force fifteen years ago. I'm a private investigator now."

"So what are you doing here?"

"I'm here to see a woman named Selma Onderdonk."

"Oh Selma, Selma's great. How do you know her?"

"I don't. Her brother hired me—"

"Oh my God, that's right—her granddaughter." Naomi checked her watch and sighed. "Selma's a nice woman and this has been real hard on her." Naomi stood up. "Listen, I hate to do this, but I got to run. Promise me we'll get together." She stood up and pulled me into a tight embrace. "Here." She handed me a business card. "Call me, okay?"

We hugged, and ten minutes later I was on the fourth floor looking for room 411.

The Treelane was like a cross between a hospital and a dorm. As I wandered through the halls I got a chance to look in the residents' rooms. In the dayroom a group of people were watching a soap opera, or at least they were pointed in the direction of the TV. In another room a tall, painfully thin young woman in black stretch pants and a flowing leopard top was leading an exercise class, encouraging her elderly students to, "Stretch them muscles, kids, we don't want to get flabby!" In yet another common room, three women, deep in conversation, sat at a table sewing what looked to be a quilt.

When I found room 411, it was empty. I paused in the doorway.

The room was the same twelve-by-twelve-foot square allotted to all the residents. Beige tiled floors, two windows, beige blinds, wood-veneer armoire, two chairs, one bed, and one of those hospital rolling tables you can pull over yourself while in bed so you can eat or play solitaire, or whatever.

But Selma's room looked different. First of all, unlike most of the other rooms I'd passed, it was a private room. Secondly, she had taken the time to make it hers. A colorful rag weave rug covered the floor, a huge vase with silk flowers sat beside the armoire, and there was a bookcase loaded with books and photo albums. She also had a small parsons table that fit nicely under the windows, which she apparently used as her desk. Selma's space showed that she had gone to some lengths to make the room her home, as opposed to just a room in a home. But still, in the shadows, the room lost its own identity and became like all the others; small, lifeless, and claustrophobic.

"Can I help you?" An agreeable voice came from behind me.

I swung around and was met with a diminutive woman whose face had the lines of someone accustomed to laughing. She cocked her head to the right and repeated her question.

"Selma?" I asked with incredulity. If this woman was ninety-two, I wanted to know what yogurt she ate.

"Not quite." When she smiled her whole face seemed to settle into place. "But I can show you where she is."

"Thank you." I followed behind her, wondering if I ought to apologize for having mistaken her for a nearly one-hundred-year-old woman. I decided it was best to leave well enough alone.

As we hurried up the hallway I saw that my guide's posture was absolutely perfect, not an easy boast for a woman of her age, which—after closer inspection—I put to be somewhere around seventy. The same age my mother would have been.

When we got to the end of the hall, we turned left and went down another corridor I hadn't seen before. At the end was a glassed-in sunroom that had once been a large terrace. It was a bright, cheery room that felt like it was in another building altogether. Though there was activity everywhere you looked, the room was peaceful. At one table a foursome was playing cards. In the middle of the room was a young woman with a one-year-old, surrounded by several residents—all taking turns holding the baby. A man in a robe was sitting by himself at one end of the room. At first glance he looked engrossed in the book on his lap, but a second look revealed that he was sound asleep.

Without a word, my guide escorted me to the other end of the room, where I found Selma Onderdonk hunched over a piece of stationery at a small writing table.

"Selma." She gently laid her hand on Selma's shoulder.

Enoch's sister twisted her whole upper torso so she could turn and see who was standing beside her. When she was contorted into what looked like a really uncomfortable position, she looked over the rim of her glasses and said, "What? Oh, Beatrice." She twisted slightly further to glance at me, but turned her attention back to her friend.

"You have a visitor." Beatrice stepped back and lifted her hand toward me as a way of an introduction.

"Oh?" Selma twisted back around to her writing paper and placed her pen down. She then carefully swiveled around in her chair, and brought her legs to the side so she could maneuver out from the desk. I watched as Beatrice helped Selma up off her chair and over the fifteen paces to an intimate seating arrangement in the sunlight. Not a word was spoken between them, but the way they moved together made me think this was a routine they both knew well. It also made me wonder what my body would feel like at ninety-two. Would all the exercise I subject myself to now work against me as an old woman? Would the aches and pains I am oh-so-familiar with now ultimately contort my body into a pretzel of arthritic pain?

When Selma was settled, Beatrice left us alone.

She didn't look like a Selma, though I don't know what a Selma looks like, per se. I suppose I expected a Golda Meir double, with wiry hair, a bulbous nose, and thick eyebrows. Enoch's sister was none of those things. She was short and slender, wore makeup and earrings, and was dressed in loose gray woolen slacks, a sweater the color of maize, and big black sneakers. Her black-rimmed glasses were shaped like TV screens and magnified her eyes, making her look baffled or confused, which, I was soon to learn, she wasn't.

"My name is Sydney." I sat on the edge of my seat and leaned toward her. "Sydney Sloane. Your brother, Enoch, is a friend of mine."

Selma listened with her head cocked slightly to the right, as though she favored that ear. "Well, dear, any friend of Enoch's is a friend of mine. Now what brings you to this stuffy old place?" Selma smiled and extended a veined, bony hand, taking mine with a surprisingly firm grasp. Her skin was dry and her hand felt almost too big in mine, but when she touched me, it was as if an electrical current shot straight to my heart. I have always had a warm spot for the elderly. Maybe it's because I lost both my parents before they could qualify for senior status, or because my Aunt Minnie and I are best friends; hell, it could simply be because one of these days I'll be old and want to be treated with respect, but whatever it is, when Selma Onderdonk took my hand, I felt an immediate connection.

"I'm a private investigator, Selma. Enoch's hired me to find out what happened to Jessica."

She held on to my hand without muttering a sound. Finally she tightened her hold and leaned toward me. "Jessica didn't kill herself. I also know in my heart that Michael wouldn't hurt her."

"How do you know that?" I asked.

She let go of my hand, placed her hands on her knees, and studied me carefully. "I know love, and I know he loved her with all his heart. You cannot murder someone you *really* love." She arched an eyebrow and nodded once. "Wanting to end the pain for someone you love, like this euthanasia business—that's one thing—but *murder*? Like this?" She pushed the corners of her lips down and shook her head. "No way." She wet her lips and said, "You think I'm a nutsy old lady, don't you?"

"No. No, I don't." I couldn't take my eyes off hers. "But I need to ask you a few questions about both Jessica and Michael, if that's all right . . ."

"Of course it's all right. Anything."

As I took a small spiral notebook out of my bag I asked, "When did you last see Jessica?"

"The day she died. She had just come back from California and she was visiting me here."

"That was a Wednesday?"

"That's right."

"Did she come with Michael?"

"No. It was during the middle of the day and he had office hours and rounds to make at the hospital. He's a doctor, you know."

"I see. Did you have a long visit that day?"

The visiting baby in the middle of the room let out a gleeful cry, which distracted Selma. The room was mesmerized by the baby. When she finally answered, she seemed momentarily confused and mumbled, "Jessica was here."

"Do you remember, did she stay long?" Though it's never easy to question immediate family members when they are in the throes of mourning, it was particularly hard for me with Selma. I don't know if it was because she was so old, or because she simply looked so vulnerable and I wanted to protect her, but the fact is, hard though it may be, the questions had to be asked.

"Can you tell me about your visit with Jessica?" I gently tried to bring her back to me.

"She was excited. Some good news about her work."

"So she was happy? In good spirits?"

"Oh yes, but she was always happy. Did Enoch tell you that I introduced them?"

"Jessica and Michael?" Just seeing the excitement in her eyes made me smile.

"Yes!" Clearly this was a story Selma enjoyed telling.

"No. Tell me."

Selma proceeded to reminisce about her granddaughter, starting with Jessica's childhood and ending with the story of how Selma had played cupid for the two young people. As she segued from one story into another, Selma shared her love and loss with me, trying to use her memories as a balm. But it was impossible, because she couldn't avoid coming back to her loss, and each time she did, her eyes made me want to reach out and promise her that nothing would ever hurt her again. Before we knew it the Treelane staff was herding the residents in for lunch.

"Oh dear." Selma sighed when a young man told her it was time to eat. "I never thought I'd say this, but, aside from jelly beans, food has gotten boring. I used to love to eat, but now . . ." She made a sour face. "It's in the taste buds, you know."

"What do you mean?"

"Well . . ." She held out a hand and I helped her out of the chair. "The older you get, the less sensitive your taste buds are. If food has no flavor, you lose interest in it. There's a gal here, maybe ten years younger than me, who loves the food here. She says it doesn't matter that everything tastes like sawdust to the rest of us because it reminds her of her mother's cooking, so she loves it!" Selma laughed until she started coughing.

"Careful, now." I gently patted her on the back as I walked her through the sunroom to the dining room.

"Oh, I'm okay." She squeezed my hand again and sighed loudly. "I wasn't much help today, was I?"

"Sure you were." I spoke the truth. People think that as a private investigator, I know exactly what I'm looking for when I ask to talk to them. But the fact is, nine times out of ten, when I'm starting a case, nothing could be further from the truth. Essentially, I begin with a blank canvas. Then someone comes along and throws a subject on it . . . in this instance, a murder victim. So now there's this image of a dead woman lying in the middle of an otherwise stark white canvas. The investigation process is a matter of filling in the composition. In a way, my talk with Selma gave me a pastel wash for a background.

When Selma asked if I'd be back, I told her yes.

"It gets lonely here. Not that the people aren't nice— they're just so . . . old!" It was something my dad would have said, and the thought of him made me ache, just a little. I missed my folks.

When I left, the fourth floor was assembled for a lunch of tomato soup, melba toast, and stewed prunes. No wonder their taste buds were in revolt.

Their lunch did, however, remind me that aside from a cup of coffee after my swim, I hadn't eaten yet and I was hungry. The Village has an overabundance of restaurants, cafés, and unusual fast-food stores, so I decided to start uptown on foot and see what crossed my path. I didn't know what I wanted to eat. The only thing I knew for sure was that I didn't want prunes.

Three

On a quiet little side street, just north of the Tree-lane, I came upon Feastings, a catering company that had once belonged to a childhood chum of mine. I stopped there hoping to see the current owner, Tracy Warren, but was told that she was working a party. I learned that business was so good she was looking for a larger space and that a newspaper had recently given them a rave review. Always one to support friends and small businesses, I ordered an herbed chèvre with grilled eggplant and roasted peppers on sourdough for myself, a tuna salad with lemon sauce and capers on whole grain for Kerry, and a filet mignon with arugula, asiago cheese, and horseradish sauce on an onion roll for Max. After I tossed in a bag of chips and three sodas, the bill came to nearly thirty-six dollars, including tax. With prices like that it doesn't take a genius to figure out why McDonald's has sold more than twelve zillion burgers.

Over lunch the three of us discussed business and I learned that one of our new undercover operatives, Louie Perez, had screwed up a sweet hotel deal we had contracted for the last three months. Louie was one of four operatives we had working undercover at the Madeline Hotel. Working in security, he had apparently slipped a note under a Hollywood film director's door. His girlfriend, a film student, had begged him to get her number to the director. He did it the only way he knew how.

"Now why on earth would he do that?" I asked rhetorically, but Kerry answered it anyway.

"Love will make you do crazy things. Just look at yourself." She looked at me.

"Me? What does this have to do with me?" I asked.

"Right, Sydney, like you loan your car to everyone. I don't think so." Kerry stretched over from her seat on a director's chair and passed the chips to Max.

"My car?" I stopped mid-bite.

"The message is right there on your desk. Leslie called to say she took your car because she needed to drive a client out to Long Island. Knowing you and your car, I'd have to say that was a *big* act of love."

I have an '81 Volvo that became all mine when my ex, Caryn, moved to Ireland, almost five years ago. This is not a car I share, especially with Leslie, who likes to drive automatics with both feet at the same time. As much as I love her, there is no getting around the fact that Leslie should never have been issued a driver's license.

I filled my mouth with the eggplant sandwich to keep it shut.

"Well there you go." Max propped the opened bag of chips at his side and dug in. "The mystery of love. Sydney loans a perfectly wonderful car to a perfectly miserable driver, you suddenly dress like it's Halloween every day, and Louie not only gets his ass fired, but could cost—no, I guarantee you, *has cost*—us a small fortune. We won't see any of the money they owe us. And not so much as an apology from him." This last part seemed to upset Max most.

"When did you talk to him?" I asked.

"I haven't. And right now I don't want to. Tell us what happened at the retirement home."

"Nursing home," I corrected him.

"Is there a difference?" Kerry asked as she folded her sandwich paper into a one-inch square.

"Sure there is. One's for retirement and one's for nursing. Anyway, I met Enoch's sister, Selma, and she's wonderful. The possibility that Jessica killed herself is a nonissue, and she insists that Michael couldn't have done it because he was so much in love with Jessica."

"Oh please, the paper is filled with people who kill for love," Kerry dismissed as she started back to the outer office.

"That's not love," I said to her back. I then turned to Max and asked, "You think the *if I can't have you nobody can* school of murder is about love?"

"In a convoluted way, sort of. Self-love. But the question is, do you agree with Selma?" Max crumpled his sandwich wrapper and tossed it into the wastebasket.

"Well, it's too soon to tell. But theoretically? I know *I* couldn't kill someone I really loved. I have to work with the assumption that Michael didn't, either."

"Oh, before I forget, Enoch called," Max told me as he kept his eyes trained on the street.

"Why?"

"Well, he said he's afraid that you're going to get Selma all stirred up. But it was very strange, I mean there we were on the phone, and I suddenly got a sense of him I never had before."

"What do you mean?"

Max took a deep breath and swung his legs around to the floor. "He seemed, I don't know . . . old."

"He *is* old."

"I know, but he never *seemed* old. He's always been like a peer, you know what I mean?"

"Yeah, I do. Remember that family reunion I went to maybe six years ago? My Uncle Hap hit me like that. I remembered him as this virile, strapping man, and when I saw him, he was still handsome and he had a lot of energy, but he had aged. Which made me feel incredibly old."

"Enoch actually seemed a little confused. I don't know, it just felt uncomfortable." I could practically feel Max's unease.

"Maybe it's always been there, but we never noticed before because we always see him at social events," I suggested.

"No." He dismissed this with a flip of his hand. "Minnie's not *old* and she's old, you know what I mean?"

"Minnie's different." At eighty-one my aunt is an exceptionally vivacious woman, but she always has been, ever since I can remember. Sure, her body has aged, but her mind has always been sharp. Then again, so has Enoch's.

In the silence that followed I could swear I heard us both aging. The thought that we are all getting older is not a new one for me, but one I try not to dwell on. I figure I'll age, whether I think about it or not. Now, as we sat there I could hear my skin wrinkling. It was a sobering sensation.

"Speaking of aging, Max, is it true that as men get older their hair grows out their ears instead of their heads?" I asked, pulling out the office and home numbers Enoch had given me for Michael Callahan.

"That's right. Gravity. Same reason women suddenly spurt facial hair."

"Bummer. You see, I think this would be a perfect world if we all just went bald, every single one of us. After a certain age, body hair should just pop right off. One less thing to worry about. You know—" I stopped myself.

"What?" he asked, stifling a sly smile.

"Nothing."

"Oh no you don't. You said *you know* . . ." he prompted me to continue.

"Okay, well, I know this sounds really tacky, but when I was talking to Selma, I was riveted on this one patch of hair on her chin, and I kept thinking, *Someone ought to do something about that.*"

"You'd think she could feel it." Max understood exactly what I meant.

"Absolutely. Not only that, but I mean, if I was old and couldn't see it—or feel it—I'd want someone to yank it the hell out of there."

Vowing that in the future we would be each other's personal hair scouts, we returned to the business at hand.

Max said, "I think I should focus on the Louie situation and try and salvage our relationship with the Madeline, and you should follow up on Enoch's case. Also, it's renewal time at the Hackle Corporation, so one of us is going to have to visit them within the next few weeks. Unfortunately it's not as simple this time as it has been for the last two years. Harvey Johns called today and said that (a), we can't simply renew the contract this time, and (b), we have to talk with the head of the company, who happens to be in the Middle East."

The Hackle Corporation is a company Max and I have been working with for the last several years. They manufacture gas masks, and because much of their business is conducted in the Middle East, they like to provide protection for their executives located there. On average we have four bodyguards working full-time in the Middle East year round. They've become a little gold mine for us, and they were not a client we wanted to lose.

"Why do we have to meet with Hackle?" I asked, discovering a pile of phone messages on my desk.

"I think he wants to see the brains behind the brawn. Who knows, and who cares? He's a great client, and the objective is to make him happy, happy, happy."

"Shit," I muttered as I read through the calls and reread Leslie's message. "I can't believe she took my car."

"You didn't give it to her?" Max stood up and stretched.

"No. I'm embarrassed to say it, because I'm not a selfish person by nature, but I would never give my car to Leslie, especially for a drive out to Long Island."

"I don't blame you. I wouldn't either, and my car's crapola."

To say that I was experiencing mixed feelings would be

an understatement. On one hand, I felt like a heel for being anxious that my love had taken my car. What is mine should, by all rights, be hers. However, on the other hand, Leslie is, without a doubt, *the* worst driver I have ever known.

"I should just let go and let God, right? She took my car, and there's nothing I can do about it now, right?"

"We could have an APB put out for her."

"Ha-ha," I said without any enthusiasm.

I picked up the telephone receiver and waved to Max as he returned to his own office. I punched in Leslie's office number, got her machine, and decided, given the way I was feeling, it was best not to leave a message. After all, what could I say? That she had taken the car without so much as a "May I?" really bothered me, but it bothered me more that I was bothered by it at all; after all, she's my partner, my mate, my spouse of two years. Two years, and you would think I'd just say, "Hey honey, go ahead, it's all yours," but the simple fact is, Leslie drives like she got her license at the Bumper Car Academy in Carnival Land.

I had to deal with first things first; I needed to meet Michael Callahan. I dialed his office number on the off-chance that he might be there. A young, lilting voice on the other end of the phone told me that he wasn't in but asked, "Would you like to make an appointment with Dr. Miller?"

"Yes, I would." As a matter of fact I wanted to meet all the people in Michael's office, especially the ones who had been with him the day Jessica was killed. Although I was essentially working for him—albeit through Enoch and Selma—it would have been awkward if he was there when I interviewed his staff.

"Okay, I can make an appointment for you next week, is that all right?"

"No. I need to see him today."

A slight pause preceded, "Is this appointment for *you*?"

"Yes it is."

26

"Could you tell me exactly what the problem is?"

"No. I'd prefer to tell the doctor." I'd never done that before, and it felt terribly freeing. As a patient I usually give receptionists all my gory health details, forgetting they're not nurses.

My reticence, however, did not please the receptionist, and my punishment was to be put on hold for ten minutes. When next I heard a voice it did not belong to the young receptionist. The tone was brisk, the register lower, and the accent nondescript.

"This is Dr. Miller, can I help you?" Her tone implied that I was interrupting really important stuff and this had better be good.

"Dr. Miller, my name is Sydney Sloane. I'm investigating Jessica Callahan's murder and I was wondering if you could spare me some time today."

I do believe I had her attention, though there was an extended silence at the other end of the line.

"I'm afraid I have no time today. How about tomorrow morning?"

"That would be fine."

"I'll put you back through to my secretary. Have her squeeze you in around ten. Okay?"

"Ten is good, thank you."

"Officer, what did you say your name was, again?" she asked.

"Sydney Sloane," I said, and added, "but it's not officer." Unfortunately she had already popped me on hold before she could hear my qualification. Oh well, I guessed I'd have to tell her face to face.

Next I called Michael's home number in Brooklyn Heights. To my surprise he answered on the sixth ring.

"Hello?" The voice at the other end was cautious.

"Hello, Michael?"

There was a pause. "Yes."

"Hi Michael. My name is Sydney Sloane. Selma Onderdonk asked me to call you." Nothing on the other end.

27

"I'd like to drop by and see you, if that's all right."

"Well . . . I'm not really up for—"

I cut him off before he could object too strenuously. "I can be there in half an hour and I won't take more than fifteen minutes of your time." I waited for a response. "I'm a private investigator, Michael. Selma's hired me to help you."

He sighed and gave me directions to his house.

Four

I am convinced that Brooklyn Heights was settled by Dutch greengrocers. How else do you explain streets named after fruit? It can't be easy to say "I live on Pineapple between Cranberry and Orange," and yet people pay a small fortune to say just that.

Michael Callahan did better than that. He lived in a private corner house with a garage, which meant he had paid more than a small fortune to live in the urban answer to Camelot. In the Heights, as in most older districts in New York, houses are sandwiched side by side, from one end of a block to the other. The Callahan residence was indistinguishable from the other buildings on the block, except for two things. One, the garage, and two, the front door was painted an amazing shade of sea-green. Though most of the houses on the street had long ago been converted into apartments, there are still a handful that are private residences.

I climbed the five steps to the front door and rang the buzzer. As I waited, I surveyed the street that, like so many New York neighborhoods, easily evoked the time when horses pulled carriages along cobblestone streets and the city was a safe place to live. Brightly colored leaves blanketed the sidewalk and a woman with a baby in a Snugli pushed a red shopping cart filled with groceries. The sun was warm, and streaks of lavender and pink raced across the sky. All in all it was a perfect day to be alive.

I rang the doorbell again, and before my finger was off the bell, the door flung open. I was about to say hello but instead I was met with a flattened palm in my face, shoving me hard against the side wall of the entranceway. The meaty hand belonged to a large man in a big hurry. My first instinct was to reach out and grab for him, but I missed. As luck would have it, however, a second fellow was right on his heels. This one I was able to grab hold of. He was a young carrot-top in jeans and a white shirt with huge splotchy-red cheeks and a sweaty head. I grabbed his collar and tried to pull him toward me, but he jerked me forward. I wasn't about to let this kid go. I jumped on his back and held on for dear life as he raced down the stoop trying to buck me off with every step.

I figured if these two schmoes were running from the Callahan residence, there was trouble. I tightened my left arm around his neck, brought my right hand over his forehead, and tried to apply the brakes, using the equestrian principle and pulling his head back. Fact is, he was hauling ass out of there, whether I went for the ride or not.

"Let go." He strained through clenched teeth. He tried to pry my hand off his head, but I wasn't going anywhere. I squeezed my knees against his midriff and let out a loud cry for help. It wasn't the busiest street in the world, but *someone* had to be watching.

He stopped suddenly and tried to throw me off his back. I slipped, but held tighter to his neck. I was in an awkward position now, with half my body clinging on in horseyback and the other half losing grip. As I tightened my hold on his neck, he choked for air. The last thing I wanted was to strangle a total stranger, but for all I knew he was bolting because the good doctor was dead inside his fine house. As the only witness, I felt it was my duty to hold on for dear life and ride this young man as far as I could.

So much for good intentions. Before I knew what hit me, someone pulled me off the redhead and tossed me into the air like I was a ball. I hit the sidewalk, however, like a ton of bricks. The first gorilla must have doubled back to help his pal when he saw I was a fixture. Big as he was, all the first guy had to do was slip his massive hands under my armpits, and with one good pull, peel me off Carrot-top like I was a Colorform toy. I landed on my right side and felt like I'd shattered just about every inch of my body.

"Ah shit, sorry," said with the hint of a brogue, was the last thing I heard before the two of them took off in a waiting car: a rusted white station wagon I hadn't noticed until it was too late. The plates in the back were missing along with the right brake light. A worn bumper sticker read "Honk If You Love Jesus."

I lay on the sidewalk for several minutes after they'd gone, assessing possible injuries and wondering if any of the neighbors had been concerned enough to call the police. Aside from having the wind completely knocked out of me, a scraped elbow, and a rip in my new jeans, as far as I could tell I was fine. I saw curtains flutter across the street, but no one seemed to be in a hurry to help the lady lying on the pavement.

Once on my feet, I saw that the door to Michael Callahan's house was wide open. This time I wasn't going to take any chances. As I approached the doorway, I put my hand in my bag and wrapped my fingers around my gun, a Walther P5 Compact 9mm. As soon as I stepped over the threshold, I was standing in a large foyer, a room in itself. An oval mirror hung over a table to my left, and the table-top was covered with untouched mail. A glance in the mirror assured me that all things considered, I looked pretty good. I was having a good hair day.

I cautiously entered the house, an open, warm, traditional space with the living area to the left as you walked in and a staircase to the right. Straight back were the kitchen and backyard. Sunlight poured into the house, making it feel as if nothing bad could ever happen within these walls.

I had a feeling that Frick and Frack hand't left a party

of twelve behind, but I'm a firm believer in better safe than sorry. I checked out the closets, living room, and dining room. While I was in the dining room I heard a high-pitched whimper. I followed the sound to the kitchen and found a man I assumed was Michael Callahan, sprawled out on the floor, his head in a puddle of blood. A cream and biscuit–colored puppy was sitting by his feet, crying and nosing his legs as if to say "Okay, you can get up now."

I put my gun back in my bag, put the bag on the table, and took a good look at the man on the floor. There was a lot of blood, but it all appeared to be coming from a small gash on his head. I took a cloth off the butcher-block counter, soaked it with warm water, and went back to him.

"Michael?" I gently cleaned the blood off his face. I figured when all was said and done he'd be the proud owner of a nasty black eye and, possibly, a broken nose. Chances were good that he wouldn't need more than a Band-Aid for his head. In other words, the St. Christopher medal hanging around his neck had either done him no good, or saved his life.

"Michael." I patted his face to bring him back. "Come on, Michael, wake up," I said more firmly.

The puppy came to my side, put her big paw on my thigh, and cocked her head to the left and then the right. Despite Michael's blood and my own physical pain, the puppy made me smile. She had big brown eyes fringed with cream-colored lashes, floppy ears that threatened to stand straight up, a huge square black nose and black lips that curled up into a smile. She moved cautiously to her master's side and gently licked his face.

The man on the floor slowly came to. When he was awake enough to moan I asked, "Dr. Callahan?"

"Yes." The word caught in his throat. He coughed and reached for the back of his head. Once he came to he looked both stunned and a little frightened.

"I'm Sydney Sloane. I spoke with you earlier?" This

seemed to register. "I'm going to help you up, okay? Now you've got a little cut on your head that looks worse than it is, all right?"

He was rallying quickly, and as a result it was relatively easy getting him off the floor and onto a kitchen stool. Still, he looked ashen.

I put a damp paper towel over his cut, placed the fingers of his right hand over it, and said, "Press." He did as he was told. "Do you have any idea who those men were, Dr. Callahan?" I opened the freezer door and took out a bag of frozen peas.

"No." His right eye was closing, but deep shadows underscored the other eye, which was almost the same color green as my own.

"Not a clue?" I asked.

"No."

"Did you let them in?" I asked, handing him the peas. "Put that on the back of your neck for a minute, and then on your eye."

He mumbled something unintelligible as he leaned onto the counter, both hands holding some part of his head.

"I'm sorry, I missed that."

"I said, I let them in."

"Maybe we should call the police."

"No," he said firmly.

"Dr. Callahan . . ."

"I appreciate your concern, Ms. Sloane, but this really is a personal matter." He straightened up and put the peas on the counter.

"Put that on your eye." I motioned to the peas. "So you *did* know them?"

"Let's just say I know why they were here." He covered his eye with the peas, slowly rose from his seat, and went to the back door to let out the dog.

"Why?"

He stood at the back door and turned to me. He looked awful. His pretty starched shirt was ruined with his blood, his right eye was reduced to a slit, and his straight brown hair was a matted mess. But despite it all, his smile was like a little gift.

"I can't tell you that," he said softly.

"Why not?"

"Because it has nothing to do with anything."

"I see. Do you normally mind people using your head as a battering ram?"

He offered me a wry look, and I realized that Michael Callahan embodied every stubborn, charming Irishman I'd ever known. "Are your people from Ireland, Doctor?" I asked, wondering if there was a connection, since the gorilla who had tossed me to the ground had a brogue as thick as molasses.

This seemed to confuse him. Finally he said, "A long time ago. Why?"

"I was wondering if maybe your visitors were cousins, or distant something-or-others."

"No relation."

"Where's the hydrogen peroxide?" I asked, knowing I wouldn't get anywhere questioning the doctor about his assailants. He knew who they were and he wasn't about to share that information.

Once I doctored the doctor, I suggested we sit somewhere he might be more comfortable. My own body was beginning to stiffen from my run-in with Michael's pals, but I expected the Advil I took would dull the pain in no time at all.

Michael led the way back into the living room, with me and the puppy close behind.

Though the household furnishings were traditional, the accents and splashes of color were clearly Mexican. Brightly painted masks, native carvings and fanciful wall hangings, shawls used as throws over otherwise monochromatic furniture, all helped to create a distinct sense of home and humor. I settled on a sofa that faced a well-used fireplace. Above it there was an enormous wooden carving of a woman painted pink and lime green, with big orange lips and Medusa-like hair.

When I sat down the puppy scurried up my legs and into my lap. She jiggled and jockeyed to get closer to my face, almost frantic to leave kisses.

"Friendly little bugger, isn't she?" I held her at arm's length as she struggled to lick my face.

"That's Auggie." Michael told me, taking a seat in an armchair far enough away from me to feel reasonably safe.

"What kind of dog is she?"

"Mutt. Half golden retriever and half Samoyed."

"How old?"

Michael shrugged. "I think maybe five months now. I'm not sure. She was really Jessica's dog. Jessie brought her back from California." He made a loose gesture with his hand, "She'll calm down in a minute or two." I put her down next to me, and both Michael and I smiled as Auggie raced from one end of the sofa, checked Michael out, and then ran back to me, a goofy little smile plastered on her face the whole time.

"So, no matter what, you're not going to tell me who your two friends were, are you?" I pulled at the knee of my jeans where I could see the scrape past the tear.

He shook his head gingerly, keeping the paper towel in place.

"Selma has hired me to help you, Michael. She believes you didn't kill Jessica." I paused in case he wanted to join in. He said nothing. "Can you tell me what happened the day Jessica died?"

He looked blankly at me and finally asked, "How is Selma?"

"As well as can be expected, I suppose, given that she's just lost her granddaughter. She's worried about you." I waited before asking again if he could tell me what happened on the day Jessica died.

"No." He removed the paper towel and checked to see if he was still bleeding.

"I beg your pardon?" I wasn't sure if he had understood my question. For the longest time he looked completely vacant, and I wondered if the wallop to his head had done more damage than I initially thought. The bleeding had apparently stopped, and he proceeded to fold the paper towel over and over and over.

Auggie, who had cuddled up in a ball at my side and was fast asleep, snuggled further under my thigh.

Michael finally said, "I sincerely appreciate what Selma's trying to do, but I don't need your help."

"I think you do."

"Well, as I said, I appreciate your concern, but . . ." He left the thought unfinished.

"But what?" I waited for an explanation. When there was none, I forged on. "Forgive me, Doctor, but I'm a little confused. If what I've been told is true, the DA has a strong, albeit circumstantial, case against you. That would concern me if I were you. You leave the office early on the day your wife is murdered, there are several hours unaccounted for, you refuse to cooperate with the police or even your own counsel."

He said nothing, but had the good grace to look uncomfortable.

I wanted to point out that it also concerned me that his face was being used as a punching bag, but I knew that he was a hair's breadth away from asking me to leave, and I needed answers.

"Is it true you refused to tell the police where you were at the time of your wife's death?" Fortunately Enoch had given me the particulars in great detail, so I had an overall idea of Michael's situation.

He met my gaze, but said nothing.

"Is it true you initially refused to seek legal counsel?"
Nothing.

"Are you prepared to spend the rest of your life behind bars?"

It was almost imperceptible, but he winced and then

crossed his legs. He was wearing expensive socks and no shoes, a luxury I was certain he wouldn't enjoy in jail. Until you take them away, people don't even consider the simplest pleasures of freedom.

"Did you murder your wife?"

He sighed and let his shoulders down. "What difference does it make?" he mumbled.

"I'd say it makes a big difference. You see, if you didn't, then someone is getting away with your wife's murder. That disturbs me, and I didn't even know her."

Michael squeezed his fist around the bloodied paper towel and said, "I didn't kill Jessica. I loved her."

"Good. Then let's find out who did kill her. Shall we start with your two recent visitors? Might they have had anything to do with her death?"

"No."

"You're certain?"

"Absolutely."

"Okay. Did she have any enemies, or people she rubbed the wrong way? Maybe a neighbor or a business associate? Can you think of anyone, anyone who would have hurt her?" I asked.

He bit his lower lip and shook his head. "Jessica was spectacular. She was wild, playful, fun, energetic, caring, so deeply caring. She was truly one of the nicest people in the world. She didn't have a mean or malicious bone in her body. She was my friend. How could I ever hurt her?" He barely had the words out, when Michael Callahan broke down. I suspected this was the first time he had cried since losing Jessica. He deserved his privacy, but the best I could do was look away. He used the soiled paper towel to hide his face. When he spoke again, his voice was so soft, I had trouble hearing him at first. "Everyone liked Jessie, even Arnold Nussen, and he's got a reputation for hating everyone. But how do you not like a cartoonist?" His good eye traveled to the wall across the room. I turned and saw a

37

gallery of framed black-and-white cartoons and family photographs.

"Arnold?"

"Her agent."

Auggie whimpered in her sleep and rolled over onto her back. Her legs stayed straight up in the air, and she looked more like a stuffed animal than a real dog. I rubbed her smooth pink belly and thought how much my four-year-old nephew, Andy, would like this dog.

"Selma said that Jessica had recently spent time in California. Could there have been a problem there?"

"No, they loved her there. I'm telling you, she wasn't like most people, she made friends wherever she went. Everyone loved her." His voice cracked.

"Obviously not, Michael. Someone killed her." Even I could hear how cold and insensitive I sounded, but the fact was, Dr. Callahan couldn't have it all ways. His wife was dead, the victim of murder. Someone, somewhere, didn't like her enough to kill her, and if he didn't help himself real soon, he'd be paying for it.

"What was she doing in California?" I softened my tone.

"Developing animation for a movie. Her friend Mary was producing the film and gave her the opportunity of a lifetime. She was thrilled."

"Did she commute at all between the East Coast and the West Coast during that time?"

"No."

"Where did she live?"

"In Sherman Oaks. Her friend Donna had arranged for her to rent a furnished apartment there."

"Donna's a friend of hers in California?"

"No. Here. They've been friends since childhood."

"I see. Was Jessica there long?"

"In California?" he asked. "No, no, not too long."

I knew how long Jessica had been in California and wondered how long Michael thought was not too long.

"A month? Two?"

"Yes, a month or two." He looked away from me and cleared his throat. At that very moment it seemed that something shifted inside Michael Callahan.

"Selma said she left in the middle of June."

"No, it was later."

"Are you sure? As Selma remembers it, she went into the nursing home the second week of June, and Jessica left for California a week later. Does that sound right?"

He stared at the sleeping puppy. It seemed as if a part of him were missing. Finally he said, "If Selma said that, then she's probably right. Despite her age, she's a sharp lady, she would know." He wouldn't meet my gaze, which, I have learned over the years, is a bad sign.

"And Jessica came back . . . ?"

"Two days before she died, which was six days ago, so just over a week ago."

Since we were now in mid-October, that meant Jessica had been in California close to four months.

"Four months is a long time. Did she seem different when she came home?"

"No. Well, maybe. Maybe she was a little more . . . confident. This job had been a real boost for her ego. As wonderful as she was, Jessie always had a hard time believing in herself. Especially as an artist."

"And things between you two were . . . ?"

"Good. Great. It was good to have her back."

"And she was glad to be back?" I asked.

"Yeah, sure, I think so. I mean, she had mixed feelings, which we talked about, but that was perfectly natural. She had just come off working in an exciting new area for her. In California she was identified as Jessica Callahan; the artist, the boss, the creative woman."

"And here?"

"Here it depends upon who you're asking. If you ask *me*, she was Jessica, the artist, my wife, my friend . . ." He trailed off and then continued, almost as if in a daze,

"Other people might have seen her as a friend, a doer, a good neighbor, someone who always reached out to help people . . ." Michael stopped and inhaled sharply, his hands balled into two small fists.

After several moments, he started talking again. "Anyway, she was happy there. I think her work there made a difference to her."

"Are you a diabetic, Michael?"

He nodded. "Yes. I am. And yes, Jessica knew how to administer an injection, though there was never any cause for her to do so, and yes, there was insulin in the house, and no, none of it was missing when she died. You know, many people have diabetes. Many people have insulin in their homes. Even Donna has diabetes."

"Donna, her friend since childhood?"

"That's right."

"Yes, well, many people are not her husband, who refuses to say where he was when she was injected with the insulin." I could tell from the way he pulled back, physically, that I might have overstepped the invisible boundary between which questions may and may not be asked. I forged on ahead. "Do you think there's even a remote possibility that Jessica killed herself?"

"Absolutely not."

"Why not?"

"She was too curious, too full of pepper."

"And yet you gave me the impression before that she was a woman who often felt insecure."

"Thanks to our society, most women I know have problems with self-image, but that doesn't mean they're suicidal. Look, Jessica loved life, and I'd be willing to bet my life that she would never—*could* never—have killed herself."

His wager landed between us like a boulder. He continued quickly. "Besides which, she never would have injected herself with insulin, *that* doesn't make any sense. I mean, just for the sake of argument, if she did want to kill herself—using carbon monoxide—she would have taken a fistful of barbiturates first to knock herself out.''

I was beginning to like Callahan. How could you not like a man who understands that our society still has a problem with how we support the female ego? "Do you have barbiturates in the house?" I asked.

"No, but they're easy enough to get hold of."

"Do you know if the police found the syringe?" I asked.

"No, I don't."

"Who were you with when Jessica was dying?" I figured as long as the man was talking, I'd give it a shot.

The iciness of Michael Callahan's glare told me clearly that, whether or not he killed his wife, he was capable of murder. It also made me think I'd hit the nail right on the head.

I held his gaze, like a game of dare. It wasn't until Auggie twitched awake and nearly rolled off the couch that I looked away. I caught her body in one hand and cupped the back of her head with my other hand.

"She likes women." Michael said, pulling on a pair of Hush Puppies that had been under the coffee table.

"I beg your pardon?" I asked, wondering if he meant that Jessica liked women and this was somehow related to her death. Auggie was back to exploring the land of sofa, bouncing from one end to the other. She paused, flopped down next to me, and let out a big yawn.

"The puppy. She likes women." Both of Michael's feet were now safely tucked into their shoes. Auggie stretched and slipped onto the floor.

"Well that's nice. But I don't see how that has—"

Michael glanced at his watch and cut me off. "I'm afraid we've run out of time. I really must get going."

It's not impossible to help people who won't help themselves, but they sure as hell make it a whole lot harder. "Michael, I'm not the police and I am not your attorney."

"Yes, well, you should know your line of questioning is almost identical."

"And you should know that unless you want to spend the rest of your life behind bars, you're going to have to answer some difficult questions. I'm here because a frightened old lady who just lost her granddaughter doesn't want to lose you, too. Aside from her brother, you see, you're all she has left. Now, she's hired me to prove your innocence, and whether you like it or not, that's what I plan to do." He stood uncomfortably before me with his hands in his pockets, his eyes cast to the floor. "Do you understand that I'm on your side?"

"Yes." His single-word response was barely audible, but then he straightened his back and said, "Perhaps if you didn't waste your time trying to prove my innocence, you just might find who killed Jess."

"Unfortunately, these things work hand in hand, so it's not a waste of time. Quite the contrary. Don't forget you're about to be tried for the murder of your wife. Your wife. Selma's convinced if you really love someone, you can't kill them. She says you really loved Jessica."

"I did."

"Then please tell me where you were at the time of her death."

"I have to get to work." He sounded deflated and tired. The puppy dodged in and out of Michael's legs, chasing her own tail.

"Hear me, Doctor, take it in; I'm on your side." I repeated.

He shook his head as he bent down and rubbed Auggie between the ears. "Sydney, I appreciate what both you and Selma are trying to do, but you have to understand, I believe in preordination. Long ago I learned to put my trust in God, because God is the only one who can guide me and judge me." He scooped the puppy up and tucked her under his arm. From my vantage point, I could see that as little as she was, her paws were the size of canoes.

"I don't want to guide or judge you. I just want to help you." I stood up.

42

"I don't know that I want your help."

"Why? How do you know it wasn't preordained that I should be put in your path to help you?" I figure it didn't matter whether it was God or karma or happenstance that brought us together, the fact is I was there, offering to help him.

"Let me think about it," he said as if he honestly meant it. Less than two paces apart, we studied each other for the longest time. His left eye was swollen almost shut and his nose was beginning to swell, but he was still a handsome man. Finally he rubbed his right cheek against Auggie's neck and walked to the fireplace. "Just for the record, I want to know who killed Jessie more than anyone." Though I couldn't see his face, his voice was weighed down with painful resignation. "It's just that . . ." When he turned back to me I had a premonition that whatever it was he was holding inside was going to undo him in the end. "There are some questions I simply cannot answer. I just can't. And if that means that I go to jail for killing Jessica, then I have to believe that that's what's meant to be." He put Auggie down and patted her fanny.

"Well, that's a lovely speech, Doctor, but do you have any idea what it's *like* in prison?"

His jaw twitched as he kept his eyes trained on the dog.

"Your recent incarceration was nothing. I can promise you that prison is about three hundred times worse than your wildest nightmares. Think about it." We weren't getting anywhere, and I knew it. I had already learned what I had hoped to from my first meeting with Michael Callahan, and experience has taught me that staying any longer would just alienate him for future questioning. "And on that pleasant note, I'll be leaving." With that said, I stepped forward to shake his hand.

"You know, Jessica would have liked you." He held my right hand in both of his.

"And I'm sure I would have liked her." I looked down and saw that the puppy had a big fuzzy banana in her mouth

43

that she was getting to squeak by banging it against my leg. She pushed the banana at me, frantic for a playmate.

Before I left I gave Michael my card, along with my home number in case he changed his mind and needed to talk. I also got the name and number of Jessica's recent employer, along with a handful of people he knew she had either seen, or spoken to, during the last few days of her life. Maybe one of her girlfriends knew something that Michael didn't. It isn't uncommon that a man or a woman tells friends something he or she hasn't told a spouse. Lastly, I got the number of his attorney. "It would help if you told him to expect a call from me," I suggested at the front door.

"No problem." He paused and cleared his throat. "I, ah, I just want to thank you for caring enough to want to help."

"It will work a lot faster with your cooperation," I reminded him before he ushered me out the door and I found myself, once again, on his stoop, looking up and down the charming and deserted Brooklyn street. I wondered how many people—if any—had seen my run-in with Michael's earlier visitors. I looked at the window across the street where I had seen the curtains move before, but all was still.

One of the people Michael suggested I talk to was their next-door neighbor, a Rosalynn Hayes. I figured as long as I was in the neighborhood, I would knock on the door. No one was home, though, and I decided it would be best if I called before meeting her.

After walking only two blocks to the subway, I felt the impact of having been slam-dunked on the sidewalk. By the time I reached the Clark Street station, the whole right side of my body was aching. On the train headed back to Manhattan, I started my case list. One thing was for sure, my meeting with Callahan had provided more questions than answers. This is when the first spark of a case starts to kindle everything around it. This is when the fun begins.

Five

I was anxious to get back to the office and get on the computer, but I could feel my body stiffening from my run-in with the Brooklyn goons. An abbreviated workout might be just the thing to loosen the joints.

I got out at Thirty-fourth Street and hurried over to Tina's Gym, a home away from home for me. My friend Zuri, who is a renowned boxing coach and fixture at the gym, was in Thailand on vacation, but Tina was behind the desk when I walked in.

"I thought you'd be in today," she said, looking up at me through the dirtiest glasses in the world.

"Why's that?" I leaned on the counter.

"Because I had a dream about you last night." She placed a worn white towel on the countertop.

"A good dream?" I rested my elbows on the towel.

She made a face. "Who can remember? Yesterday I spent half an hour looking for my glasses, which, of course, were on top of my head. You know, I had a great uncle who had Alzheimer's. Scares the hell out of me. After he got it, he became the singularly most dangerous man I ever knew."

"Well, you know they say there's one good thing about Alzheimer's."

"What's that?"

"You're always meeting new people."

Tina stared at me without cracking even a hint of a smile.

"It was a joke," I explained.

"I forgot to laugh," she deadpanned, which made me laugh.

"Say listen, you have any Band-Aids and bacitracin?" I asked.

"What's the matter, kid? Another one of your *business* engagements?" She arched her brows and smiled smugly as she handed me a box of Band-Aids and a tube of ointment.

I took the first aids and my towel. "Thank you very much. Now as much as I would love to chat with you, I'm on a tight schedule here," I said, moving toward the almost bleak locker room.

"Yeah, yeah, Sydney Sloane, gal on the go, I know." She smiled and shook her head. "If you want time in the ring, there's a gal in there looking for a partner. Big, pretty blond, her name is McGuinnis."

I held up my hands in protest. "Not today, thanks. I need to stretch more than anything. She any good?"

"Oh sure, she's one of Zuri's students," Tina said as the front door opened. Three people came in and I slipped out and made my way into the locker room.

No one was in the locker room when I got there, which was good. I suffer my share of bumps and bruises as a result of my work, but it's not something I need to share with the world at large. I needed to take a private look at my knee and elbow, which were now beginning to burn. In the bathroom I surveyed the damage and applied ointment to my scraped elbow.

There wasn't a Band-Aid big enough for the abrasion on my knee, so I just washed it with soap and water and cut the frayed area around the jeans so the wound wouldn't be irritated when I put my pants back on.

I keep workout clothes in my locker at the gym, which Tina lets me toss in the laundry with their towels. The loose shorts and T-shirt allowed me the freedom of movement I needed to give myself an hour of yoga. Granted, it wasn't my usual workout in the gym, which ordinarily consists of aerobics, shadowboxing, some time on the bags, and an occasional round or two in the ring with Zuri. At that moment I needed to gently stretch the muscles and joints that had just taken a pounding from my spill in Brooklyn Heights.

By the time I left Tina's I felt refreshed and limber, ready to tackle the matters at hand.

I was anxious to input the results of my conversation with Michael Callahan, get the big picture, so to speak, and make a game plan.

As I came up from the subway at Eighty-sixth Street, I was enveloped by the elixir from a local coffeehouse. I picked up a large cup of joe and headed to my office. Passing the corner deli I decided the coffee would be lonely by itself and needed something to go with it, something chocolate, or cakey, or both. All the Saranwrapped sweets looked old and stale, so I settled for a package of Yodels and wondered if any of my friends would ever admit they still ate this crap.

Once at my desk, I took out my spiral notebook with notes from Enoch and Selma, and the names and numbers Michael had given me of the people Jessica had seen or spoken to during the last few days before her death.

Michael had given me five names: Jessica's friend and last employer, Mary Douglas; her neighbor Rosalynn Hayes; her friend Donna Frost, and her agent, Arnold Nussen, the man who, ostensibly, didn't like anyone. The last name on the list was Michael's attorney, Marshall Tucker. I put them into the computer with a brief sketch of who they were and what their relationship was to both Jessica and Michael.

Next I read through my notes with Enoch and put them into a comprehensive order; there was information that dealt specifically with Michael and some pertaining to Jessica.

47

What took longest were my notes on my meeting with Michael. Though he was trying his damnedest not to be read, I got the general impression that Michael Callahan was a good man. Instinct told me that he wasn't responsible for his wife's death, but several factors made me uneasy about the doctor. That he was willing to go to jail for a crime he professedly didn't commit was bad enough—but that it was for the murder of his wife, his mate, a woman he insisted he loved, that really bothered me. Why would he be willing to do that? I jotted down a few possibilities:

1. He knew who did it and was protecting him or her.
2. He hired someone to kill his wife.
3. He's hiding something not related to Jessica's death.

It was a short list, but I knew all three were plausible. If he did know who killed his wife, and he loved Jessica as much as Selma thought, and he professed, then why would he protect the person? He might have hired someone to kill Jessica, but then again, why? Was it only lip service that he thought the world of his wife and insisted that no one could ever mistreat her because she was loved by all? It also disturbed me that Michael hadn't known how long Jessica was in California. How do you not feel the four-month absence of someone you love, someone you live with, sleep with?

I got up from my desk, walked to the windows facing Broadway, and took up the watering can. As I watered the plants along the window ledge I wondered if Michael really didn't know how long Jessica had been gone, or if he was just playing a game I didn't understand. (It is amazing how many people confuse stoic and stupid, and think vulnerability is a social disease.) This made me think about his face having been used as a punching bag, which brought me to the last consideration, that he was hiding something

48

not the least bit related to Jessica's death. But then, if he was hiding something totally unrelated to his wife's death, why not just tell the police, tell me, and let us all look for the real killer?

Hypothesis is all well and good, but I needed solid information. I emptied the watering can and went back to my desk, where I put on my reading glasses and picked up the phone.

Enoch had given me the number of Detective Jacob Stavinsky, who was handling the case. I caught him in, and when he heard that I had been hired by the victim's grandmother to prove the suspect's innocence, he exhaled a sardonic laugh. "That about sums up our society, doesn't it? Here you have a guy who's guilty of murder, but because he's connected, and he's rich, he's going to get away with it."

"No, no, that's not what we're after here. I want the truth, and I thought you could help me find it."

Stavinsky laid out his investigation clearly and succinctly, sharing his views as well as the pertinent information. It was, as far as he was concerned, an open-and-shut case. I thanked him for his help and found myself hoping he was wrong. Selma believed with all of her heart and soul that Michael could never have hurt Jessica. During our interview at the Treelane, she had been passionate about two things: her love of Jessica and her conviction of Michael's innocence. I didn't know Selma from Eve, but I realized, in retrospect, that she had touched me in a place few people do. With any luck, we'll all get old before we die. I'd like to know that when I'm in the final stages of my life, there will be someone out there who will take me seriously. Someone who will care. Someone who will be my voice like Jessica had been for Selma.

I called Mary Douglas, Jessica's last employer, and left a message on her machine with both my home and office numbers. Next was Rosalynn Hayes, their neighbor. This time there was no machine. The phone rang ten times before I decided to give up and call later. Next on the list was Donna Frost, Jessica's good friend. There was a machine on this phone, but a mechanical voice informed me that the tape was full when it beeped for me to leave my message. I was batting zero. Arnold Nussen, her agent, was the last one on the list. I called him and nearly jumped for joy when I was connected to a real, live, breathing person. The secretary put me through as soon as she heard I was calling with regard to Jessica Callahan.

"Nussen here." The voice over the phone brought to mind the Chunky candy commercial man from my youth, nasal and whiny.

"Hello, Arnold, my name is Sydney Sloane." I explained why I was calling. "I was hoping we could get together."

"Sorry kid, no can do. I'm a busy man. In half an hour I'm leaving for the airport. I have a client in Toronto who needs me to hold his hand through a contract signing."

"When will you be back?"

"I leave Toronto tomorrow, fly to Florida to visit my mother in the hospital, I'm there for four days and then I'm in Seattle for a week. If you can wait I can see you when I get back."

I don't like telephones as it is, and I avoid them like the plague when I need to interview someone, because people can lie so easily when you can't see them. I prefer eye contact and a chance to read body language. However, it wasn't to be with Arnold Nussen. "I understand you talked to Jessica the day she died."

"I talked to Jessica every day. She was an angel. Very talented lady."

"Could you tell me when you last spoke to her?"

"'Bout eight o'clock on Wednesday morning. She called to tell me about a call she got. Mary was talking to her about a possible offer. That was Jessica, though, she never did anything behind my back, unlike other people I represent. Let me explain something to you, it's the nature of

50

the business for clients to think they can make a deal without me and save themselves the measly commission I take. What they don't remember is that I'm there to look out for their best interests, to get them the best deal possible. Jessica's one of the few who gave me respect.''

"What was the offer Jessica was talking about?"

"Her friend Mary Douglas—you know her?"

"I know of her. We haven't talked yet."

"Yeah, well, Mary and Jessica just worked together and from what they both said it was like a marriage made in heaven. Mary was the best public relations person Jessica could have had. She saw Jessica's potential and told everyone about her work. I don't know the name of this last guy, but he was from England—I think—and he had an idea and the budget for an animated film, all done on computer."

"Computer? I thought she was a cartoonist."

"She was. That was the thing about Jessie, she was a very well-rounded artist. She started with these little cartoon characters—doing cards and then little strips in the local papers—then she discovered an interest in computer animation and the 3D programs they have. You know from this stuff?"

"No, not really."

"It's the future, I'm telling you. Anyway, this is the direction she was headed. She still did her strip on paper, but it was clear that this lady was going to make a killing in the computer business."

"Did she actually meet with this man from England?"

"I don't think so, but I don't know. She told me that she was planning to meet him with Mary, but she wasn't sure when that would happen."

"Can you tell me anything about the day she died?"

"Not really. Like I said we talked at eight and she was going to call me later when she knew more."

"So you don't know what she had planned for the day?"

51

"Only that she was going to see Selma, that's her grand-mother. They were very close."

"I know."

"Have you talked to the old gal? How is she?"

"It's not easy to lose a grandchild."

"Tell me about it. My kid brother died in Vietnam and my mother never got over it."

I mumbled something appropriate and asked, "Your relationship with Jessica was solid?"

"The best. Simply put, she was one of the most honest, talented people I will ever know. You didn't know her?"

"No."

"Too bad. She was special."

"Can you think of anyone who might not have shared your opinion of her?"

"Absolutely not. Lemme tell you, if someone didn't like Jessie, they were an asshole, if you'll pardon the language."

Despite all the rave reviews, there was one simple fact: Someone, somewhere had disliked Jessica Callahan enough to kill her.

I glanced at my watch and was amazed to see that it was already almost six. I dialed Callahan's attorney, Marshall Tucker, figuring I would leave a message and run a better chance of getting an appointment for the next day. I was surprised when he answered the phone personally. I told him who I was.

"Right." I could hear him snap his fingers. "Michael's detective. Just talked to the little man a while ago and he mentioned you. Now, I'm sorry, but did you say you were calling *for* Mr. Sloane or that you *are* Mr. Sloane?"

I paused. "I am calling for myself, Mr. Tucker. My name is Sydney Sloane."

"Right. Good. Now then, what can I do for you . . . Sydney?"

"I was hoping you could spare me some time tomorrow.

52

I have a few questions I'd like to clear up regarding Dr. Callahan.''

"Wish I could, but have a problem with that. Little thing called confidentiality.'' His words were clipped and came out in little spurts.

"I won't ask you to divulge any confidences. But if we're going to prove his innocence, we'll need to help one another.''

"Okay. Point well taken. Shoot.''

"Have you any free time tomorrow?'' I asked, not about to do another interview over the phone.

He exhaled and said, "The only time I could give you would be at seven-thirty. In the morning.''

"That's fine.''

"It is?'' He sounded surprised. "Good. I like to get things out of the way before I start my workday.''

It bothered me that Marshall Tucker didn't consider Michael Callahan's case part of his workday, but I wasn't about to put him off by confronting him with it, at least not now. We agreed to meet at his Madison Avenue office.

As soon as I hung up the phone my stomach let out a loud roar. I pressed my hand into my belly and tried to soothe the rumblings as I dialed my home number. There were two messages on the machine. The first one was enough to floor me. It was from my ex, and close friend, Caryn, who lives in Ireland and studies sculpting with world-renowned Liam Greene. "Sydney, damn it, I was hoping to catch you. You're not going to believe this, but I'll be in New York in late November. Imagine that? I'll only be there for two weeks and I insist on seeing you two. Listen, I'll call you back in a day or two. God, I can't believe I missed you. Well, I can't wait to see you. And to meet you, Leslie. Ta.'' That voice hadn't changed since I first met her. Twenty-one years, it didn't seem possible. I was a rookie cop and she was having her first show at a gallery in Soho, which is before Soho was the chic haven it's become. In those days people still responded with alarm when they knew you were *going to Soho*. It was September, and it was raining, and my friend Peggy Dexter had dragged me along to the show at the not yet, but soon to be, trendy gallery. I remember standing in front of one large canvas of varying shades of red with two homogeneous shapes outlined in the foreground, embracing. I don't know why, but I was mesmerized by the piece. "Do you like it?" The voice was cold and playful at the same time. I looked over, and there, standing off to the side with her arms crossed tightly over her chest, was the most beautiful woman I had ever seen. She literally took my breath away.

I played the message back a second time, more to hear her voice than anything else. It had been close to five years since Caryn and I had seen each other. I missed my friend, the woman who had gone from being my passion to being my family, and now knew me better than anyone, except probably Leslie. I was also excited at the prospect of Leslie and Caryn meeting. Okay, excited and maybe a little nervous.

The second message was from Leslie. "Hi babe, listen, I just left a message for you at the office, but I wanted to tell you that I have been given the opportunity of a lifetime. I was at my eight o'clock with Mrs. Reed, when who should walk in but François Bouchon. It turns out François and his wife, Mancini, have just bought a place in Amagansett and they're looking for one person to oversee the decorating. This could make my entire career. Mrs. Reed *insisted* they use me, and François said that today was his only free day and since he likes to get things done *maintenant*, we should pop out there right now and take a look at it. Naturally I can't say no. Anyway . . ." She took a deep breath here and let the words tumble out. "I said we should drive out there and then he said, 'Oh you have a car?' and without even thinking I said, 'Oh sure,' because I don't know why, because I think maybe I was showing off, anyway I have to pick him up in a few minutes and I wanted to tell you firsthand that I'm taking your car, but

54

you shouldn't worry, because I'll be very, very careful. And I'm really sorry I haven't been able to get you directly because I know how you feel about your car and my driving, but I promise you I'll be like Mario Andretti, only slow." She paused for a breath. "I love you. I should be home by eight, the latest. Wish me luck." A mechanical voice informed me that this call had come in at 10:09, just about the same time I was headed to the Treelane Nursing Home.

I did not listen to this call a second time, but I did smile. And then I asked the machine why François Bouchon— whoever the hell he was—had the money for a house on the tip of Long Island, but didn't have a car to drive them to it.

I picked up an order of Tandoori chicken with extra cilantro sauce at the India Garden Restaurant on Amsterdam, after having decided to spend the night mapping out an actual game plan for the Callahan case. Calculating that a round-trip drive out to Amagansett, including two hours for work and lunch, would take only eight hours, tops (and not the nine and a half she had estimated in her call), I half-expected Leslie to be home when I got there. This was why I bought two orders of garlic naan, a soft bread that melts in your mouth, and two salads.

As it turned out, I came home to an empty apartment. My spirits sank when I called out her name and was met with only silence in return. The heart is a funny thing. I think in the back of mine, I was hoping that Leslie had come home, was feeling deep remorse for having taken my car without asking, and wanted to make it up to me with champagne, or a massage, or something equally as appealing. But there was nothing except the dull thudding of the bass from a car stereo on the street below. Ever since Leslie moved in two years ago, the place feels painfully vacant when she's not there.

I opened the garlic bread and carried it with me to the room I had turned into my at-home office when I renovated the apartment nearly a dozen years ago. I am an anomaly among my friends, most of whom have been transplanted to New York from places like Michigan and Montana. The apartment I call home has been in the family for over forty years now and I have no intention of ever moving. In my youth, this had been my brother's bedroom. It is the smallest room in the apartment and I've learned that changing the looks of a space doesn't change memories. I thought about David as I inhaled the naan. The last time I had seen him he smelled like garlic. Garlic and bourbon.

There was only one message on the machine, and clearly it was a wrong number. Someone named Boz was late for a five-thirty meeting. I rewound the tape and checked my watch. I had missed the news, but I would be able to have dinner with *The Simpsons*.

I kept the phone at my feet throughout dinner, hoping Leslie would either walk through the door or at least call and let me know where she was. Since it was closing in on 7:30 and she had probably left the city at 10:30, that meant she had been gone nine hours. Even with traffic at a standstill, it wouldn't take her more than four hours one way . . . Where the hell was she?

I turned off the TV, dumped my empty dinner containers into the garbage, and wandered around the apartment. I switched on an Annie Lennox CD and sang and danced along to "I Can't Get Next to You." I was supposed to be constructing a game plan, but instead all I was doing was feeling my lover's absence, as well as my growing concern for where she was. This would not do.

I went back to David's old room and tried Mary Douglas again. Still no answer. I didn't leave another message because I didn't want to seem like a pest, not yet, anyway. Next I called their neighbor, Rosalynn, whose number was busy. This was promising, at least she was home. Next I called Jessica's friend Donna Frost, whose machine had been full when I had tried her before. Her telephone exchange put her in my neck of the woods. She picked up on the first ring. I explained who I was and that Selma had hired me to look into Jessica's death.

"How can I help?" she asked warily.

"I was wondering if I could meet with you, take maybe half an hour of your time. I just have a few questions."

I left a note for Leslie, and by 8:30 I was sitting at a small marble-topped table at a local coffeehouse, waiting for Donna Frost. Vivaldi was playing softly in the background, and the smell of cinnamon and coffee was almost intoxicating. I was leafing through a copy of *Bon Appétit* when I heard my name.

"Sydney?"

I looked up.

"I'm Donna," she said.

I was stunned.

Six

Donna Frost was six feet, five inches tall and absolutely exquisite. Her legs practically traveled the length of
her entire body, her features were chiseled to perfection,
and she carried every single inch with the air of an aris-
tocrat. Heads turned to watch this vision of beauty as she
gracefully took the seat across from me. She wore black
stirrup pants, short boots, a low-cut pink mohair sweater,
and a black jacket. She was breathtaking.

She was also a he.

"Thanks for meeting me on such short notice," I said
as I took in the commotion her mere presence had created.

"I'd walk through fire for Jessica." She smiled sadly up
at the waitress and placed an order for a double espresso
and banana cream pie. "I eat when I'm depressed."

I didn't think it was my place to mention that as a diabetic, banana cream could kill her. I had to assume she
knew that.

She pulled her large purse up onto her lap and I took the
opportunity to study her carefully. Aside from her large
hands, there was nothing about Donna Frost that read male.
Not even a noticeable Adam's apple. She took a pack of
Merits out of her bag, and I wondered why, compared to
most transvestites I've known, I feel about as feminine as
Milton Berle. Then again, compared to most transvestites

58

I've known, Miss America and Uncle Miltie would be about even on the fem-o-meter.

"Do you mind?" she asked, holding up the blue-and-white pack of cigarettes. I looked around and was surprised to see that more than half the coffeehouse was smoking.

"Please, go ahead." Unlike most ex-smokers, I still enjoy the smell of burning tobacco.

Donna lighted her cigarette and inhaled so hard I thought she was going to take in the table, napkins, and my decaf. She closed her eyes on the first exhale and when she opened her eyes, told me, "My husband won't let me smoke in the apartment. Actually he thinks I quit, but—" She waved her cigarette casually, as if to finish her thought.

I've never understood smokers who think they're pulling the wool over their partners' eyes, unless, of course, they're smoking one cigarette in the middle of the day with a Listerine chaser. Either that or they never get close enough for their mate to know. Donna's bloodred lipstick rimmed the white filter of the cigarette, and I realized that I didn't want to know how close she got to her mate.

"Selma hired you?" she asked and continued without waiting for a response. "How is dear, poor Selma, my God, how horrible this must be for her. I saw her the day after Jessie—" She stopped and brought a shaky hand to her mouth. Nicotine is an amazing drug. By the time she pulled the cigarette away from her mouth, the shaking had stopped; she dropped her shoulders and asked evenly, "Why did Selma hire you?"

"She doesn't think Michael killed Jessica. She wants me to prove it." I took a sip of water and put the glass back down on its old water ring.

Donna snorted a laugh, blowing smoke out of her nostrils like a cartoon bull. "Selma's a good woman, but don't forget, she's over ninety."

"What does that mean?" I reached inside my jacket pocket and pulled out a small notebook.

"It means . . ." She paused as the waitress put the espresso, pie, and two forks on the table. "It means she's a dear old lady, but she may not be the best judge of character. Don't forget she comes from a time when women bought all that bunk about happily ever after."

"I take it you don't share her fine opinion of Michael."

Donna parked her cigarette in the glass ashtray and plucked the lemon twist off the demitasse saucer. "Who told you to call me? Selma?" She smoothly twisted the lemon into her cup and retrieved her cigarette, never once taking her eyes off me.

"No. Michael."

She arched a finely tweezed brow and took a drag, blowing the smoke overhead. "I'm surprised."

"Why?"

"Michael doesn't like me much. He couldn't stand the fact that Jessica and I were so close." She put down her cigarette and picked up the demitasse cup, which in her hand looked like it had been taken from a children's tea set.

"Why?"

Donna sipped her coffee and studied my face. After she had placed the cup carefully back on the saucer, she asked me, "What kind of detective are you?"

As it was a question open to interpretation, I decided to interpret it openly. "A good one. Why?" Her response was to arch *both* of her perfect eyebrows as she reached for her fork, feigning apathy. I hate when people do that. It's like saying, "Oh, you're a detective? Detect." Comics must get it all the time: "Hey, you're a comic? Say something funny."

"Oh, I see, a challenge. Okay. Michael doesn't like you because you're taller than he is?"

Her smile was worth the aggravation. "You're getting warm." She dug her fork into the tip of the pie.

"Actually I'm quite hot, but I didn't think the purpose of this meeting was to play games."

She toasted me with her fork and said, "Touché" before

slipping the banana cream pie into her splendidly shaped mouth. I knew I was staring, how could I not? Here was a magnificent-looking woman, with a penis. I reached for my coffee cup.

"How did you meet Jessica?" I asked as she gestured to the extra fork for me to help myself.

"We go waaaay back. Freshman year, high school. For the longest time she was the only person in the world who seemed to understand me." She pushed her fork at the pie. "Jessie stuck with me when no one else in school would even talk to me, and you have to understand she knew everyone. She risked her popularity to be my friend. Kids can be so cruel." She put down the fork and retrieved her cigarette. "But we lasted, she and I. I was even her bridesmaid."

"Seriously?" I couldn't help but smile.

"Oh my God, yes, it was *wonderful*. I mean, who else *but* me?"

"How did Michael respond?"

"Okay, I suppose. If he had any objections, I never heard about it. Quite honestly, I think if he had said no, she probably wouldn't have married him." From all I had heard about Jessica, I didn't doubt it. "I tell you, we were divine."

"I'm sure you were. Can you tell me about her state of mind, recently? Was she in good spirits or low? Maybe California was—" I started to prompt her, but it wasn't necessary.

"California was the best thing that could have happened to her. I went out there in August—"

"You were there?"

"Of course I was. My best friend was at a high point in her life then. You think I didn't want to share it with her?" She took another mouthful and put the fork down. "You'd think her loving, doting husband would have shared it with her as well, but in case you didn't know it, doctors are more important than mere mortals." She dabbed the corners of her mouth with a paper napkin. "As far as I'm concerned, Jessie deserved more than she ever received, and that's across the board. What happened for her in California was very exciting. She was defining her career, but more than anything else she was finally starting to believe in herself. You would think of all the people in her life, her husband would have supported her with more than lip service, wouldn't you? She's gone close to what, five months and he can't even swing a weekend out there? That's not right."

"Are you saying you don't think Michael loved her?" I asked as the waitress poured me more decaf.

She rested her elbow on the table and leaned onto it. She exhaled an enormous sigh. "No. I may not be crazy about Michael, I might even be a little jealous of Michael, but I do think he loved her." She tapped a thumb nail against her teeth before adding, "All I'm saying is that he showed it when it was easy. Which is like every other man I've known in a relationship. As long as the spotlight's on him, he's oh-so-supportive and everyone *kivels* that he's in touch with his feminine side, but let me tell you, as soon as that focus shifts, watch out, and believe me, I know what I'm talking about."

"When you say, 'Watch out,' what are you saying?"

She responded with a facial shrug.

"Are you suggesting that he might have actually killed Jessica?"

She ran her fingertips along the marble tabletop. "Who knows? Maybe. I certainly wouldn't reject it as a possibility; after all, the police seem to think he did it. Besides, there's just something incredibly sleazy about that guy." We looked at each other for about four seconds before she laughed self-consciously. "Which is exactly what he would say about me, I know. I know." She slipped another cigarette out of the pack and rolled it between her fingers like a miniature baton.

"What do you mean by sleazy? He seemed pretty strait-laced to me."

"Honey, some of the sleaziest people I know are the most straitlaced, church-on-Sunday, right-wing Republicans you'll ever meet."

An image of Newt Gingrich popped into my head and quickly vanished. "So on one hand, you say you believe he loved Jessica, and yet you also think he was capable of murdering her. The two thoughts seem somehow antithetical."

"I believe that most people, with or without intention, kill the things they love most. It's human nature. That's *really* what separates us from the rest of the animal kingdom."

It was a point of view that diametrically opposed Selma's earlier conviction that we cannot kill those we love. I lean toward Selma's point of view, but then again, I've seen a lot of evil committed in the name of love. But that's just it: *In the name of love* doesn't mean beans.

"When did you last see Jessica?" I asked.

"The day she died. We had coffee together before she went to see Selma." She tapped the filter of the cigarette against the tabletop.

"What time was that?"

She gave this some thought as she picked up the lighter and lighted the cigarette. "About nine-fifteen, nine-thirty. I was late—as usual. She called me early, maybe seven o'clock, and she wanted to see me." She exhaled blue smoke. "Actually, she was taking Selma out to lunch and asked if I wanted to go. Unfortunately I already had lunch plans, so we agreed to meet for coffee down in the Village, before she saw Selma."

"How was she?"

Donna outlined her mouth with her fingers as she stared at her half-eaten pie. Finally she said, "Jessie wasn't having a great day. Insecurity, mixed feelings. You see, on one hand her career was just taking off, but on the other she was worried about Michael. She was excited about the possibility of working on a film in England, but she was afraid that Michael was drifting. True to her style, she talked herself into believing either that it was all in her head or that it was her own doing and she could correct it. By the time we finished coffee, she had convinced herself that she had created something out of nothing.''

"Why?''

"Oh please, because 'Michael is one of the most even-tempered, kindest men on the planet.' '' Her falsetto impersonation of Jessica was accompanied with hands clasped chest high and batting eyelashes. "This is enough to make even a Sandra Dee aficionado, such as myself, sick to her stomach.''

"So you talked about work and Michael. How was she when you left her?''

"She was fine. She was going to go over and meet Selma.''

"What time was that?''

"About eleven. I called her later in the day, but . . .'' Donna became perfectly still and stared at the tabletop. "You have no idea what a huge hole there is inside me right now,'' she told the ashtray. She then looked up at me, almost surprised by my presence. "Death is not one of those things you become inured to, you know what I mean? I mean, I've lost a lot of friends to AIDS—three ex-lovers in the last two years alone—but . . .'' Her beautifully sculpted features seemed suddenly to lose their definition. "I miss her so much.'' She breathed evenly.

One of the hardest things about my job is to distance myself from people and their pain. It would have been inappropriate for me to reach out and touch her, and yet it was my natural instinct to do just that. I reached for my coffee instead, and nodded sympathetically. The room suddenly seemed to swell with noise; silverware clanging against dishes, laughter, voices getting louder and louder in an attempt to be heard above the din, the music, the hiss of a cappuccino machine. I felt the sound crowd in around us and squeeze.

By a quarter to ten I was on my way home. My thoughts, as I hurried from the restaurant, were not about Donna Frost, drag queen extraordinaire, or even about Jessica Callahan. The only thing on my mind, as I practically jogged the four blocks, was my concern that something had happened to Leslie. It wasn't like her not to call. I was sandwiched between anger and fear as I literally ran the last block and up the three flights of stairs to our apartment.

I opened the door to the apartment, stifling my natural instinct to call out to her. I could feel the place was empty, and my heart felt as if someone had injected me with ice water. I raced to the answering machine and saw that there were three messages. The first one was the same wrong number. The second call was from Naomi Lewis, my friend at the Treelane Nursing Home. I jotted down her number and wrote a note to call her first thing in the morning. The last call was Leslie. By the time her message had finished playing, I marveled that I hadn't pulled the damned thing from the wall and tossed it out the window.

"Hi honey, listen, I know it's late and I'm *really* sorry, but it has been a crazy day. Just so you know, I'm going to stay out here, maybe even for a few days, but here's my number. Call me. I love you. Bye."

I had half a mind to not call and let her sweat it out waiting for me, but the fact was, I had just been catapulted from concern to anger in a millisecond and I needed to tell her how pissed I was. I dialed the number she had left and asked for her room number.

"Hello." It was said with a breathy, almost girlish quality that did not sit well with me.

"Hello." The word caught in the back of my throat.

"Sydney!"

"You sound surprised." She couldn't miss the anger in my voice.

"Listen, you're probably upset, I know, but I can explain." She paused, and I decided that rather than rush at her with a flurry of words, as I have been known to do in the past, I would instead let her sink herself.

"Are you there?" she asked.

"Yes."

"You're mad, all right, I understand. I know I should have called earlier, but I really thought I'd be coming home." She held her hand over the receiver and said something to someone else in the room.

"Excuse me?" If I looked in a mirror I would have probably seen that my blond hair and green eyes had turned the same color as my face, which, if the heat emanating from it was any indication, was crimson. "What did you say?" I asked.

"Nothing. François wants to explain what happened— no it *wasn't* your fault," she said to someone I assumed was François. In her room. Late at night.

"You have thirteen seconds to tell me what's going on," I said with remarkable control.

Leslie paused. "Let me call you right back."

"Call back? I don't think so. I think you can talk to me in front of your newfound pal." Years of police and detective work kicked in and I realized there was the possibility—remote though it was—that she was being detained against her will. "Wait a minute. Are you all right?"

"Yes," she said almost warily.

"Seriously, Leslie, is he holding you there against your will?"

"Oh don't be ridiculous," she said in a way that made me feel like a fool.

Not being one to hang up on others, I squeezed the receiver in my hand and said as coldly as I could, "Is my car okay?"

The pause confirmed for me that, indeed, my car was not okay, and that was why my lover was spending the night in a hotel, over a hundred miles away, with a rich, married Frenchman who could afford a house but not a car. Leslie,

66

I guessed, was fine because she was calling from a hotel room and not a hospital. It is amazing how much can go through one's mind in a split second.

"What happened to my car?" My voice was flat.

"They promise it'll be fixed by tomorrow."

"What will be fixed?"

"Just . . . a little . . . dent, it's really no big deal, honestly. I bet you wouldn't even have noticed it, but François felt responsible and so—"

"Why did *François* feel responsible, Leslie?"

"Well, because . . ." She took a deep breath. "Because he was driving." She sighed.

The silence that descended between us was so utterly complete that it felt as if I were alone in the universe. I am by nature a generous woman, but my car—which is the only car I have ever owned—is something of which I am most protective. Knowing that Leslie was standing in the same room with the man who had dented my car, a total stranger who thought he could charm me with his accent or his explanation, only made me seethe.

"Let me explain," Leslie started.

"Okay." I sounded dangerously calm.

"Well, let me call you back in a little while."

"Why dear? Can't you talk in front of your little French friend who likes to test crash cars?"

"No."

"Then why don't you ask him to leave so that you and I can talk?"

"I can't."

"You can't?" I paused, for only a moment, but in the quiet I could literally feel my blood starting to boil. "I see. Let me rephrase it for you, Leslie, you can't or you won't?"

"Sydney . . ." She sounded tired and irritable.

"Don't bother to call back, Leslie. I have an early-morning meeting and I don't have time for your games. I don't know how you could be so disrespectful of *my* needs while you seem to be bending over backward to satisfy this prick you don't even know. What I find most disturbing is that you seem to care more about making a dollar than hurting me. I didn't know that about you.''

''Sydney . . .''

''Good night.'' I said, hoping, of course, that she would turn to Frenchie and tell him that she had to finish her call with me and would he please leave. But she didn't. When I banged the receiver back into the cradle, I knew that this was one of those situations that probably had a perfectly reasonable explanation, but egos would be bruised and feelings would be hurt as we struggled to get down to the nitty-gritty.

I knew she'd call back, she had to. Neither one of us had ever hung up on the other before, and I knew if it was upsetting me as much as it was, it had to be upsetting her more, because this whole thing was her fault. I went to the kitchen, certain the phone would ring by the time I reached the Britta water pitcher. Why she let a total stranger drive my car—especially knowing how meshugeneh I am about the damned thing—was beyond me. Unless, of course, he had driven with her for more than three miles and thought his chances for survival were better if he took over the helm. I spilled the water over the counter and onto the floor. By the time I cleaned up my mess she still had not called.

I was not going to let this make me crazy. Since I had a 7:30 meeting with Marshall Tucker, I decided that early-to-bed was a good idea. While I readied myself for bed, the phone remained silent. Though I was starting to obsess that Leslie hadn't called me back, I turned off the light at 10:43. I wasn't going to let it ruin my sleep. To ensure that, I turned off the ringer on the bedroom phone. Let her call. Let her call and wonder where I was.

At 1:15, I was still awake. I turned the ringer back on, turned on the light, went to the office, checked to see if she had called in case I hadn't heard it, and found that she hadn't. How could she have not called back? What the hell was she doing? She should have felt so bad that no matter what time the arrogant French man who totaled my car left, she should have called. I was wide awake, halfway to the kitchen, and not just a little upset, so I treated myself to a post-midnight snack of rye toast with brie, which I ate in bed while reading. By 2:30 I had finished Barbara Kingsolver's *Animal Dreams* and decided Leslie was in the doghouse for life.

Marshall Tucker was exactly what I expected. He wore a navy-blue Armani suit with a faded pink shirt and suspenders, was très tan, and had slicked his fine head of black hair under what I guessed was a tube and a half of glue. He wore a thin gold wedding band on his left hand, along with a gold Rolex watch and an enormous ID bracelet.

I accepted his offer of coffee and, while he went to get it, took the time to examine his office. It was a room that said, I am the boss, but I'm cool; I ski, I run the New York Marathon, and I have three children and a pretty wife. In the gallery of photos along one wall, Marshall proved that he believed himself to be very photogenic, as he was featured in every single picture.

"Here we are." He handed me a mug that boasted the firm's initials: TNDR, which stood for Tucker, Nylor, Druby, and Ross.

"Thank you." I followed him to his desk and put the mug on a TNDR coaster.

"So." He plopped himself down like a casual kind of guy, and nodded once. "I'm at your disposal. What can I do?"

"How long has Michael Callahan been a client?" I scribbled in my notebook to make sure my pen still had ink.

"I've known Mike maybe fifteen years. We met when we were kids at Columbia." He punctuated this information with a brisk nod.

"Columbia?" I acted sufficiently impressed to stroke his ego. "Medical and law? Aren't the campuses far apart?"

"Yeah, but we met as undergraduates and then continued to play squash together."

"So you know Michael pretty well."

"Oh sure. I was there for him when his folks died—"

"His parents died?"

"Oh yeah, it was awful. Mike was a junior when the accident happened. They were coming back from a vacation overseas and the plane went down."

"That's awful."

"Yeah. The horrible thing is, Michael convinced his mom to take the trip. His dad loved to travel, but she was afraid to fly. She would have been happy if she never left Queens."

"That's where Michael was raised?"

"That's right. It was tough. He was an only child, so when his folks died, he didn't have a sibling to help him get through it. He didn't have anyone. It really was pathetic. We all tried, but with something like that?" He shook his head. "There's really nothing anyone can do to help you through that."

"How long has he been a client?" I repeated my initial question.

Marshall reached for his coffee. "Long time. Since the beginning."

"It seems pretty clear that Michael's resisting help. How do you plan to defend him?"

"If you do your job, I won't have to." He smiled smugly as he brought his coffee up to his mouth. When I didn't respond, he slumped into his seat and said, "It would be imprudent for me to discuss strategy with you. As I mentioned on the phone, I respect my client's confidentiality. Besides, legally, I'm not allowed to discuss Michael's business with you."

"Michael is my client, too. Why did you agree to see me?"

"Quite honestly, I thought if there was *some* way I could

help . . ." He leaned further back into his chair and crossed his legs. "After all, Michael and I are friends."

Marshall Tucker was sending me crossed signals, which—giving him the benefit of the doubt—I supposed were a result of his good intentions. He wanted to help his friend but he was bound by the ethics of his profession to answer nothing and offer less.

"Do you know Michael well?" I asked, trying a different tactic. Ethics or not, I needed some answers.

"Yes. I thought so."

"Thought?"

He nodded.

"Does that mean you no longer think that?"

He sipped from his cup and when it was clear that he wasn't going to answer that question, I asked, "Did you know his wife, Jessica?" I asked.

"Oh yes. It's a terrible loss. Jessica was a lovely girl." It was hard to tell if he meant what he said or was just talking platitudes. Tucker stared into his cup as if he was deep in thought. Then he suddenly sat forward, leaned his elbows on his desk, looked me dead in the eyes, and said, "I apologize if I've wasted your time, Ms. Sloane, but I'm afraid all I can tell you is that Michael was arrested for suspicion of murder and released on one hundred thousand dollars' bail yesterday morning. We will do everything in our power to prove his innocence."

"You sound like you're practicing for reporters, and quite convincingly, I might add." I didn't budge from my seat. I don't know what had happened in Marshall Tucker's head when I asked him about Jessica, but clearly something was triggered off. "Mr. Tucker, just for the record, you and I are fighting the same battle."

"Are we?" His cryptic response irritated me. Why the hell can't people just be direct?

"Well, *I* was hired to prove Michael Callahan's innocence. You're his *defense* attorney. I would assume that places you and me on the same team."

71

He leaned back again and rested his chin on his fist. "We are on the same team."

"Good. Now, Michael doesn't seem to want anyone's help, yours or mine. As his friend, as his attorney, is there any way you could explain that?"

He gently ran his fingertips against his lips and sighed. "I will tell you one thing. I'm concerned."

"Why?"

"Well, what little contact I've had with him since Jessica died . . ." He paused and gave me a stern look. "This is strictly between the two of us, Ms. Sloane, is that understood?"

I nodded.

"Mike's different. It's like he's turned to stone."

"And that's unlike him?"

"Absolutely. He's always been a woman's man, if you know what I mean. Warm, funny, gentle, *accessible*, and he's a great doctor—the kids love him—he's our pediatrician. As a matter of fact, my wife is always complaining that I should be more like him." He swiveled his chair to look out the window. Most of his view was other office buildings that were only starting to come to life.

"You think he killed her, don't you?" I asked the back of his chair.

"I didn't say that." He kept his back to me.

"No. You didn't." He didn't have to. Marshall Tucker had been deliberately transparent. His allusions read loud and clear that he was trying to point me in a direction without having to take responsibility.

"Just a few more quick questions." I said, knowing that his back to me meant several things, one of them being that as far as he was concerned, our meeting was over.

He sighed.

"Do you know if Michael was seeing anyone outside his marriage?"

"What?" He swiveled around in his chair and gave me a look of sheer incredulity.

72

"I said do you know if Michael was cheating on Jessica?"

"Of course I know. Absolutely not. Aside from the fact that he adored her, he's the kind of man who lives his life by a strict code of ethics."

"I see. Does that code of ethics include murder?" When Marshall didn't respond, I continued. "One of the most interesting things I am learning about our client, Counselor, is that he seems to be a man people love but don't really trust. No one doubts his deep love for Jessica, but at the same time, no one denies the possibility that he might have killed her. I find that both disturbing and fascinating. Don't you?"

"I thought you were out to prove Michael's innocence."

"I am. I just hope it doesn't preclude the truth."

When I left Marshall's law firm the streets were teeming with office workers hurrying to their jobs. In the sea of faces that sped past, if there were three who looked happy, it was a lot. Everyone just seemed to be racing from one place to another but not enjoying it very much. Which brought to mind Marshall's assessment of Michael Callahan having turned to stone. It was an interesting comment, as far as I saw it. On the one hand I had a ninety-two-year-old woman who believed wholeheartedly in the doctor's innocence, but on the other hand, his own attorney and his wife's close friend had both made it clear that they were inclined to see Michael Callahan as a guilty man.

The Madison Avenue bus was packed. I excused and pushed my way to the back of the bus where I found a pocket of air space, which I claimed. Had I worn sneakers I would have walked crosstown, but I had dressed, instead, to inspire confidence from a lawyer. What a silly thing to do.

Seven

Max was on the phone when I walked into the office. He grimaced to indicate that this was not a good call and I gestured that I'd be in my office. I grabbed a cup of coffee and saw that the answering machine light was blinking. There were three calls. The first one was from a woman named Roz Porter. She was definitely not a happy camper and left a bizarre message. "I'm trying to reach Sydney Sloane. This is Roz Porter. Look, if I don't hear from you, I'm just going to have to go to the pound. I made it clear that I can't do this again right now, it's too hard on the kids. Call me." Her number started with 718, which put her in any borough but Manhattan.

The second call was Mary Douglas, Jessica Callahan's friend and employer. If the machine wasn't on the fritz, her call had come in at three in the morning.

The last message was from Leslie, and she sounded miserable. She left the number of her hotel, which proves how well she knows me. I had deliberately left her phone number behind, not wanting to be tempted to call her during the day.

I scribbled out a quick list of calls to make.

My curiosity was piqued by Roz's call, but first things first. As soon as I hit my desk I called Marcy Franks, who happens not only to be Max's girlfriend, but an incredibly reliable source of information as an officer with the NYPD.

"Hey Marcy, it's Sydney."

"Sydney, what a nice surprise." Said with only a touch of sarcasm. Marcy and I both know that I only call her at the office when I need help.

"You busy?" I asked, pulling out the telephone book.

"I'm always busy. What's up?"

I told her I was working on the Callahan case and asked if she could get me something on it, if only the names of the officers. She promised to check into it and call me as soon as she had anything.

Mary Douglas had her machine on, but I left another message telling her to call me at the office. Finally I couldn't hold off anymore and dialed the East Hampton number Leslie had left.

I let the phone ring once, twice, and hung up before anyone answered.

A loud voice in the back of my head called out, *Chicken.*

In the same area of my cerebrum, the voice of reason responded, *I have more important things to do than chase after Leslie right now.*

And yet, even as I was saying this to myself, I was reaching for the phone again.

She should be calling you! The reasonable voice pulled my hand away from the receiver like it was on fire.

Oh for crying out loud, you're too old for these games, call her.

The voices volleyed back and forth like that, with me reaching and pulling back from the phone, like I was a marionette.

Finally, as if an omen sent from the powers that be, the phone rang. I answered. "CSI, may I help you?"

"Yeah, can I talk to Sydney, please?" The voice was both angry and familiar. It was the woman on the answering machine. Roz. I'd forgotten to call her back.

"Speaking."

"Don't you return your calls? Hang on a second." The caller put her hand over the mouthpiece but I could still hear her yelling at Howie to leave his sister's ears alone. "Sorry about that." She said when she returned. "I'm Roz. Michael's neighbor? I'm calling about the dog."

"Dog?"

"What do you mean *dog* like you've never heard the word?" she asked, her voice getting noticeably tighter.

In the back of my mind I had the sinking feeling that I knew what this woman was going to tell me. "Who is your neighbor?"

"Michael Callahan." She said through what sounded distinctly like gritted teeth.

"Roz? Rosalynn Porter? I thought your name was Hayes."

"Porter's my married name. I use both."

"I was going to call you today."

"Well isn't that nice? Listen, I'm doing you guys a favor, you know. I told Michael it was a bad idea for me to take this dog again because the kids are getting attached, but he promised me you'd be here. Now you're acting like you don't know what the hell I'm talking about. Howie, leave the puppy alone."

"Michael gave you his dog?" This call was not going well.

There was a long silence on the other end of the line. Finally she said, "Look, I took this dog when he was arrested because he had nowhere else to turn. But I'm going to tell you, I don't like being taken advantage of. Children get attached too quickly . . ."

"Wait a minute, where is Michael?"

"That's the nine-million-dollar question. My husband's convinced he's in Brazil." Rosalynn Hayes-Porter went on to explain that shortly after I had left Michael's the day before, he went over to her place with the dog and told her that he had to leave town unexpectedly, but that a friend of his—Sydney Sloane—was going to come by and pick up the dog by five o'clock. Since I didn't have a key to his place he asked Roz to take care of the dog until I arrived.

"I warned him that I would not get stuck with this dog. It was hard enough for us when I agreed to take her while he was in—Howie, leave-the-pup-py-a-lone! Christ, hang on." I listened as the receiver on her end tumbled to the floor and then her distinct shriek at Howie to stop putting cereal in the puppy's ears. A quick survey of my feelings let me know that there was a slow burn on the rise. I didn't know if I was angrier that Michael had skipped out on his bail (which only made the jerk look guilty), or that he thought he could just saddle me with his dog. "Sorry about that," she said on her return. "Kids. So." She took a deep breath. "You don't know what the hell I'm talking about, do you? He never even told you, right? That son of a bitch. Dennis told me he wasn't right."

"Who's Dennis?"

"My husband. He's a therapist. He warned me that Michael was off the deep end and I was just asking for trouble."

"And Michael didn't tell you where he was going?"

"No. All he said was that he had to leave town unexpectedly. We've been friends a long time, so I thought I could trust him, but Dennis was right. Well, screw it. I'll figure something out."

"Wait a minute." I needed to meet with Rosalynn anyway, because Michael had told me that she had seen Jessica on the day she was killed. But the doctor's word was questionable at this point. "Rosalynn, when did you see Jessica last?" I could hear her wondering where I was coming from. "Did you see her the day she died?"

"Yes," she said mistrustfully.

"And what are you planning to do with the dog?"

"What am I going to do? I don't have any choice. I'll have Dennis take her to the . . . you know." Though she lowered her voice it was clear that Howie was hanging on his mother's every word. At the mention of the "you know," he started screaming and crying that he wanted to keep the puppy.

77

Hearing Howie wailing long distance made me sympathetic to his mother's plight. I could just picture this poor woman in her kitchen, a white telephone receiver tucked between her chin and her shoulder, one kid in a highchair, the other hanging on her legs screaming about the puppy, while the puppy happily raced around the room vacuuming up all fallen scraps.

"Wait a minute. I'll take her." It was as if I was possessed; the words were out before I could stop them. Me with a dog? Impossible, and yet it was distinctly my voice uttering those three crucial words: "I'll take her." And do what? I wanted to add, but good sense prevailed and I refrained from having a lengthy discussion with myself.

"Oh my God, that's great." Rosalynn's relief was lost under the din of her child's vocal protest. Again she put her hand over the receiver and tried to reason past Howie's screams. Finally she blew the kid into silence by screeching, *"Shut up the lady's gonna take it!"*

We agreed that I would be at her place by three o'clock that afternoon.

I was exhausted when I went to Max's office.

"You know, I've been thinking . . ." I took the seat directly across from him.

"I love it when you think." He didn't look up from his *Times* crossword puzzle.

"Thank you. I've been thinking that you need something."

"You're right. I do. I need a new car, a vacation and a four-letter word for algae."

"Scum?"

"No."

"Kelp."

"No."

"A puppy."

"A puppy? What's that?" He glanced up from the paper and counted out too many fingers. "It's more than four letters."

78

"I think you need a puppy. As in dog, man's best friend. Bowser. Fido. Spot." None of these words seem to trigger anything mildly resembling interest.

"I think not. As in no, negative, not on your life."

"It really is a cute dog, Max. Her name is Auggie."

"Auggie? Auggie is not a good name, Sydney. Right off the bat you have to change her name."

"I kind of like it. It suits her."

"I'm telling you, if you want to get rid of this dog—which I assume is what you're trying to do—you need something better than a cartoon name. Wasn't there an Auggie Doggie on *Quick Draw McGraw?*"

"Of course she'd name her dog after a cartoon!" I tapped my fingers against my forehead. "She was a cartoonist. The name is perfect for the dog."

"Well I don't want it anyway. I had a dog once. That was enough."

"When?"

"When I was married. It didn't work out."

"Really?"

"Yeah. She couldn't stand me. She used to pee on me every time I came in the front door."

"But that was nothing, you shoulda seen the way the dog greeted me." I wiggled my eyebrows and mimicked Groucho Marx.

"You're stealing my material." Max glanced up from the puzzle he was pretending to fill in.

"Okay, I'm out of here." I got up and saw that Byron De La Beckwith's photo on the dartboard had been replaced with a badly drawn cartoon stick figure, which was, I knew, Max's handiwork. I assumed the dart-riddled page had something to do with Louie.

"Can I expect to see you in today, dear?" He leaned back and put his feet up on his desk.

"Probably, but you can never tell. Surprises abound. Why just now we lost Enoch's sister's grandson by marriage."

"The doctor?"

"That's right."

"He's gone?"

"Eyup. Which makes it a tad harder to believe in his alleged innocence."

"Speaking of which . . . ?"

"I met him yesterday."

"And?"

"And I liked him. But not everyone does."

"How's that?"

"When I arrived at his house, a couple of Irish boys were just leaving."

"Bad boys?"

I nodded. "Yes. Not only did they rough up the good doctor, but they gave me a couple of bruises that I'm hiding under my detective attire." I looked down at my outfit for the day; Cole Haan leather driving shoes; loose, pleated green slacks; a low-cut silk blouse, and a flecked woolen blazer. Despite my classy, womanly look, I knew my right elbow and knee were sporting huge bruises from my spill the day before.

"Are you okay?" He put down the paper and got very serious.

"I'm fine."

"Maybe I should—"

I cut him off. "No you don't, we agreed that you would take care of Louie and the Hackle contract."

"We did not."

"Sure we did."

"No, no. I agreed to take care of *Louie*, but not the Hackle contract. That's definitely your area of expertise."

"You're such a baby. Speaking of Louie . . ." I poked my thumb in the general direction of the dartboard. Max nodded. "I can assume from your artwork that things are not progressing in a positive vein?"

"He is a hateful, stupid man. Despite my charm and persuasiveness, we will, I am certain, lose the Madeline.

Right now it's a matter of trying to salvage back pay.''

"If anyone can do it, Maxo, you can. And seeing as though you're being such a good sport about taking that on, I will deal with Hackle, but first I want to find out why our friend jumped bail.''

Max clicked his tongue against his teeth. "I hate when that happens. Any ideas?''

"Well, clearly he's hiding something. When we met yesterday I thought he was protecting someone else, but who knows?'' I stretched and let out a big yawn. "Talking to him is like pulling teeth. I mean, here we have a man who doesn't seem to care if he goes to jail for his wife's murder—but at the same time he swears he didn't do it. He loved her but he's willing to spend his life behind bars for her murder . . . a murder he allegedly didn't commit.''

"I like it.'' Max nodded.

"Me, too.''

"You sure you don't need help?''

"Nah, all I have to do is find out where he was when she was murdered and who she was with before she was killed. Easy.''

"Right. Well, I'll just sit here and vegetate all day.'' He sighed as he went back to the crossword puzzle.

"You do that.'' I got to my office door and said, "By the way, how about moss?''

"Moss? Hart, famous playwright.''

"No, moss as in a four-letter word for algae.''

"M-o-s-s, excellent. Thank you.''

"Anytime. Hey, don't work too hard.''

"I won't.''

Somehow I knew I could count on that. What the hell? It was Indian summer and we had just given away three months for nothing. More than three hundred man-hours and we had collected only a portion of the fee. Just the thought of it made my stomach hurt.

Eight

The ground-floor offices of Drs. Callahan and Miller are located in a brownstone on a side street in lower Manhattan not far from the Treelane Nursing Home. The waiting room felt more like a cluttered living room than a doctor's office. The walls were lined with shelves of books, a centrally located coffee table was lost under piles of magazines and kids' books, and one section of the room had been clearly designed as the children's corner, with pint-sized table and chairs and toys that had seen better days, but were being put to use by two three-year-olds having a tea party.

Three young women were crammed in behind the counter, each one occupied with a task. They reminded me of ants or bees working with precision and utter focus. The shortest and roundest of the three noticed me first. From her melodic Jamaican accent when she asked if she could help me, I knew she was the one I had spoken with the day before.

"Good morning. My name is Sydney Sloane. I have an appointment with Dr. Miller."

All activity behind the counter came to a momentary halt as the other two worker bees stopped to look at me. In small offices it's impossible to keep a secret; evidently they all knew who I was and why I wanted to see the doctor. I smiled in greeting.

"You'll have to wait." She gestured to the couches behind me and squeezed out what I took to be a smile.

I glanced at the seating behind me and counted two women and three children. I turned back to my Jamaican friend and asked, "May I ask you a question or two?" I flashed my private investigator's license and tried to shield us from the rest of the room with my back.

Her dark brown eyes flashed from my license to her two friends beside her. "Is this about Dr. Mike?" she asked mistrustfully.

"Yes."

"He's a good man," she warned me quietly with her voice and her eyes.

"I know that. I'm his friend. What's your name?"

"Daphne."

"Daphne, were you here the day Dr. Callahan's wife died?"

"Yes."

"Can you tell me anything about that day?"

"What about it?"

"Well for starters, how would you describe Dr. Callahan's mood?"

"Good." She pouted.

"He was preoccupied," offered a second woman behind the counter. She gave me her opinion without so much as glancing up from her paperwork.

"Really? Was that unusual?" I looked from Daphne to her coworker and back again.

Before either woman could answer, the third woman behind the counter pointed to me. "Miss? Dr. Miller will see you now." She pointed to a door to my immediate right. "Go right in there."

I paused, wanting to pursue this conversation, but was quickly ushered into the office.

When I entered, Hannah Miller was sitting behind her desk, wrapping up a phone call. The first thing I noticed about her was that her pale blue eyes were so close together, they nearly appeared as one Cycloptic oculus in the middle of her head. The second thing I noticed was that she was wearing a very wrinkled navy-blue sailor dress with a crooked bow under her white jacket. Not a sight that instilled confidence. If I had been there as a patient, I might have backed out the door with a "Gosh I suddenly feel fine," but I wasn't, so I nodded a silent greeting.

She motioned for me to sit across from her in the only other seat in the room. I did as I was told and quickly discovered that an enormous air conditioner behind the doctor was blasting frigid air directly at the visitor's chair. Since it was October, I could only assume Hannah was prone to hot flashes. That's nice, a patient comes in for a stomachache and leaves with pneumonia. I studied the doctor as I inched my chair away from the wind tunnel. Her fine blond hair was parted in the middle and hung flat on her long head, tucked behind two large ears. She was a nail biter and she wore no rings. I had about twelve dozen photographs of me in high school sporting a very similar look.

"Now then," she said as soon as she ended her call. "You are Officer Sloane?" Her small round mouth hid a set of crooked teeth.

"Sydney Sloane," I said as I handed her my license.

She looked at my ID and, without giving it back to me, said with distaste, "You're a private investigator."

"Yes."

"Why didn't you tell me that on the phone?"

"I tried to, but you put me on hold—"

She cut me off. "I don't like deception." She tossed my ID back onto the desk as if it had cooties. "I'm too busy for this nonsense."

"I didn't try to deceive you, and I don't consider this investigation to be nonsense. Also, I don't know if you understand, but I'm working *for* Michael, not against him." I didn't move.

"Michael hired you?" She raised an almost invisible eyebrow.

"No. Jessica's grandmother did. She wants me to prove he's innocent."

"Fine. Look, I've told the police everything I know, which is nothing. I am incredibly busy, what with Michael out of the office—"

"He told me yesterday that he was returning to work."

"Well, he's decided that he needs time to sort through things, and quite honestly, I don't blame him." She pointed to my ID. "Now if you'll just—"

"Dr. Miller, I assume that you and Michael are friends as well as partners, am I right?" She gave me a condescending nod. "Right now he could use all the friends he has. You see, if I don't prove that he's innocent, he's going to go to jail for a long time for a crime he probably didn't commit. But between his unwillingness to help me and his friends' reticence, I get the feeling that I'm trying to jumpstart a case here that no one gives a damn about, not even the accused.

"Now if you really don't want to answer my questions, I'll leave. But you should know that if you do that, as far as I'm concerned, you're contributing to his incarceration."

Hannah studied her fingertips as the air conditioner droned noisily behind her. Finally she looked at me, brought a finger to her mouth, and said, "What do you want to know?"

"For starters, where is he?"

She pressed her lips together, shook her head, and shrugged. "I don't know."

If she was telling the truth I would vote for Pat Buchanan in the next election. "You don't know where he is, or you don't want to tell me where he is?"

"I don't know where he is." She picked up a stray piece of paper from her desk and glanced at it. Right. If she was telling the truth, I'd *sleep* with Pat Buchanan.

"Is there an extended family that he might have turned to? Aunts or cousins?"

"No one. I don't know if you know this, but his parents

were killed when he was younger. It's very sad, his mother was the only child of an only child, and his father was an orphan.''

"Michael was from Queens?''

"That's right. Astoria.''

"When did you last see him?''

"Yesterday.''

"What time?''

She frowned. "Around five, maybe? I don't remember. But sometime in the early evening.''

"Where?''

"Here. He stopped by to tell me that he wouldn't be in for a few days. He said he needed some time to sort things out for himself.''

"Do you know what it is he needs to sort out?''

"He was just falsely arrested for the murder of his wife,'' she said coldly. "I'm sure he has any number of things to sort through, emotionally. At least, that's how I interpreted it. We didn't discuss it.''

"I see. You realize that by leaving town he is actively jumping bail. That doesn't look good.''

"Maybe he didn't leave town.'' With her snippy attitude alone, Hannah Miller was actively wooing my bad side. However, she had a point, and it bothered me that this was a distinct possibility I hadn't even considered.

"Maybe not. Tell me, Doctor, if Michael were to have stayed in town, where would he have stayed?''

She looked mildly surprised. "At home, I would suspect.''

"And if not there?''

She scratched the back of her neck with the nubs of her fingernails and shrugged.

"What about your place?''

She exhaled a laugh of contempt and affected an air of boredom. "Michael is *just* my friend.''

"I don't doubt that.'' I looked away from her and studied my notepad.

86

"I don't know where he is." She sulked.

"Okay, then can you tell me anything about the day Jessica died?"

"I honestly don't know what to tell you. It was a normal day at the office, nothing unusual until we heard that Jessica was dead. You should know that when the police questioned me they twisted everything I said and made it sound like I thought Michael did it."

"Do you?"

"No!" The color rose to her cheeks.

"Did you know Jessica?"

"Of course I knew her." She shifted impatiently in her seat. "Michael only started *dating* her four years ago."

"And they were married for how long?"

"Two years."

"How did you and Jessica get along?"

"Fine." The doctor gave one shoulder an unenthusiastic shrug.

"Did you like her?"

"Jessica and I are very different from each other." This was the first reaction to Jessica that hadn't been a rave review.

"Really? How so?"

"Have you met any of her friends?" she asked, with more than a hint of derision. I thought of Donna Frost and met her look with a blank stare. "Well . . ." The doctor sat up straighter and leaned stiffly toward me. "I'll tell you what I told the police. If anyone was responsible for Jessica's death it was herself. I'm not saying that she committed suicide, but if you saw the people she called her friends, you'd know what I'm talking about." Hannah's smugness made her face look somehow longer and thinner.

"I don't understand."

"They're what you would call a . . . flamboyant group of people, if you know what I mean."

"Oh, I see. Jessica and Michael had eccentric friends, is that what you're saying?"

She shook her head ever so slightly. "I'm saying that *she* had flamboyant friends. Michael isn't like that."

"Like what?" I could tell Dr. Cyclops found me as frustrating as a three-year-old who is constantly intoning, "Why?"

"Jessica was the type of person who didn't really understand boundaries. Personally I don't think she showed the best of taste or judgment, especially insofar as how her social life could have affected Michael's career."

"So, Michael didn't like her friends?" I prompted her.

"Michael is a very tolerant man. More so than I would have been if I was in his shoes. I mean, she would bring home stray animals and *people*. I remember one time several of us had been invited for dinner and when we showed up, Jessica had completely forgotten about her dinner party because she had plucked a bag lady off the street and taken her to a shelter, where she had to spend hours wading through red tape to get this woman settled. A total stranger. Can you *imagine* that?"

I couldn't, but clearly not for the same reason as the doctor.

"Michael was amazingly gracious. We all showed up, she hadn't done a thing toward dinner, and his reaction was to say that it was no big deal and then he took us all out to a restaurant. That's just *one* example of her social ineptitude. She was a very strange woman."

We should all be so strange, I thought.

"Do you think one of her strays or her friends killed her?"

"I don't know who killed her, but I don't believe for one minute that Michael did, whereas I wouldn't be surprised *if* one of her friends were responsible."

"Who?"

Her close-set eyes grew wide. "I don't know. It's just a theory, a hypothesis. I wouldn't be so foolhardy as to give you *names*. Look, I'm convinced Michael didn't do it and I just want to show that there are other options."

"I agree. Now, Michael left the office early on the day Jessica was killed. Do you know where he went?"

She paused. "No." She picked up a rubber ball and started squeezing it.

"What sort of mood was he in that day?"

"He was in a fine mood. There was nothing extraordinary in his behavior." Between squeezing the ball, the coldness of her response, and the fact that she was keeping her eye on the ball and not me, I was willing to bet a years' worth of wrinkles that Hannah Miller was lying again through her crooked little teeth.

"So it was just like any other day?"

"Yes."

"Except that Michael left early."

"It happens."

"Often?"

"No."

"Was there any time in the recent past when he left the office early?"

"Yes. He had a patient, a young boy with AIDS he was treating. He became emotionally involved with the child, and several times Michael left the office early to be with him. And, of course, Michael was with him on the day the boy died."

"When was that?"

She shrugged. "A month ago."

"Your hospital affiliation is with . . . ?"

"St. Mary's. Just a few blocks away."

"Both you and Michael are with that hospital?"

"That's right."

"What time did Michael leave last Wednesday?"

"Around two."

"And you?"

"Me?" She flashed me a look of disbelief. "What are you suggesting?"

"Nothing. I'm simply asking what time you left the office that day."

"Five-thirty."

The intercom buzzed one long ring. The sound ricocheted off the four walls and pierced my eardrums. Dr. Miller plucked the receiver off the phone and flatly said, "Yes. It's all right, Daphne, we were just finishing up here." She said this into the telephone, but looked directly at me.

As I tucked my ID back into my wallet, I asked Hannah for a contact at the hospital.

"What for?" As she stood, the wind current from the air conditioner blew her fine hair forward onto her face.

I explained that for any investigation to be thorough, I had to touch all bases. Dr. Cyclops gave me two names at St. Mary's. Though the interview had been helpful, Hannah Miller knew a lot more than she was letting on, and I was looking forward to finding out what, exactly, that was.

I had a feeling that I was going to have better luck piecing together Jessica's last few hours than Michael's missing ones. I also had a hunch that Jessica's friend Mary Douglas was a good place to start.

Knowing that nine out of ten pay phones on the street are worthless, I used the phone at the front desk in the doctor's office. Mary's line was busy, which was promising. I then called Max and learned that Marcy—his girlfriend and police pal—had called back with some basic information.

"Tell me, tell me." I pulled my notebook from my bag and tried to fold myself out of the way of patients signing in.

"First of all, I have the name and number of the detective working on the case as well as the first officer."

"Okay." I had already gotten the detective, Jacob Stavinsky's number from Enoch. I noted Patrolman Greg Minor and his precinct number in my book. "Okay, good. Next?"

"Cause of death was carbon monoxide poisoning."

"Yes." This confirmed what Enoch had told me the day before.

"Time of death is set between noon and four."

"Okay."

"The deceased was discovered by a neighbor at five-fifteen." Again this confirmed Enoch's information.

"Do you know who?"

"Let's see, a Dennis Porter."

"Really?"

"Yes."

"Good." I already had plans to meet with the Porters that afternoon and retrieve Auggie.

"The deceased's husband, Michael, showed up at six-thirty. When—"

"Excuse me, are you going to be long?" A wide woman with teased black hair and red lacquered lips tapped my shoulder and pushed her face into mine. "I have to make a call." She blinked her phony lashes at me and added, "I've been waiting for you to get off." Her face contorted into what I assumed she meant to be a smile. When I didn't respond quickly enough, she added, "It's like you're monopolizing, okay?"

I don't know if I was more intrigued by her gall or by her greasepaint, but, having gotten the gist of Marcy's information from Max, I asked him to check the city hotels for the missing doctor. I then thanked the women behind the desk, who each made it a point to give me nothing more than a fleeting glance, as if eye contact with me would turn them into stoolies. It's not easy being an investigator.

My objective now was to piece together the hours between eleven—when Jessica had left Donna Frost after their coffee date—and five-fifteen—when her body was discovered by Dennis Porter.

I turned west and found myself walking toward the Treelane Nursing Home. I knew that Jessica had seen Selma that day, but the time frame was still a little foggy. En route to the Treelane, I remembered that Selma had mentioned she liked jelly beans. I picked up a bag from a candy store and passed two pay phones that proved to be useless. However, on the third one I struck pay dirt. Not only was the phone working, but I was able to get a line through to Mary Douglas.

She agreed to meet me at her apartment on the Upper East Side at 12:30, which gave me more than enough time to meet with Selma and start connecting the dots.

Nine

The Treelane receptionist with big hair remembered me from the day before and we made small talk as I signed in. I learned that Naomi's office was on the second floor and she was in all day. Since I hadn't returned her call the night before, I decided to kill two birds with one stone.

The fourth floor was quieter than it had been the day before. I went to the sunroom first. There were two ancient women sitting side by side at the table where the foursome had played cards the day before. They were deep in conversation, holding hands. When I poked my head in the room the one with red hair looked up and smiled.

I smiled back at her, stepped into the corridor, and practically bumped into an elderly man with enormous, hairy ears, standing expectantly, just to the side of the doorway. "Hi," I greeted him warmly.

He looked as if he had been caught. His eyes grew wide and he looked from his right to his left and then back at me. "You don't scare me." He finally said, obviously mustering up every ounce of courage inside him.

"That's good," I tried to reassure him. "I wouldn't want to."

"Oh sure." He started to back away, but then decided against it. Instead he pushed up his unshaven chin at me and cackled, "You're all alike."

Before I could find out who this global "you" was, he turned his back on me and shuffled away.

I found Selma in her room. She was sitting on the pea-green leatherette chair, looking smaller than she really was. The blinds were closed, blocking out all sunlight, and leaving gray shadows that hung in the room like hovering ghosts.

"Selma?" I said softly, afraid of startling her. "May I come in?" I asked, inching my way into the darkness.

She took in a big breath and exhaled a slow "Yes."

I stepped into the room and squatted in front of her. "It's Sydney. I brought you some jelly beans." I searched her eyes, hoping to see the same glimmer that had been there the day before, but she was different.

She looked startled at the little white paper bag and then took it with an arthritic hand. "Jessica always brought me jelly beans. I have my own teeth, you know, so I don't have to worry about sugar." She sounded far away.

"Good for you." I squeezed her hand gently. "I'm going to open the shades, Selma, okay? It's a beautiful day out there and you could use some light in here." I got up, went to the windows, and opened the blinds. Sunlight inched its way into the room until finally the place was flooded in light.

Selma kept her back to the windows. I brought a chair with me and joined her.

"What's up?" I asked, as if we were longtime friends.

She shrugged and kept her eyes on the white bag in her hand. "I have a friend, a very nice woman, all she ever talks about is how she wants to die and be reunited with her husband." Selma shook her head. "She has family who love her, reasonably good health, but she tells me all the time she wants to die. I'm ninety-two, I never felt that way." Selma looked at me and I saw her eyes were blood-shot and drooping. She reached out for my hand. "Today I understand how my friend feels."

The fact is, as hard a concept as death is for me, I can

understand being ready to call it a life. But I hardly knew Selma well enough to say, "Yeah, well, soon." So I leaned toward her and clasped her hand in both of mine and decided to go the pep-talk route. "Selma, you don't want to die. You have Enoch and Michael and now you're stuck with me, and all of your friends here."

"Michael?" She looked confused.

"Jessica's husband?"

"Jessica should be here soon." Because she looked away from me I couldn't tell if she was playing a game with herself or if she really believed this. It didn't matter, though. She looked vulnerable and frail and I just wanted to hold her in my arms and tell her everything would be all right. But I didn't know what that would mean. I thought of my own parents and wondered, what if they had lived to frailty?

"Jelly bean?" She pushed the bag in my direction.

"Thanks." I opened the bag, took out a candy, and offered her the bag.

She glanced behind me. "Mother doesn't like me to eat candy." She looked in the bag and carefully selected two black jelly beans. "I always save the pink ones for Ennie." She popped a licorice in her mouth and smiled in a way that let me see exactly what she had looked like as a little girl.

"Ennie?" I asked.

"Enoch." She had the demeanor of a ten-year-old.

For the next five minutes Selma was a little girl whose little brother was a nuisance. Then, without a blink of an eye she seemed to be back to her old self.

"I was talking to Mr. Sherman earlier. Poor man, his son died several months ago." She leaned toward me and whispered. "He was a bigshot, a lawyer. Too busy to visit his father." She paused. "Heart attack, just like *your* father."

"Sorry?"

Selma looked panicked. "Jessica, oh honey, I'm sorry. I never told you." She grabbed my hand in a viselike grip.

Her eyes were pleading and I could see that her tongue was stained black from the candy.

"It's okay, Selma," I said gently.

Why is it so much harder to watch old people and children in pain? She cried, and I let her hold me thinking I was Jessica. And, I did what I thought Jessica would do, I absolved her of all transgressions, real or imagined, that might have taken place between them.

I stayed half an hour longer and Selma bounced between confusion and reality the whole time, addressing me as Jessica one minute, and myself the next. This was fine by me, I was happy to bounce right along with her. As Sydney I asked about her last visit with Jessica and she told me that they had not had lunch together as planned because Selma had an upset stomach. She also said that Jessica had arrived at 11:00 and left at 3:00. Unfortunately, given her emotional state, I didn't know if I could trust this information. I figured, however, that since the Treelane kept a log of all visitors, Naomi might be able to provide the details for me.

When I left, Selma thanked me—Sydney—for the jelly beans. I doubted she would remember my visit.

The elevator smelled like antiseptic and mothballs, provoking a gag reflex from me. I held my breath the sixty seconds it took to descend two floors and wondered if the elderly residents knew that they had probably the slowest elevators in the whole of Manhattan. Maybe they didn't notice, or didn't care. Maybe they napped between the fourth and first floors.

I got off at the second floor, asked an aide where I'd find Naomi, followed her directions to a T, and found myself standing in the doorway of an empty staff lunchroom.

"Can I help you?" a familiar voice asked from behind. I turned and saw the woman who had led me to Selma the day before.

"Well, hello there," I said as soon as I saw her friendly face. "Remember me? We met yesterday when I was lost."

"Of course I remember you. You're Selma's friend."

"That's right. Believe it or not, I think I'm lost again," I said, glancing back into the lunchroom. "Unless, of course, this is Naomi's office."

She was polite enough to chuckle at my joke and said, "They ought to provide visitors with maps. Miss Lewis's office is just down the hall. Come on, I'll take you there." She took two baby steps back, pivoted, and made a crisp turn up the hall. No question, this was one efficient lady.

"Thank you. At this rate someone should assign you as my personal escort."

"We aim to please at the Treelane."

"So it seems." I couldn't help but notice as we wove our way through the halls that the initial directions I had been given to Naomi's room were completely backward.

"Do you . . . live here?" I asked as she led me down the antiseptic-smelling corridor.

"No, dear, I don't. I work here, I'm a volunteer. My name's Beatrice. And yours?" She didn't miss a step as she held out her hand to me.

"Sydney." I took her hand as we hurried down the hall.

"What a marvelous name for a girl. Well, Sydney, here we are." Apparently they had converted one of the resident rooms into an office. Naomi was sitting behind her desk with a cup of coffee in one hand and a bunch of papers in the other. She was scowling as she read.

"Knock, knock," Beatrice said without actually knocking.

When Naomi looked up, her face relaxed and she drew the corners of her mouth up into a wide smile. "Bea, I'm glad to see you found my friend before she got into trouble. Beatrice is our unofficial welcome wagon, Sydney." Naomi put down her coffee and papers and stood up behind her desk.

"She's been more like the cavalry."

"Beatrice Carson, Sydney Sloane; Sydney, Beatrice." Naomi made a formal introduction.

"Naomi, dear, we're way ahead of you." Beatrice patted

Naomi's arm. "I didn't know that you two were chums. I thought you were friends with Selma." She addressed the last part to me.

"Oh, Sydney's friends with everyone," Naomi chimed in.

"Isn't that swell? Well, you two girls have a nice visit." With that said, Beatrice fluttered a little wave of her hand and was barreling back up the corridor, calling out a cheery good morning to everyone she passed.

"She's quite a character," I said as I followed Naomi into her twelve-by-twelve-foot office. Sunlight was pouring in through the single wide window. When Naomi stood behind her desk, which was in front of the window, she was surrounded by an ethereal glow.

"Beatrice Carson is as sharp as a tack and twice as pointed." She sat down and gestured to the chair in front of her desk. "She is also one of the nicest women in the world."

"I was stunned when she told me she works here."

"Oh yeah, she's a volunteer, though I'd gladly pay her, she's so good to our residents."

"I thought she *was* a resident."

"Bea is seventy-one and fit as a horse."

It flashed through my head that had she lived, my mother would have been seventy-one.

"She's amazing. She lives in an apartment not far from here. She's not ready for a nursing home. I'm surprised, though, that the two of you got on so well."

"Really? Why?"

"I don't think she takes to most young people."

"Young people. You say the sweetest things." I alighted on the chair like a fifties glamour queen, rolling my shoulder, crossing my long legs, and patting my hair.

Naomi let out a gruff laugh and reminded me that age is relative. "Speaking of relatives, how's your sister?" she asked.

"Nora? Good. She lives in a big house in Baltimore with

a rich husband, a vintage Mercedes, and a Republican voting card.''

"There's nothing wrong with Republicans," she said, sounding a little like a Stepford Wife.

"You're a Republican?" I was floored. Naomi had been one of the most outspoken hippies in our high school.

"No, of course not. But I married one." Her smile was brilliant. "What can I tell you? He was great in bed."

"Is he still?"

"Oh sister." She did a little jiggle in her chair and laughed, "My man is my medicine."

It was wonderful to see that life had been so good to Naomi. We spent the next half-hour playing catch-up. It wasn't surprising that it was like picking up right where we'd left off more than twenty years earlier.

Only it wasn't twenty-odd years earlier, when our biggest dilemma was whether we should lose our virginity in high school with the rest of the girls or hold out for love . . . or at least college. Now Naomi had two mortgages, two daughters, and two cars. I had one apartment, one car (which was God knew where), and one murder to solve.

"So, how well do you know Selma Onderdonk?" I asked, getting back to business.

"Pretty well. Actually, very well. You see, I try to make it a point to know all the residents here. Naturally some I get to know better than others, but . . ." She trailed off as she rummaged through her top right drawer and pulled out a red-and-white tin of Altoid mints.

"And Selma, I take it, is one of those you know better than others?"

She nodded and offered me a mint.

"Thanks. So let me ask you, is Selma senile?"

Naomi smiled indulgently, closed the mint tin, and put it away. "Selma can be a little forgetful. Why? Did she get lost on you today?"

"Well, it wasn't a big deal, but first we were back at the turn of the century, and then I was Jessica . . ."

"But with ample sprinklings of reality to spice up the conversation and totally confuse the hell out of you, right?" Naomi laughed. "Don't you love it? Old age. A glance into our own futures; your body giving out on you, your joints turning into big gnarly things, your eyes clouded over so you can't see where the hell your mouth is for your lipstick. All of a sudden, one day you're sitting there watching TV, because it's too hard on your eyes to read, and the next thing you know you're sitting in a puddle of your own urine." She said this all with a lightheartedness that seemed inappropriate.

"Not everyone disintegrates." I knew that; after all, I'd started *The Fountain of Age* by Betty Friedan.

"Don't you believe it, cookie, you start disintegrating from the second you're born."

"Well, I'd like to take this opportunity to thank you for your insights, unsought though they may be." I stood up to leave. "And though it's been fun, I'm going to take these rapidly aging bones out of here before they turn to dust before your very eyes."

Naomi flapped her hands in a downward motion. "Wait, wait, wait, sit down, you just got here."

I did as told and said, "You have a skewed view of things, Nai."

"Absolutely not, I'm just a realist. I look at it this way, Sydney, we don't all have to deteriorate when we get old, but we all have to age, and ultimately die. Now the fact is, we can enter old age with our eyes shut, or we can try to understand it so that when it does happen, God willing, we're not so frightened. I have a lot of little chickens here in my coop, and I can tell you, the ones who have the healthiest attitude are the ones who can laugh at themselves—and life, and death."

"And Selma?" I asked.

"Oh, Sel knows how to laugh. She's someone I would have liked to have known when she was young." The phone rang and she waved it off. "My voice mail can pick it up." She leaned back in her chair, crossed her arms over her stomach, and nodded to me. "You afraid of getting old?"

It was a simple question but I felt bombarded with a thousand answers. I went with my gut reaction. "Yes, I suppose I am."

"What scares you most?"

Right, like pick one thing out of a zillion and make that the most frightening. Was it the physical or emotional I feared most? I stumbled like an idiot and shook my head. "I don't know. Maybe the unknown. Or being helpless. I mean, I've been young all my life, old isn't something I know."

"Right. Like those sorry old bones don't creak when you've been sitting in one position for too long? Or what radio station do you listen to now? When was it that James Taylor and America became easy listening? Or how about buses, do you find yourself debating before you offer your seat, waiting for people who are *really* old? Or sight." She plucked the glasses hanging from a chain around her neck. "You got a pair of these in there, my dear?" She motioned to my bag.

I laughed, knowing perfectly well that my reading glasses were readily available in the outside pouch of my bag.

"Uh-huh, but you're telling me old isn't something you know." Despite all our talk about age, when Naomi smiled, we could have been back in high school. "So, in answer to your original question—is Selma senile?—Selma is old and every now and then she gets confused, but for the most part she is a savvy, together, active lady. Why?"

"Well, I guess I'm not used to actually having a conversation with someone who's *really* old." I stopped and was amazed at the truth behind what I had just said. "I mean, my aunt is eighty-one, but there are no gaps in her conversation. She's as clear as a bell."

"Minnie?"

"Yeah."

"God, I remember Minnie. She was *always* old."

Naomi's impression of Aunt Minnie took me only slightly by surprise. To me, Minnie has always been more like a peer. She's my aunt—and my elderly aunt at that—but her energy and wit have always kept me on my toes. As I sat in Naomi's office, I wondered where Minnie would be in eleven years, which was the difference between her age and Selma's. Would we be engaging in a conversation that took place in a time warp, or would she even be around? Oh no, this was not a train of thought I wanted to ride at that very moment.

I bit into the Altoid mint that I'd parked in the back of my mouth, and it felt as if my tongue and teeth had caught on fire. This must be the refreshing concept of mints.

"Anyway." When I inhaled, the air made my mouth feel like additional solvents had been added to the already-present flames. "Like I told you yesterday, I'm investigating the death of her granddaughter."

"Mmhm."

"I understand she was here the day she died."

"That's right."

"Did you see her?"

"Briefly."

"Do you let family members take their parent, or whoever they have here, out for dinner or shopping?"

"No. We prefer to tie the elderly to wheelchairs and play bumper cars with them."

"Ha-ha. Not funny."

"Of course it's funny. You should see them. And the best part is, they don't remember a thing!" Naomi opened her desk drawer again and took out another mint.

"Did Jessica take Selma out for lunch that day?" I chose to ignore her teasing.

"I don't think so."

"Can you find out? I need to know what time Jessica got here and when she left."

102

"Didn't you ask Selma?"

"Yeah."

"Don't trust the old gal, eh? Well, she would have had to sign in, so I can find out what time she got here, but the time she left might be an estimate. Is that okay?"

"Anything would help. Did you know her?"

"The granddaughter?" She shook her head. "Not really. I met her when Selma first moved here in June. But then we didn't see her for a long time. Months, I think."

"She was in California." I explained, almost defensively for a woman I didn't know.

"That's what Selma said."

"You know, it just occurred to me, but do you have counselors here to help Selma with this loss?"

"Oh sure. We have two people on staff."

"Full-time?"

"No, part-time."

"Are they good?"

"I like to think so. I hired them."

"I didn't mean that the way it sounded."

Naomi smiled. "That's okay, I'll get even."

"Is one of the counselors working with Selma?"

"I believe Judy's tried to talk to her, but I don't know how or even if they've progressed. Remember, people Selma's age are not nearly as inclined to talk about their troubles—especially to a therapist—as our generation. And you should know that as much as I love you, if I *did* know, I wouldn't tell you. You know how I feel about boundaries and privacy."

"Still an issue?"

"No. But I have a deep respect for it, personally as well as professionally, for which I can thank Demon Woman of the East." She took a deep breath.

"How *is* your mom?"

"Older. Meaner. Thinner."

"I see things haven't changed."

"Actually, they have. I no longer expect her to change

103

and, I finally understand that just because she's my mother doesn't mean I'll become her.''

"Wow. I'm impressed.''

Naomi winked. "That little tidbit of insight took me fifteen years and untold thousands of dollars to come by.''

"But it was worth it.''

"Absolutely. And now, as much as I want to keep schmoozing with my long-lost friend, I should get back to work.'' She leaned forward and rested her hands on her desk. "By the way, I called you last night. Did you get my message?''

"Yes. Is everything all right?'' I stood up and lifted my bag off the floor.

"Everything is fine. It's just that I *might* have a minor job for you, and I was wondering if you wanted to dine with me and my Republican tonight. You could even meet the baby Republicrats—which is what they are, seeing as though they're both too young to vote and haven't chosen a party—though I tend to think the younger is leaning toward socialism.'' She had moved out from behind her desk and was leading me to the elevator.

"I'd love to but I have a date with a dog tonight. Oh wait a minute, what a great idea, how would your girls like a puppy? She's really sweet. Cute, fuzzy, housebroken.'' I didn't know if the last detail was true, but I knew it would be a real selling point.

"Oh yeah, they'd love one.'' She pressed the elevator button.

"That's great! I have one I could bring you tonight. Her name is Auggie and she—''

"No.'' Naomi put her arm through mine and tugged. "We have had a chameleon, two gerbils, a turtle, a parrot, a cat, *and* four goldfish, all of which the girls said they would take care of, and all of which I have had to feed, water, clean, find and flush. I assure you, Mom does not want a dog to walk in rain, sleet, hail and snow.''

"What about the Republican?''

"Him? He can walk himself."

"Dang. I have to find a home for this puppy."

"And I'm sure you will."

"Can I have a rain check for tonight?" I asked.

"Absolutely."

"Wait, what about this job you're talking about?"

"Minor stuff, I assure you it can wait. In the meantime, if I think of anyone who would want a puppy, I'll give you a call. Also, I'll check into the Onderdonk lunch thing for you. Call me tomorrow."

The world's slowest elevator door inched open and I stepped inside. "Thanks, Nai." I nodded to my fellow passenger, a woman leaning on a walker in the corner of the elevator. She wore a housedress and floppy slippers, and clutched a metal walker for dear life.

"Anything for a friend." Naomi said. "Except a dog. Oh, and Sydney?" She held open the elevator door. "Auggie's a really bad name for a dog. You should try Buster or Molly or something. You might have better luck unloading it."

"I'll keep that in mind, thanks." I waved good-bye as the door jerked shut, and smiled at the walker woman. She glared at me and smacked her lips. When the elevator finally reached the ground floor I held open the door for the grump and discovered why the Treelane had the slowest elevators. If this old gal moved any slower she would have been going in reverse. Halfway over the threshold of the elevator she looked around and barked at me, "Is this the third floor?"

"No, it's the first." I said politely, though I was anxious to get the hell out of there.

"What?" she snapped, squinting at me.

"It's the first floor." I raised my voice so she could hear me.

"First floor! I wanted the third floor!" she yelled at me, white-knuckling her walker.

I was tempted to tell her, "Oops, my mistake this *is* the

third floor,'' but not only could I see the fortune-teller receptionist watching us in the concave mirror above the entrance door, but I figured if I did that, it would come back and plague me in my old age. So instead I patiently held open the door while she very, very slowly turned around and shuffled back into the car. I pressed the button for the third floor and suggested she take along reading material for the ride.

When I hit the street I could feel the tension cramping my shoulder blades. My lower back was beginning to ache and my head felt immobile, as though it had been riveted to my neck. The sunlight seemed to burn right past the ultraviolet protection of my sunglasses and felt like it was engraving cataracts right onto the old eyeballs. It was happening. I was getting old right before my very eyes and there wasn't a thing I could do about it.

Ten

Mary Douglas lived in a twenty-eighth-floor apartment on Third Avenue in the Sixties. Unlike her friend Jessica, whose home was warm and inviting, Mary's place felt more like a movie set. The floors were marble, the furniture leather, the lighting halogen, and the southern view went as far down the avenue as the eye could see. Very clean.

She met me at the front door and led me down four marbled stairs into her sprawling living room. Sprawling is not a word normally associated with apartment dwelling in New York City, but this place was not the norm. The floor-to-ceiling windows heightened the feeling of being airborne, which is not a sensation I particularly relish. A magnificent ebony grand piano dominated the far end of the room.

She was finishing up a call in the other room and suggested that I make myself comfortable. I took care to steer clear of the view and focused on everything else but. The glass and chrome shelves were filled with well-worn books revealing an eclectic taste in reading. On a table in front of the shelves was a stack of four or five books including the autobiography of Beryl Markham; *A Year in Provence*, by Peter Mayle; the Winchell biography by Neal Gabler; and a book of poetry by Jewelle Gomez. Photo-trophies were scattered throughout the room; Mary with various celebrities ranging from Barbra Streisand to Ed Koch. In all the pictures Mary was beaming, but looking off to the side—away from her celebrity cohort—as if to make sure people were taking notes.

When she returned we went to the conversation area in the living room, which was fashioned with a black stone coffee table, maybe twelve feet square, surrounded by a leather sofa, loveseat, and two armchairs. I sat on one end of the sofa while Mary took what was clearly her seat; an armchair with black metal tables on either side—one with a phone, the other with a lamp and a stack of books and manuscripts. She sat on one leg and draped the other leg over it.

"So, how can I help you?" She asked.

"As I told you, I'm investigating Jessica's death. What I'm trying to do right now is get an idea of what happened during the last few days of her life, especially the last few hours. Can you tell me when you last saw Jessica?"

"Two days before she died. We actually flew back from LA together."

"So you didn't see her the day she died?"

"No."

"Did you speak with her that day?"

"No, but I did talk to her the night before." She reached down into the cushions of her chair and pulled out two knitting needles, a ball of orange yarn, and what looked like the start of a sweater. "Do you mind? It always calms me down."

"No, go right ahead."

I watched as she quickly wound yarn around her left index finger and laid the sweater in her lap.

"Your last conversation . . ."

"I was trying to set up a meeting for her with this film producer from England."

"Did you?"

"No. But it didn't matter, because he was coming back in a week or two and they would have met then. He was anxious to work with her." Her knitting needles tapped out

108

what sounded like a Morse code. "And you can't blame him because Jessie was amazing. Years ago she took an interest in computer art and ultimately computer animation. She taught herself everything from scratch and when we needed animation segments for the film I just produced, I knew that the cartoon characters she had already created would be perfect." Mary's hands moved like a blur between the needles and the orange yarn.

"She did all the animation for your movie?" I asked innocently.

"No way. She designed the animation, the characters, the storyline, and oversaw the artists, but we used a company called BarkingFish Productions to do the actual animation." She continued knitting.

"You know, don't you, that Michael was arrested for Jessica's murder?"

"Yes, but he didn't do it."

"How do you know?" I asked with a flicker of hope that she knew where he had been between two and five-fifteen that day.

"I know it here." She held a fist between her breasts.

"What else did you and Jessica talk about that night?"

Mary continued knitting, and I was beginning to wonder if she had heard me, when she finally said, "Nothing much, just the same old stuff. Who's pregnant, who's having an affair, new restaurants, the ballet—she loved the ballet—oh, and Selma. We talked a little about Selma."

"In what respect?"

"Jessica was concerned because Selma told her someone was stealing from her at the nursing home."

"Stealing? Stealing what?"

Mary raised her brows and pushed the corners of her mouth down. "Money, I think."

"A lot of money?"

"I don't know."

"You said Jessica was concerned. Can you be a little more explicit?"

"Well, she was pissed. You don't take advantage of an old lady like that. I mean, the way *I* looked at it was that Jessica's paying a small fortune to make sure that Selma's taken care of properly. The way *Jessica* looked at it was that Selma was her only family, and Jessica was *very* protective of her. As a matter of fact, when I first talked to her about working together in California, she was reticent because she said it would take her away from Selma. She felt that because the nursing home was a new thing for Selma, she needed to be there for her. Fortunately Selma and Michael set her straight."

"How so?"

"Michael promised to visit Selma every day and Selma promised to die if Jessica didn't go to California." Mary smiled sadly. "Selma's a good woman." Mary's soft features suddenly grew dark.

"What is it?" I asked leaning slightly toward her.

Mary dropped the knitting in her lap and covered her eyes with her hands. "I haven't called Selma. I've tried to, but every time I pick up the phone, I just can't. Christ, what's wrong with me?" All composure faded as she folded into herself and sobbed uncontrollably. I went to the kitchen and snapped a few sheets of paper towels off the roller. Mary Douglas needed to cry. I handed her the floral-patterned towels and sat quietly until hiccups replaced the sobs.

"I'm sorry." She blew her nose into the towels and wiped her eyes.

"Don't be."

"I can't believe how selfish I've been."

"Don't be so hard on yourself. My guess is you were just afraid."

"Of what?" She gathered the knitting in one hand and tossed it on the coffee table.

"Death. Loss. An old lady's pain. Your own pain." I paused. "I could go on."

"Don't."

I didn't. I left Mary Douglas just a hair after one-thirty. As I headed back to the subway, I realized that the beautiful October day wasn't touching me. Instead, I found myself walking right into a low-grade anxiety attack. I had to talk to my Aunt Minnie, and I suddenly needed to know how my big sister, Nora, was.

Because the Transit Department is in a perpetual state of ripping up the street with jackhammers, I stopped at a pay phone inside an office building and dialed Minnie's number. My chain-smoking, feisty aunt may be diminutive in physical size, but she is an enormous presence in my life. Having lost both of my parents before I was thirty, I think Minnie made a deal with the powers-that-be that she would hang around for the long haul. She's the kind of family you would pick, if given the choice, the way, over the years, certain friends become family. It makes sense that whenever I'm feeling blue or vulnerable, or anxious, I turn to her. Her machine picked up, and I left a message asking her to join me for dinner.

Next I pulled out my address book and looked up my sister's number in Baltimore. She answered on the second ring and suspiciously asked why I was calling in the middle of the day.

"Because I missed you."

There was a pause. "Really?" She sounded sweet and innocent, two adjectives I would not normally use to describe her.

"Yeah. As a matter of fact I'm calling you from a pay phone."

This bit of information elicited another higher-pitched "Really? Is everything okay?"

"Yes." I wanted to tell her that I missed Mom and Dad, too, but I couldn't. I knew if I did I'd only start crying. Instead I said, "Actually, I'm working on a case involving old people and, why, it made me think of you."

Eleven

St. Mary's Hospital is directly between where I was and where I was headed. I had an hour and a half before I had to be in Brooklyn Heights to pick up what was no doubt going to be the biggest mistake of my life, so I decided to stop by the hospital and find out what I could.

Before I even made it inside the dark, imposing structure, I was stopped dead in my tracks on the sidewalk, causing a humorless man in a cheap business suit to bump into me. He growled, "Watch where you're going, asshole." However, had I been doing that I would have missed the car illegally double-parked outside the side entrance to the hospital.

In Manhattan alone there must be eight thousand identical cars for hire as "gypsy" car service wagons, but I knew I had hit pay dirt with this old thing. The rusted white wagon was the very same one that had been parked outside Michael Callahan's house the day before. I would have recognized the bumper sticker anywhere: "Honk If You Love Jesus." As I approached the car I could see that the back license plate was still missing.

I walked up to the empty car and first went to the front of it. Dingdingdingdingding! The sirens were going off in my head. Not only was there a New York State license plate hanging precariously off the bumper, but there was a round yellow sticker affixed to it that enabled the driver access to the local garbage dump in the Town of East Hampton. I was looking at gold, plain and simple, which meant that I was that much closer to finding the two boys who had used Michael Callahan's face as a punching bag. Feeling almost giddy with good fortune, I noted the number and then looked inside the car. The red interior had suffered over the years, but other than that, the owner seemed to keep it in good shape. The headliner sagged like a harem tent, and a string of rosary beads hung from the rearview mirror. In the backseat was a copy of *Suffolk Life*, a weekly paper printed for Long Island residents. The newspaper was crumpled in such a way that I was unable to see which part of Long Island this particular edition hailed from, but given the garbage sticker, I was willing to bet my rent-controlled apartment that it was East Hampton. I first discovered this little newspaper through Leslie, whose mother used to have a house out in Montauk, the farthest point out on Long Island. I knew from her that this giveaway publication was zoned to specific areas and wasn't just shipped out from one end of the Island to the other. Folks in Hauppauge would get the Hauppauge news and folks in Montauk would get the Montauk news.

I eyed the glove compartment, knowing that if the driver of this vehicle was like many others I know, he or she would keep the car registration in there. There was only one way of getting to it. I had to open the door.

From the little metal posts just the other side of the window, it was clear to see that the owner had forgotten to lock it. Then again, judging from the looks of the car, this might have been a deliberate act in hopes that someone might steal it.

I looked up the block. People hurried up and down the crowded narrow sidewalk. I noticed a gaggle of smokers loitering outside the hospital door. It has always seemed to me that there are an inordinate number of smokers in the health care profession. I once asked a friend—who happens to be a cynical gynecologist—why so many doctors smoke, and he told me there were several reasons, ranging from God complexes to the other extreme, a total distrust in their chosen profession. At that moment, all the smokers seemed to be interested in everything but a forty-year-old woman standing beside an ugly station wagon.

There were no passersby who seemed disturbed by my close proximity to the car, no one who even seemed to give me a second glance. Two security guards stood near the smokers' circle, deep in conversation, their laughter rising above the ordinary street noise. One of them looked at me and smiled. I, of course, smiled back. The Irish gal in me knew that the unlocked car was a gift from the powers-that-be and I would be the fool to ignore the offering.

I slipped my fingers into the handle of the driver's door and pressed my thumb onto the latch. A tingle of excitement went through me when I felt the lock give and the door pop open. With studied nonchalance, I opened the door, bent down, rested my knee on the driver's seat and leaned into the car.

I reached into the backseat and flipped the paper over. The paper was from East Hampton, which is where Leslie was at that very moment. The cosmos works in mysterious ways.

I left the paper where it was and reached across the front seat with my sights trained on the glove compartment. My fingers were literally centimeters away from all the goodies that lay behind the car drawer when suddenly I felt the very distinct sensation of someone tapping three times on my buttocks.

With the speed of sap in December, I eased myself back, planted my right foot firmly on the ground, and slowly ducked out of the car. With every movement I made I prepared myself for the defensive. I was still feeling my last encounter with the passengers of this vehicle and I wasn't about to be tossed on my keister again.

I was ready to turn and face the gorilla who had plucked me off the ground like I was a feather, or Carrot-top with the rosy cheeks, both of whom would tower over me. So when I ducked out of the car and twisted around, I was already looking up in anticipation, my hands ready for a fight.

Instead I was face to face with a woman, no more than five feet, three inches tall, who was wearing the all-too-familiar—and yet oh-so-flattering—brown uniform of the Manhattan meter maid. Generally speaking, these civil servants are referred to as Brownies, because of the color of their spiffy attire.

Her stubby arms were crossed over her chest, and she kept her head cocked to the right as she watched me emerge. Maybe she had never seen a human move quite so slowly before, but the smile on her face convinced me that I was, indeed, entertaining her. Though her mouth was closed, two sharp points of teeth poked out just under her upper lip. Her cap sat crooked on her head, and wild tufts of black hair looked like they were trying to escape from under her chapeau.

I was mesmerized. Not only had I never seen a person who looked like the embodiment of the word *befuddled*, but I had never in my life seen a woman with so much facial hair. I tried not to stare at her upper lip but it was impossible.

"What are you doing?" she asked, scrunching up her face. She scratched at her lower lip with her two teeth tines.

An honest answer would have been "Breaking and entering," but I smiled and tried to look stupid. "What do you mean, Officer?"

She pursed her lips and shook her head. "Nice try." Her dark eyes sparkled. "But you still have to move the car." She backed up a step and fluttered her hand, shooing me back into the car.

What to do, what to do. "It's not my car," I said, scratching the side of my face like a perplexed farmer.

"Then move your friend's car, but get it outta here." Again she scraped her buck teeth against her lower lip.

I stared mutely, trying to figure out what my next step should be. I knew that the longer I hung around this car the more my chances increased of coming face to face with Frick and Frack, a prospect that didn't particularly upset me, but one I wanted to be quite prepared for.

I nodded and smiled at the little Brownie, hoping she would take that as an agreement and leave, but she stood in place and rocked back and forth on her worn heels.

"In thirty seconds I'm going to give you a ticket," she warned with a crooked smile.

"I told you, it's not my car." I looked up and down the street again, then back at the gaggle of smokers. "Besides, I don't have a key." I tried to sound as helpless as I could, without reducing myself to whining.

"Is that so?" She sounded skeptical.

"Absolutely."

"Then waddaya call those?" She made a sharp gesture to the inside of the car. I followed her point and was amazed to see that the idiot who owned this wreck had left the keys dangling in the ignition. I was equally amazed that the idiot who makes her living detecting hadn't noticed it.

"Keys."

"I suggest you use them."

It might have been simpler for me to get in the damned ugly thing and drive it away, but the fact is, I wasn't up for committing car theft. Breaking into a car was one thing—that I could try and talk my way out of—but stealing a car was another thing altogether.

"I can't drive." I shrugged and held up my hands in a *what can you do?* kind of gesture. "But I can get my friend, he's right inside. His father's in the hospital. They're really close, you know?" I tried to sidestep her and move toward the hospital. "Two seconds. I'll just be two seconds."

She smacked her lips and let me pass. I hurried into the hospital entrance and disappeared into the dark building. I slipped to the side of the doorway and watched as she patiently waited for my return. After several minutes she shook her head, pulled out her ticket pad, and walked to the back of the car. She had, I knew, given me leeway one never gets from a Brownie, and I was kicking myself that I had to waste good meter maid karma on some schlemiel who leaves his key in the car.

By the time she was finished, I had created a mental list of possibilities—ranging from Alzheimer's to espionage—as to why a seasoned New Yorker would leave keys in the car. Then again, this car was from Long Island, which could explain all that.

The Brownie pulled up the windshield wiper on the driver's side and with a flourish positioned the fresh ticket. The wiper blade snapped back into place. Before heading off to her next adventure, she took great care rearranging her hat, this time squarely on her head with the beak only a hairsbreadth away from the bridge of her nose. I got the impression she was killing time, waiting for an irate driver to come screaming out of the hospital and verbally attack her for giving him a ticket.

After what felt like an hour, she finally reholstered her ticket book and sauntered away from the station wagon. I waited several minutes before starting back to the car. Before I was out the door I spotted a robust but slightly stooped elderly man who stepped out between two parked cars and went directly to the station wagon. A small shopping bag dangled limply from his right hand. His gray and white hair was shorn into a crew cut, and judging by his leathery complexion, he was accustomed to working outdoors. I guessed that he was hovering between seventy and seventy-five, though he had the look of a man who had worked hard all his life and had probably aged prematurely. He reached for the ticket, crumpled it off the windshield, and tossed it on the ground, like the thoughtless boob he probably was. Next he opened the car door and threw the bag into the front seat. He then rooted around in his pants pockets looking for what I guessed were the car keys. He spent a confused minute patting his four pants pockets, one shirt pocket, and three jacket pockets before finally bending down and glancing at the ignition where I knew the keys hung forgotten and secure.

The man moved in slow motion. He settled himself behind the wheel of the car, ran his fingers through his coarse hair, straightened the rearview mirror, pulled a cigarette out of his inside jacket pocket, and let it hang lazily from his lips before finally lighting it and starting the car. He cut off a spanking new Mercedes as he pulled into traffic and turned onto Sixth Avenue. I turned back and went into the hospital.

Dr. Cyclops had given me the names of two people at the hospital, one in administration (who I quickly learned was on vacation), and the other in pediatrics, where they worked.

Once on the seventh floor, I stopped at the nurses' station and asked for Sheila Nivens, the second name that Hannah Miller had given me.

"Peck, you see Nivens today?" a nurse making notations on a clipboard asked her nearly anorexic associate, who was peeling an orange.

"Nivens? Oh yeah, she's around." Her bony fingers worked like a razor under the dense peel. The sweet bouquet of citrus smelled more like a car deodorizer than anything natural.

The nurse with the clipboard sighed and rolled her eyes at me. "Hang on, let me see if I can find her." She slid the clipboard into a metal file holder and ducked into a doorway behind the nurses' station. I watched Peck complete her surgery on the orange and painstakingly dissect the sections, laying them out before her on a paper napkin. I figured if it took me that long to prepare a snack, I'd be a hundred pounds lighter, too.

After a good five minutes the other nurse returned and Peck was washing her hands on a moist towelette before digging in.

"Nivens is on lunch break. Can you come back after three?"

I couldn't, but was told that I could probably find her in the cafeteria. Apparently a creature of habit, Sheila Nivens always sat at the same table when she had lunch.

"Sheila's a nurse?" I asked as I was leaving.

With a mouthful Peck said, "Sheila's *the* nurse."

I looked to the other woman for a translation and was told that Sheila Nivens basically ran pediatrics. "Us minions help the old gal, but my guess is this place would fall apart without the General."

"She's been here so long they built this *building* around her," Peck offered, slipping a second section of orange into her small mouth. It was not a pretty sight.

I thanked them for their help and waited what seemed to be forever for an elevator. I found Sheila Nivens sitting alone at the table to which I had been directed. She was a thickset woman with thinning white hair, drooping jowls, and penetrating eyes. When I asked if I could join her, she glanced at the roomful of empty tables and asked why.

"Are you Sheila Nivens?" I asked, pulling out an orange plastic chair and sitting across from her.

"Yes. And this is my lunch hour, which I use to eat and catch up on the news." She pointed to the newspaper laid out before her. A cup of coffee, nestled on a paper napkin atop a saucer, held down one corner of the paper.

I flashed my ID at her and explained who I was and what I wanted from her. She took a deep breath, shook her head slightly, and folded the paper.

"Dr. Callahan is one of the most dedicated doctors I have ever known, and I've been doing this a long time."

"I don't doubt that. I'm on his side."

"So what do you think I can do for you?" She placed the folded paper on the seat beside her and brought the coffee closer.

"I was hoping you could tell me something about last Wednesday. Do you recall seeing him?"

119

"No. I know he had done early rounds, but he wasn't here when I was on duty."

"Are you and Michael close?"

"Well, we don't go out and shoot pool, if that's what you mean, but we have a close and respectful working relationship."

"Is there anyone else on staff with whom he was particularly close?"

"Do you mean romantically?" She leveled a gaze at me.

"Not necessarily, though if he was—"

"I'm a damned good judge of character, Miss Sloane, and I can assure you Dr. Callahan had no romantic interest or involvement on pediatrics." She arched a brow. "I make it a point to keep my eye on *everything* that affects my floor. Do you understand?"

"Yes, ma'am." Nurse Nivens demanded respect and got it. I cleared my throat before asking, "Were there other staff members with whom Michael was notably close?"

"Yes. He and Hannah Miller are very close."

"His partner."

"That's correct." She brought the coffee to her lips and swallowed. "Ach, it's cold. I hate cold coffee."

"May I get you a fresh cup?" I offered.

"No, no, I have to get back to work in a minute." She glanced at the large clock on the wall above the doorway.

"Was there anyone else he was close with? Someone who might help shed a little light on where he was last Wednesday, or how he had been feeling prior to his wife's death?"

"Haven't you talked to him about where he was or what he was feeling?" It was a pragmatic question from a no-nonsense woman.

"Yes, I have. Unfortunately, Dr. Callahan isn't helping himself. As a matter of fact, I get the impression that he's protecting someone."

"Then isn't that his business?" She placed the coffee cup and saucer on the tray.

"Yes, it is. However, I don't think he knows what life in prison is like. Have you any idea what prison would be like for a man like Dr. Callahan?"

She studied my face without moving a muscle, and I had the distinct impression that Nurse Nivens did indeed know what life would be like in prison for a man like Dr. Callahan. "I don't know how anyone else can help if he's not willing to help himself, but, from my observations he was close with Hannah, Milt Brown, and Mary Grace. However, I don't think that he had a social connection with anyone in pediatrics other than Dr. Miller."

"Milt Brown?" I asked.

"One of the physical therapists on staff. Very funny man."

"Is he here today?"

She raised her brows. "No, it's his day off."

"Mary Grace?"

Nurse Nivens pulled the tray in front of her. "Mary Grace is on leave."

"Since when?" I asked.

"Not long. A few days ago." She took the newspaper off the chair and put it on top of the dirty dishes.

"Really? Do you know where she went? Or why?"

Sheila Nivens squinted at me and let out a boisterous laugh.

"What?" I asked.

"Forgive me, Miss Sloane, but I read people for a living, and I can tell you, you are barking up the wrong tree. Mary Grace and Michael are just friends. But to answer your questions, I don't know where she went, but I suspect it was time for a vacation."

I could feel my cheeks flush. It isn't often that I am so easily read by an interviewee, but since I had been, I decided to follow it through.

"Just for the sake of argument, how can you be so certain that Dr. Callahan and Mary Grace weren't . . . social?" I asked without missing a beat.

"Because Mary Grace is a nun." With that said, Sheila Nivens stood up with her tray and added, "I like Michael Callahan. I'll do anything I can to keep that boy out of prison, and not because I like him, but because he's innocent." She winked at me. "I know people. If he killed his wife then pigs can fly."

By the time I left the hospital I knew I would be late for my date with Auggie Doggie and Rosalynn Hayes-Porter, but in New York City I always give people fifteen minutes leeway. Tardy or not, I knew Roz wanted to see me almost as much as, if not more than, I wanted to see her.

Twelve

I passed Michael Callahan's house en route to his neighbors, the Porters. The imagination is a powerful place to wander. Only twenty-four hours earlier I had been inside the beautiful house and felt the life that Jessica and Michael had infused it with; the splashes of color, the family photographs of happy times, the comfortable furnishings, the puppy racing from one end of the house to the other. Despite the fact that I had walked in on the aftermath of violence and that only a week earlier Jessica had lost her life in the garage, when I had been there the day before the house still held a positive energy. Passing it now, I realized there had been a change. Whether the transformation was all in my mind or if a cloud had appeared over the actual structure, I can't say, but there had indeed been a change. The Callahan residence looked darker and more foreboding than the other buildings on the street. I could see it becoming the house on the street that terrified the local kids, the house that would become a dare.

Less than twenty minutes late, I reached Roz Porter's front door. I rang once and from the other side of the door I could hear the children and puppy yapping in unison. Oh the excitement that a doorbell produces.

The door swung open revealing a woman with long, wiry salt-and-pepper hair and small eyes the color of charcoal. On her hip was perched a round-faced baby whose pudgy little fingers were becoming increasingly tangled in Mommy's hair.

"Roz? I'm Sydney."

"Oh my God, you have no idea how glad I am to see you." She pulled the door open, stepped back, and asked me to come in. "No Meggy, don't pull Mommy's hair." She held the child secure with one arm and tried to disentangle herself with the other.

Auggie came racing out from the back of the house with a little boy in hot pursuit. Poor dog. The little boy—no doubt this was Howie—was doughy and awkward, his movements hampered by the fact that his pants were inching down his backside like a plumber or an electrician in training. He chased after Auggie, whining to his mother, "He won't wait! Make him stop."

As if seeking refuge, Auggie practically threw herself into my arms. Howie stood before me, looking up, his arms outstretched, whimpering for me to give him the dog.

I smiled down at the little cretin and assured him that Auggie seemed fine right where she was.

"We were just about to have a treat." Roz told me as she led the way into the kitchen. There was no question that the Hayes-Porter home was one with children. Toys were scattered everywhere. Crayola artwork lined the walls, once cream-painted. The wall-to-wall carpet in the living room was deeply spotted and stained, and the vacuum cleaner sat in the middle of the room, abandoned seemingly mid-task.

The kitchen was the hub of activity in this household, and as a result it looked as if someone had taken the room, put it in a Cuisinart, and set the thing on pulse. I figure life is chaotic enough, my home has to have some sense of calm. It is one of the reasons I chose not to have children. I couldn't stand the idea of a life in a constant state of sticky mess.

When the kids were quieted with fruit roll-ups and cookies, Roz gave me the lowdown on Auggie, who was still nestled safely in my lap. She was, for the most part, house-trained. "When Howie squeezed her once, she peed on him, but I don't think that's her usual behavior." I glared at Howie as he sucked down his fruit treat, managing to get half of it smeared on the area surrounding his mouth. He caught my glare and smiled in response.

Auggie done, I approached the topic of Jessica, trying to be circumspect because of Howie.

"We need to talk," I said.

"Oh please, this is like all I've been talking about. Howie, go finish *The Lion King*."

"No!" He pushed out his lower lip.

"Yes." She hiked the little one off her hip and slid her into an elasticized harness that hung in the frame of a doorway. Once secured into the rigging, the child looked momentarily stunned but then began bouncing up and down in delight.

"No! No! No! No!" Howie marched in a circle, his arms pumping in time to his chant. He watched me out of the corner of his eye.

"Stop it," Roz said as she wiped off the table where he had stuffed his little face.

"No! No! No! No!"

It's boys like this who grow into men who make me oh-so-glad to be gay.

"No! No! No! No! No! No!"

Roz grabbed Howie by the arm, dragged him into the living room, and within seconds the kid's exposed heinie was planted in front of the television, and the electronic baby-sitter was officially on duty. It was not a solution I would have pegged her for and I was duly impressed. When she returned, I told her as much.

Roz shrugged. "After a while he's just in overdrive. He'll be asleep in a few minutes." She paused. "Either that or he'll have set the place on fire."

I put Auggie on the floor and took my notepad out of my bag. Auggie curled up in a ball at my feet and sighed contentedly as Roz filled her dishwasher and told me about the day Jessica Callahan died.

Roz had seen Jessica leave the fateful morning, though they had not talked. Roz had been putting laundry away when she happened to look out the window in Howie's bedroom, which is on the third floor and looks out onto the Callahans'.

"It was maybe quarter to nine in the morning. I saw her pull out and drive away. I didn't think anything of it, like my God, this is going to be the last time I ever see this woman. That's not how most of us approach life, but then again, maybe it should be." She rinsed glasses and lined them on the counter above the dishwasher. "That's why I tell Dennis 'I love you' every time he leaves or we end a phone call, you know what I mean? Who knows if he isn't going to get hit by a train on the way to work?" I thought about Leslie. The last time we had spoken I had hung up on her. I could feel guilt slowly oozing into my consciousness. Rosalynn pulled out the top rack of the washer and loaded it like a professional domestic maven. "He's afraid I'm going to pass my neurosis on to the kids, but all it takes is something like this for me to look at him and say, " 'See? See what happens?' " She stopped loading long enough to raise her palms to heaven and nod knowingly.

"When did you last talk to Jessica?"

"The day before she died. She brought the kids presents from Disneyland and she wanted Howie to meet the puppy. She loved that little mutt." Roz glanced at Auggie as she continued loading the dishwasher.

"What kind of mood was she in?"

"Good. She was excited to be cooking in her own kitchen again. She did say it was weird being back in the city. You know what it's like, you constantly have to be on guard here. I think that's why she drove into Manhattan instead of taking the train, which she normally would. Anyway, she was planning on making brisket with yams and apricots, stuff she never would have made in California."

126

"Was there anything disturbing her about . . . Michael? Or Selma? Work? Contracts?"

Roz gave this some thought. "No, but . . ."

"What?"

"I think she might have been concerned about Selma. Unfortunately I had Howie with me, so I couldn't give Jessica my undivided, but she said something about Selma being ripped off maybe by someone on the staff there. You know, now that I think about it, she was mad. She rarely got mad."

"Was there anyone at the nursing home in particular she mentioned?"

"No."

"Did you see Jessica again on the day she died?"

"I didn't see *her*, no."

"What does that mean?"

"It means I could have sworn I saw the garage door close, but I didn't see either Jessica or her car for that matter."

"What time was this?"

"Around three-thirty, quarter of four." On the top rack of the dishwasher, she wedged a plastic sip cup between a measuring cup and a plastic container. "It must have been closer to three-thirty because the baby-sitter had just left and I only have her until three-thirty on alternate Wednesdays." The Tupperware couldn't take the strain and popped out of its place, shooting into mid-air, barely missing Roz's head. This delighted the pint-sized bouncer, who clapped her hands together and boinged a little jig. Auggie picked up her head, wagged her tail, and put her head back down.

"Did you see anyone in front of the garage or near it when you looked out?" I asked.

"No. Well, wait, that's not altogether true. There was an old lady carrying a canvas shopping bag, but she was the only one. This street can get pretty deserted during the weekdays. That's why you have to keep such a close eye on the kids." She retrieved the plastic projectile.

I wondered if losing Howie wouldn't be a little like "The Ransom of Red Chief." "Have you been in her garage before?"

"Sure, lots of times. I keep the kids' winter toys in there. Jessica and I were good friends." Aside from these statements of fact, Rosalynn didn't seem particularly moved by the loss of her friend. She scraped at a spot on the countertop.

"Is there a door leading directly into the house from inside the garage?"

"Yeah, it's off the kitchen. Have you been there?"

"Yes."

"There's a sliding door in the kitchen?" she asked as she shoved one last bowl into the dishwasher. I nodded. "Well, right next to it, there's a door that leads into the garage. The garage door is automatic.

"Do you have keys to their house?"

"Yeah." She looked suspicious. "Why?"

"I'm trying to prove Michael didn't kill Jessica, which means I have to find out who did. It would help if I could have a look at the garage."

"You said you were there yesterday. Didn't Michael show it to you then?"

"We had limited time and other things to discuss. I hadn't anticipated he would disappear the next day."

"I suppose not." Roz stepped into the doorway and looked in on Howie. She smiled lovingly. "Sound asleep."

"You could come with me," I suggested as I tried to move my foot out from under the sleeping pup.

"With these two?" She went to the baby and continued her thought in kootchie-coos. "I don't think so, do you, wummywum. My widdle big girl." The baby was in heaven. Mommy, a bottle, and a good bounce, what more could a kid ask for?

"Would you give me the key, then?"

She sighed and ran her fingers gently over her lips. "To be honest with you, it makes me a little uncomfortable."

She came over to the cluttered table where I was sitting and pulled out a chair. Before actually sitting she studied the tabletop, slapped her forehead, and said, "I can't believe I never asked you if you want something to drink. I'm sorry."

"No big deal," I assured her, feeling Auggie shift on my feet and resettle herself, leaning heavily onto my shins.

"I have a fresh pot of coffee. You want some?"

"No thanks."

Roz poured herself a cup and told me, "I just feel a little uneasy letting you in there. I mean, Michael screwed me over, I know, and I know that he's probably really messed things up for himself by running away, but the fact is, my friends gave me a key to their home because they knew they could trust me."

"I want to find out who killed your friend—" I started, but was cut off before I could finish.

"I know that. I do. But I don't know you from a hole in the wall. For all I know you could be a part of this network of burglars who, you know, steal things."

I stared at her. "Roz. Michael told you about me, didn't he?"

"Yes."

"He trusted me enough to give me Jessica's dog, right?"

"Yes."

"And you know that in some way I am a part of things right now, right?"

"Yes."

"So, what harm could it do if I took a look in their garage?"

She sipped her coffee and gave this some thought. The baby gurgled and made a delicate sound that was accompanied by a foul smell. It is amazing to think that a thing that small can make such a big stink. Roz threw her head back and fanned the air in front of her. "Whoa, that's my girl." She got up and promptly slipped the baby out of the bouncing chair, into her arms.

"Okay, I'll tell you what. If you watch Howie while I go upstairs and change her, I'll give you the keys as soon as I come back down. Okay?"

Roz's little game of *Let's Make a Deal* annoyed me, but I went along with it. What was to watch? The kid was sound asleep and there didn't seem to be any chance that I'd be forced to shoot him for misbehaving.

Fifteen minutes later I was standing in the Callahans' garage, letting my eyes adjust to the light. After examining the oil patch in the middle of the floor, Auggie proceeded with her own investigation and happily sniffed her way around the dimly lit room.

Their car was missing, which meant that either Michael had it, or—more likely—it had been impounded so the police could look for evidence. I made a note to ask Marcy if the police had it and then spent a good fifteen minutes poking around the excessively well-organized space that had been used exclusively for the car and storage. There were no work benches or peg boards filled with carpentry tools, no sign of any hobbies like painting or drums, or even exercise equipment. There were just boxes, all stacked precisely, all taped closed with regimental order and all clearly labeled with the same boxy print. In black Magic Marker the cartons were tagged MIKE: CHILDHOOD, JESS: PICTURES, SELMA'S KITCHEN STUFF, PORTER TOYS. Someone was just a wee bit compulsive here.

I wandered the circumference of the room, impressed with not only the orderliness, but that someone—probably Jessica—had taken the time to paint the cement floor to look like grass. Not just a flat slap-on of green paint, but a work of art that actually created an optical illusion of grass blowing in the breeze. Here and there she had painted a clump of daffodils and iris ready to bloom. It was just the sort of thing that made me want to know the person who had put the time and energy into such a project.

I looked high and low, but there was nothing to be found in the Callahan garage other than a toolbox (filled with proof that neither Jessica nor Michael was very handy around the house), a coffee can with old paint brushes, two empty recyclable cans, and the cartons, which I could not legally open, nor would I want to.

Auggie, in the meantime, was on the scent of something. She pushed her massive paws under a wooden table and whined until I squatted down on all fours and looked under the table. A ratty old tennis ball was the cause of such excitement. I looked at the ball and then at the puppy's smiling face—her black lips were literally pulled up into a smile—which was all it took to make me melt. She cocked her head from one side to the other as she looked from my face to the goodies that she knew were hidden under the table. I wasn't about to lie flat on the garage floor to retrieve a ball, so I looked for something to fish it out. I found a yardstick stuck between two boxes and batted it out. A tinkling sound accompanied the ball. The puppy pounced on the ball, paused, reared back on her hind legs, and pounced on it again. I got off my knees and put my foot down on something hard and round. I lifted my foot and found a little bronze button, about the size of a nickel, shaped like a heart. This must have been under the table with the ball. A delicate pattern covered the face of the button, and I wondered if it belonged to Jessica Callahan. I could imagine her getting out of the car, schlepping bags of groceries into the house, and not even knowing the button had popped off her jacket or sweater—it was too delicate for a jacket. She had probably disocvered the loss only later, when there was no hope of finding it.

The button made me think of Leslie's mother, Dorothy, who collects notions and buttons and pins. I knew this was something the collector in her would love. I also knew that taking anything from a crime scene was illegal. I put the button on the table and called out to Auggie as I pulled her leash from my jacket pocket. She came when she was called and sat before me while I attached the leash to her collar. As I prepared her for the great outdoors, she held the tennis ball firmly between her sharp little teeth, and I wondered if giving the puppy the ratty ball could be considered tampering with evidence.

"What do you think, Auggie? Did someone kill Jessica with that nasty old ball?"

Auggie cocked her head from side to side and listened to me carefully, never once taking her eyes off mine. She then pushed up her nose and tossed the ball to me. There was no question about it, this puppy was wrapping me around her dewclaw, and I was falling like a ton of bricks.

I rubbed her playfully behind her floppy ears and gave her back the saliva-drenched ball. What the hell? If this ball was primary to the case, at least I'd know where it was. As far as the button was concerned, I knew that Jessica would no longer have a use for it, and it was just a button. I picked it up and slipped it into my pocket, knowing it would find a good home.

Next to the garage door was a side door that led to the street. I turned the knob, but it didn't budge. I let myself out through the house entrance, but not before taking the time to stop and glance through the Callahans' two floors of rooms, furniture, photos, papers, and life. Nothing I saw jumped out at me and yelled, *"Yoo hoo, clue here!"*

By the time I returned to the house next door, Howie was up, and any calm that had existed during his naptime was shot. I asked Roz when I could talk to Dennis and was told that I would have better luck calling him at the office, to which she gave me the number. What with Auggie and the bags containing her food, toys, bowls, and brushes, I let Roz call a car service to take me from the Heights to the Upper West Side, destination home sweet home.

In the low backseat of the beat-up Pontiac, Auggie proved that cars and puppies are not the best of combos. She lost her cookies twice (into a towel that Roz had given me, anticipating the inevitable), and finally fell asleep in my lap as I smiled at the snarling taxi driver in the rearview mirror.

Thirteen

It took me close to twenty minutes to get Auggie from the car into the apartment. Everybody and his uncle wanted to stop and cuddle with the puppy, except Mrs. Jensen, one of my more colorful, elderly neighbors, who has become the building mascot in my eyes.

"What's that?" she barked at me, training her water gun at my chest and nodding to Auggie, who was all over the doorman.

"A dog," I answered, preoccupied with my juggling act, trying to hold on to the pup and her bags, and still not get the soiled towel on anyone or anything.

Mrs. J squirted me once with the water pistol and said, "I know that, partner. What *kind* of dog?"

I told her—and the three other people who had gathered around Auggie—that she was half golden and half Samoyed.

"Reindeer." Mrs. Jensen nodded knowingly. "The Samoyed herd reindeer, that's what their job is." Auggie scurried between Mrs. Jensen's legs and cried happily. Mrs. Jensen seemed not to notice. She crossed her arms under her sagging bosom and asked, "Are you going to see to it that he gets to do the work he likes best?"

"She's still a little young, Mrs. J. I don't want to mess with puppy labor laws." I inched my way toward the elevator.

"I don't blame you!" she shouted. "And you better not let her pee here." Mrs. Jensen pointed to the tiled floor. "That disgusting wrinkled thing pees here every single solitary day. Disgusting!" Mrs. J turned to the doorman and confided that she shoots the old Sharpei with her water gun when its owner isn't looking.

By the time I closed my front door I was exhausted. My first instinct was to call out to Leslie and show off Auggie, but again the place felt vast and empty. I knew well enough not to be worried about her, but despite my previous ire, I missed her, missed seeing how she would have responded to Auggie.

I brought Auggie's bags into the kitchen and started to unpack. Her food went into one of the lower cabinets. The toys—which were a huge assortment ranging from Miss Carrot, the Carmen Miranda of rubber squeakies, to partially gnawed rawhide bones—were tossed into a large basket in the office. I didn't know what to do with her bed. I stood in the hallway, turning first to the bedroom, and then to the kitchen. It wasn't as if I intended to hang on to this dog. This was merely a layover for her. I may have saved her from the dog pound, but I didn't have the room, time, or energy for a pooch. I directed myself back to the kitchen, where I put her fleece mat bed in the corner of the dining area. I went back to finish unpacking and caught Auggie out of the corner of my eye. She went directly to her bed, curled herself around several times, flopped down, flattened her chin on the bed and finally let out an enormous sigh. At the bottom of the last bag was a plain white sealed envelope with my name printed neatly on the front. I opened it and slipped out a white sheet of paper. Folded inside the letter was a green check that fluttered to the floor. I retrieved the check as I opened the letter and read:

Dear Sydney,

Thank you for your time and interest with regard to my situation. Please understand, however, that I am

*a man who needs to manage my own adversities. I
know that you want to help, so please, give Auggie a
good home. Enclosed is a little something for your
trouble.*

> Sincerely,
> Michael Callahan

I read it once and I was angry. Did this smooth-talking
Irishman honestly think I wouldn't see through his malar-
key? First he flatters: "I know you want to help," like I'm
doing this simply out of the goodness of my heart. Then
he makes it sound like he's doing me a favor by dumping
his dog on me. I know you want to help, so hey, I'll let
you do this for me. Oh thank you, thank you. Last, but not
least, the final flourish: a check, which, in other circles, is
also known as a bribe.

I read the letter again and found myself fuming. Who
did this jackass think he was, or—more importantly—who
did he think *I* was? Yin and yang being what it is, the first
thing I did was question if he would have played this silly
little game had Max been dealing with him. Judge and jury,
I decided the answer was no and vowed not only to find
him but to return his check, along with a piece of my mind.
That he would insult my integrity with a bribe was one
thing, but to insult my intelligence was another.

I looked at the check and caught my breath. Michael
Callahan's guilt gelt would have more than made up for
the substantial loss we were taking as a result of Louie's
shenanigans at the Madeline Hotel. I held proof in my hand
that Dr. Callahan was so anxious that I stop my investigation he was willing to pay and pay handsomely. I knew
if I showed the ten-thousand-dollar check to Max he'd take
it, deposit it, and tell me to go after the newly departed
doctor. I folded it in half and slipped it into my back
pocket.

I still didn't think that Michael murdered his wife, but I was more convinced than ever that he knew who did. Why else would he be willing to take the rap for it, and offer me hush money?

But whom was he protecting? And why? Was he being blackmailed? Did passion play into this somewhere, and if so, how and with whom? Though I could easily envision his partner, Dr. Cyclops, as a woman capable of murder, I couldn't imagine her and Michael in a passionate relationship.

I needed to organize my thoughts, and since I wasn't at the office where I put everything into the computer, I sat at the round oak dining table, and made notes regarding the case on index cards. Auggie came over to me and sat by my side with her head on my knee, not begging, but in need of something. I patted her head and rubbed her behind the ears. She issued a low, guttural growl. "Show me what you want," I said, for lack of anything else to say to her. Her ears perked up, she cocked her head and started toward the kitchen. Stunned to have gotten any response, I followed her. She went straight to her bowls and nudged one of the empty dishes. Water. I'd forgotten to give the puppy water. Christ, no wonder I didn't have pets of my own. How could I forget to give her water? It was a good thing she didn't have to rely on me for air. As she lapped up the water, I oohed and aahed that she had had the smarts to tell me what she wanted. Bright dog, this here Auggie. I bent down and hugged her and promised that if it was the last thing I did, I would find her a home worthy of her. She liked this and showered me with kisses. Sloppy puppy kisses, which I wiped off when she became preoccupied with chasing her tail and wasn't looking.

Just as I returned to the table to sort through the index cards, the doorbell rang. Whoever it was had a heavy finger and was impatient, two traits in doorbell-ringing technique that I don't admire. Auggie, however, was thrilled at the idea of company and puppy-barked her way to the door.

I was surprised to see that the culprit with the heavy finger was Naomi Lewis.

"I'm glad you're here," she said, hoisting her briefcase off the floor.

"Naomi," I said, trying to keep Auggie off her nylons. "What the hell are you doing here?"

"We have to talk." She walked past me into the foyer. I followed her as she made herself quite at home in my home, dropping her pounds of paperwork in the foyer, and continued on to the living room.

"Wow, you really changed the place from when we were kids, didn't you? It looks great." She took off her raincoat, tossed it on a chair, and studied the living room. The room she would have remembered from the past had been crammed with dark, heavy pieces of furniture and walls lined with books, books, and more books. When I claimed the apartment after my father died, I turned the living room into an uncluttered, calm space.

"Why didn't you call?" I asked as I shooed Auggie off the white sofa.

"I did, woman. Don't you listen to your messages? First I called you at work and your partner told me you would probably be here, so I left a message here telling you I was on my way over." She paced the room, taking in the place with an anxious eye.

"What's up?"

"Well, you know me, Syd, I'm not normally a suspicious person, but if someone hits you in the head with a mallet, you'd be a fool not to at least take a look at the stars floating around in front of your very eyes, right?" She kept pacing back and forth, her hands flapping at her side as she moved.

"What are you talking about?"

She took a deep breath and let her shoulders relax. "I

don't know, but I'm afraid there's something's wrong at the Treelane.''

"Okay." I motioned for her to follow me into the kitchen. "You want something to drink?"

"You have a beer?"

"I think so. Come on." I went into the kitchen and told her to have a seat at the dining room table, where we could continue our conversation.

She landed heavily on a chair and sighed.

There were two beers in the refrigerator. I pulled one out, and took it and a glass to the table.

"Thanks. Okay, where to begin?" She pressed her lips together until it looked as if she had none and then started. "Over the years Treelane has had some minor thefts, silly things like supplies, napkins, soap, small change, you know how it is. You expect that no matter what business you're running because essentially, people like to steal, they think they deserve it, you know?" She rubbed Auggie, who was relentlessly vying for her attention. "Personally, I don't care if someone steals a roll or two of scratchy toilet paper, however, as the proverbial buck stopper, I have to deal with it, and so, every time I've known there was a problem, I've been pretty good at getting to the root of it and putting an end to it. But today is different." She poured beer into the glass and watched the head rise and fall.

"Is this about the cash thefts from residents?"

"How did you know about that?" She paused as she brought the glass to her mouth.

"Apparently Jessica Callahan was upset that someone was taking money from Selma."

"Selma, too? Why didn't they say something to me?" Naomi said with a defensive edge.

I shrugged. "I don't know. Maybe Jessica planned to talk to you later."

"How did you find out? Did Selma tell you?" She sounded almost hurt.

"No, one of Jessica's friends told me."

"Well that's great, just great." She finally brought the glass to her mouth and took a long swallow.

"So, you've recently discovered that someone is stealing from the residents?"

"Yes, but that's not why I'm here. First we have to go back in time, okay? A year ago I had another problem with theft, but it wasn't toilet paper or small change. It was drugs."

"What sort of drugs?"

"Have you ever heard of Haldol?" Naomi asked.

"No."

"It's an incredibly strong depressant, and not one we use often, but it was in the cabinet because one of our patients at the time required it."

"How much was missing?"

"A bottle, maybe twenty-five pills."

"What did you do?"

"First I had a meeting with the heads of security, medical, and nursing. Now, like any other medical facility, the only people with direct access to medication are the nursing staff and the doctors." Naomi took a sip of her beer. "As a result of the meeting, we limited access to the medication, which meant that only the head nurse for each floor had a key, as well as the two resident doctors. At the same time there was a young woman who was new to the staff, and, unfortunately, she had a history of shoplifting from when she was in high school. Glenn Von Striker, who's the head of security, didn't like her, he didn't trust her. Now believe me, if this girl was going to steal drugs, Haldol would not have been the flavor of choice, but I wasn't in a position where I could take a chance, so I had to fire her. I told her that due to finances, we had to cut back on staff. I'm sure there was no connection between her and the missing drugs, but either way, the end result was that the stealing stopped. For a while. Then four months ago it happened again, only this time, oddly enough, it was digitoxin that was missing."

"The heart medicine?" I asked.

"That's right. During a routine inventory check, it was discovered that some was missing."

"Do you know who took it?"

Naomi shook her head. "No."

"Is Digitoxin a dangerous drug?"

"Sure. Any drug can be dangerous if it's not administered correctly. Christ, vitamin A has been known to kill."

"Really?"

"Yes, but anyway, the drug was missing, so we changed the locks on the medicine cabinets again and beefed up security. Now, with both the Haldol and the Digitoxin, it wasn't as if anyone was taking great quantities, and it's not as if *either* of these drugs is something you would find a dealer pushing on the streets. So, who's taking it and why?" She paused as if expecting me to answer.

"I don't know."

"Neither do I, but the fact is, they were isolated, essentially minor incidents, and I knew that security was on it. Again, nothing happened for a long time and quite honestly, I had forgotten about the thefts." She gave me a *what can you do* look and took a sip of her beer.

"So, this is why you called last night?"

"No. I called you last night because someone's stealing from my chickens. But you already knew about that, didn't you?" It sounded like an accusation, but I chose to ignore it because Naomi was always the kind of kid who liked to control things. My knowing something about her realm—without her having told me—must have been disconcerting.

"Last night I figured you and I were thrown into each other's paths again for a reason. Who knows, maybe you're here to figure out who's stealing from my little chickens. After all, you're an expert, right? I thought if nothing else, being an outsider, you might have a different perspective. You see, I'm not pleased with the internal investigation. I mean, it's been going on too long now, maybe close to a month. For all I know, someone in security could be responsible." I watched Naomi bring the glass to her mouth again, her face suddenly flattened and serious.

"You didn't race over here to consult with me on petty theft, did you? What's *really* on your mind?" Though many years had passed, I still knew how to read my old friend. There was some other reason for her unexpected visit.

"At about four o'clock this afternoon one of my senior nurses told me that we're missing drugs again." She shook her head. "Again, not a great quantity, and a strange choice." We stared at each other and I knew what the next word out of her mouth would be. "Insulin."

Fourteen

Naomi finished her beer and I brought her a fresh one. Auggie was sleeping comfortably on Naomi's feet, and the woman upstairs was practicing piano. Badly. But she was improving.

"Have you told anyone about this?" I asked, returning to the table with a beer for her and a glass of red wine for myself.

"No. When Phyllis told me about the theft, I don't know, but it hit me like a ton of bricks." Naomi looked like a kid in detention as she clutched her glass of beer.

"You think that was the insulin used to kill Jessica Callahan?" I asked.

"I don't know." She bent down and rubbed Auggie's head. "But that is how she died, isn't it?"

"Sort of. Jessica was killed a week ago. When was the insulin taken?"

Naomi looked chagrined. "The last check was a week and a half ago. Everything was accounted for." She took a deep breath.

"What?" I asked.

Naomi shook her head and said, "Look, I'm not a paranoid person by nature, and I don't go looking to stir up calm waters, but, Sydney, I feel in my heart that something is terribly wrong. I can't go to Glenn with this."

"Why not? He's your head of security."

"He's also bizarre. Look, Glenn Von Striker's been there a lot longer than I have and he's always had an issue with authority. That, coupled with the fact that he's a chauvinist, doesn't make for an easy working atmosphere between us. Not to mention he's the kind of nut who does surveillance by cutting holes in newspapers and watching people from behind them." She leaned back in her chair, slipped off her shoes, and rubbed Auggie's belly with her feet.

"You're exaggerating."

"Cross my heart." She did. "But there's more."

"What?"

"Well, this could be a figment of my imagination but . . ."

"Go on."

She leaned forward and rested her elbows on the table. "When Phyllis came to my office today and told me about the insulin, I had a flash on this man, Robert Sherman."

The name Sherman rang a bell, but I couldn't place it.

"His father, Sol, is one of our residents. Robert was in his fifties, a very successful Wall Street broker. He had his father admitted to the Treelane maybe three years ago."

"He's dead." I remembered Selma's passing comment when she was in and out of lucidity during my visit earlier that day. *I was talking to Mr. Sherman earlier. Poor man, his son died several months ago. He was a big shot, a lawyer. Too busy to visit his father. Heart attack, just like your father.*

"That's right. How did you know?"

"Heart attack?"

"I think so. Okay, so maybe I'm crazy, but maybe, maybe there's some sort of connection here."

"Why do you think that?"

"Robert Sherman was found behind the wheel of his car." She paused. "I mean, I know it could have been merely coincidental, but wasn't Jessica Callahan in her car, too? Don't even say it." She held up her hands. "I've been telling myself over and over that hundreds of people probably die behind the wheels of their cars every day and I just happen to know of two. You think I'm crazy, right?''

''Quite the contrary. I think you may be brilliant. Do you know if there were any other deaths related to the Treelane residents when the digitoxin was taken?'' I could feel the energy inside me surging. It was hard to sit still.

She shook her head. ''No, I don't. But I do know that no one *at* the Treelane died because of it.''

''How can you be so certain?''

''Because in the month after the theft, the only death was Hortense Ginsberg, and she died of natural causes.''

I shot her a questioning look, knowing that if someone wanted to, they could administer digitoxin in such a way that it would look like a heart attack.

''Believe me.'' She pooh-poohed me with a wave of her hand. ''At ninety-eight and given her state, it was a blessing. She went quietly in her sleep.''

''Remember that guy who considered himself an angel of God and went around killing old people?''

''Yeah, but Robert Sherman wasn't old. Neither was Jessica Callahan. She was what? Thirty-something?''

''Thirty-eight.''

''You know what kills me? No pun intended,'' Naomi said. ''I know that looking into something like this is just begging for trouble. Robert Sherman probably had a heart attack because he was in his fifties, stressed out, and out of shape. I'm a lunatic to be thinking the two are connected, but I can't stop thinking, *What if?* And that's making me crazy.''

''You can't ignore your gut reaction. If you're anything like me, once the seed is planted you won't be satisfied until you get some answers. Let me ask you, was Michael Callahan on staff at the Treelane?''

''The man's a pediatrician, Sydney.'' She rolled her eyes and cracked a smile for the first time since barging in on me.

''I knew that.'' I fished a pen out of the pile of index

cards on the table and found a fresh card. "Is Sol Sherman still a resident with you?"

"Yes."

"Does he have family?"

"He has a daughter in Montana. But it's his daughter-in-law, Betty, who's listed as the person to call in case of emergency."

"Do you know her?"

"I've met her a few times. Once when we admitted Sol, and once after Robert died. Stop making faces, Sloane."

"Well, why is it that old people are forgotten in our society?"

"They remind us of what's to come."

"So you stick 'em in a home and forget about them?"

"That's not as pervasive as you might think. But you're right, it does happen."

"If my folks were alive and needed to be in a home, I'd visit them all the time."

"I don't doubt that. But that's you. And that's them. Everyone has a different story. Imagine Lori Falduchi going to visit her father in a nursing home?" We had both gone to school with Lori. Every weekend her father would get drunk and beat the hell out of the kids. One night he used a knife and blinded Lori.

"In other scenarios, reversing the role of parent/child is never easy . . . some people can't handle it. It's not that they're evil, they're just scared. Conversely, I know one woman who visits her grandmother three times a week; she brushes her hair, puts makeup on her, reads to her, brings her special treats, and her grandmother doesn't have a clue. But you're right, most people aren't like this woman, most people figure, why schlepp all the way over to hell and gone when they won't even remember? It's frustrating. They get depressed."

"So the bottom line is, Betty doesn't visit Sol."

"Not that I know of. No."

"Do you have her number?"

145

"Not on me. But I can get it for you." She looked contemplatively in her glass and finally said, "I can't afford to start a scandal here, Sydney."

"I understand."

"I mean, I don't want you calling Betty Sherman and telling her you want to dig up old Robbie so we can have a look-see into the cause of his death, and, oh by the way, we think someone at the Treelane killed him."

"I promise you I won't," I said, though I knew that there was every likelihood that, ultimately, this scenario would be a reality. For the present, however, I could work with the hypothesis that someone at the Treelane had access to the insulin that might have killed Jessica Callahan, as well as the opportunity to commit that murder. Motive was a problem, but I had enough to start with. I was ready to roll up my sleeves and get to work when the phone rang.

I plucked the receiver off the kitchen wall phone and offered a distracted "Hello."

"Don't you bother to call in anymore, dear?" Whenever Max adds a "dear" to a sentence, it's a sure sign that I'm in trouble.

"Hey, Maxo, any luck with the hotels?" I asked, referring to his task to check hotels for Michael Callahan's whereabouts.

I listened as he breathed.

"You still at the office?" The clock on the wall read 5:45.

"Yes."

"You busy tonight?"

"Yes."

I was getting impatient with my partner's monosyllabic responses. I knew I was walking on thin ice, but I didn't know why.

"I'm going to pick you up in ten minutes and take you to Minnie's, where we have both been invited for dinner." He was warming slowly.

"Minnie?" I might have forgotten that I had called her

146

earlier, but knew I hadn't made plans for dinner. "I don't understand."

"Apparently in your outdoor travels through the day, you called Minnie for a dinner date. Well, she returned your call and said that she was cooking. I explained that Leslie and your car were on vacation but that I would be happy to fill in as your date. This, naturally, thrilled Minnie, as she is a thoroughbred among women and appreciates a stud when she sees one."

I glanced at Naomi, who was scanning the index card notes I had left on the table when she first arrived.

"Max, I'm on to something and I need help," was my gracious response.

"Now?"

"Yes." I gave him an abbreviated update on what Naomi had just handed me. When I was finished he issued a low whistle.

"That's interesting," he said.

"I think so, too. You in?"

"Of course, I'm in. But we have to eat and Minnie's already made dinner, so I suggest we go there, chow down, and then spend the night working."

Minnie was used to my racing in and out when I am hot on a case, so I knew she would understand. My only problem was the dog, who was happily dozing on Naomi's feet.

"Hang on," I told Max and covered the mouthpiece. "Hey, Naomi." She opened her eyes and looked at me sleepily. "Naomi, that's Auggie." I pointed to the pooch warming her feet. "Auggie, Naomi. Now that the two of you have been properly introduced, do you think you could take her? Just for tonight?" I quickly qualified, so as not to frighten her away.

Naomi leaned forward and looked down at Auggie. "Hello, Auggie." She leaned back and looked at me. "Nope."

"I don't mean forever. Just for tonight?" I was beginning to plead.

147

"No, Sydney. I have two daughters, a Republican, and a hundred and fifty chickens to worry about. Enough is enough. The kids see this dog and they'll drive me crazy, begging to keep it, which I won't. Then I'm the bad guy. No."

I mumbled, "Selfish," and got back on the phone. "What time is Minnie expecting us?" I asked Max.

"Six."

"Call her and tell her we'll be late. We'll pick you up in twenty minutes, but be waiting downstairs, okay?" I hung up before he could finish asking who *we* was.

I fed Auggie, who inhaled her dinner in under twenty seconds; slipped into a pair of sneakers; grabbed a few plastic bags to scoop the poop, her leash, a puppy toy to entertain her at Minnie's, and a couple of treats. Naomi, Auggie, and I walked downtown on West End Avenue, as it was less congested than Broadway and I discovered that Auggie—like any sensible dog—had no desire to do her business on pavement.

When we hit Eighty-third Street, Naomi and I said our good-byes and I promised to call her first thing in the morning.

"Naomi, you did the right thing," I reassured my dejected friend as I hugged her.

"Really? Then why don't I feel better about it?"

"Doesn't always work that way. Get some sleep, you look beat."

Max was waiting in front of the building when we arrived. Despite his previous pooch protests, I could tell he was smitten with Miss Auggie from the moment he saw her.

"Who's dis?" Max Cabe talking baby talk, would wonders never cease? He bent down and let her jump up on his knees.

"Auggie. You want her?" I offered him the leash.

"This the puppy you were trying to pawn off before?" He took the leash and we started toward Central Park.

"That's right."

"She's great."

"I know. She's beautiful, friendly, good with children and old people, a real diplomat among her peers. All that and she's housebroken, too. There's only one small flaw."

"As I recall that was her name," Max said, tugging on her collar, trying to get her to heel.

"That's not the problem. It's her eating habits. They should have named her Oinker."

"Puppies eat fast. How old is she?"

"Six months?"

"Has she had all her shots?"

"I don't know. Why?"

"Because she can get distemper if you walk her on the streets before she's had all her shots."

"Well, we don't have much choice now, do we?"

We hurried through the park as fast as we could, but it still took us half an hour, which meant we were already late for Minnie. Four vacant cabs passed us before one finally pulled up and said a dog was no problem.

We made it to Minnie's Park Avenue apartment by a quarter to seven, with earnest apologies and one tired pooch. The wine was breathing and Minnie was so thrilled to have a puppy in her home that she practically forgot Max and I were there. The second she saw Auggie, she was down on her knees rubbing noses with the pup. Max offered her a hand up, which she waved away. "If I couldn't get up, I wouldn't go down, but thank you, Max, your mother raised you well." She braced herself on the seat of the bench in the foyer and rose with energy and grace. She then stretched up on her tiptoes and let Max give her a bear hug. As I hung up my jacket, I watched the two of them. Minnie looked great in her black slacks and big red sweater covered with a butcher's apron; why, you could have mistaken her for a seventy-year-old. I thought of my recent conversation with Naomi as Minnie patted my face and said, "Nice outfit, but you look like hell." For some odd reason, this reminded me of Leslie, whom I was now beginning to miss. A lot. It had been literally years since we had gone this long without talking.

In the kitchen, Max poured the wine and I took the lids off pots and pans to get an idea of the menu: lamb chops, potatoes Anna, sautéed spinach, and chopped salad. Bliss. Minnie shooed me away from the stove and made me sit on a stool by the counter, out of her way and, therefore, out of trouble. In the meantime, Auggie followed Minnie like a homing device. As I watched the two of them, it occurred to me that a match between Minnie and Auggie might just be made in heaven. They say pets keep people young.

"Max says you have your doubts about Michael's innocence. He's a very nice boy. I'm stunned he's in such trouble." Minnie went to the oven and pulled out the casserole dish of potatoes. Just the aroma of the crusty, buttery potatoes was adding weight to my hips. I inhaled deeply, and realized that I was starving.

"Once the authorities find out he's skipped town, he'll really know trouble." I tugged the heel off a loaf of semolina bread.

"Where on earth would he go?" Minnie mused as she dunked a piece of bread in the lamb juice. She shoved the chops back into the oven, closed the oven door, and turned to Auggie.

"Don't give her people food," I said with a full mouth.

"This is my home, Missy Sloane, and I can do as I like." She turned to Auggie, held up the alluring treat, and gently said, "Sit. Sit now." When Auggie put her tushy on the floor I felt like a proud mom. "Good puppy." Minnie praised her as she gave her the treat. She wiped her hands on her white apron and turned to me. "So with all this work, why did you get a dog? It's so unlike you."

"This is Michael's dog." I looked out at two nonplussed faces. "That's right, kids, Michael thought that I'd be the perfect baby-sitter for Jessica's dog. The only problem is, he never asked if I wanted the job.''

"So how did you get her?" Max asked, handing me a glass of Merlot.

I sighed. ''Michael's neighbor, Roz, was going to take her to the pound. I had to interview the woman anyway, and I couldn't let a puppy rot in a cage, so I told her that I'd find a home for Auggie." Hearing her name, Auggie came to me, tail wagging a mile a minute.

"This dog would not rot in a cage," Minnie observed, quite sensibly.

"Maybe not, but a trip to the pound can be very traumatic for a dog.''

"Oh sure, she might hook up with a pit bull and that would be it." Max gave Minnie her glass and took the bottle into the dining room, where Minnie had already set the table.

"You know, Min, I thought maybe *you* would want Auggie," I casually suggested.

She smiled slyly and shook her head. "Oh no you don't, my dear. This is *your* responsibility. I had a cat once and that was enough. If I want a pet, I call Enoch."

"Where *is* Enoch?"

"Home. We decided we were seeing each other too often.''

"*We* decided?" I asked as Max came back into the room.

"*I* decided." She took the chops out of the oven and pressed them with an index finger, checking for doneness. "Look, I don't want to rush into anything here." She switched off the oven and asked Max to hand her a platter.

"Rush into anything?" I teased my father's eldest sister, who is the only person I know who's made a habit of rushing.

"Don't you be fresh."

"For crying out loud, you've been seeing the man for almost two years. Two weeks after you two started dating you took a vacation together. You celebrate all the holidays together, I would imagine you've—"

"That's enough." She cut me off, blushing ever so slightly.

"Why Minerva Sloane, I don't think I've ever seen you blush."

"It's high blood pressure," she quipped. Max held the tray while Minnie piled it high with chops and spinach. I was charged with taking the salad and bread to the table while Max was entrusted with the potatoes, lucky boy.

At the table, with plates and glasses full, Minnie picked up where we had left off. "We were talking about Michael. Where is he?"

"If I knew that, he wouldn't be missing and I could reunite him with his sweet, little, friendly, housebroken puppy who seems to be oh-so-happy in these Park Avenue digs."

"Won't work," Minnie said as she started in on the spinach. "I assume you've begun looking for him." There was an archness in her tone that reminded me of my mom.

"Well, my illustrious partner is checking all the hotels in Manhattan and I know that the guys who visited him yesterday hail from out on Long Island. East Hampton to be exact."

"What about family?" Max asked as he cut into a chop aromatic with rosemary and garlic.

"Not a soul. Apparently both of his parents died in an airplane crash when he was in college and there was no one else."

"Oh dear, that's right. I had completely forgotten. Such a shame," Minnie said.

Auggie curled up next to my chair, heaved a sigh, and fell fast asleep.

I told them about my visit to Michael's, the hospital, the license plate, the old man with the bag, my talk with Roz, and my pit stop at the Callahan garage. I didn't go into Naomi's recent visit because Max and I would go through it later and Minnie didn't need all this information.

"I think it's a pity," Minnie announced when I was through. "They were such a sweet couple."

"You knew her?" I asked.

"Oh sure, Enoch and I had dinner with the two of them a few times. I was even at their wedding, but that was just after Enoch and I started dating. I didn't even know them then."

Max pointed to the last lamb chop. "Anyone want that chopster?"

"Chopster?" Minnie and I asked in unison. "Far out, man," I continued, "wanna brewsky to go with it?"

"I don't like you, Sydney," Max enunciated clearly.

I handed him the lamb chop and polished off the potatoes, making myself only mildly sick with all that fat sloshing around inside me. A high colonic, that's what I needed. One of them babies, and I'd feel as good as new.

"So you were at their wedding?" I asked.

"Oh yes. It was very nice. Small, but as I recall the food was really quite good." As Minnie makes her living writing cookbooks this was a four-star review.

"Do you remember her bridesmaid?"

"Donna? Now there's a sweet boy. He was the one who got Enoch and me tickets when Rosemary Clooney was sold out at the Rainbow Grill."

"*Donna's* a sweet boy?" Max asked.

"I should look so womanly," I told him. "So you thought they were a sweet couple?" I asked Minnie.

"Well, I think Selma's insistence that Enoch do something to prove Michael's innocence only demonstrates how much she believes in him. That's quite a testimony to the young man, I'd say."

"So you don't think they were maybe a little mismatched? From everything I've heard, he seems pretty straitlaced and yet her best friend is a transvestite."

Minnie gave this some thought before answering. "Well, I suppose he was a little conservative compared to her, but

I think that enhances a relationship. Differences often balance things out, don't you agree?" Again I thought of Leslie and sighed.

"I couldn't agree with you more," Max said as he licked his fingers.

As if on cue, as soon as Max finished dinner, Auggie woke up and started talking to us.

"She wants something," I explained with a tinge of pride.

"Food, probably." Minnie leaned back in her chair and nodded. "That's what happens when you feed them from the table."

"I didn't feed her from the table. She was asleep."

"Maybe she wants water," Max suggested.

"She has a bowl in the other room," Minnie said.

"Maybe she has to go out." I considered. All eyes were on Auggie. "Okay, Aug, show me what you want. Show me." Minnie and Max were duly impressed when Auggie went directly to the door.

"That's good. She wants galoshes," Max said, noting that the door Auggie had approached was, in fact, a closet.

"You're jaded, Mr. Cabe," Minnie said in Auggie's defense.

"But in love with you, Minnie. Always and forever." He blew her a kiss.

"You know, Max, if you were thirty years older, I think I would actually marry you. But as long as you're here, would you mind taking Auggie for a walk?"

"Me?" he sputtered. "It's *her* dog."

"I know that, dear, but I have something I need to ask Sydney." She winked at him as if there was some private joke I wasn't privy to.

I smugly handed him the plastic bags and her leash. The sight of the leash brought about great excitement from the puppy, which only further chagrined Max.

"I'm *only* doing this for you, Minnie. And for the record,

I'd marry you in a second. You have something I've always wanted."

"Wrinkles?" she suggested.

"Nope. A big, inexpensive apartment on Park Avenue. And your cooking. It was great, as always." He took the leash and glared at me. "I'll be right back."

When he was gone I returned to the table and asked Minnie, "What's up."

"That's what I want to know."

"What do you mean?" I reached for my water glass and felt like I'd been caught, but I didn't know what for.

"Your message today led me to believe you have something on your mind."

I paused, remembering how I had felt when I left Mary Douglas's apartment. The moment, however, had passed, and I didn't want to feel the loss and fear I had experienced earlier in the day. Now I needed to focus on the matters at hand.

"Your sister called today." She filled in the silence.

"Ah ha, so that's it. That old snitch." I slumped back in my chair and rubbed the base of my glass along the tablecloth. "It was a moment. It passed."

"You know what they say about bullshitting a bullshitter."

When I didn't respond she said, "Sydney, I expect you to be as honest with me as you have always been. Life is too goddamned short for us to have to fish the truth out of each other—especially if we don't have to, which we never have and I don't expect to now."

"Could you be a little more direct, please." I finished my water and reached for the pitcher.

"What's up? Really."

"Okay." I stalled for time by pouring more water in each of our glasses. "For the first time I'm really thinking about getting old." I said this more to my glass than to Minnie. How do you tell a woman who's forty years your senior that you're thinking about getting old and not expect her to tell you to go suck an egg? More importantly, how do you tell your best friend, your surrogate mother, that you've spent the last twenty-four hours subconsciously worrying about losing her? "And I guess spending time at the nursing home makes me think about, I don't know, everything." For the first time since I had confided in Minnie that I lost my virginity at the ripe old age of eighteen, I felt shy with her.

"Are you worried about me?" She looked me straight in the eyes.

"Not worried. But it's something we've never *really* talked about. In passing, yeah, but not . . . I don't know."

"Honey, aging is inevitable, if we're lucky. But not all people get *old*, if you know what I mean. Talk about misconceptions! I mean, yes, there comes a point when you don't have the same elasticity of flesh and a hundred chin-ups is out of the question, and one should deal with the practical matters, for example, what would my wishes be if I was on life support?"

"Pull the plug?"

"That's right. But I suspect it isn't that that you're concerned with right now, is it?"

"I don't know," I answered honestly. "I never think of you as getting old, but you're eighty-one years old. I mean, I know the changes that *my* body's going through right now. I can't imagine what you're going through."

"I appreciate your concern, dolly, but honestly, aside from some aches and pains that started when I was your age, I've never felt better. I feel confident, capable and more creative than I have in years. Our society is so afraid of aging, but most people don't have a clue as to what it's really about. Not all of us get senile and wet ourselves, you know," she said, reaching for her glass. "Don't be afraid of it, my dear, either for yourself or me. Now tell me one thing."

"What's that?"

"Where's Leslie? You two aren't fighting, are you?"

"Why would you ask that?"

"Max said she took your car and went to the Hamptons. Was she upset?"

"No, she went on business." I ran my fingertips against the hair on an eyebrow.

"Oh dear." She took a deep breath and leaned back in her seat.

"What?" I asked, alarmed.

"You're doing that annoying thing with your eyebrow. You only do that when you're really upset."

I put my elbows on the table and cupped my chin in my hand. "I hung up on her last night."

"Oh dear. That's unlike you."

"She let her client drive my car, he got into an accident serious enough to warrant at least an overnight stay in a garage, the client was in her room last night, and she wouldn't ask him to leave so we could discuss it."

"And that makes you feel justified?"

"Well, yeah. Don't you think?"

"It's a car, for cryin' out loud." She clearly could not get worked up to see my side of this.

"It's not about the car, Minnie, it's about communicating with each other, openly, honestly . . ."

"Which you severed the second you hung up on her. Let me tell you something, whether she was wrong or right in taking the car or letting this client drive it, you know she didn't do it maliciously. And you know she's crazy about you. Don't forget, 'He who is loved is rich.' " I nodded and recited her father's favorite adage along with her. "When you get home tonight, you hug that girl and tell her you love her. You hear me?"

"I love you, Minnie." I reached out and took my aunt's surprisingly solid hand in mine.

"I love you, too, dear."

"And I love you both," Max said from the doorway. "Are we getting maudlin from the wine or is this just a moment between women that a man couldn't possibly appreciate?''

Auggie came racing over to me, a smile plastered on her goofy little face. I took her into the kitchen and wiped off her paws and privates with a paper towel. It was a lesson I had learned from one of my friends whose dog I'd cared for. Dogs are creatures of habit. Once they get used to the routine, it's easier to keep them—as well as your apartment—clean.

By the time Auggie and I returned to the dining room, Max and Minnie were clearing the table and Max was explaining that we had an evening of work ahead.

"Does that mean no dessert?" Minnie said as she handed me a stack of dishes.

"We can't," I said at the same time Max asked what it was.

"Eclairs." She waggled her eyebrows, knowing that she had hit nerve central.

Max and I both swooned.

"Can we take them to go?" I asked sweetly.

"To go? What do I look like, a Chinese restaurant?"

"No," I said with mock sincerity. "Does she look like a Chinese restaurant, Max?"

Max studied Minnie. "No. Not Chinese. She looks more like that drive-in I took you to in Chicago for your birthday."

"Super-Dawg?"

"Yeah, that's it. She looks like a well-dressed little hot dog."

"Very funny. Here." She had already packed the dessert for us to take with us. "I know you two knuckleheads well enough to be prepared. Now get out of here, I have things to do."

I don't know why, but at that very moment I wanted to cry, to just wrap my arms around my aunt and tell her how much I love her. Instead, I took the bag of goodies and asked Max what he planned to have for dessert.

158

Twenty minutes later we were back in my apartment. I was breathlessly hoping Leslie would be there upon my return, but she wasn't. It was almost nine-thirty, and I made a beeline to the office to check the answering machine, which I had neglected to do when I was home before. There was one message. It was from Leslie. My car was almost fixed, and she had decided to give herself a few days— *alone*—at the beach. If I was still talking to her, I could call the same number as before. Just the sound of her voice made me smile. I quickly dialed the number, but there was no answer in her room. I left a message saying I would call later.

On my way to the kitchen to make coffee for a long night ahead, I passed Max, who was in the bathroom washing his slacks from where Auggie had tossed her cookies in the taxi. Auggie sat with him in the bathroom as he lectured her on proper car etiquette, which included no vomiting, no blocking the rearview mirror, and no unexpected loud barking. As much as Max complained, I could tell that it was only a matter of time before he asked for Auggie's paw in holy dogimony.

Fifteen

By the time we settled at the dining room table, I had made coffee, put the four eclairs (oh, Minnie is bad) on a plate, and arranged the index cards into three columns: MURDER, MOTIVE, and WHERE IN THE WORLD IS?

Under the MURDER card, I had stacked about a dozen notes, all related to the evidence surrounding Jessica Callahan's murder, including date and time of death; actual cause of death; how she had been found and where; who she saw and spoke with on the day she died, as well as a card marked *Suspects.* So far only one name had been noted there: Michael.

This led to the MOTIVE stack where there were four cards, simply marked *Greed, Passion, Jealousy,* and *Revenge.* The last stack of index cards—WHERE IN THE WORLD IS—was dedicated solely to Michael Callahan.

"Is Marcy working tonight?" I asked Max as he came in, with Auggie happily taking up the rear. I was pleased to see that she didn't look the least bit contrite after their bathroom chat.

"No. Why?" He had helped himself to a pair of my sweatpants, which were only a tidge too small.

"She could find out if the Callahan car has been impounded. If it hasn't, that means Dr. Mike probably has it and she could get me a description of the car as well as a plate number."

"She could, indeed. Anything else?"

"Yeah, I have the license plate number for that station wagon. Do you want to call her?" I fished in my bag and pulled out my handy-dandy spiral notebook where I keep all notes, large and small.

"Yeah." He grabbed the mug of coffee I had set out for him and said, "Thanks. Decaf?"

"Nope. I figured at your advancing age, you could use a stimulant to stay awake."

"Caffeine gives me gas." He tapped in Marcy's number on the kitchen phone and smiled impishly.

"Lucky me," I mumbled as I shuffled through all the cards. On a fresh card I wrote in fine print everything that I could remember from my conversation with Naomi. As I did this I listened to Max woo Marcy. Over the years Max has mellowed and come to realize what a find he has in Marcy, but there was a time when she was only one on a long list of gals in the old corral. Over the last few years Max has focused his attention more and more on Marcy and let the other women fall by the wayside (a decision hailed by all the other important women in Max's life, including me, Minnie, Kerry, Leslie, his mother, and his sister, Joy).

I listened carefully as he gave her the information regarding both Callahan and the white station wagon. I also left the room when he dropped his voice and flirted like a schoolboy making a date for a movie and heavy petting. Auggie followed me to the bedroom, where I, too, slipped into a pair of sweat pants. While in there I showed Auggie a picture of Leslie, "She's my partner and she's mad at me right now. Waddaya think?" Auggie sniffed the frame, licked it, noticed her tail wagging behind her, and quickly lost interest in Leslie.

By the time I returned to the kitchen, Max was off the phone and working his way through the eclairs.

"So, what did Marcy say?" I asked, pushing a pile of paper napkins in front of him.

"She said she'd have something for us first thing in the morning."

"Okay, let's do it." I said.

"You got it."

In the next hour we went through everything that I had learned, and added Naomi's information. In October of this year Jessica Callahan had died. Robert Sherman's death was placed in June. The digitoxin theft happened in March. If we could determine a death related to the Treelane in that time period, we might be able to establish a connection. We decided that the best way to approach this was to divide and conquer. As it was there were four immediate questions to answer:

1. Who killed Jessica Callahan?
2. Where was Michael Callahan at the time of his wife's murder?
3. Where was Michael Callahan now?
4. Who was stealing drugs from the Treelane?

As there were four problems and three of us—including Kerry—to tackle them, it was easy to compartmentalize the work list, and make it less daunting. It made sense to have Max look into a possible connection between Jessica Callahan's death and the Treelane. Seeing as though people there already knew me, it would be easier to bring him in undercover to get into not only the patient files, but the staff folders as well. Naomi could hire him to help with filing, which would give him access to the records, which would be a start.

Initially he would focus on the months of October and November of the prior year, when the first theft had occurred. Not knowing what he would actually be looking for, we decided that he should focus first on hirings and firings during that time period. Next focus would be on June and July, when the digitoxin was stolen. We decided that—again—he would focus on who was hired and fired

162

during that time first, and then try to find out if any of the residents had lost a relative. We were grasping at straws, and we knew it, but needles in haystacks is usually what our work is about.

With her connections at the city morgue, Kerry would be in charge of finding out exactly what killed Robert Sherman. After that, if Max was able to bring files out of the Treelane, she could help him wade through those.

In the meantime, I would focus on Michael Callahan. Max and I were both convinced that the doctor knew a lot more about his wife's death than he would admit. Max had checked most of the better hotels in New York City, and come up empty-handed. Though we knew it was an impossibly long shot, we decided to keep Kerry on the next day, as well as have her get an autopsy report on Robert, and trace Michael's hospital buddies, Milt Brown and Mary Grace. If we were going to find Callahan, we had to be methodical, which meant going through every single bit of information we had on him. Limited though that information was, we've both done this enough to know that the pointer which would set us in his direction had to be right under our very noses. We just had to look harder. Max was writing up a profile of Callahan and polishing off the last eclair when the phone rang. It was 10:38 and I was in the middle of making a fresh pot of coffee.

I knew it was Leslie. Who else could it be at that hour? And when did barely eleven at night suddenly get to be *that hour*? Naomi was right, old was slipping up right behind me without my even being aware of it. It started with listening to soft-rock radio stations, then needing reading glasses, on to aching bones, and now this, phone curfews. My head was filled with noise when I plucked the receiver off the wall and answered with a cheerier hello than I felt.

There was a pause. I imagined Leslie looking at the receiver and marveling that I was actually chipper.

"Um, Sydney, please." The voice was male, but so soft I had trouble hearing it clearly.

"This is Sydney." I paused. "Can I help you?"

"I'm looking for Sydney, um, Sloane?" His voice lilted up at the end, turning his statement into a question.

"You found her."

A longer pause followed, but I listened intensely. He was still on the other end of the line, and I had the feeling that if I spoke, I'd frighten him away like a hummingbird at a feeder.

Finally he started again.

"Michael Callahan needs help," he enunciated very clearly.

"Is he okay?"

"He needs help," he repeated, emphatically.

"Where is he?"

He covered the receiver and called out to someone. When he came back, he gave me an address out in Montauk.

"Is this a hotel?"

"No."

"Is he okay?"

Again there was silence.

"Who are you? Where can I—"

The next thing I heard was the very distinct sound of the receiver being set back into it's cradle. I stared at the phone before finally hanging up.

"What?" Max asked, pulling at the snug waistband of the sweatpants.

"There's a man in Montauk who's looking out for Michael Callahan. I have his current address." I held up the piece of paper. "He says Michael needs help."

"No shit." Max sat back into his chair and shook his head. "When you least expect it, manna comes from the heavens above." He smiled. "I love it. So, when do you leave?"

"Now," I said, feeling my energy and the caffeine kick in simultaneously.

"Really? How? If I'm not mistaken, you're without wheels." He stood up. "You know you can have mine if

164

you want it.'' With a top speed of forty-five miles an hour, Max's '78 Chevy was, at best, an impractical choice of transportation.

"Thanks anyway, but this is why we have rental cars. And car services. And taxis." I had already pulled out the phone book and was reaching for the phone.

"Good. You rent a car or a driver or whatever the hell you're going to do and I'll be right back. I don't know how you wear these sweats, they're killing me. They're like a girdle.''

As soon as Max left, I dialed a local car rental company I've done business with in the past. Most places in the city closed, I knew, at around eleven, and I was cutting it short, but the cosmic joker was working with me and this place was open until 11:30. It was 10:45. I had scads of time. Max came in as I was tossing the coffee pot and plates into the dishwasher.

"Any luck?" Max asked, wiping the wet spot on his thigh where Auggie had left her mark earlier.

"Yup. I just have to clean up here and pack a bag. Want to puppy-sit while I'm gone? It'll only be for twenty-four hours, tops." I wet a sponge and started wiping all eclair crumbs from the counter. It was an ounce of precaution, as Manhattan is notorious for roaches. No matter how clean you are, or how many Roach Motels you put out, chances are you'll find a few strolling across the floor when you turn on a light late at night.

Max glanced down at Auggie, who was snoozing peacefully half on, half off her bed.

"Think I'll pass."

"You can't pass. She gets car sick."

"She'll be fine. Here," He opened a cabinet and pulled out a metal bowl. "Most dogs give you a few hiccups' warning before they lose it. Just slide this under her face and you'll be fine. Stop that.'' He took a sponge from my hand and directed me out of the room. "Let me do this; you go pack.'' Max took over KP and I went to the bedroom, where I changed back into my street clothes, started packing an overnight bag, and placed another call to Leslie. Still there was no answer, so I left a message saying I would be there later that night.

When Max and Auggie walked into the room I picked up where we had left off. "Maxo, you have to keep the dog."

"No."

"Max." I urged him to face facts. "The poor thing gets car sick; most hotels don't accept animals, and God knows what's going to happen to me when I'm out there. I may not be able to get back to her for hours. It's not fair to Auggie."

"Life is not fair, Sydney." He sat on the foot of the bed and watched me toss jeans, underwear, boots, sneakers, slippers, and a tee-shirt into the canvas satchel.

"But she's a puppy, Max." I felt like I was six and a half trying to reason with my big sister, Nora, that it wasn't fair that she owned 90 percent of the family cat and I could only own the tushy.

"Give her to Leslie. She's out there, right?"

"Why are you being such a poot?" Done in the bedroom, I hurried back to the kitchen.

"Look, I don't need to get attached to a dog. If you leave her with me I'll only get attached and then suddenly I'll be saddled with a dog I don't have time for and it'll only make me feel guilty. I don't need any more guilt. I get enough every time I talk to my mother."

I started to repack her original shopping bag, when I caught her out of the corner of my eye, sitting in the corner, cocking her head from one side to the other, looking sad and perplexed. I scooped her up into my arms, nuzzled her face, and told her secretly that she had nothing to worry about, I wasn't going to abandon her. "Fine." I said to Max in a tone I hoped would instill deep guilt. "That's just fine." I handed him Auggie and emptied her water bowl,

166

which I dried and put into a bag along with toys, bones, two towels, and the metal bowl.

"Do you have any cash?" I asked, having gone through my pockets and wallet and collected a lump sum of twenty-eight dollars.

"Yeah." Max tucked his hand into his back pocket and came out with a wad of bills. "How much do you need?" He peeled off three twenties and paused.

"A couple thousand should do it." I took the five twenties he offered and nodded to his money. "You know, it's dangerous to carry so much money."

"Yes, Mom."

"Don't Mom me."

"Yes, dear."

"That's better." I took another forty from him and slipped it in my back pocket. "You never know."

"So, what's your game plan?" Max asked as I packed an extra eight-round magazine for the Walther and tucked it safely in my bag. "Think you'll need that?" he asked, motioning to the ammunition.

"I hope not, but the Girl Scout in me says be prepared."

"Don't forget maps," he suggested.

"They're in my car—" I started to say, but caught myself. "Right. Maps."

"So, game plan?" He followed me back into my office, where I keep all things cartographic.

"Considering the way the caller sounded, I think I have to go directly to Michael—"

"If he's still there."

"Right. If he's still there. Or ever was."

"You won't get there until after two in the morning."

I checked my watch. Max was right. It was just past eleven, which meant that if I left the city proper by 11:30, it would still take me two to three hours to get to Montauk, even at this hour with no traffic, which would place me out there at 1:30, 2:00. "Well, let's not tarry. Will you at least help me get all this shit to the rental place?" I asked, hook-ing Auggie's leash to her collar. Despite her sleepiness, I could see that she was anxious.

"Seeing as you put it so nicely, how could I refuse?" Max took the two puppy bags and her bed and started for the door.

"Now I know what schlepping a toddler feels like. Next thing you know I'll be taking a stroller on a stakeout."

Half an hour later, I was sailing east on the Long Island Expressway with Auggie's chin on my thigh. I had the radio dial tuned in to a previously recorded talk show, starring Clifford Bartholomew, a champion of nonsense and prejudice whom I had once had the displeasure of meeting. The show started with Bartholomew asking his listeners: "Does anyone know why these knuckleheads in the Order of the Solar Temple did themselves in, in Canada and Switzerland? And furthermore does anyone *care*?" I knew I had had enough talk radio when the subject matter had spiraled to the point where callers were actually giving emotional responses to the query, "Are people who own African pigmy hedgehogs as household pets demented?" The moment I switched off Bartholomew and put on classical music, Auggie let out an enormous sigh and pressed her big paw against my knee. I was, I knew, falling helplessly in love, and there was nothing I could do about it, which is probably how Jessica Callahan felt every time she looked at Auggie.

An hour and forty-five minutes later I entered East Hampton, pulled over, and called Leslie. It was, I knew, too late to be calling anywhere, but I had no choice. The phone rang fifteen times before a sleepy, curt gentleman answered and put me through to Leslie's room.

She had been expecting the call and picked up before the first ring finished. I told her to meet me downstairs. Not knowing what to expect in Montauk, I couldn't take Auggie with me, Auggie, my good puppy, who had kept her cookies intact for the whole of the trip.

Leslie was waiting in the parking lot when I arrived.

When I saw her I was overwhelmed. Sure, there was a part of me who was still pissed at her for having taken my car and driven off into the sunset with an arrogant Frenchman. But then there was the me who was like a little kid at Christmas with the best present in the world right before my very eyes. Auggie jumped out of the car and raced past her to do her business in the bushes that surrounded the parking lot. Stars crowded the clear sky above and all I could hear was the sound of waves crashing on the shore in the distance. No traffic. No sirens. No nothing. It was beautiful.

Without a word we slipped into each other's arms, and I felt like I was taking my first deep breath since she had gone. And when I inhaled, it was Leslie I was breathing in; it felt like home. "Why didn't you call?" she whispered, the very sound of her voice like a caress.

"I did." I held her at arm's distance so I could see her face. "I missed you," I said, seeing Auggie in my peripheral vision, pouncing on something in the grass.

Leslie cupped my face in her hands and kissed me in a way that told me how much she had missed me. "You didn't call me all day." She rubbed her cheek against mine.

I fell into a second kiss before saying, "We have a lot to talk about."

"I know, but I'm glad you're here. However, the real question is, who is this sweet baby?" She was radiant as she bent down and picked up Auggie, who was happily scurrying between our legs.

"This is Auggie. She's between homes."

"Oh my God, she's gorgeous." Auggie was smiling, there's no question about it. Her black lips were pulled up into what could only be described as a grin and her black eyes were dancing with delight. She squirmed happily in Leslie's arms . . . who could blame her?

"How long do I have you for?" she asked me as she nuzzled Auggie.

"About thirty-eight seconds. I have to go to Montauk."

"Montauk? I thought you came out here to be with me."

I looked into her big blue eyes and decided the middle ground was definitely the route to take. Honest, but kind. "I'm on a case," I said gently. "Enoch Zarlin's hired us—"

"Minnie's Enoch?"

"Right. It turns out that his grandniece was murdered and her husband's the most likely candidate. Enoch wants us to find out who really did it."

"Wow. Well, can't you go to Montauk in the morning? There's a double bed upstairs with our names on it." Given the choice between a nice warm bed with my lover or a dark, cold drive out to Montauk, I was tempted to put Michael Callahan on hold until morning.

"I wish, but I can't. Can you take her upstairs?" I asked, taking Auggie's bags out of the car.

"They don't allow pets." Auggie sighed and rested her chin on Leslie's shoulder.

"Who's to know?" I asked.

Leslie took a step closer to me and said suggestively, "You never make things easy, do you?" She nibbled on my ear for punctuation.

She smelled faintly of lavender, and I would have liked nothing better than to burrow my face into the soft warmth of her neck and go to sleep. Instead, I heard the caller's insistent voice in the back of my head and whispered, "I have to go. Let me help you upstairs with Auggie and then I'll take your key, okay?" I kissed her neck and gently pulled away, rubbing my cheek against hers. "This way I won't have to wake you later."

She held tightly to my jeans jacket and pulled me back. "You better wake me."

And so it was I found myself back on the road, wondering if it would have been wiser for me to have slept until sunrise and then gone looking for the doctor. On the one hand, I knew that losing five hours could make the difference between solving a case or not. On the other hand, I didn't know what the hell I was walking into. For all I knew, I could have been headed to a bogus address in Montauk. So what the hell was I doing?

Michael Callahan needs help. The man's soft voice kept echoing in my head, pushing me forward to the end of the island and, I hoped, the end of my hunt for Michael Callahan.

Sixteen

It is no secret among my intimates that I don't like bugs or mushrooms. A lesser known fact about me is that I am, I confess, afraid of the dark. This is a little tidbit that, as a private investigator, I am not anxious to share with the world.

Mind you, it is not *all* dark that causes me concern; for example, I need to sleep in total darkness. However, the dark of night in a rural area, surrounded by nothing but open spaces and shadows, is something altogether different. I could never feel completely safe in an area without street-lights.

The drive to Montauk was dark. The sky was teeming with stars, but there was no moon, and though the effect at any other time—or with another person—might have been romantic, it was, at that moment, spooky. As I passed the town of Amagansett, I realized that I was, indeed, the only car on the road. I also didn't know where, exactly, I was going. I pulled onto the shoulder of the road and decided it was time for one of the maps Max had wisely suggested I bring. Instinctively I went to take the flashlight out of the glove compartment, but immediately remembered that this was a rental car, not my car, which meant there would be no maps, no mints, no napkins, batteries, flashlights, hand lotion, fresh Tootsie Rolls, or packets of salt, pepper, and sugar hidden inside.

I finally found, and flipped on, the overhead light. I looked out the window and saw only my own reflection. It was late and I looked tired and drawn. It was then I realized two things. First, that I had left my makeup case in the bathroom at home, and, second, that I was parked in what felt like the most isolated spot on the face of the universe. Shrouded in absolute darkness with a wall of trees no more than ten feet away, I had the presence of mind to remember that toothless madmen with sharp axes hide in trees such as these. I locked all four doors.

I finally found the street I was looking for on the map. It figured that it was one of those roads that people who live out here relish; secluded, quiet, and close to the ocean. I drove another ten minutes, before turning off the two-lane highway and bumbling through a grid of badly marked streets.

I finally saw a black mailbox with a reflective red house number painted on the side, the same number the man on the phone had given. The house was masterfully hidden behind twenty feet of dense brush and trees. As tired as I was, I couldn't help but notice that someone had done a very nice job with the planting to make it look absolutely natural. There were hemlocks and some kind of knobby, gnarly-looking pine tree that, in the light of day, would bring Dr. Seuss to mind, but in the dead of night was more like the spooky swamps. Patches of wildflowers were tucked away here and there. Though the foliage was there to give the house privacy, it was also enough to conceal me from the house. I was able to see that there was a car in the driveway and I deliberated whether to park my car on the side of the road, or pull into the driveway behind the Toyota.

There was, however, no real debate here. I turned off the headlights, cut the engine, and pulled in behind the other car. I rolled down my window and listened to the treetops blowing in the breeze.

From where I sat I could see that there were several large

spotlights affixed to the front of the house near the eaves. I assumed that these were movement sensor lights and as soon as I came within range I would be lit up like Christmas in Sheboygan. The idea of light exploding over the grounds as soon as I set foot on the property was one I could whole-heartedly embrace, but given the nature of my visit . . .

I stopped in my stationary track. Come to think of it, what *was* the nature of my visit?

Michael Callahan needs help. The man's imploring voice had conveyed an urgency that made me think he needed assistance immediately. But it was now more than two hours later and I was sitting in a darkened driveway in the middle of the night in the middle of nowhere. I sighed, resigned to the fact that no matter how much I might have wanted to back-pedal at this point I was here and I was going to see this through.

I opened the car door and bravely followed the pathway to the house entrance. I felt relieved when the motion light flicked on, but when a twig—or was it a branch or even a tree?—snapped in the brush behind me, my heart leaped halfway out of my chest. Composure lost, I bolted to the porch, reminded of a summer day on my grandmother's farm in Wisconsin back in the 1950s. It was dusk and we kids had been called in to get ready for bed. My sister, Nora, ran ahead of me and looked back with terror etched on her face. "The Boogeyman! The Boogeyman!" she cried as she sped past me. "He's behind you!" Being the baby, and recently convinced by my two siblings that I was really adopted and now in a trial period, I knew that my time was up; there was no way I could make it to the front door without the Boogeyman getting me first. I did the same thing any sensible five-year-old on warranty would do; I sat down and cried.

Tempted though I was to take my gun out of my bag, instinct told me not to. Though I handle firearms wisely and well, with Boogeymen looming in the background, I didn't want to take any undue risks.

The front door was locked. By now my eyes had adjusted to the darkness, and I walked around the side of the house, where I saw that the back wall of the living room was really floor-to-ceiling French doors that led to a brick patio, looking out onto the sea. Sheer white curtains hung loosely over the windows that exposed the large room, painstakingly furnished in Early American Beach.

I worked my way past the doors, trying each one to see if the Cosmic Joker had seen fit to leave one lock unlatched. As I neared the final door, I overlooked a large ceramic planter, tripped, and went flying into the cheerful patio furniture. It is impossible to literally hit the bricks and not make noise or get hurt. I did both. Before I had even rolled around to a sitting position, I heard the door behind me open slowly and the unmistakable metallic click of a rifle being readied to fire.

"Why don't you stop right there?" a low male brogue suggested as I held my shin and rocked back and forth on the cold, damp bricks.

Without turning around I knew that someone Irish was pointing a really big gun at me. I took several deep breaths to subdue the pain in my shin and nodded so he knew I had heard him.

He flicked on a light inside the living room, casting a yellow glow onto the patio and lawn. My shadow became an eerie silhouette against the ground.

Unlike when I was five and the Boogeyman loomed behind me, I couldn't simply cry and have Mom come out and save me, assuring me that everything was fine and wasn't I a silly little girl to think that anyone would adopt me.

Now there was no one to save me. Then again, now that I was finally confronted with an actual Boogeyman, I didn't feel as if I needed saving. Pain does wonders to ward off fear. I looked out at the ocean and felt a controlled calm wash over me. I told him, "I'm going to get up now."

"Slow. Very slow," he warned me.

I did as he suggested, not only because he had a gun, but because I didn't know what might be behind me.

Standing there, with the glare of the lamplight behind him, I turned and saw the driver of the "Honk If You Love Jesus" station wagon standing in his BVDs, baggy tee-shirt, and bare feet. An old Winchester rifle rested on his right forearm. His left hand was balled into a fist and pressed into his rib cage, as if he had heartburn. He looked tired and bored as he squinted at me. "What do you think you're doing, little girl?"

At close to five feet, eight inches tall and a hair past forty I consider myself neither little nor a girl; however, I knew that this was something Mr. Honk If You Love Jesus wouldn't appreciate, so I decided to let it pass. I stood there wide-eyed, dragging out the moment while I ran a mental checklist.

The image of the man before me did not jive with the decor, so I came to the conclusion that it was not his own hearth and home that he was protecting with an old hunting rifle. Ergo, he probably had as much right to be here as I did. Clearly he didn't know me from a hole in the wall, which meant that he probably hadn't seen me scuffle with Carrot-top and his bully cohort. I screeched, "Oh my God! What are you doing aiming that thing at me. What are you, crazy?" I limped around the patio, calling, "Help me. Help me. Oh my God, there's a crazy man here. I just come to see a friend and my God, a woman's not safe anywhere!"

Mr. Honk couldn't have been more chagrined. He shushed and shushed and when it was clear that I wasn't going to shut up until he put his gun down, he went back in the house, where I could see him, and carefully placed it on the dining room table.

"Now shut the hell up!" he yelled when he returned empty-handed.

I did. Said with a brogue, "Shut the hell up," is positively charming.

"That's a very nice accent," I said, leaning against the patio table to rub my shin. "Is it real?"

He shook his head, rubbed the back of his neck, and moaned, "Ah Chhrrist, jost what ah need, anoother noot."

"Where's Michael?" I asked.

He squinted at me. "Who are you?"

"An old friend. Who are you?"

"An old man." He said this as if a truer word were never spoken.

The fact is, he was old, but standing there in his BVDs, he was in better shape than a gaggle of men I know at half the age.

"Where's Michael?" I asked again.

He looked at me, then looked away, keeping his left hand pressed into his stomach. "He's not here," he finally said.

"Where is he?"

"You know, it's bloody cold out here." He looked up at the sky and rubbed his arms. "Come on in before I catch me death."

Once inside I saw that the house had a grossly different feel from Michael and Jessica's Brooklyn house. It was as if a compulsive with a fistful of money in one hand and a decorating magazine in the other was responsible for the end result, the studied casual beach house. It was not unlike many of the houses out on the East End, but it was definitely not a place for the old man who stood before me. I envisioned him in a worn, plaid easy-boy chair with a can of beer in hand and a television table at his side.

He took the gun off the dining table and motioned for me to have a seat. Instinct told me that he wasn't planning on using the rifle on me, but I didn't want the damned thing within arm's reach.

"Put that over there and I'll sit down," I said, pointing first to the rifle and then to one of the three sand-colored sofas in the living room.

He acted as if this was one of the most unreasonable requests he'd ever heard, but complied. When the gun was out of reach, I sat and felt a cool breeze on my back as it wafted in through the screen doors.

"Now, who are you and what is it you'd be wanting with Dr. Callahan?" He joined me at the table.

Now it was my turn to squint. "I don't think so."

"What?" He clasped his hands and sighed.

"First of all, I don't think my business with Michael is any of your business. Second, why should I tell you anything? You won't even tell me who you are."

"I told you I'm an old man."

"Right, and I'm Agnes Moorehead. Now, where's Michael?"

"Missy, you and I could be spending the month chasing our tails, so one of us has got to budge a little. I'm an old Irishman, set in me ways and as stubborn as the day is long, so I suggest you be the bigger person, and tell me what business you'd be having with the doctor." Again he pressed the heel of his palm into his sternum.

"Are you all right?" I asked, nodding to his obvious distress.

"Just a little heartburn, that's all."

"Okay." Instinct told me that if I didn't get the ball rolling, we would be watching the sunrise together from these very seats. "Michael is my . . . brother . . ." The old man didn't seem to notice that I faltered on the word *brother*.

However, this little tidbit of false information did seem to jolt his adrenaline. Without uttering a word, the old man snapped back into his chair, turned absolutely ashen, was suddenly pouring sweat, made a nasty guttural noise, and then stiffened. Instinct screamed that he was having a heart attack.

This was not good.

I eased him on the floor and started to administer mouth-to-mouth resuscitation. It took several minutes, but I had him breathing long enough for me to run to the kitchen and call 911.

By the time I returned, his eyes were open and he looked

confused. I knelt beside him and assured him that everything was going to be just fine.

His breathing was shallow as he shook his head slightly and murmured, "I'm sorry." This consumed energy he didn't have and I told him to be still, that help was on the way. He whispered, "Tell her I'm . . ." and then exhaled his last breath.

I tried CPR this time, but it didn't work. I didn't hear any sirens in the distance, so I gave up hope that the ambulance team would be able to bring him back around. One second he was a lovely brogue; the next he was dead. Death is not something with which I have ever been very comfortable. Not that many people are, I suppose, but I've seen a lot of it and I have never been easy with it. This time was no different, except now there were complications. Big complications. I was in a bail jumper's house in the middle of the night with a half-naked, dead old man whose name I didn't even know. I had a sneaky feeling that this was not going to go over very well with the local police.

Seventeen

I admit I considered leaving before the ambulance arrived, but that would have been unethical, and as an ex-police officer, I have a high regard for the way things ought to be. I had little confidence that the local constabulary would believe that Mr. Honk and I were merely having a pleasant conversation at two in the morning when he just keeled over and died in his undies, but I knew I had to stay and tell them the facts. One thing was certain, I owed it to myself to gather as much information as I could before they arrived.

A quick search of the three-bedroom house confirmed that Michael was nowhere to be found. In the kitchen I discovered that Mr. Honk's real name was Patrick Delaney. He had left his worn wallet on the kitchen counter with a driver's license that listed a P.O. box in Southampton. He carried no credit cards and had thirteen dollars and change. In the kitchen I also found Mr. Delaney's freshly washed clothes in the still-warm dryer. Why he felt compelled to wash his clothes in Michael's house at two in the morning, I didn't know, but it made me deeply curious. I methodically started searching the house, looking for anything that might point me in Michael's direction.

The master bedroom—a frightening affair with bold floral prints and wicker, wicker, wicker—proved that Michael had been there recently. On an oversized wicker armchair

I found the clothes he had been wearing when I last saw him in Brooklyn, and the wastebasket had new garbage, including tissues, cotton balls still damp with what I assumed was hydrogen peroxide, Band-Aids, and green floss, no doubt the minted variety.

As I nosed around, I was struck by how very different this house felt from the doctor's city house. The city place was a home, whereas this residence was simply a house, and schizophrenically furnished at that. The living room—aside from several unfortunate tchotchkes—reflected the Beach House scene to a T, whereas in the bedroom there was actually a large wicker clothes hamper shaped like a chicken. The wicker nightstand on one side of the bed had a stack of books including a mystery by Umberto Eco, a weathered copy of *The Religions of Man*, several books on theology, and two versions of the Bible. I was thinking, *That'll put you to sleep*, when I heard a car pull into the driveway. I looked out the window over the bed and saw Delaney's white station wagon blocking my car. I watched through the lace curtains as one of the two men with whom I had had a run-in the day before walked past the motion detector and was bathed in white light. He was definitely the bigger of the two, the one who had tossed me to the ground like I was a handkerchief. He sauntered across the front lawn, and from the cut of his jaw, his hairline, and the fullness of his bottom lip, I was willing to bet my shoes that he was related to the dead man in the other room.

I went to the front door to meet him. Halfway up the three concrete and brick steps, he saw me standing at the door and stopped short. He looked momentarily stunned, but quickly recovered, squinted past me into the house, and then back at me.

"I know you," he said cautiously, as if he couldn't remember if I were friend or foe.

"We might have run into each other before," I said, opening the door.

His eyes drew into two tight slits as he worked to place me.

"Where's Pad?" he asked shoving past me into the house.

I assumed Pad was an affectionate nickname for Dad, who, I knew, was lying dead in his panties no more than twenty feet away.

"Listen, there's something you should—" There is no easy way to tell a person that someone he loves has just died, and in this instance, I didn't have to. The big guy stomped past me into the living room, where he would had to have been blind not to see Patrick Delaney.

As soon as he saw the lifeless body a sound caught in the back of his throat, almost delicate. I couldn't see his face, as his back was to me, but in less than two steps he was kneeling at Patrick Delaney's side. I kept a respectful distance.

"Pad?" He cupped the old man's face in the palm of his hand. "Paddy, come on, man, what are you doing?" He moved his right hand to his father's left shoulder and gently shook it. Slowly the panic started to pinch into his voice. "Dad? Come on man, this isn't funny." He issued a short laugh as he placed his left hand on his father's right shoulder and aggressively shook the old man. "Goddamn it! What the hell's going on here?" With his back to me all I could see were his clenched fists, massive arms, the white tee-shirt straining against the muscles in his back, and his close-cropped, relatively small head of red hair.

I didn't have to see his face to know that it was probably registering and rejecting an awful truth all at the same time. Death is the one of the few things that is guaranteed in life, and one of the last things we're ever prepared for.

You would think that common sense would have prevailed here. Knowing as I did that this man was not afraid of violence, and that I was the only other person in the house with his dead dad, you would have thought that I'd do the smart thing and haul ass out of there. But no, I didn't. I'd like to say that this was one of those moments when I saw the headlights coming and I was transfixed in place, but that wasn't altogether true. The fact is, I knew I had to be there when the police came. What can I tell you, I make mistakes. At that very moment, the moment when he was totally absorbed in his grief, I could have disappeared, just slipped out and locked myself in my car until the police arrived, but I didn't.

His breath caught in his chest and he screamed at his father to stop fucking around. He then brought his dad to his chest, hugged him, and let loose a cry so tragic that it could only come from loss. He laid his father back on the floor, bent into himself, and came up screaming and flailing. His powerful arms shot out from his body like metal blades. I had, I knew, missed my window for departure.

Patrick Delaney's son was in pain, and for him this meant striking out. He stood up and started with the sofa nearest him, kicking it with all his might until it moved a good four feet away and butted up against the sofa where Delaney's rifle rested. I held my breath for fear that he would see the rifle and just start shooting. By this point he had started to get out of control and I had no choice but to freeze in place.

He started swinging randomly, grabbing whatever he could get his hands on and smashing it against the walls. Fortunately there wasn't all that much that the Callahans had left out. A vase here, a paperweight there, ugly little figurines that were better off as shards. He swung blindly, his face contorted and wet with tears.

In the middle of a swing, he saw me. He stood halfway across the room from me, poised for a fight with one fist raised just over his right shoulder and the other in front of him. There was one split second that passed between us, one split second before recognition, and then hatred, washed over his face.

"You." He panted. "You're the one from Brooklyn." His face was red and sweaty.

I slowly lowered my hands to my side and said as gently as I could, "Listen, I lost both of my folks, I know what you're going through."

His eyes practically bugged out of their sockets, which I took as a sign that this was not the right thing to have started with.

"Who the fuck are you?" he demanded. "What did you do to my father?"

"Nothing." I felt it imperative to answer the second query first, given that he was on a road I would have preferred he didn't travel. That I was somehow—even remotely—responsible for his father's death was not an impression I wanted to leave him with.

"What do you mean, nothing?" He seethed. "The man's dead, for God's sake. What the hell did you do?" By now he had brought his hands down in front of him, but they were still balled into enormous fists and his veins looked like steel under taut flesh. While it is impossible not to admire such definition and tone, I was feeling a growing concern for my physical well-being.

I decided that the best defense is a good offense. I pulled myself up to my full five feet seven and a half inches and gave him back his aggressiveness full force, "Just what is that supposed to mean, what did I do? I tried to save his life."

"How? By killing him? Now, who the hell are you?" he screamed as he inched closer to me, kneading his fists.

I started to move to my right, positioning myself closer to the front door.

"My name is Sydney Sloane. I'm an investigator." I left out *private* in case he had a passing respect for authority.

"And?" He wiped his mouth with the back of his hand and moved closer.

"And I want to know what your relationship is to Michael Callahan," I said impassively, which I thought carried an amazing weight of authority. I gauged his every movement, and readied myself for the defensive. If he was going to pounce, I'd be ready. The last thing I needed or wanted was a two-hundred-pound heavy-weight messing my hair.

I watched him carefully and I could literally see his emotions shift. In the blink of an eye, he pushed all grief and pain aside and replaced it with hell-bent lust for revenge. And, in this depraved game of tag, I was It. With a speed and grace I never would have anticipated, he dove for me as if he were sailing for a line drive between second and third. I knew he went low so that he'd slide toward the front door, so I jumped forward out of his reach. As he crashed into a trestle table by the front door, I was swinging around and running back toward the master bedroom, where I had left the sliding door unlocked for easy access the next day, should need be. Halfway to the bedroom, I heard the lamp from the trestle table hit the floor with a crash. The big guy let out a sound that must have been human but sounded otherworldly. As I crossed the threshold to the bedroom I swung the door shut but Godzilla was only a matter of steps behind, and I heard the nauseating sound of his fist meeting the door.

I was nearly past the bed when he tackled me and we went flying onto the loud floral comforter. Just the sheer bulk of him knocked the air so completely out of me that I thought I would flap around the room like a popped balloon. He wrapped his arm around my waist and once we were half on, half off the bed, he pulled one leg over my thighs and tried to straddle me. I was stuck on my side with my right arm pinned between me and the bed. Godzilla had his entire weight on me and not only could I feel the veins in my arm flattening into useless ribbons, but as he leaned on me a sharp pain shot through my left breast, causing me considerable discomfort.

"Get off me," I snarled through clenched teeth, slapping at his face with my free hand.

He leaned his weight onto his left knee, releasing the pressure on me, and then slid me up onto the bed like I was nothing more cumbersome than a two-by-four. Now that we were this close I could smell the beer and sweat on him and guessed that his bloodshot eyes probably had little to do with grief for the dead man in the other room.

Despite his weight, I freed my right hand and pushed his face away, smushing his nose so he resembled a pig. This only incited him further.

He released my waist, clamped both my wrists, and pinned them on the bed. I bucked and struggled under his weight, trying desperately to work us to the edge of the bed, where I had at least a passing chance of extricating myself. This only induced him to press his full weight on top of me, leading, of course, with his groin.

"Wait . . . wait." I let my body go limp. "What the hell are we fighting about?"

"We're not fighting now, are we?" He lifted his right knee and tried to tuck it between my legs. As hard as I resisted, he was still bigger and stronger than me, and within seconds, he had my left knee pushed up as if I were preparing to do a round of bicycle kicks.

"For Christ sake, asshole, your father just died!" Given his body language, I couldn't help but come to the nauseating conclusion that grief had stimulated his desire for female companionship. This couldn't be happening. I couldn't have suddenly gone from being an object of rancor to being one of desire. Given the two choices, I would have opted for rancor. I may have understood that his aggressiveness was born of shock, but I didn't give a damn. The fact was, I had a two-hundred-and-twenty-pound bully treating me like a rag doll for the second time in two days, and I didn't like it one bit.

It was clear by this point that guilt was probably my most logical weapon.

"What would your father say?" I cried out as I fought to free my hands. He paused long enough for me to know I had hit a nerve. "He's probably watching you . . . right . . . now."

At that precise moment the phone rang and scared the hell out of Delaney's son, who literally sprang off me as if he had seen the ghost of his old man. As he leaped to the left, I fell off the side of the bed onto the floor.

The unexpected ringing split through the night that was already beginning to resemble a journey into the Twilight Zone. *Imagine if you will an autumn night. A lone woman ventures into a sleepy town and meets a man, a simple man in his underwear. Little does she know, she's just entered Montauk.*

The phone rang again. We were both frozen in place, me on the floor with an army of dust bunnies and him on the bed. We both watched the phone on the wicker nightstand as if it were going to jump up and dance around the room. The answering machine kicked in after the second ring.

It was as if the world had stopped and all the chaos was put on hold. Neither of us moved a muscle as we listened to the whirring and clicking of the machine. I don't know why he didn't move, but I feared that as soon as I flicked a finger he'd be on me like a magnet. I was aching from our scuffle yesterday and figured that if the police didn't arrive before the call was completed, I still had the wondrous tool of guilt, that universally effective weapon. Finally a familiar, stiff voice filled the room from the little gray box. "Hello. You've reached the answering machine for Dr. Hannah Miller . . ." Answering machine for Hannah Miller! Of course, now all the wicker and floral designs made sense. This was Michael's partner, Dr. Cyclops's house, not the Callahans'. When her mechanical message ended, there was a beep and then, "Michael? Michael, it's Hannah, pick up. Come on, pick up for crying out loud." Hannah Miller's nasal voice chafed on top of an already-difficult night. "Look, I know you're there and we need to talk. You scared me before and not picking up the machine is just childish." There was a long pause that she filled with an exaggerated sigh. "I'm not kidding, Michael, if I don't hear from you by seven, I'm coming out there. Trust me, I can help you, I always have, haven't I?" Another sigh and then, "I'm home. I'm up. Call." Click.

Godzilla and I looked from the phone to each other. This fortuitous interruption had taken the air out of his sails. He flopped onto his back on the bed, covered his eyes with his right arm, and said, "I'm going to kill that son of a bitch."

"Who?" I asked softly as I inched my way to the sliding door, sweeping up dust bunnies with my behind. Though the tension between us had been dissolved a bit, I wasn't about to let my guard down, especially with a guy as volatile as this one.

"Your friend Callahan." He kept his eyes shielded with his arm. "This has been the worst fucking week of my life and it's all that cocksucker's fault."

"What did he do?" I asked, genuinely curious.

He exhaled a huff of air and rolled over onto his left side, facing me. "I'm still trying to figure that out. But when I get my hands on him again, the fucker's dead meat." Just the thought of this seemed to stir him into action. He kicked himself into a sitting position and scooted himself to the end of the bed. He studied me carefully and asked, "Just who is Callahan to you?"

"I told you, I'm an investigator. I want him just as much as you do. Probably more."

He let out a dull laugh. "I don't think so. Why do you want him?"

I shook my head. "It doesn't work that way."

"No?"

"No. You see, before I give *you* information, you have to give me something."

"Is that right?" he said with a crooked grin.

"That's right." Having studied theater in my long-ago past, I felt certain that I was radiating self-confidence with just a touch of arrogance. Underneath, however, I was flinching because I could sense that Godzilla was on the brink of another emotional shift, which could only result in physical force.

"What do you want to know?" He studied his nails, chose the index finger on his right hand, and started nibbling at the cuticle.

"I want to know where Michael is and why you want to kill him."

His face clouded over. "I don't know where he is."

"I don't believe you."

"Too bad. I answered your question." He moved to the cuticle of his middle finger and began grazing.

"Why do you want to kill him?" I pushed onward.

"No, no, I answered one for you, now you answer one for me." This little adolescent game seemed to be taking his mind off his troubles, including his dearly departed dad in the other room. "Why do *you* want the slimy son of a bitch?"

"I have a check that belongs to him." I thought of the ten-thousand-dollar check in my back pocket and Michael's inept attempt at bribery.

"Yeah, right." He spat a piece of cuticle onto the floor and said, "This is getting us nowhere."

He was right, so I decided to lay some cards on the table. "Did you know that Michael was recently indicted for the murder of his wife?"

He looked at me out of the corner of his eye and grunted in the affirmative.

"Did you know his wife?" I asked, hoping that a game of twenty questions might provide some answers.

"No. Did you?"

"No." I took a deep breath. "I was hired to prove his innocence . . ." I let the thought linger, anticipating his skeptical response.

I was surprised when this information elicited nothing more than a thoughtful nod. "Who hired you? Him?"

"No. His wife's grandmother."

Godzilla needed a moment to connect the dots. Finally he thundered, "You've got to be joking!" He started chewing anxiously on his cuticle.

"No, I'm not. Why? Do you know something I don't know?"

He practically bounced up off the bed and pointed a finger at me. "I don't know anything, do you understand that?"

"No, not really. You act like you know a whole lot." By now I was up on my feet, my back against the wall, braced for trouble.

In two leaps, he was standing in front of me. "You think he's not guilty?" It was an accusation more than a question. He pressed his palms against the wall behind me, trapping me between the wall and himself.

My face was a mask of cool and calm, but I was angry more than anything else. I hate bullies.

"I don't know if he is or isn't. I'm just paid to find the truth."

He leaned in toward me until our noses were practically touching. "The truth is he's a scumbag." Godzilla was clearly agitated and I worried that with his uneven breathing, excessive perspiration, and flushed complexion, I was about to witness another death in the family. Just what I needed to top off a perfect day.

"The truth is," he continued, "that looking into this maggot's life could only screw things up for a lot of other people. Good people."

"Like Patrick Delaney?"

He looked confused at first, and then stunned. The color washed from his face and he pushed off the wall. He made a beeline for the bedroom door, and, I assumed the front door. I, however, knew that the sliding door in the bedroom faced the side of the house closest to the driveway. I slammed back the slider and the screen door and bolted outside, hoping to cut him off.

As soon as he hit the front yard, the lights went on. He was halfway to his car, but all I had to do to catch up to him was jump over the deck railing and run two car lengths. Easy.

Unfortunately the autumn leaves had already begun to fall and there were a handful on the deck. My heel came down hard on one, at an angle that sent me skidding on my bottom from one end of the deck to the other. Tears filled my eyes as I heard the station wagon start up and peel out of the driveway. These tears were not because Godzilla had gotten away or abandoned his dead father. I knew he and I would meet again in the near future; it was his business if he felt karmically at ease leaving me alone with his dead dad. No, I was crying because, having skidded along Hannah Miller's stupid, worn deck, I had turned my bummy into a pincushion, and it hurt like hell. Enormous splinters of pressure-treated wood stuck out of my jeans like I was a porcupine in training. I lay in a fetal position and tried to reach back and pluck out the larger splinters, blaming Hannah Miller with each and every sickening extraction, not unlike how Godzilla was blaming Michael for his troubles.

After what felt like an eternity, I was able to pull out the five largest splinters, get to my knees, and then my feet, just in time to see a police car pull into the driveway, past my car, and onto the front lawn. The motion light went on and I could see that the tires of the car had already dug deep ruts into Hannah Miller's front yard, proving that there are times when justice does prevail.

Eighteen

The first officer out of the car was the driver, the man in the duo and a good-looking one at that. He squinted up at me, with his hands on his hips, and asked, "Did you call the police, ma'am?"

"I called an ambulance half an hour ago." I tried to straighten my back to make my posture reflect my vexation, but with my bottom sporting enough wood to make a box of toothpicks, it was impossible.

He nodded once and motioned to his right. "The front door?"

"That way." I pointed to my left. "I'll let you in." Walking was a painful exercise, that reduced my mobility to baby steps. By the time I made it to the living room, both officers were in the house. The driver was standing between me and the very dead Patrick Delaney. His badge identified him as Officer Shelton. His partner was already bent over Delaney. From behind, the second officer reminded me of one of those lawn ornaments with the gardener bent over, bottoms up.

I had completely forgotten the behemoth's tantrum and now saw just how suspicious the broken lamp, shattered tchotchkes, and disarrayed seating looked.

"We're real sorry it took so long, miss. The ambulance will be here shortly. They had an accident. Hit a deer. We got here as soon as we could."

"Oh dear Lord, Bob, it's Paddy Delaney." The other officer was a woman. When she turned around I marveled that this very round, squat individual had ever made it past the rigorous training required to become a police officer.

Officer Shelton, still with both hands on his hips, stepped over to the body, looked down and shook his head. "That's a shame. Damn fine man." He then pulled a quilt off the back of the sofa and placed it over Patrick's face and upper body.

The lawn ornament waddled over to me, nodding to the broken lamp, and asked, "What did you say your name was?"

"I didn't. But it's Sydney Sloane."

"Did you get that Bob? Cindy Stone."

"Sydney." I corrected her. "As in Greenstreet. Sydney Sloane."

Her name tag read Gimber, and when she asked where the phone was I pointed her toward the kitchen.

"Is this your home, Ms. Sloane?" Officer Shelton asked, taking out a small notebook and pen.

"No, it's not."

"You're visiting?"

It was a simple question, but I knew what was going on in his head . . . the same thing that would have been going through mine if I were in his shoes. It's three in the morning, there's an old dead man—whom they know—in his underwear with a woman who's walking like she's an advertisement for Preparation H in a house that doesn't belong to either one of them.

"Was there a problem here?" He motioned to the broken lamp.

I chose not to follow his gaze and answered the question from a different angle. "Aside from the fact that a man had a heart attack and died? No."

He made a point of sizing me up carefully before asking, "Why don't we have a seat?" He moved the skewed sofa back into place.

The idea of sitting was about as comforting as bathing in lye. I grimaced weakly and followed him to the sofa, shuffling as gracefully as I could.

"Are you all right?" he asked, looking at me as he moved right toward the fallen couch pillow that was covering the rifle.

"To be perfectly honest with you, Officer Shelton, I've had better days." I was exhausted and I knew that I had to find a way to explain all this. But how? The whole truth and nothing but the truth? *I'm looking for this man who allegedly killed his wife and is somehow connected with Mr. Delaney here, whose son just happened to drop by and had something more pressing to do than to wait for you. As a matter of fact, you might even know him seeing as though you're about the same age and you knew old Paddy here . . .* No, I didn't think so.

"Well now, looky here." Bob Shelton uncovered the rifle and picked it up, checking my reaction as he did so. I hoped that with my arched brows I looked as surprised as he, but I didn't think so.

He brought the rifle to his nose and sniffed at the firing mechanism. "Can you explain this, Ms. Sloane?"

"No," I said honestly.

"This is Paddy's hunting rifle."

"I didn't know that."

"He and I have hunted together. Deer."

"I beg your pardon?" My mind swerved as I tried to rest my knee on the edge of a sofa. This movement tugged my pants against my fanny, which pressed the remaining splinters more deeply into my muscle and no doubt my bloodstream.

"We hunted deer." He explained.

"Oh, dear." The pain was making me nauseous. Maybe if I held my breath it might not hurt so much.

"That's right, we have a lot of deer out here," he informed me as he checked the gun. "This gun was recently fired."

"Well, not in my presence."

"Will you have a seat, Ms. Sloane?" he asked as he made sure the gun was empty.

"I don't think so, but thank you."

"Where are you from?" He perched on the arm of a sofa.

"Manhattan," I tried to say casually, knowing how the locals feel about the Manhattanites who come in and take over their town each summer. The summer people are the ones who keep the locals afloat, financially, but they can be arrogant, rude and piggish. The last thing I wanted was to alienate Bob and his sidekick, Officer Gimber.

"I see. And what brings you out here?"

"I came to see a friend."

"And who would that be?" he prompted me.

"Michael."

"Michael who?"

"Callahan." There was no reaction from the officer, which led me to believe that he didn't know Michael was under indictment for the murder of his wife. This was good, one less area of confusion. I wasn't being difficult on purpose, but with each question, I had to decide how much to answer. I figured at this juncture, less was enough.

"And this is Michael Callahan's house?" he asked.

"Well, no. This is his friend's house."

"Who would that friend be, do you know?"

"Hannah Miller."

"And where is Hannah Miller right now?" This man had the patience of Job.

"In the city."

"And how long have you been here, Ms. Sloane?"

I glanced at my watch. "An hour? If that."

His smile was crooked, but not without its charm. He nodded, as if this were the norm with a kook like me, and made a notation in his book.

"Isn't it a little unusual to go visiting at this hour?"

I shrugged. "I didn't leave the city until eleven, eleven-thirty," I said as if this were an answer to his question.

"You realize, Ms. Sloane, that this situation is what you would call a bit unorthodox, or out of the ordinary."

I nodded and pressed my lips together.

"Can you tell me what happened here tonight?"

"Yes. I came looking for Michael, your friend Paddy answered the door, and a couple of minutes later he had a heart seizure. I performed mouth-to-mouth resuscitation, revived him, called an ambulance and came back to him, but he died a minute later. I tried CPR, but it was too late."

"And the rifle?"

I sealed my lips, shrugged and made my eyes wide. "You know more about that rifle than I do."

"Un-huh. And the broken lamp? Can you explain that?"

"I'm afraid not." If I explained that then I'd have to explain Paddy's son and his sudden, inexplicable departure, and probably everything else associated with my presence here. All I wanted was to be somewhere safe where I could rid myself of the thousand and one splinters.

"Tell me, was he dressed like that when he answered the door?" He flipped a page in his notebook.

I wanted to say, "Absolutely not, I undressed him after he died." Instead I begged his pardon and asked him what he meant.

"Did he open the door in his underwear?"

"Of course he did. I don't understand the question."

Bob blushed slightly and shrugged. "Paddy's always been a bit of a ladies' man . . ."

"You've got to be joking," I said with unmasked queasiness. "I mean, I'm sure he was a very nice old man, but he's hardly my . . . type."

"Carl should be here in a few minutes," Officer Gimber informed her partner as she entered the room. "He's on East Lake." She stood at Paddy's feet and stared down at the old man's pale legs sticking out from the quilt. "Just what was your relationship with the deceased?" she asked me, giving her partner a sidelong glance.

"I never met him before in my life. I—"

She interrupted me. "Is that so?" Well, I wonder about that, miss. Only good friends call Paddy *Paddy*. It was a show of intimacy with him." She winked as a means of punctuation. "If he didn't know you, didn't feel *close* to you, you had to call him Patrick, not even Pat. Isn't that right, Bob?"

"The man died fourteen minutes after we met," I said by way of explaining I didn't know the ground rules in his life.

"Then how did you come to call him Paddy?"

"Because you two did. What are you, Barney Fife?" I knew it was the wrong thing to say, but my ass hurt and she was a moron.

If looks could kill, Barney would have made a direct hit.

"Mitz, why don't you go check the rest of the house?" Bob interjected before she could think of another stupid thing to say and irritate me further.

I watched the partners engage in a silent dialogue that ended with a huffy-puffy Mitzi waddling off into the hallway.

"Where is Michael now?" Bob asked.

"I don't know. He wasn't here when I arrived," I said.

"Was that your car in the driveway?" he continued.

"The Ford is, yes."

"And the Toyota?" Officer Bob continued to scribble away in his notepad.

I had assumed initially that the Toyota was Michael's car. The only car I associated with Paddy was the beat-up station wagon his son had driven off in. For all I knew, Paddy could have been the proud owner of the new Toyota.

"I don't know."

"Where will you be staying out here, Ms. Sloane?"

"I have another friend staying at a hotel in East Hampton. I'll stay with her."

"How long do you plan on staying here?"

"Just a day or two. But I hadn't expected this." I motioned to Paddy. "Does this change my plans?" I asked, feigning innocence.

"Maybe. But right now, I know it's late and you must be tired. If I could just ask you—"

"Bob." Officer Gimber was holding on to the master bedroom door frame and leaning out into the hallway, looking like her feet didn't even reach the floor. She was able to infuse a simple, monosyllabic word with enough officiousness to create a clear picture of who she was. "Could you come here, please, there's something I think you should see." Gimber made it sound like there was a stash of dead bodies in the bedroom, when I knew perfectly well that there was nothing. Nothing but a decorator's nightmare and a messed-up bed.

My already bleak spirits sank lower. A messy bed was not going to go over well with these two.

Bob excused himself. While they were gone I tried to extract another splinter. He returned as I was picking at a particularly prominent chunk of timber.

He smiled uncomfortably and tried not to look at me.

"A splinter," I explained, lamely.

"How'd you get that?" he asked with a sympathetic smile.

"You don't want to know." I waved my hand in a pooh-pooh gesture, knowing perfectly well it was just the thing he *would* want to know.

We stared at each other for the longest time while I could hear Officer Mitzi Gimber in the other room on the phone.

"As I was saying before I left, I can imagine how tired you are."

"Wiped."

"Yes, well, I'm afraid I'm going to have to ask you to stay in town until we can investigate this thoroughly . . ."

"I understand."

"The detectives should be here any second, but I can see how tired you are and I don't see any reason to keep you for questioning right now. However, I'd like your word,

Ms. Sloane, that we'll have no trouble finding you tomorrow should we need you, and I expect we will."

I gave him my city numbers as well as the name of the hotel where Leslie was staying. In turn, he gave me the number of the police station, should I be thinking about changing locations. I was more than relieved not to have to explain what had happened since my arrival at Hannah Miller's. Bob Shelton was, at that moment, an angel in my eyes. I retrieved my bag from the dining room area and tried to walk like a normal person, but found it impossible. With each movement my black denim jeans shoved the woodlands deeper into my flesh. By the time I reached the front door, Officer Gimber had returned and was leaning against the wall trying hard to look mean and threatening; however, she only came across as wide and pouting.

I wished her a fond farewell and Officer Bob offered to escort me out to my car. I couldn't tell if he was flirting or out to get information, but as it was still pitch-black out there, I welcomed the company.

"I don't understand what Mr. Delaney was doing here," I said helplessly.

"Well, ever since Paddy retired a few years ago, he's become invaluable to the people who own summer or weekend houses out here. In an area like this, burglary could easily soar—it doesn't—but it could because there are so many empty, well-stocked houses for so much of the year. We do our jobs and keep an eye on things, but Paddy had a great racket. He'd take in mail, water plants, and generally make it look as if there was a more regular presence in the houses he watched. For example, when it snows out here, it's real easy to see who's here and who isn't. Well, Paddy would get one of his boys to shovel the driveway and a path so it looked as if someone was living there. I suspect he was here looking after the property for the owner."

"One of his boys?" I asked as we slowly made our way to the car.

"Paddy and Suzy were Irish Catholic." He laughed. "Everyone always teased them that they created a township on their own with their offspring. Suzy died two years ago. Cancer."

"I'm sorry."

"Oh yeah, it's been hard on Paddy."

"I can imagine. But at least he had a big family. How many children are there?"

"Twelve?" he said with a pained expression. "Something like that. Nice kids, all of them." We walked past the police cruiser and the motion light went on. "So, now let me ask you a question, okay?"

"Okay."

"How did that bed get all messed up like that?"

I shrugged. "Maybe Paddy was sleeping on it before I got here."

He stopped, turned to me, and shook his head. He held out his hand and opened his palm. In it lay a gold and ruby clip-on earring, half of the set I had been wearing when I arrived at the Miller manse.

I automatically reached up and felt my right lobe. It had fallen off during my scuffle with one of Delaney's progeny. I couldn't figure out if Shelton was handing me the earring or simply showing it to me.

"Oh great," I said with heightened enthusiasm. "I was looking all over for that."

"I bet you were."

"Where did you find it?" I plucked it off his palm and clipped it back onto my earlobe.

"In the bedding. You want to explain?"

"Well, I did go to the bathroom in there. It might have popped off then."

He furrowed his brow and shook his head. "Try another. This could prove entertaining." Though he had me by the short hairs—so to speak—there was something gracious and generous about Bob Shelton. Either that or he was a larcenous kind of guy with something up his sleeve I couldn't see in my state of physical discomfort.

I had several choices. I could make up entertaining little stories until the ambulance arrived, at which point I could slip away and answer his question the next day. I could tell him the truth about the Delaney kid, who apparently went to the John Wayne school of male emotions. Or I could tell another truth that was related but not direct.

"I had nothing to do with your friend's death. I tried to save him." I opted for door number three.

"I believe that. However, you're obviously a bright woman. You can see how bad this looks, can't you?"

"I think so."

"A recently fired rifle, a dead man in his skivvies, a beautiful woman who appears to have a big splinter in a strange location, signs of a struggle in the living room, and a bed that looks like it recently saw some serious action. Now, what would you think if you were me?"

I stared at him mutely. Chances were if I wasn't exhausted or in pain and dreading the thought of sitting in a car, I might have come up with something imaginative and plausible, but I was and I didn't.

"I thought so." He slipped his hands onto his hips and nodded. "You make sure you stick around tomorrow, you hear me." He sounded like the generic dad on any of the sixties sitcoms, and though I felt compelled to respond like Eddie Haskell, with a perky *"Yes sir,"* I was able to refrain. I simply nodded.

A shiver went through my body as we neared my bubblelike rental car.

"Someone just walked over your grave," was his superstitious response to the chills.

"Ah yes, and a comforting thought at that." I limped to the driver's side of the car and turned back to Bob, who was standing next to his patrol car on the front lawn. "You have my word that I won't leave town without contacting you."

"Thank you." He rocked back on his heels. "You get some rest now."

"Oh yeah."

"Oh, and Ms. Sloane?"

"Yes?"

"You might want to see a doctor about your problem. Your backside looks like a cactus." He pulled up his shoulders and made a sour face. "We have a fine hospital facility in Southampton."

"Thanks." I grimaced as I lowered myself into the car. Each splinter seemed to attach itself to the seat fabric. As I tried to jockey into a more bearable position, I memorized the license plate of the Toyota. Tomorrow I would have information from Marcy that would confirm whether this was Michael's car. If it wasn't, it would be easy enough to run a check on whom it belonged to.

If it *was* Michael's car, then where was he and how did he get there? And where had the younger Delaney gone off to? What could have been so important that he would have left his father behind with a total stranger? I turned the key in the ignition and pressed my foot gently on the gas pedal, sending pinpricks of pain shooting off like fireworks into my thighs and lower back. *This is not good*, I thought as I backed into the pitch-black street. I pushed against the backrest and tried to lift my tush up off the seat, keeping my weight on my left heel as I used my right foot to accelerate and brake.

By the time I made it to Leslie's bed, I was exhausted. Both Auggie and Leslie picked up their heads when I arrived, but neither of them thought to get up and greet me, which was just as well, because all we needed was for Auggie to start barking.

In the bathroom I was able to see for myself just what damage I had suffered. I considered bathing it in hydrogen peroxide—which I never travel without—but realized that, like it or not, I needed help. Unable to perform an act of seductive awakening, I simply bent down and kissed Leslie's neck. She moaned softly and arched her back. "More," she murmured with her eyes shut. I placed my lips on hers and was only slightly surprised by her response. Without opening her eyes, she reached up and drew my hand under the sheets.

"I want you," she whispered.

"I want you, too," I said softly.

She lifted the sheets.

"No, not here." I took her hand and coaxed her out of bed. "In the bathroom."

"The bathroom?" She followed without opening her eyes. Auggie lifted her head off the blankets, stretched out on the bed, and sighed back into sleep.

"There's something I want to show you." I led her slowly.

"What?"

"My tush."

She smiled in her fog and mumbled, "I love that tush."

"Good thing."

And so, at three-fifteen in the morning, with tweezers and a needle, my love and I performed the very intimate act of extracting twenty-four various-sized splinters from my backside while I told her about my evening's activities.

By the time we finally hit the hay, Leslie was no longer in the mood. She gave me a peck, then rolled over onto her side and cuddled a down pillow. As I lay there holding Auggie and listening to Leslie's soft snoring, I tried to make a mental list of everything I had to do. I was entering day three of the investigation and felt in my bones that something was about to break, but not without a lot of prodding. The clock read 3:58. If I were going to get a jump on things, I had to be up by seven. I fell asleep with the number seven affixed firmly in my mind's eye. Seven. Seven. *Seven.*

Nineteen

Is there anything more enticing than the aroma of fresh coffee first thing in the morning? I was awakened not only to the magnificent bouquet of coffee and toast but to the gentle touch of something tantalizing on my lips, something wet. Without opening my eyes, I ran my tongue along my lips and was treated to the taste of sweet coffee. Slowly I cracked open my left eye, then my right, and saw Auggie sprawled across my legs, Leslie washed and dressed sitting beside me, and sunlight pouring ceaselessly through lace curtains, casting intricate patterns on the floor.

Leslie dipped her finger into the coffee cup and again brought her wet finger to my mouth. I licked it sleepily, smiled, and stretched. Or rather, *tried* to stretch. It was curtailed due to a number of physical ailments, not the least of which was nasty stinging in my fanny. There was also a bump on my shin from having tripped over the planter the night before, a scrape on my knee and one on my elbow from Brooklyn Heights, and a stiffness in my lower back that hadn't been there the day before. I was falling apart.

Leslie put the cup on the night table and leaned over to kiss me. She hovered.

"Despite the hour of your arrival, it's very nice to be back in the same bed with you, my love." Her kiss was a gentle caress.

"What time is it?" I asked behind closed eyes.

"Nine-thirty," she said softly, slipping her hand under the covers.

My body jerked into high panic. "Nine-thirty?" I shot up into a sitting position and just as quickly jerked onto my side. I reached for the clock, as if seeing it would make a difference.

Auggie issued a grumpy, muted woof, and Leslie, accustomed to such behavior, leaned back on her elbows and gave me plenty of room.

"Jeez, I can't believe—why didn't you wake me?" I asked, grabbing the coffee cup and taking a grateful gulp.

"Because I stupidly thought you needed sleep. Silly me." She grabbed two pillows, stacked them at the foot of the bed, and put her head on them.

"Thank you for the coffee," I said disagreeably. "Did anything interesting happen while I was asleep?"

"Yes."

"What?" I perched gingerly on the side of the bed as I examined my leg. I had a bump the size of a golf ball and the color of a plum, and a scraped knee that was pink and cranberry. At least I was color coordinated.

"The garage called and said that your car would be in mint condition by three this afternoon."

"It would probably be a good idea if we didn't even approach that conversation just now." Having slept past seven, I was feeling cranky and in no mood for car talk. I opened the drawer to the nightstand and looked for a local phone book.

"Let me explain . . ."

"I gave you a chance to explain the other day and you didn't want it, or don't you remember?" I found the phone book, and a Bible.

"It wasn't the right time."

"You couldn't call back?"

"I was with a client. You said you had an early-morning—"

"Bullshit." I dismissed her as I flipped through the white

205

pages looking for Delaney. "You were wrong. It was after ten and he should have left you alone to sort things out with me."

"But he didn't."

"You're a big girl, Leslie. You could have asked him to leave. You always make your needs known to me."

"It's not the same thing and you know it. He's a client and you're my family." The tone of her voice told me loud and clear that we were treading on very thin ice.

"Actually, it is the exact same thing. It's about respect." I glanced up at her from the phone book. "The only difference is he is a rich man dangling a big fat carrot in front of your face whom you *chose* to treat with more respect than me. It was a choice on your part and, in my opinion, a very bad one." I found the Delaney clan with no problem.

"Oh no you don't. I'm not going to let you turn this into a *rich people are dysfunctional and don't know how to treat anyone with respect* diatribe," she warned me.

"I didn't say that." I looked for my bag, which I had conveniently tossed by the bedside before going to sleep.

"You didn't have to. Now, I know this is something we have to deal with, but I don't think that now is the time or place, so if you don't mind, I'd appreciate your changing the subject before you fray my nerves."

"Fray your nerves," I repeated, unable to hide my smile. "I didn't bring this up, but I will change the subject. Did anything *else* interesting happen that I should know about," I asked, leaning down to get my bag.

"I made an appointment for you to see the doctor for your heinie. They expect you at noon." She tucked her arms under her head.

"Doctor?" I folded over the page with the long list of Delaneys and looked for a pen, as well as my glasses, in my bag. "Thank you anyway, but noon's right in the middle of the day." I knew that once I was out, the only doctor I would be stopping for was Michael Callahan.

206

"Yes sir folks, and next week the little lady will learn her colors."

"Ha-ha. What you don't understand is—"

"I understand, all right," she cut me off. "What you don't understand is that he could see you at noon, so noon it will be."

"I have two things to say to you. One, I don't know that I really *need* to see a doctor, and two, I don't have *time* to see a doctor." I pulled my reading glasses, pen, and spiral notebook from my bag and set them beside me on the bed.

"Is that right?"

"That's right."

"Well then, I have one thing to say to you. This is not up for discussion. You *will* see the doctor. You don't know what it looks like back there."

I test-wiggled my bottom on the mattress. "You know, it doesn't feel as bad as I thought it would. Look at me, I'm sitting without difficulty."

"Un-huh, and you're sitting on a soft mattress with a bare butt. Think of panties, slacks, and scratchy upholstery on hardwood."

"Why would I think of scratchy upholstery on hardwood?" I held up my hand. "No, don't answer that." Suddenly ravenous, I dropped my bag back on the floor and peeled open an individual container of strawberry jam, which I slathered on some toast. "So, what exactly did this supercilious Frenchman do to my car?" I polished off the first piece of toast.

"Uh-uh, sister, we are not going there. I'll talk about anything else, but I am not about to engage in a fight with you. I'll talk about the successful poop I got from Auggie this morning, or even the call from Max, but I refuse to talk about your car, which, by the way, François has already paid for in full," she said, pointedly blasé.

"Max called *here*?"

"Yes."

"When? I didn't hear the phone ring." I wiped the

crumbs off my fingers and reached for my notebook.

"You were tired, Sydney. That's why I didn't wake you until now."

"Thank you." I could tell from the strain in her voice that the ice upon which I tread was cracking. I slipped my glasses on the tip of my nose and nodded. I had before me a writing implement, a notebook, the phone book, and breakfast. I was ready. I studied my lover as she absentmindedly petted Auggie, who had inched into her lap. Ten years my junior, Leslie is one of the sexiest women I have ever known. Her allure may be simply that she is completely comfortable with herself or perhaps she is just everything I find appealing in a woman, both physically and emotionally, but it wasn't until we had moved in together that I learned not only how loving and kind she is, but how well she knows me. I see living with her as a kind of gift.

She pulled a scrap of paper out of her back pocket and unfolded it, reading her notes.

"Let's see, Max called at around eight this morning and said to tell you he talked with Naomi Lucas—"

"Lewis," I corrected her.

"Whatever. He's going to see her today."

"Good." I retrieved the coffee cup and drained it. "Is there any more coffee?" I asked.

"Yes, over there." She pointed to the other night table. I reached over and grabbed it while she continued. "He said to tell you that Kerry has already made a call to her friend at the morgue for Robert Sherman?" She looked at me questioningly.

"Excellent." I poured the coffee and asked if she wanted some. She didn't.

"Kerry doesn't have anything yet, but promised she'd have more later today." Leslie flapped the paper in the air and said, "I also have the number for Betty Sherman right here. Be nice and I may give it to you."

"I'll be nice." I ran a finger along the bottom of her

bare foot. Whether I admitted it or not, the extra few hours of sleep had done wonders for my disposition.

"Oh no you don't. Let me finish first; otherwise, you'll just give me a hard time later." She tucked that same foot under my thigh. "Max said to tell you that he spoke with Marcy. You know, I haven't seen Marcy in forever. Ask them over for dinner next week, okay?"

"Okay."

"Anyway, Marcy said that the car was no longer impounded and that it's a—"

"—white Toyota Camry, license plate number—" I cut her off and reeled off the license plate from the car in Cyclops's driveway the night before.

"I'm impressed." She suppressed a big smile and nodded once.

"Thank you. Did Marcy mention the station wagon?"

"Yes. He said there was a wagon registered to a Patrick M. De—"

"—laney." I finished the name for her. "Is there an address better than a post office box, or maybe a phone number?"

"Just a P.O. box in Southampton."

"Anything else?"

"Max'll be out all day but Kerry will be in the office. He has her tracking down Milt Brown and Mary Grace, as well as finishing his search of the hospitals."

"Excellent."

"Who are Milt and Mary?"

"Friends of Michael's. They may know where he was when his wife was murdered."

"Wow. I can't believe Enoch's granddaughter was killed."

"Grandniece."

"Either way," she mumbled as she handed me the piece of paper she had been reading from. "That's about it."

"Good. Thank you." I pulled the phone book onto my

lap and slipped my reading glasses onto the bridge of my nose.

"So what's next?"

"Next, I've got to get out of here." Between East Hampton and Southampton, there were at least fifteen Delaneys listed in the phone book. Three were the initials P and one was Patrick, but it was Patrick Q., not Patrick M. Delaney.

"What do you mean you've got to get out of here? Where are you going?"

"First I'm going to pay my respects to the Delaney family, and then I'm going to find Michael Callahan. Let me ask you a question. If you didn't have a car out here, how would you get around?" I was thinking of Michael Callahan's car sitting in Hannah Miller's driveway.

"Bicycle. Walk. Bus, though they're few and far between. Hitch—"

"You would hitch?"

"No, *I* wouldn't, but I thought the question was global." She squinted at me. "Why? Are you planning on taking your car back and making me walk?"

"My car." The reminder that my poor car was so near and yet so far did not sit well with me. I ripped out the page in the phone book that listed the Delaney clan.

"Are we going to start with this car again?" she asked, her voice sounding ready for an argument.

Before I could answer, someone knocked at the door, which made the dog bark and sent me flying butt-naked into the bathroom.

"Take the dog, take the dog," Leslie hissed as I tried to shut the door.

"No, no, no, you keep her. It's not like you can pretend she's not here."

"Damn it, Sydney." She turned back into the room and wagged a finger at Auggie, who couldn't have cared less. Quite the contrary, Auggie was terribly excited at the idea of company. The knocking persisted. "I'm coming," Leslie finally barked at the door as she grabbed hold of Auggie.

That's when I shut the bathroom door and decided to leave the management to Leslie.

Auggie's barks calmed after several seconds and I started my morning bathroom routine, straining to hear anything that might be coming from the other room, like "Take your dog out of these rooms at once!" Though Leslie is perfectly capable of handling management objections to a puppy in her room, I decided to wait until they left before taking a shower.

After what felt like a matter of seconds, Leslie knocked on the door.

"Have we been ousted?" I asked.

"No. You had a visitor."

"I did?" Immediately Officer Bob Shelton sprung to mind.

"Yes. A woman named Rosalie. She said you were with her father last night when he died?" She gave me a look asking for confirmation.

I nodded as I started past her back into the room. "Where is she?" I asked to the empty room.

"She left. She was on her way to make the funeral arrangements, but she just wanted to thank you for having tried to revive her father. I asked her if she wanted to talk to you directly, but she didn't."

"What do you mean she didn't?"

"She didn't. She was emphatic that I not disturb you. I told her you were only cowering in the bathroom from the puppy police, but she didn't care. She said she was in a hurry and asked me to pass her thanks on to you. That was it."

"Shit," I mumbled as I headed back into the bathroom to shower.

"So, you were with her father when he died?"

"Yeah. He had a heart attack."

"Why didn't you tell me?" She pulled the toilet cover down and sat.

"I did, in this very bathroom last night." I turned on the hot water tap.

"No you didn't. I would have remembered that."

"You were half asleep."

"I remember how you got the splinters and about the police. I don't think you told me about this man. You know, your problem is you don't share."

"I do so share. I let you use my car, didn't I?" The water was beginning to steam, so I turned on the cold-water tap and held my hand under the shower head.

When I turned to face her, she was shaking her head, and a crooked little smile was just playing on her lips. I wiggled my eyebrows and blew her a kiss before I stepped into the shower, where I looked down at my body. It's damned tight, and normally I am proud of my body, but that morning, looking down at my odd array of bruises, bumps, and scrapes, I cringed.

The next thing I knew, Leslie pulled back the glass sliding door and joined me in the shower. For the first time in over two years, I felt suddenly shy with her. She is ten years younger, ten years tighter, and ten years softer than I am, and it showed. She slipped into my arms and said, "Your body looks color-coded, dear."

I turned us around so her back would face the shower spray and protect my fanny from pinpricks of pain. Her black hair gave in to the rush of water and fell gently over her face. With her arms securely wrapped around my waist, I pushed the hair out of her eyes and kissed first one, then the other. She raised her mouth to meet mine and for the first time in several days, I felt my love's body against my own, a sensation I sorely miss when we are apart from each other. She took the soap and massaged me from head to toe, bathing and loving me with each and every touch of her hand and lips. When we moved from the shower to the bed, Auggie was waiting patiently just outside the bathtub. She followed us into the bedroom and slept under the bed while on top of it, Leslie and I made love.

I knew I was losing time looking for Michael Callahan, but I also know that life is too short to pass up love. If I couldn't take an hour out of my life for making love, then something was wrong.

Then again, as soon as we finished, I was hurrying around the room readying myself for the day ahead.

"So did this Rosalie Delaney say where she was going?" I asked, picking up where we had left off preshower.

"Just to a funeral home. She had to make arrangements." As we talked Leslie slipped into a pair of linen slacks, a tee-shirt, and an extra large vee-necked blue sweater.

Fully dressed, I retrieved the notes Leslie had taken during her call with Max, and made sure that I could read her handwriting. "Can I use your makeup?" I asked, catching a glimpse of myself in a mirror and remembering that I had left mine in the city.

"Sure," Leslie said, picking up the phone.

"Who are you calling?" I asked from the bathroom.

"I have a client out here who was thinking of getting some work done. She told me if ever I was out here I should call. Well, I called yesterday and she said we should get together today sometime."

I listened as Leslie connected smoothly with another one of her excessively rich clients. They discussed François and Mancini Bouchon and how Leslie was going to be designing the interior of their new house on Further Lane. They talked about the work that this client, Courtney, wanted, and they discussed Auggie, now labeled as the "sweet new addition to the family."

This set off sirens in my head. I stood in front of Leslie and shook my head no while pointing to Auggie, who was curled up in her lap. When she tried to ignore me, I mouthed "No," while holding up my hands in front of me as if to stop an oncoming thing, which in this case was the addition of a dog to our happy, but humble, home.

Leslie waved me away and finished her conversation

213

with Courtney, whom she was to meet in half an hour.

"We are not keeping this dog," I told Leslie as soon as she ended her call. "This dog is a visitor in our lives."

"Who said you get to make *all* the decisions? I don't remember anyone asking me what *I* thought."

"But I didn't *get* the dog, I *got* it, there's a difference."

Leslie stared at me and then looked away shaking her head.

"You know what I mean. I told you, you have to think of this dog like it's Margot's dog Zack, or Carmen's cat Charlie; we're just taking care of her. That's all."

"Sydney. This dog has no home to be returned to. From what you and Max told me, this is *not* a comparable situation at all and you know it. And, adding insult to injury, you never once asked me what *I* thought one way or the other. You just show up in the middle of the night with a dog and expect that I'll go along with whatever you say. Well I'm saying no, Sydney. N-O. I have grown attached to this puppy and I want to keep her." With that said she swung her bag over her shoulder and reached for Auggie's leash.

"Just what did Max tell you?" I asked lamely.

Leslie let out an exasperated sigh and shook her head. "You're nuts, you know that?"

"Look, we don't have the time for a pet. Especially in the city."

"Sydney, we both have jobs where we can bring her to the office with us. We're our own bosses, remember?" She checked her watch. "Look, I'm running late. I'll see you later. Oh, and Courtney wants us to stay at her guest house while we're here. She insists."

I took a deep breath and decided that to maintain peace I would go along with this Courtney thing. First of all, Leslie was right; I had just thrust Auggie upon her without so much as an if-you-please, and that wasn't fair. Second, it was only a matter of time before the management was wise to the presence of the cutest puppy in the universe.

214

Leslie gave me a quick kiss as she handed me Courtney's number, along with the doctor's name, address, and number. Then she and Auggie left me flipping through the Yellow Pages. Between the two directories covering the area from Southampton to Montauk, there were five funeral homes I could choose from. On the third call I found Delaney in Southampton. I checked my watch and knew that if I hurried, chances were good that I would be able to reach the funeral home while his daughter Rosalie was still there.

Before leaving, I stood at the door to the room, feeling like I was forgetting something. I went through a checklist of things I might need: gun, address book, keys, sunglasses, wallet with identification, and money . . . Everything was there. Then it hit me. Auggie. I realized that it was Auggie I was missing. It also occurred to me that, like my Volvo, Leslie had taken my dog. *The* dog. Auggie wasn't my dog, I reminded myself as I closed the door behind me. She was the dog whom I planned to find a home for. Maybe a home out here by the beach, where there's room for a dog to grow. Not like the city, where she'd be cramped in an apartment and spend most of her waking hours indoors. That's no way to raise a dog. People—sure. But dogs? Why, it's positively inhumane.

I checked myself out in the gilded hallway mirror. Loose black slacks, white tee-shirt, beige silk jacket, and soft brown flats. I looked like a woman with the wrong-colored shadow and blush, ready to extend condolences for a man she never knew.

Twenty

It was a magnificent day for a wake at the beach. There was not a cloud in the sky, the air was crisp, the seagulls were soaring, and the small town looked like the idyllic seaside hamlet that it is. The wooden houses along the main road, all complete with either wraparound verandahs or front porches, bring to mind the 1600s, when the town was first developed. Back then, these were farmhouses with acres and acres of farmland stretched out behind them. Now if each house sits on an acre or two, it's a lot of property, but it doesn't diminish the charm.

My plan was first to meet Rosalie Delaney, who seemed, judging from the nature of her visit, to be more accessible and rational than her brother, King Kong. Depending on what I learned from her, I would return to Hannah Miller's and try to find out where the wandering doctor had gone off to. I wondered how much evidence would be left, thanks to Mr. Kong's outburst. It could have been so easy. The police had simply come to remove a dead body, the body of a man they happened to know and love, a man who could do no wrong. However, given the state of the house when they arrived, my guess is they went through it with a fine-toothed comb, not knowing what they were looking for, but looking nonetheless. There had to be a logical reason why Paddy Delaney, and not Michael, had been at Cyclops's summer house. There also had to be a reason that Paddy was toting a rifle.

I was surprised the police hadn't yet visited, but as I wasn't leaving town, I felt no need to contact them. Had I been Officer Bob the night before, I wouldn't have let me go so easily. There were too many unanswered questions.

In the parking lot, I carefully lowered myself into the Ford, rolled down the windows, and slipped on a pair of sunglasses. No question about it, I needed an air pillow. A right turn onto 27 would take me to Southampton (and the rest of the United States for that matter). As I was about to turn I saw the rusted white station speed by, headed west. It was the "Honk If You Love Jesus" mobile that had belonged to Paddy Delaney, the same car Godzilla had been driving the night before. I took a right onto the road and congratulated myself for this cosmic stroke of good luck.

I trailed the car for several miles before the driver turned left through a wrought-iron gate, into the parking lot of what looked like an old estate, which I had always thought was a Yoga retreat. It was still an estate. A left turn would bring me into the manor grounds or allow me to park, illegally, in a place where I would stick out like a sore thumb. I parked across the way on Highway 27, and turned off the ignition. Though my sight lines were partially obstructed by the stone pillars on either side of the gate, I was able to see a muscular young man emerge from the driver's seat. It was not my friend from the night before. With a lethargic, sloping gait, he moved toward the entrance of the building.

It was Carrot-top—the fellow I rode piggy-back in Brooklyn Heights only two days earlier. Seeing him again, even from this distance, I was able to draw the conclusion that Carrot-top and Godzilla were brothers. Before he even made it to the last step, the large wooden door opened and he disappeared into the darkness beyond.

A stakeout. I hadn't been on one of these in a long time. All I needed was a thermos of coffee and a bag of junk food. As I had neither, I took in the sights with an eye for detail: a large gaggle of geese lounged on the lawn of the estate, a yawning, one-armed man rode a tractor-mower and cut the grass on the far side of the mansion, and on one of the stone pillars there was a small bronze plaque, which, from my distance, I couldn't read. No doubt it identified the place or told of its history, which I was curious about. If I got out of the car and read it, I ran the risk of Carrot-top taking off and leaving me in the dust. If I made a U-turn and parked in front of the grounds—where there was no parking—I ran the risk of getting a ticket from one of the vigilant traffic officers who religiously protect and defend the thirty-mile-an-hour speed limit on the East End.

I decided that I was fine where I was and let my thoughts wander. I wondered what—if anything—Max might find at the Treelane and if he would check in on Selma while he was there. I knew, of course, that he wouldn't. Selma. Selma made me think of Minnie, and Minnie made me think of our exchange the night before and how the future is something we never discuss. Less than twelve hours earlier, I had witnessed a man die. A sobering thought. And though I was not thrilled that the cosmic joker chose to have me be the sole witness to his passing, the fact is, it was quick. Paddy Delaney went just the way I would want to go, fast and without fear.

Sitting there, on a glorious autumn morning, contemplating death, I wondered if Selma gave it much thought, and if it scared her. Just as Minnie came waltzing back into my head, the door to the house opened and Carrot-top came storming out. I couldn't tell if he was squinting or crying, but he headed like a bullet to the station wagon. His face was beet-red and free of the lethargy that had seemed to weigh him down before. In its stead was a frenetic energy that made him look almost comical.

A young woman ran out from the shadows behind him, reaching out to him with one hand, clutching her chest with the other. Anguish, pain, and rage were reflected in both their faces. I was completely drawn into the drama being played out for the one-armed landscaper, who didn't even notice.

Carrot-top grabbed for the handle of the car door, missed, banged the roof of the car with his fist, and made a deep dent just over the driver's seat. The woman cried out what looked to be "Stop!" and, at a good ten paces away from him, reached out to him with her other hand. By now he had opened the car door, thrown himself inside, and slammed the door shut with such force that the side view mirror went flying onto the graveled driveway. When he tried to start it, the car let out a screech that was loud enough to get the landscaper's attention. A second attempt got the engine going, and he peeled out of the driveway, sending pellets of gravel spitting back at the woman, who had sunk to her knees and was bent into her own embrace.

There was no traffic headed west, but Carrot-top had made a right and was headed east. I had to think quickly. The station wagon was getting away from me, but I wasn't so sure I wanted to follow, considering that a motionless woman was in the driveway, a woman who had to have *some* answers and probably wouldn't beat me up if I asked her a question or two. I pulled into the westbound lane, made an immediate U-turn, and pulled into the driveway.

Another woman from the house was already rushing out to help her friend. I felt helpless as I approached them. The second woman, who was older and had a round, friendly face with wide, red cheeks, looked up at me as she helped the younger woman to her feet. The older woman shook her head at me and made it clear—without saying a word—that I should keep my distance.

It's my natural instinct to help, which may be why I wound up as a detective in the first place. I can't watch someone struggle without reaching out a helping hand. I dug my fists into my pockets and watched the two women from behind my dark glasses. The younger woman was sobbing uncontrollably and fell into her friend's arms with complete abandon. "Why?" she moaned into the woman's shoulder. Over and over she repeated, "Why? Why? Why?" In a matter of moments the two women were safely inside the house, the massive wooden door closed tight between us.

I looked up and saw the one-armed landscaper paused on his tractor, smoking a cigarette. He looked at me and blinked once. Both of us, voyeurs, abruptly looked away from each other. It felt as if we had already shared too much.

I climbed back into the car and pulled quickly out of the driveway. I knew that someone at the Yoga-Zen-Buddhist retreat—or whatever it was—would be able to answer my questions later. However, if I was going to catch Rosalie Delaney at the funeral home, I had to haul ass—a thought that, given my state, I didn't relish.

I found the Manning Funeral Home without too much trouble. In small towns the funeral homes are always the biggest, prettiest houses on the block, which is something I understand, but have always considered a bit of a waste. In reality, the dead don't care and the living have to treat the space with an almost surreal solemnity. On top of that, the resale value has to be dreadful. Once it's been a funeral home, how many people would ever buy it for a family house? "Go on now, Johnny, go play in the old embalming room."

A huge wraparound verandah encircled the house, and the front door opened onto a foyer that faced a narrow staircase. Much to my surprise the wooden floors hadn't been covered with dark carpeting, nor did damask drapes hang heavily over the windows. Lace curtains fluttered gently in the breeze coming through the open windows and plush carpet runners ran from the foyer into the back of the house, up the stairs, and to the entrance of what was now a waiting room. I was amazed at how warm and inviting the place was. It could have been a bed-and-breakfast rather than a board-and-box. I was standing there admiring the way the light played through the curtains and patterned the floor when a soft, friendly voice greeted me.

"Good morning. Can I help you?" I looked up and saw a woman, about my age, wearing a shapeless dress that reminded me of the seventies. She was all angles, with sharp features and straight, straight hair parted in the middle. The soft calico dress hung loosely on her wiry frame, creating a jarring, yet comforting effect. Unlike the stiff mortician greeting I'm accustomed to, her smile was so genuine and warm, I got the impression that she was actually glad to see me.

I took off my glasses. "Yes please. I understand that Patrick Delaney is in your . . . care?"

She nodded and said, "That's right. Were you a friend of Paddy's?"

"I was actually looking for his daughter," I said with a half-nod and what I felt sure was a sympathetic expression.

"Rosalie?" Her smile dimmed briefly as she sized me up. I nodded. "May I ask why?"

"I was with her father when he died," I said confidentially. I had a feeling that this little tidbit of information would open all sorts of doors for me in this establishment. Not a thought to dwell on.

Her body relaxed. She reached out, gently placing her fingertips on my arm. "I'm sorry, I didn't mean to sound so harsh, but Rosie's a personal friend and this is a difficult time for her."

I patted her hand and assured her that I understood. "Is Rosalie here?" I asked.

"Oh yes. She's just working out the final arrangements with Bob. Bob's my husband. This is our business." She gestured to the building around us. "My name's Fran. You are . . . ?"

"Sydney. Sydney Sloane."

There was a momentary awkward silence. Simultaneously we started talking.

"Your place is—" I started.

221

"Would you like some—" she started.

We both stopped, chuckled, and said, "Go on," at the same time.

"Rosie will be a little while longer. She and Bob just got started. Do you want to wait?"

"Is that all right?"

"Oh sure." She took my elbow and steered me into the waiting room. "Would you like something to drink?"

"No thank you. So . . ." I scanned the room for the most comfortable chair. "Are all the Delaneys here?" I asked, gesturing to nowhere in particular.

"Oh no, just Rosie."

"Really? I thought it was a large family," I said, casually adjusting myself on the side chair I had chosen for the padding.

"It is. Thirteen of 'em. But when their mother died a few years ago, Rosie really took over. We went to school together, so I can tell you that even as kids she had a huge responsibility. I mean what would you expect? She was the eldest daughter in an Irish Catholic family. She's also the most practical in the lot." Fran looped her hair behind her ear and sighed. "So you were with Paddy when he died?"

I nodded. "That's right."

"Montauk, was it?"

Again I nodded. "That's right."

Fran nodded. We listened to some kids in the street playing. Apparently Scooch was cheating and this upset Darlene.

"I heard that it was fast. It's always a blessing when it's fast." She leaned forward as she spoke, her hands clasped tightly in her lap.

I said nothing.

"It was your friend's house where he died?" she pressed on ahead.

I cleared my throat and looked around. It was a large room with two identical light blue chesterfield sofas facing each other, separated by a plain cherry wood coffee table.

Vases of flowers were scattered throughout the room, and framed antique maps covered the walls.

"Did Rosalie tell you all this?" I finally asked.

"Some. Why?"

"Quite honestly, I feel like I'm getting the third degree." I chuckled uncomfortably and made my eyes as wide as saucers.

"Oh dear, I am so sorry." She brought her hands to her chest. "It's my sister, Claire. She's married to one of the ambulance drivers who went to the scene." She paused. "I just sounded like a silly gossip, didn't I?"

I smiled. "Don't worry about it."

Off in the distance a phone rang once, twice. On the third ring, Fran excused herself and went to tend to business. I was relieved when she left because it meant I could stand up. Despite the padded side chair seat, my backside was starting to feel like it had been splattered with hot oil.

Fran never came back. I sat there for another twenty minutes flipping through a boating magazine someone had left behind and listening to Scooch and Darlene alternately clash and then squeal with delight as they became partners again.

I was on my feet when Rosalie Delaney stopped in the doorway. She was a sturdy-looking woman with surprisingly dark shoulder-length hair. Her brown eyes were swollen and bloodshot but honest and direct.

"You're Sydney Sloane?" Car keys dangled from her hand.

"Yes. Rosalie?"

She nodded but stayed glued to her position at the door. We spent the next several moments sizing each other up. She was carrying an extra twenty pounds or so, but was the type of woman who made it look sensual and not sluggish. However, this was not a woman to cross. Her pain and apparent exhaustion notwithstanding, I had no doubts that Rosalie Delaney was a woman who liked to be in control.

"I'm sorry about your father." I offered my condolences.

She stuck her keys in her jacket pocket and looked down at her black flats. When she looked up she acknowledged my words with a slow, tired blink, then turned and walked out the front door. I followed and found that she was waiting for me on the verandah, with her eyes now hidden behind a pair of sunglasses.

"I understand you came to see me." I decided to get the ball rolling.

She pulled a pack of cigarettes out of her bag. "That's right. I didn't expect you'd follow me, though. Especially not here." She tucked the filtered end of a cigarette between her lips and added, "I don't know that I appreciate that." The cigarette twitched up and down as she spoke.

"I'm sorry, but I thought you and I needed to talk." I watched as she cupped her hand around a stick match and lighted her cigarette. She squinted to keep the smoke out of her eyes and started down the three porch steps.

"I don't like to air my family business in public." She was like a little engine chugging up the sidewalk. I kept up with her accelerated pace.

"I haven't done that."

"Everyone here knows that if you need to make something public, you tell Frances Manning in confidence."

"That may be, but I didn't tell her anything." I objected. "She knew a lot and when I asked her how, she told me that her brother-in-law worked on the ambulance team that responded to my call for help for your father. Hey." I grabbed her arm as she began to turn and cross the street. Ashes jerked off the end of the cigarette. "I'm not the enemy. I tried to save your father."

She studied me good and hard before asking me to remove my hand. "Thank you." I didn't know if she was responding to my words or the release of my hand, but she nodded to a bench by the side of the wide street. "Why don't we sit down for a minute?"

Down the street Scooch and Darlene were still at play. I was able to put faces to the disembodied voices. Scooch was seven, towheaded, and determined. Darlene was around the same age, freckled, and sporting at least eight different-colored florescent Band-Aids, all on one leg. It was a fabulous look.

Rosalie Delaney crossed one leg over the other, and her arms under her chest. She looked out at the street as she exhaled blue smoke.

I wanted to sit on a hard, slatted bench almost as much as I wanted root canal without Novocain, but I had no choice. Ms. Delaney was hostile as it was, and I didn't know why. Towering over her would hardly help the situation. A slight wave of nausea washed over me as soon as my heinie made contact with the bench. Wonderful, for the rest of my life I'd be allergic to pressure-treated wood.

"What do you want?" She stared straight ahead as she spoke. I was starting to feel like I was in a James Bond movie where two apparent strangers meet on a bench and exchange dangerous information and cool gadgets.

I turned toward her, lifting one cheek off the seat, and reminded her, "You came to see me."

"I said what I had to say to your friend."

"What is with your family?" I asked, both in pain and fed up with the Delaney demeanor.

"*My family*? I'd say that's the pot calling the kettle black, wouldn't you?" She tossed her cigarette into the street.

"I don't know what you're talking about. One minute you come to my hotel room, ostensibly to say thank you, and then the next thing I know you're acting like I've done something wrong."

"Is that right, Miss *Private Detective*?" She seemed to expect a reaction, but as there was nothing to react to, I simply waited. She leaned closer to me and lowered her voice. "Let me tell you something, the police may not know who you are, but I know all about you."

225

"You do?"

"Yes, I do."

"And just what is it you know?"

"I know you're a private investigator, which you neglected to tell the police. I know you roughed up my father because you think he had something to do with a woman's death."

"That is an absolute lie. Why don't we start from the beginning. First off, who's feeding you this information?"

She pursed her lips and looked back out at the street.

"For the record, I never touched your father, other than to administer mouth-to-mouth and CPR, which I think you know, or else why would you have come to my hotel to *thank me*? And also for the record, I think it's fascinating that neither you nor your brother has even asked about the last few minutes of your father's life, which I happened to share with him. If that was my dad, you bet your ass I'd want to know every last detail. It makes me wonder what the hell you two are trying to cover up that's so much more important than your loss."

She swallowed hard and tried to fight the tears, but it was a losing battle. She pulled a thick wad of tissues out of her purse and cried silently as Scooch and Darlene taunted a newcomer to their play, a little guy named Dalton.

After several minutes she took a deep breath and whispered, "You're right, of course. This whole situation has me sick to my stomach."

"Talk to me. I might be able to help."

She shook her head. "Matt will have a fit."

"Matt?"

"My brother."

"The one I met last night."

"That's right. He doesn't trust you."

"Unless he has something to hide, he has no reason not to trust me." I paused and decided to push on ahead. "Was Matt involved in the death of Jessica Callahan?"

226

"Absolutely not!" She dug nervously into her bag and pulled out the cigarettes.

"Rosalie, plain and simple, the fact is your family is connected to the Callahans and I need to know how." Smashing Pumpkins blasted from a passing vintage Mercedes. "Let me give you a little background, so that you know I'm on the up and up. Michael Callahan has been accused of killing his wife. Jessica Callahan's ninety-two-year-old grandmother believes that Michael is innocent and has hired me to prove it. I'd say that's a big vote of confidence for a man who refuses to defend himself, which he does." I shifted cheeks, sending a shock of pain tingling along my thigh. "I met Michael for the first time the other day, after your brothers—I'm assuming the other kid there was a brother—had just finished beating him up. Now why, I ask myself, would these two men have such a big grudge against the doctor? When I asked Michael, he refused to answer. Perhaps more importantly, I got the impression that he would have protected them. That's odd, wouldn't you say? Protecting the men who had only moments earlier rearranged his face? Now, over the years, Rosalie, I've learned that people protect other people for only a handful of reasons. Love. Guilt. Fear." I watched as she exhaled the smoke through her nostrils. "I can assure you, Michael was not afraid of your brothers, and logic tells me he's not in love with them either. So, I take this information, and I put it in the back of my mind because in the meantime, Dr. Callahan disappears. He's not in a good position to do that because jumping bail is frowned upon in most states." I paused to see if she was still with me. The nicotine had calmed her, and she turned to me as if to say, "Well go on." So I did.

"Proving Michael's innocence is my responsibility, and it bothers me when the person I'm trying to help resists me. Now, I not only have to prove his innocence, but I have to find him, and, naturally, my quest took me to the hospital where he works. Do you know who I saw there?"

227

Rosalie jerked as if I had startled her. She tossed the cigarette into the gutter and said, vaguely, "No, who?"

"Your father. Was your father aware of his sons' extra-curricular activity the day before at the Callahan house in Brooklyn?" I shrugged as I asked the hypothetical question, "I don't know. Was it your father behind the wheel when his boys took off after beating Michael? I don't know. What was your father doing at St. Mary's the next day?" I shrugged. "Had he stayed overnight or did this elderly man make a potentially six-hour round-trip two days in a row? Again, I just don't know. I assume that he knew Michael, because last night I received a phone call telling me that Michael Callahan was out here and that he needed help; when I arrived at the address I had been given, Michael was not to be found, but your father was. I arrived at about two in the morning at what I thought was Michael Callahan's house and there was your father, in his BVDs, aiming a rifle at my head."

"It wasn't loaded," Rosalie said as she slumped against the back of the bench.

We studied each other, silently acknowledging that something had shifted between us. We were no longer enemies.

"Even if it had been, I got the impression that he wouldn't have used it."

She took a deep breath, held it in, and nodded.

"I wasn't with your father more than fifteen, twenty minutes before he died. In the short time that I spent with him, I noticed that he seemed to be in mild pain, like he had heartburn." I paused. "Do you want to hear this?"

"Yes, please."

"He had a heart attack. I was able to revive him and called 911. When I came back—I take it he was a stubborn man?" I interrupted myself.

Rosalie smiled sadly and nodded as if to say, "Oh yeah."

228

"Well, when I came back he tried to tell me something. I told him to be still, but he insisted."

"What did he say?" She sounded like a scared little girl.

"He said, 'I'm sorry. Tell her I'm sorry.' " I paused as Dalton ran screaming behind us, with Scooch in hot pursuit. "Do you know what he meant?"

With her hand pressed to her lips and her eyes squeezed shut, Rosalie Delaney was either trying to seal herself in or keep the world out. Unfortunately life doesn't work that way. At some point she would have to breathe. At some point she would have to open her eyes and see that nothing had changed. At some point she would have to uncover her mouth, and when she did, I would be there waiting to hear the truth.

Twenty-one

"Thank you." Rosalie patted her eyes and took a deep breath. "I needed to hear that. Sometimes . . ." She studied her lap as if she were checking a cheat sheet. "Sometimes you just don't know what to believe. And this has been one fucking unbelievable week."

"Do you know what your father meant?" I asked again.

She shrugged. "Matt is afraid of you, you know."

Whether it was a calculated shift of focus or not, I thought it was interesting that she chose to change the subject from her father's last words to her brother's fear. Wrong or right, I decided that the two were connected. "Why would he be afraid of me?"

"Oh, I think it's about family honor . . . male pride . . . tradition." Though she sounded exhausted, her voice was strong. "Christ, I could use a drink." She rubbed her eyes.

I am fond of gin and love my red wine, but I've never been one to drink at brunch let alone breakfast, and drinking to lessen emotional pain is—as I see it—a defective smoke screen.

"Come on, I'll buy you a cup of coffee, or tea."

Rosalie led the way to a plain little restaurant just a block and a half from Manning Funeral Home. Here she was greeted warmly, and with sympathy. "News moves fast in a town this size," I commented after we had settled down at a darkened booth in the back.

230

"Not nearly as fast as a rumor. If you're raised here, you know everybody, and I mean everybody. For example, Mitzi Gimber was one of the officers you met last night, right?"

"Yes." How could I forget the human lawn ornament?

"Well, Mitzi's telling everyone that she thinks you're a man who actually likes to dress up like a woman and wear cosmetics."

I let out an appreciative laugh. "She thinks I'm a transvestite?"

"Oh I doubt that, but she didn't like you and this is her way of getting even. She came up with the worst thing she could think of and decided you were it."

I could think of any number of things worse than being a transvestite, like an investment banker or a Republican. Or a lawn ornament look-alike with no sense of humor. Oh, those stone-throwers.

"It's a small community and those of us who have lived here forever know that Mitzi's always been like that, even as a kid."

The young waitress brought us both coffee and placed a toasted corn muffin in front of Rosalie. "Buns says you got to eat this."

Rosalie looked over at the man behind the counter, who had greeted her when we arrived. "Thanks, Buns," she called out to him. He winked, nodded, and hurriedly went back to work.

"You want something, miss?" The waitress turned her shy, pale blue eyes on me.

"No, thank you." When we were left alone, I said to Rosalie, "About last night . . ."

"I sincerely appreciate your candor out there." She nodded to the front door as she tore open two sugar packets and poured them into her coffee. "I understand that you would like me to reciprocate. Please understand, it's not that simple."

"Why not?"

"It has to do with loyalty, I think."

"To . . ."

Her eyebrows went up as she sipped two-handed from her cup. "Family. Friends. Self," she said when she put the cup down.

"I'm sorry, but I'm a simple gal. What you're saying is a bit esoteric for me. Could you maybe be a little more specific?"

She looked around to make certain no one was listening to our conversation. "Okay, for *myself* I would like nothing better than to tell you everything I know, which would probably set you in the right direction if what you told me outside was true—and I believe it was. I'd also like to because confession's always so freeing, but the fact is, I can't. I can't because whatever I tell you will have an impact on a lot more people than just me, especially with regard to my family, and I would never do anything to hurt my family, or the family name." Her voice went up on the last part, as if she was trying to convince herself more than me.

"As for friends?" She shrugged her shoulders. "People like to talk and my family business is private."

"So, I don't get it. What are you telling me? That you will or won't help me? I mean, either way I'll get the information, because that's what I do for a living, but I have no intention of blasting your secrets to the public if that's what you're concerned about. What would I gain by doing that? If you don't mind a blunt observation, I think the real thing you seem to be afraid of is gossip." I finished my coffee and wanted more, but waved off the waitress.

"You don't live in a small town. You don't know how gossip can affect your life."

People like to see Manhattan as a huge anonymous place where no one talks to anyone else and lives are lived in little capsules. This is simply not the case. It's relatively small—about thirteen miles long by maybe four miles wide—essentially a place where neighborhoods become small towns. In my neighborhood, I've taken the brunt of gossip and rumors, and I've learned that people talk and people forget. It doesn't really matter. Hell, look at Peewee Herman. People talked, they assumed his career was over, and now he's back, but this time on prime time.

I pinched off a piece of her untouched corn muffin and tasted it. "So what you're saying is, you'd rather an innocent man go to jail for the murder of his wife while the real killer runs free, as long as it doesn't run the fine Delaney name through the mud. Does that sum it up accurately?"

Rosalie rested her elbows on the table and leaned toward me. "You don't understand," she said under her breath.

"I think I do. As a matter of fact, I think I hit the nail on the head and that's what's got you so angry."

"I'm not angry."

The waitress came up and refilled our cups, then lingered, slowly clearing away empty sugar packets and wiping up crumbs. Rosalie stared at the tabletop and I smiled at the waitress until she left.

"I am not angry," Rosalie repeated as soon as the girl was out of earshot.

I dismissed that delusion with a wave of my hand. "Of course you're angry. Your father just died. That in itself is enough to make you angry. But you and I both know that something else is eating away at you, Rosalie, something you know is not right. Tell me what it is. Tell me who your father was apologizing to when he died." She said nothing. I persisted. "What is it that Matt's so afraid of? What does your family have to do with Michael Callahan, and where the hell is he?" I was practically whispering, but out of the corner of my eye I caught the counter girl watching us intently.

"Michael Callahan is back at his friend's house." Her voice was hoarse.

"Since when?"

"Since . . . now." She checked her watch. "He should

be there by now." I waited for her to continue. There are times when it's best to just let go.

"I met him for the first time last night," Rosalie mumbled. She was going to open up, but because she was having mixed feelings about it, her words were strained. "I had heard about him, but I'd never met him. He's a very nice but totally screwed-up man, you know." She looked up at me from under her dark brows and continued softly.

"I can tell you that from what *I* know, he had absolutely nothing to do with his wife's death. I can also tell you that he's okay, physically, and has no intention of leaving the state. As far as I know, his plan is to go to trial, even though he didn't kill her."

"Why?"

She stared at me for a long time. "He has his reasons."

"Yes, that much I know. Everyone knows that Michael Callahan has his reasons, including his wife's grandmother—who hired me—but no one seems to know what those reasons are. Tell me, is it *you* he's protecting?" I asked, feeling certain that it wasn't, but getting tired of the cat-and-mouse game.

She exhaled a hollow laugh. "Right. If it was me I'd have no problem telling you everything. My problem is that my mother taught me to respect other people's privacy."

"Really? What did your father teach you?" I needed to get a rise out of her, needed to shake her just enough to rattle some information out of her.

"My father was a good man." Her eyes flashed with anger. Shake, shake, shake.

"Your father felt the need to apologize when he died. Who did he feel guilty about? If it wasn't you, who was it?"

"What if it *was* me?" she countered, sloshing her coffee into the saucer and onto the tabletop as she put down the cup. Good. She was getting rattled.

"Come on, Rosalie, who's the emotional cripple everyone has to protect?"

If Rosalie wasn't so concerned with gossip, she would have decked me right then and there. As it was, without another word, she grabbed her bag and flew out of the restaurant. I quickly tossed a few bucks on the tabletop to cover the coffees and a tip and hurried after her.

Out on the street she was already halfway to the corner when I caught up to her. If it wasn't for the condition of my buttocks, I would have reached her sooner, which was sobering, considering that my living depends on a whole and healthy body. In other words, chasing after an overweight, out-of-shape, almost middle-aged cigarette smoker should not have physically challenged me.

"Either way I'm going to find out," I called out when I was four paces away from her. Given her phobia of gossip, I had a hunch that yelling would stop her in her tracks. I was right.

She swung around as if about to bat me with her bag, but caught herself, and checked the streets, looking, no doubt, for a familiar face. This is one of the many things I love about living in New York City; one is free to experience life there with total abandon. I once witnessed an abnormally tall, painfully slender, bare-breasted woman limping up Broadway at noon wearing only black tights and ballet shoes. If three people stared, it was a crowd.

"Christ, what is it with you people?" I asked, walking beside her as she turned and headed to her car. "A woman is dead!" In my mind's eye I saw Selma Onderdonk, alone, in her room, waiting for a granddaughter who would never come.

She turned on me with a force that only grief or fear could produce. I wasn't sure which emotion had triggered her outburst, but I was relieved when she yelled, "And so is my father. Why don't you just leave me alone?" She walloped my arm with a solid right.

"Because you want to tell me."

"I do not!"

"Then why did you come to my hotel room? Why didn't

you just walk past me at the Mannings'? Why did you have coffee with me?"

"Because I was stupid," she cried.

"Because you want help. Goddamn it, let me help."

Rosalie covered her face with her hands and stood there sobbing. "My father shot him," she mumbled into her hands when the crying subsided.

"Who?" I asked, leading her back to our old bench.

"It was an accident. He would never hurt anybody." The tears started anew at the thought of her father hurting anyone.

"Who did he shoot?" I asked, trying to sit on the side of my thigh.

"Michael."

"Your father shot Michael?" This was getting weirder by the second.

She nodded.

"When?"

"Last night. That's why I met him." She sucked in a breath of air that sounded like ripples.

"Who, Michael?"

"Yes, Michael." She sighed as if I was dumber than a doorknob.

"You met Michael because your father shot him?" I repeated thickly.

She nodded. "Matt brought him to my place. The last thing they wanted was to have to go to the hospital and explain what happened."

"What did happen?"

She blew her nose into a wad of tissues. "Dad threatened Michael with his rifle. He jerked—my guess is it might have been his first heart seizure—and squeezed the trigger by accident. The shot hit Michael in the arm."

I thought about this while she wiped under her eyes with the tissues. Matt, Michael, and Paddy had all been together at Hannah Miller's house the night before. But there had to have been someone else there, the same person who had

236

called me and told me that Michael needed help. The only one I could think of was Carrot-top, but then, he was the only other player that I knew. If he had participated in beating Michael up just the day before—and I knew he had—I couldn't figure out why he would call me in the city, two and a half hours away, to help protect Michael from his father. This wasn't making any sense.

"Why did Matt bring him to you?"

"I'm a registered nurse."

"So the man gets shot at close range with a rifle and he's fine the next day?" I said this with exaggerated doubt.

"It was only a twenty-two and it was just a flesh wound."

"Where was he shot?" I asked.

"Right shoulder."

"And the bullet?"

"I suspect it's not too far from where it was fired."

"Did the police tell you about finding a bullet?"

She shook her head. "No, just that dad's rifle had been recently fired. That's all."

"Did they question the gun being fired?"

She shrugged. "They did, but they think they know what he shot at."

"What?"

"Deer." She looked at me directly for the first time since having left the restaurant. Despite her angst, the mischievous Delaney gene had her eyes sparkling. Clearly, once the pain of loss had subsided, this final episode in Paddy Delaney's life was going down in the annals of their family history as a most entertaining gotcha. I, however, was not particularly amused.

"So that's it? The investigation is closed?"

She nodded.

"It can't be."

"I believe for all intents and purposes, it is. We've lived here a long time and have family on the force . . ."

I didn't want to debate about whether the police would

continue to investigate. If they weren't interested in details like the whereabouts of the bullet that ostensibly grazed Callahan, why Delaney was in his undies, how come the place came to be in shambles, and what the hell was I doing there . . . it wasn't my concern. All I wanted was to find Michael Callahan.

"Why did your father threaten Michael?"

The mischievousness faded abruptly and was replaced with timidity.

"Everything goes back to the person you all feel compelled to protect, doesn't it?" I pushed.

I watched as she wove the wet tissues around her fingers. "It's not that simple," she finally said.

"You'd be surprised." I paused. "Who is she? It is a she, isn't it?" Suddenly Donna Frost popped into my head.

"It's all so terribly tragic."

"What is?"

"That Michael's suspected of killing his wife when he's only capable of hurting himself."

"That's quite an insight for having only met the man last night."

"I'm quite a gal," she said self-mockingly.

"I don't doubt that for one second. It's obvious that your capacity to love is so great that you're willing to make yourself miserable to protect someone else. Is it worth it?"

She stared at the street and shrugged.

"You know, I had a cousin once. Everyone wanted to protect her. They were convinced—because she went through a spell of depression in her teens—that she was emotionally frail. As a result they never told her things that they thought would upset her, things about her family that she needed to know, had every right to know. By taking control away from her, they ultimately did her more damage than good. They thought they were protecting her, but they were really only protecting themselves. It was very sad; she thought she was crazy because they treated her like she was."

"What happened to her?" Rosalie asked.

"Well, she went through a bout of alcoholism, decided at forty-four to clean up her act, and is living in California with a physical therapist."

There was a long pause. I was surprised at how still the streets were. Not a sound other than some fat bluejays arguing in a maple tree.

"You need to talk to my sister, Mary."

"Okay. Where is she?"

She paused, but only briefly. "At the convent."

It hit me like a ton of bricks. "Mary *Grace*?" I asked, remembering my meeting with Nurse Nivens, who had commented on Michael's friendship with a nun named Mary Grace.

"That's right." She was stunned. "How did you know?"

My body was electrified with the excitement of knowing I'd just hit the jackpot.

"Is that mansion on Twenty-seven a convent?" I asked, standing up, ready to bolt to the rental bubble car.

"In Water Mill?"

I nodded.

"Yes. That's where she is."

I promised Rosalie that if her sister didn't want to talk to me, I wouldn't force it. But as I headed back east, I couldn't help but hope that what I had was Michael Callahan's alibi for the time of his wife's murder. Connect-the-dots had always been a favorite game of mine as a kid, along with What's Wrong With This Picture? and Can You Find the Nine Ninas in This Picture?

I thought of Selma Onderdonk and how pleased she would be to know that Michael had been exonerated of a crime she was certain he hadn't committed. Again I saw her face in my mind's eye; her eyes magnified behind huge glasses, lipstick smeared just outside the edges of her lips, her soft-spoken gentleness as a woman whose grace and dignity hadn't been sacrificed to age. I knew she would be

239

thrilled to know about Michael, but I couldn't rejoice. As close as I was to proving that he *hadn't* killed her granddaughter, I was light-years away from providing even a suspect, let alone proof of someone else's guilt. Though I hadn't actually been hired to find out who was *responsible* for Jessica Callahan's death, I knew there would be no closure—for either Selma or me—if I didn't at least try to answer all the questions.

I pulled into the convent driveway and parked in a lot next to the main building. Usually when I reach this stage of an investigation I'm charged and unstoppable. But it was more than the four thousand pinpricks in my ass that had me taking the steps slowly. I realized as I walked up the steps that I had never interviewed a nun before. Not that that mattered. I had interviewed plenty of religious folks before—why, I'd even tussled with a rotund rabbi once— but this felt different. Maybe it was because the Delaney tribe treated their sister Mary Grace with kid gloves—like my fictitious cousin in California—but as much as I wanted to get the truth, I was dreading talking to her.

I knocked softly at the thick wooden door, and waited. I knocked again, harder, this time checking the general area for a doorbell. There was none. Finally I took a deep breath, pushed my shoulders back and down, grasped the doorknob, and let myself into the Villa Madonna.

Twenty-two

"May I help you?" A long-faced, plain-looking woman dressed in a dark sweater and skirt greeted me suspiciously. She had found me wandering from room to room in the main part of the building.

"Yes. Thank you. I'm looking for Mary Grace," I said casually, hoping to sound friendly enough to be led right to the protected waif.

Her face hardened as she smiled. "Sister Mary Grace isn't receiving visitors today. Perhaps I can assist you?" She took two baby steps toward the front door.

"Actually, I need to see Mary Grace. I have something for her." I motioned to the back of the house and took a brazen step in the general direction.

"Excuse me, miss, but Sister Mary Grace isn't here." She made a sweeping gesture with her hand toward the front door, which was my cue to leave.

"Mary Grace isn't here or she isn't receiving visitors?" I gave her a look that said we both knew a nun had just lied. Big trouble.

"She isn't here." She looked away from me and stepped once more in the direction of the entrance.

"Really? Where is she?" I stayed glued in place until she turned around and looked me straight in the eyes.

"I beg your pardon?" Her voice was strained.

"I have something for her." I examined a framed painting of a beach scene hanging in the darkened hallway.

"Well, I'm sure you can just leave it with me. I'll see that she gets it." Her cheeks were growing faintly flushed and I knew that we had an A-type personality at work here.

"Forgive me, but I think Mary Grace is here and I'm not leaving until I see her."

"What did you say?"

"I said I won't leave." I gave her my back and studied a photograph of a fishing vessel from days gone by.

"You leave me no choice but to call the police." Her voice was as sharp as a razor blade.

"Sister Catherine, is everything all right?" I turned and saw the older woman who had come to the aid of the young woman in the driveway. She held a book in the crook of one arm and a fabric doll in the other.

"This rude young woman wants to see Sister Mary Grace." Catherine, who had to be my age, shot me a smarmy glance and then turned and softened her entire tone of being for the gray-haired woman.

"I see. Well, thank you, Sister Catherine, I'll take care of this." The nun's cheeks were covered with tiny broken capillaries, which had made them look rosy in the driveway.

As soon as Catherine had left, the older nun asked me who I was and just what I wanted. I told her my name and explained that Rosalie Delaney had suggested I contact her sister. She heard me out and asked me to join her as she moved toward the back of the house. "I was just going to my office."

I fell in step beside her and discovered that despite her age and size, Janet moved quickly. "I'm playing matchmaker today. I know a little girl who will give this lady a fine home." She held up the doll as we hurried through the wide corridor to the back of the house, where we entered the last room. Here there was a wall of windows facing a large pond. "I won't be but a minute." She motioned to the room before us and suggested that I make myself comfortable. Without another word she popped into an adjoining room and shut the door behind her.

I think it is a strange and curious thing that all the best property in the world seems to be owned, almost exclusively, by religious organizations. Big, huge, tax-exempt ones at ritzy addresses that attempt to portray themselves as poor with their worn yet stately furnishings. I walked to the window and took in the view. Geese were congregating on the well-manicured lawn, that stretched out to the water's edge. Weeping willows along the shore resembled languid maidens dipping their fingertips into the cool water, while above, the sky was dotted here and there with little lavender clouds. It was a scene of perfection. God's creation to be sure. Off the top of my head, I knew about four dozen city kids who didn't have an inkling that beauty like this even existed.

I was thinking about the kids in the Headstart and Big Sister programs I've been involved in when I felt a hand touch my shoulder.

"Are you all right?" she asked, her face open and warm.

"Yes, thank you. I'm fine." I gestured to the vista. "I was just thinking about several children I know who could put that lawn to good use."

"Is that so?" She pushed the corners of her mouth down and nodded slowly. "We should talk about that."

"I'd like that. But in the meantime, I need to talk to Mary Grace."

She took a deep breath and exhaled slowly. She then lowered herself onto a leather parsons chair and waited for me to join her.

"I'm happy to talk to the Mother Superior first, or whoever is in charge here."

"That would be me," she said almost distractedly.

"Well then, Mother, may I please see Mary Grace?"

"Please, call me Janet. I've asked someone to fetch her, but whether Mary Grace speaks to you is up to her."

"I see. Thank you."

"It's certainly none of my business what you need or want from Mary Grace, but as her friend, I must caution you to be kind."

"I've been warned that Mary Grace is . . . fragile?"

Janet looked surprised, stared at me in disbelief, and finally let out a fabulous belly laugh.

I smiled uneasily. "What?" I asked, feeling like I had just committed a funny faux pas.

"Mary Grace as fragile." Janet's wide grin was contagious. "I've never heard anything more ludicrous in my life."

"Really?" I wondered for half a second if we were talking about the same person.

"She is a steady, bright, wonderful young woman who happens to be in pain right now. That's why I asked that you be kind. This is not an easy time for her."

"I see."

Behind Janet I saw a woman enter the room. She was slender and pale with chiseled features. She had cheekbones Audrey Hepburn would have been jealous of, and dark, sad, swollen eyes. It was the woman I had seen in the driveway. It was Mary Grace Delaney. I stood slowly, mesmerized. She didn't look fragile. Beautiful, yes, but not fragile.

She placed one hand against the door frame while the other clutched a fistful of tissues.

Janet turned around and motioned for her to join us.

"How are you, dear?" Janet hefted herself off the chair and met Mary Grace halfway into the room, where she placed a protective arm over the woman's shoulders.

Mary Grace nodded and mumbled softly, "I'm fine." She looked tired and drawn.

"Mary Grace, this is Sydney Sloane. She'd like to have a few words with you."

At the mention of my name, there was instant recognition on her part.

"Miss Sloane understands that you may not want to talk," Janet added. "The decision is yours."

Mary Grace nodded and squeezed her friend's hand. "It's all right, Janet, thank you. I want to talk to Ms. Sloane." She moved away from Janet and seemed to float to the windows, where she stood and watched the geese. I thanked Janet for her help and watched as she went back to her office.

When we were alone Mary Grace initiated the conversation. "Thank you for coming out so quickly last night."

"*You* were responsible for the call?"

She nodded.

"But it wasn't you who *made* the call?"

"No. It was my brother Logan."

"The young redhead who was here earlier?"

"Yes. I didn't know you were here." She said this as she watched the geese.

"I'm sorry about your father." I offered my condolences and followed her gaze. A particularly large goose was taking flight. The little fatty looked like it was about to drop from sheer exhaustion after the first ten flaps, but when it was finally airborne, it was gorgeous.

Mary Grace stared out the window, her bloodshot eyes apparently focused on nothing.

"Logan said you were with Dad when he died."

"I was." I had already decided that with this Delaney daughter I wasn't going to give information until I got some. "I know how much pain you must be in right now, Mary Grace, and I'm sure it seems heartless that I'd ask you to answer questions on the day your father died, but . . . I have no choice." I was met with no objections, so I continued. "Do you know why I'm here?"

She nodded, still staring blankly out at the birds. "You're looking for Michael Callahan."

"That's right. You and he are friends?"

Her right eyebrow moved a fraction of an inch, but that was her only response.

"Do you know where Michael was when his wife was murdered?"

She lowered her eyes and pressed her thin lips together. What little color she had had when she had first walked into the room was now gone. She swallowed with difficulty and nodded.

"Was he with you?" I asked softly.

I must have waited two minutes before she finally answered. "Yes," she said.

Call it a hunch, but I had a feeling that if Michael and Mary Grace had been out to lunch or tending to the sick at the time Jessica was killed, neither of them would have had a problem telling the police. Logic, therefore, dictated that Mary Grace and Michael had—at the precise moment his wife was killed—been doing the deed, so to speak. It explained everything: his chivalrous attempt to protect her, her family's attempt to preserve her honor, his guilt, her guilt, her father's rage, her brothers' indignation, her sister's confusion. It was as if this enormous lightbulb went on in my head.

"Shall we sit down?" I asked gently. Though she was not the helpless woman I had anticipated meeting, she was hurting and it showed. Instinctively, I liked her.

Once seated, she took a deep breath and looked me straight in the eyes. "I believe I owe you an explanation." She glanced down at the bunch of tattered tissues in her hand and shook her head. Clearly she wanted to talk but was having trouble finding the right words. I looked down at my own hands and thought about sex, which was—I assumed—at the root of all this. Celibacy. Masturbation. Intimacy. Lust. Passion. Words conjured up images, like flash cards. The nun and the doctor. Images that had probably driven Paddy Delaney and his boys from shame to rage, a quick and easy step.

"Ever since I was a little girl, I wanted to be a nun." She paused and looked surprised, as if that were the last thing she had expected to come out of her mouth.

"It's okay," I reassured her. "Go on."

"My parents, especially Dad, had wanted that for me

246

ever since I can remember. By the time I was thirteen, it had become my dream," she said almost coldly as she tore apart the tissue in hand. "I won't take up your time with all the details, but a year ago I met Dr. Callahan." She stared at my neck. I ran my hand along my neck and collarbone in a casual way. But there was nothing. Just a new bumper crop of tiny skin tabs that had only started appearing in the last year . . . a little sign of aging that no one had ever bothered to mention.

I encouraged her to continue. "How did you and Michael meet?"

"I had just arrived at St. Mary's. He was one of my first friends there. He's a wonderful doctor." When she mentioned Michael, there was a visible change to her whole being, a lowering of the guard, so to speak.

"During the last several months we had a patient in the children's ward, a little boy named Todd. He had contracted the AIDS virus through his mother's boyfriend." Her hands went limp in her lap. "This poor child had a miserable life, and yet he was one of the most positive people I'd ever met. So courageous." She paused and tried to fight the tears. "The day Todd died, I was devastated. It just didn't seem right. In his short life he had known suffering and gave only joy in return." She pressed the tissues to her mouth and covered her eyes with her other hand.

After over twenty years in this business, I should probably be inured to the discomfort of sitting across from someone who is crying, but I'm not. I always want to make them feel better somehow, and I inevitably have to sit there and keep my own counsel.

"I'm sorry," she said when she had caught her breath. "Anyway, I had a hard time after Todd died. I couldn't find comfort anywhere, not even in my faith. I couldn't understand this child's suffering. He was such a special little boy. Michael knew that, and I guess initially we tried to help each other through our loss."

Mary Grace sat rigid, her slender fingers destroying the

now-worthless Kleenexes. I got the sense that Mary Grace needed to confess and—fortunately for me—I happened to be It.

"I was with Michael when Jessica was killed." She looked me straight in the eyes as if awaiting my judgment. I had none to offer.

"He hasn't told the police because he wanted to protect me, and, sadly, up until this point, I've let him. I was . . . afraid? Ashamed? Frightened? Confused? Selfish. Stupid. My father and my brothers were so concerned about my honor . . ." She looked up and at me with unabashed wonder. "I don't know what honor is. I don't know what it means. And I may not know what love is, or loyalty, or faith in God anymore, but I do know that Todd's life wasn't in vain. I do trust that God brought us together for a reason."

"You and Michael?" I asked.

The corner of her mouth twitched. "I was talking about Todd, but I'm sure God had a reason for bringing Michael into my life."

The more she talked, the more I liked Mary Grace.

"I didn't know about Michael's arrest until several days after the fact. You see, after the day we spent together, I had to leave New York. I left that very night. I came home for a few days' rest. I was confused. I needed to be alone. During that time, I made many decisions, among them not to see Michael again. One night, however, I was watching the news and I saw that Michael had been arrested." Her voice grew stronger as she opened up. "God works in mysterious ways. I was afraid for Michael, I was afraid for myself, but there was no question that I had to tell the police where he had been.

"I also knew that before I did that, however, I had to tell my family." She stared at the floor and smiled sadly.

"That must have been difficult."

"My father and my oldest brother heard only what they wanted and responded in kind. They were livid. Dad shut me out, and Matt was impossible. They had each drawn their own erroneous conclusion, and nothing I could say, or do, would make a difference to either of them." She tucked the useless tissues into her skirt pocket. "I became so confused and consumed with self-loathing I didn't know which end was up. All I knew was that I had turned my back on my faith and for that I was being punished."

I shifted uncomfortably in my seat. It might have been the physical pain in my bottom, but I had a feeling it was more that I find the concept of a vindictive God unsettling. The idea that God would want to punish us for being the only thing we can be—human—is a notion that I am convinced only man could have contrived.

"That's when I came here. I needed God's help, and I knew I would find guidance and kindness here."

"Janet seems to be a nurturing person," I said, certain that the nasty Smarmelite, Catherine, couldn't have done much for Mary Grace.

"Oh, she is. All the women here are." Mary Grace sighed, letting her shoulders release for the first time since sitting. "There was no question about what was the right thing to do; I had to call the police. But again, my family vigorously objected. They were afraid of scandal, and at my father's age, I couldn't blame him." She rubbed her hands together like Lady Macbeth washing away imagined blood. "But after having made so many mistakes recently, I knew I had to do the right thing. Whether my family approved or not, I had to contact the authorities. I also had to tell Michael what I was going to do, so it didn't make things worse for him.

"I called him at home, just after he had just been released from prison, and told him what I was going to do. He insisted I not do it. He assured me that he would find a way to prove his innocence without my having to be involved." Her knuckles were white as she continued wringing her hands. "I was confused, or maybe I was looking for an easy way out of this mess, but I . . . I promised him I wouldn't call.'' She reached into her pocket and pulled out the clump of shredded tissues again, looked at it as if to use it, and then put it back in her pocket.

"When was that?" I asked, handing her a packet of tissues.

"Thank you." She pulled out two, turned her head away from me, and blew her nose. "Tuesday."

I did a mental tally and figured out that since this was Thursday, Tuesday was the day Michael had been released from custody, the day I met him. Time flies when you're having fun.

"In the meantime, my father and Matt had gotten it into their heads that they had to meet Michael and find out what he intended to do. Dad wanted to make sure that I was kept out of it." She put the used Kleenex into her pocket with the others. "I found out last night that they had gone into the city to have a talk with him the day he was released from jail.

"I think that in reality, I didn't want to accept responsibility for my own actions. I thought that I could hide in here and everything would miraculously work out just fine. It doesn't work that way." She rubbed her palms against the skirt draped over her knees and looked gracefully down at the empty seat beside her on the sofa. She looked more like a ballerina than a nun. Her grace reminded me of the lone swan that lives in the East Hampton pond. I noticed that little flecks of tissue clung to her navy-blue skirt.

"So, when did you speak to Michael next?"

"He came out here yesterday or the day before, actually, and insisted on seeing me. The poor man is consumed with guilt." She looked as if nothing could be more absurd.

"It would seem as though he has good reason," I observed. I didn't think it was necessary for me to point out that cheating on his wife with a nun was enough to make a God-fearing, moral person feel a deep sense of guilt.

Anger flashed across Mary Grace's face.

"What?" I asked.

"You disappoint me, Ms. Sloane. I had thought you would be different." She looked away from me. "I don't know why."

"Different from what?"

"It's true that I was with Michael when Jessica was killed, but why must you all draw the same licentious conclusion?"

I suddenly felt about two inches tall. "I don't know what you mean." I managed not to stammer, knowing perfectly well I had been caught with my thoughts in the gutter . . . figures a nun would find it there.

"You know perfectly well what I mean." Her anger made her direct.

"If you mean I assumed that you and Michael had made love, you're right." Knowing that she was a woman who could deal with truth, I saw no reason to beat around the bush.

"We didn't."

"Then why did you run away? Why did you make it seem as though you had been intimate?"

"*I* didn't make it seem anything. People draw their own conclusions. I 'ran away' because to me the thought is as good—or as bad—as the deed." Her face flushed, but she didn't look away from me.

"Mary Grace, where were you the day Jessica was killed?"

She swallowed. "With Michael at his friend's apartment."

"And how long were you there? What did you do?"

"We were there for several hours. We talked." Again her face flushed crimson, but she remained steadfast.

"Talked? In his friend's apartment? Surely you see how contrived this sounds. When you're interrogated by the police—as I assure you you will be—they're going to want to know all the sticky little details. I can just about promise you that they will draw the same licentious conclusion, not because they're dirty-minded vulgarians, but because you are both acting as if you have something to hide, something to be ashamed of.''

"But we *do* have something to be ashamed of!'' she cried and hit her thighs with her fists. ''Don't you understand?''

"No, I don't. Even if you had been intimate with Michael, I don't think you're bad or have anything to be ashamed of, Mary Grace, I think you're human. People don't turn off the need for comfort and love just because they choose a profession or put on a habit, or collar. Stop judging yourself so harshly, and please stop assuming I'm going to judge you. I'm just trying to do my job and prove that Michael couldn't have killed his wife. After that I want to find out who did, and I'm running out of time, so, please, tell me what happened that day,'' I implored her.

"Our friendship had become more intense after Todd died.'' Mary Grace sounded flat, but she spoke without interruption. ''Jessica was in California and Michael didn't have anyone to turn to in his pain, so we turned to each other. Before we knew it, we both had to acknowledge that there was a certain . . . attraction between us.'' She told the story to her hands, which she kneaded in her lap.

"It was impossible to talk about it openly because we were always in a public forum. We had to talk, we had to iron it out, we had to confront it and be done with it once and for all, but in order to do that, we needed privacy.

"Michael had a friend whose apartment was uptown, away from the hospital and that neighborhood.'' She paused. ''We met at two-thirty. He brought coffee and crumb cake. We were there for three hours.'' She laced her fingers together and squeezed. ''Todd had a thing he called his life list. It was a list of things he wanted to do before he died, and he always had me adding to it for him. When he died, I realized, I didn't have a life list. Not long after he died, I was up one night thinking about him and decided to write a list of my own. Much to my surprise, I wrote 'Kiss Michael Callahan.' '' She flushed from her collar to the tips of her ears. "I tore up the list. But that day, in his friend's apartment, as we tried to grapple with our feelings, Michael did kiss me." She grimaced, but the impact of that breathtaking moment in her life was electrifying even from where I was sitting.

If I wanted to get all the information I needed before losing her, it was time to change the subject. "What happened last night?" I asked.

"Michael called me and insisted on seeing me. I owed it to him, to both of us. My brother Logan went with me to Montauk where Michael was staying. We were there maybe fifteen minutes before Matt came in with my dad." She chewed on her lower lip. "Michael was a mess. That's when I learned what Matt and Logan had done, but Michael kept insisting that it was fine and he promised me that he would be okay. You see, when we first got there, Michael gave me your card and said you were working to prove he was innocent without having to drag me into it." She glanced over at me with what I took to be hope. I said nothing.

"Anyway, my father had a bag of things I'd left at the hospital, he'd retrieved them without my permission, and he had his rifle. I knew he wouldn't use it, he just wanted to scare Michael, and that made me sick. I was enraged, but there was nothing I could do. Dad made Logan and me leave. That's when I made Logan call you." She stood up and walked to a table where there was a vase of tulips. She eased a tulip from the vase and pulled off a dead leaf. "I made him pull over on the side of the road. Logan's my baby brother and probably my closest friend. I think he was scared, he'd never seen me this way before . . . I was beside myself with fear for Michael."

I didn't know if Mary Grace knew that before her father died, he had, indeed, shot Michael. I knew it wasn't a kettle of fish I wanted to stir up. One thing was disturbing me, however, and I knew I had to address it.

253

"Mary Grace?" I said to her back. "Jessica didn't die because of you and Michael."

"No?" She rested her hands on the tabletop.

"No. You think that was God's way of punishing you both, don't you?"

She said nothing.

"For what it's worth, I may not believe in religion, but I do believe in God, and to me the foundation of that faith is love, not punishment." I stood up to leave. "I also think that people have a harder time looking inside rather than out, because we're more afraid of what we can't see. Don't be so afraid, Mary Grace. Be as kind to yourself as you would be to a stranger . . . or to Todd." I got as far as the door when I remembered Patrick Delaney's last words. "Mary Grace?" She looked up, startled, as if she had already forgotten I had ever been there. "Before your father died, he said, 'Tell her I'm sorry.' I don't know if he meant you or not, but from what I've learned about your family so far, I'd say it was a pretty good guess. I just thought you'd want to know."

Without another word I left Sister Mary Grace alone with her thoughts. I had the answers I had come for. I knew that Michael Callahan couldn't have killed his wife, because, because, because.

As I gingerly eased myself into the bubble car, I considered my options. As far as I knew, I had none. I could only head out to Montauk and have a little chat with Michael Callahan. Now that I knew his alibi, I knew that somewhere in the greater Manhattan area was the person who had really killed Jessica Callahan. I was determined to find out who that was. I was still angry that Callahan had thought he could bribe me, and angrier that he had lied to Mary Grace, telling her that I was working to prove his innocence, when in fact he had tried to bribe me to lay off the case. If Callahan had lied to her, I wondered just what lies he had told me. I turned east onto 27 and knew that I had to get gas soon or I'd never make it to Montauk. And I was convinced that there were more answers awaiting me in Montauk.

Twenty-three

There were two cars in the driveway when I arrived at Hannah Miller's Montauk house: Callahan's Toyota and a racing green Jaguar.

I parked behind the Jaguar and noticed that the grounds looked quite different in the light of day. Less daunting. I crossed the front lawn and cringed when I saw the deck on the side of the house where my buttocks had taken a beating the night before.

As I neared the front door, I heard voices in the back of the house, coming from the patio. I passed the entrance and walked around the side of the house, where I saw Michael Callahan and Dr. Cyclops. He was sitting in a chair with his back to me and she was pacing back and forth like a cat ready to pounce. A large canvas table umbrella was opened, shading the table and chairs where Michael sat nursing a cup of something. Hannah was clearly on a diatribe.

". . . she said? Please understand that you are my friend, Michael, and I worry about you. I can't understand the sense behind—" Hannah stopped short as soon as she saw me. "What in God's name are *you* doing here?" She stopped pacing, squinted over at me, and let out an exasperated sigh, as if I was the cause of all her troubles.

"Dr. Miller, do you have any idea how much trouble you're in?" I asked, joining them on the brick patio.

"Excuse me?" When she squinted, her upper lip pulled way up, exposing her crooked teeth, making her look remarkably like an albino mole.

I ordered Dr. Miller to sit down. By now I was standing next to Michael, who, apart from his black eye and swollen nose from when the Delaney boys had visited him in Brooklyn, looked none the worse for the wear. His right arm was resting in a sling, but that was the only sign that he had been shot less than a day earlier.

"*Just who do you think you are*?" To prove her indignation, Hannah stressed every word, which only made her sound like a character in a Restoration comedy.

"Sit down," I repeated coldly.

"I don't think so." Her words were like little pellets. "If you don't leave my property immediately, I'll call the police. After your involvement in whatever happened here last night, I'm sure they'd like to see *you* again."

I didn't like her, I just didn't like her.

I had a fleeting fantasy of pulling out my Walther, pointing it in her face, and shutting her up, but I knew this was only because I still blamed her for my splinter-ridden bummy. Instead, by the time she finished her threat, I had pulled a chair next to Michael's and joined him. A word to the wise: Patio chairs are not recommended seating for people with tush conditions.

"Go ahead. Call them." I gestured to the house. "I can't wait to tell them about your complicity in Jessica Callahan's murder."

"*What*?" she screamed loud enough to wake Paddy Delaney.

"Withholding information from the police is frowned upon, Hannah, especially during a murder investigation." I smiled from behind my sunglasses, knowing this would only irritate her further.

She sputtered and paced before demanding, "Michael, are you just going to sit there, or what?"

"Sit down, Hannah." Michael's voice was thin and tired.

256

Hannah opened and closed her mouth several times but fortunately issued no sounds. When she finally plopped down at the foot of a chaise, I turned to Michael and asked pleasantly, "Are you all right?" I glanced at his shoulder.

"I'm fine." He sighed with a look that said he didn't care.

"Good. Hey, I just saw Mary Grace."

He closed his eyes as if to block me out.

"I'm curious about something, Michael. Did you often lie to Mary Grace?"

"Just what are you talking about?" His jaw twitched.

I got off the chair and walked to the edge of the patio. "I believe you told her that I was going to prove you innocent and keep her out of it at the same time. Did you tell her that?"

"It wasn't necessarily a lie," he said, hedging.

"Well, considering that you had tried to bribe me to let go of the investigation, I think I'd categorize that as a lie."

"I didn't try to bribe you." He was sincerely indignant.

"Really? Well then, let's take a glance at your record for veracity, shall we?" I stood up and paced past Hannah, who was folded into herself and fuming. "I understand why you didn't tell me about Mary Grace and the Delaney clan, but beyond that I'm a bit baffled. You drop off Auggie at your neighbor's and tell her that I'll be by later that day to pick the dog up. Let's not mince words, Doctor. That was a lie. But because I'm in the middle of an investigation representing a woman I happen to like immensely, I agreed to pick up the puppy you had abandoned."

He started to object, but I put out my hands to stop him.

"I picked up the dog so I could get some answers from your neighbor and perhaps get inside your house for another look-see. There's no need to go pale, Doctor, I didn't find anything. However, when I do get the dog I find a note and a check in her bag of belongings." I stood four feet in front of him with my back to the Cyclops, who sounded like she was whimpering.

"I never once tried to bribe you," he yelled over my words. "The check was my way of thanking you for taking Auggie."

"Bullshit! You're a manipulator, Callahan, and people like you are experts at twisting the truth to fit their needs. You enclosed a ten-thousand-dollar check and asked me to back off the case in the same little thank-you note, but you want to pretend it's not a bribe? I don't like people who think they can buy me off and I don't like liars."

"He is not a liar!" Hannah Miller cried out, bringing silence to the garden, including a family of catbirds in pursuit of a squirrel. I turned and looked down at her. Her pearly white skin looked even whiter against her stained, cream-colored pants suit, and had it not been for her black sandals, she might have all but blended in with the beige chaise-longue. She white-knuckled the side of the chaise as huge tears streaked her face. "He's not a liar," she whispered.

The Hannah Miller sitting before us was neither a doctor nor a woman, a nuisance nor a witch. She was a lonely, sad little girl who just couldn't hold on anymore. Tears slipped down her cheeks as she exhaled an almost incoherent outpouring of feelings that she had obviously kept bottled up for years. It would have been embarrassing had it not been so morbidly hypnotic. It was, however, the last thing that I had expected, and, from the look on Michael's face, the effect was equally jarring for him.

Michael sat there, mute, his face completely impassive, as she carried on about having been in love with him for years, how he had made his first mistake when he married that "lunatic" and then how she tried to protect him from this last unforgivable, depraved mistake of having fallen in love with a nun.

Hannah Miller's pathetic emotional eruption might have stirred compassion or even sympathy from me, but as it concluded on such an ugly, angry note, I wound up feeling only impatience. Having been the recipient of Hannah's malediction, Michael seemed stunned but he was impossible to read. When it was over and Hannah sat there wiping her nose with her sleeve, I turned and walked to the far end of the patio away from them. As much as I didn't like the Cyclops, I knew that the two of them needed a little privacy to work through this stuff. I decided I'd give them a few minutes and walked around to the side of the house, noticing that through the hedges of evergreen, one could easily spy on one's neighbors. As I peered through the lower branches, I saw a woman with short gray hair in a colorful housedress reprimanding a feisty German shepherd who couldn't have cared less. "Taffy! Taffy get over here this minute." It was a voice I would have obeyed, had I been Taffy, but the German Shepherd continued to prance and play just beyond her reach. Her paws sounded like horse hoofs against the ground, and I wondered if Auggie would be happy in this woman's backyard with Taffy. Taffy picked up my scent and came barreling over to the wire fence between the pine trees. "That's it, I'm gonna get the stick," Taffy's owner warned. The pup and I were face-to-face and I could almost see her thinking, *Oh oh, not the stick*, as she ducked her head and scurried back to the deck where the woman hadn't moved an inch. My guess is, there was no stick.

Time up, I went back to Michael and Hannah. She had moved from her perch on the chaise and was pacing in the grass, maybe ten feet into the yard. Michael was still sitting, his cheek resting on the knuckles of his left hand.

"Excuse me, folks, I know you two have things to discuss here, so I'd like to finish up with you, Michael, if that's okay."

He looked as if he was going to be sick.

"Good. Now then, we've established where you were at the time of your wife's murder—"

"I'll deny it."

"Frankly, Doctor, I don't care what you do. As far as I'm concerned, every single person I've come in contact with regarding this case—with the exception of the woman who hired me—has got a whole subset of problems I don't even want to go near. You want to spend the rest of your life in jail for a crime you didn't commit? Do it. You don't care if the person who really murdered your wife is out there free as a bird?" I shrugged and held my palms up in an *I don't get it* gesture. "Fine. You think if you can protect Mary Grace's honor that way, good for you—it makes you a moron—but good for you."

Hannah started to say something, but I whirled on her and warned, "Don't even start." Turning back to Michael, I said, "Humor me. Let's just assume I'm going to see this case through to the end because Selma Onderdonk matters to me." He flinched but said nothing. "You may not care who killed Jessica, but Selma does, and I intend on finding it out for her. So if you could just answer a few questions, honestly, I'd appreciate it.

"Okay. Can you think of any of your wife's friends or associates who might have had a grudge against her?"

He shook his head and said, "I told you, she was well-loved."

"Oh please, she was a mental case," Hannah said bitterly.

"Shut the fuck up!" Michael shot out of his seat, causing the chair to go flying behind him. He grabbed the coffee mug and flung it against a tree. It bounced, rather than broke, and rolled onto the grass maybe three feet to the right of Hannah. Her eyes were like saucers as her hands curled into tight little fists and her shoulders squared back. "Just shut the fuck up, you sour old jealous bitch! I've had it! Had it! For years I've listened to you put Jessica down, and I didn't say anything because I knew where it was coming from and I just wasn't fucking man enough to deal with you directly. Jessica knew, too, but she felt sorry for you, that's why she put up with your snide, patronizing ways. But goddamn it, Hannie, you seemed downright fucking pleased when she died." Michael's face was beet-red and wet with tears and saliva. When he was able to breathe evenly, he continued. "You think she was a mental case because she put herself out there for other people, something you have never done in your life for anyone other than me, and even then you did it because you wanted something." He took a deep breath and turned to me. "You want to know who had a grudge against Jessie? Hannah Miller, that's the only person I know of, but do I think she had anything to do with Jessica's death? Absolutely not. I don't know who murdered Jessica and, contrary to what you might think, Ms. Sloane, I do want to find her killer. For all I know it could have been one of those sorry characters she was always helping, though it doesn't seem likely."

"Why?" I interrupted.

"Because nothing was missing. There was no apparent struggle. There were no fingerprints."

"There are three ways to enter the garage, right?"

"That's right. There's the door into the house, the garage door, and another street door, but we never use that one."

"Does the door that leads to the inside of the house lock from both sides?"

"Yeah, it's like the street door; there's a key to lock it from either side, but we only ever locked it when we were in the house."

"What about the street door?"

"We never used it."

"Do the police know which door the killer used to exit?"

"I don't know."

"Were any of Jessica's keys missing?"

"I don't know."

"How do you not know? You were arrested for this crime."

"I didn't actually participate, but Marshall would know," he said referring to his attorney, Marshall Tucker.

"Call him."

"Now?" Hannah Miller's irritating voice scratched through what had become a calm of sorts.

"Yes. Now," I said, not taking my eyes off Michael.

He nodded slowly and started toward the house.

"Oh no you don't," Hannah called out, charging toward the patio with her arms pumping widely. "You don't treat me like garbage and then think you can use me and my place. Get out of here, both of you. I am fed up." She was waving her arms now, as if to shoo chickens out of the way.

When Michael didn't say anything, I tried to open a dialogue. "Hannah, if you could please—"

"Don't you dare call me Hannah. I am *Doctor* Miller to you. And as far as I'm concerned, you can go and tell the police any damned thing you want. Complicity, my ass." She planted herself back on the patio and faced Michael. "As for you, mister, you're an ingrate and a pig, and as much as you may want to make your little friend here think that you were as good as gold to St. Jessica, the fact is it wasn't always a bed of roses. If it was, Michael, how could you have ever had an interest in that nun?" She paused to let the truth sink in.

"Dr. Miller, let Michael make this call and I promise you, you won't ever have to see me again." The prospect was, I knew, equally enticing to both of us. A long moment passed and I had a flash of Hannah Miller on the playground as a ten-year-old; pink dress, bobbysocks pulled up to bony kneecaps, huddled in play with the one kid in her class more nerdy than she. I felt a pang of sympathy for that other kid as I watched Hannah Miller roll her eyes, clap her hands onto her hips, and sigh, "Okay for Christ sake. Like this couldn't wait another hour."

Forty minutes later I was headed back to East Hampton, having found out from Marshall Tucker that all of Jessica's keys had been accounted for. He also told me that the police had *initially* speculated that the killer left through the house, using the back sliding doors as an exit. One of the doors had actually been ajar when the police arrived. They hypothesized that the killer might have then exited through the backyard, but they dropped that theory when no other fingerprints had been found in the garage or elsewhere in the house. When Michael became the focus of the investigation, all other avenues seemed to have been abandoned.

Leslie was packing up at the hotel when I arrived. Unlike people, puppies have a way of making you feel truly welcomed with their unbridled enthusiasm. Auggie was no different. She made me feel like I was her very, very, very, very, very best friend.

"Hey there. What did the doctor say?" Leslie asked as soon as I walked in.

"I missed the appointment," I admitted.

"What's wrong with you?" Leslie asked as she gathered together the few things she had purchased out here when it was apparent that she was staying.

"I was busy."

"Well, I'm sure he'll be able to take you this afternoon. Then, I think a shopping spree is in order. Courtney's guest house is perfect for a little getaway, and they're going back to Manhattan in a few days. In other words, you and I could have a nice little holiday out here." Clearly this prospect excited her.

It was then that I told her I was headed back to New York.

"You know, as it turns out, the hotel wouldn't mind our staying with Auggie. The owner said that since it's the off-season and he's fallen head over heels in love with Auggie, we could stay." She said this with her back to me as she pulled a tee-shirt out of her bag and refolded it.

I rubbed Auggie's pink belly and felt that familiar pang of guilt I often experience when trying to juggle work and my relationship.

"I can't, honey."

Leslie straightened her back and let out a big sigh.

"Is this because of your car?"

"No. Honestly."

"Because I know how you feel about your car."

"I know you do." It seemed easier for me to address her disappointment than my own feelings of guilt about not wanting her to drive my car. *It's a car for crying out loud*, Minnie's voice sang out in the back of my head. "I'm disappointed, too, Lez." I said. "It would have been nice to have a few days out here."

"Don't you think it's strange, Syd?" She turned and looked soft and sad as she knelt down on the bed with Auggie and me.

"What's that, babe?"

"Most of your life is absorbed with death."

"It is not," I defended myself automatically. Her bone of contention regarding my work had, during the last few years, seemed to mellow.

She reached out and rubbed my ankle while Auggie whined for more attention. "Don't get defensive. I'm not saying that it's bad—"

"But it's inaccurate," I cut her off. "First of all, most of my work is tedious and dull—you've said so yourself—but when it comes to cases like this, it's not death that absorbs me, but life. People left behind are hurt, and they want answers. I can't think of anything worse than not knowing how someone I loved died or who played God and killed them."

"But how can one day make a difference? And not even a full day. Just spend tonight here, that's half a day off, and then you can go back tomorrow. We could go back together. In your own car." She inched closer to the puppy and me. "I have you here now and I want to keep you."

"My client is a ninety-two-year-old woman who just lost her granddaughter. For all I know, a day will make all the difference and I don't want to take that chance." I shifted down on the bed and spooned Leslie from behind. We lay there, me holding Leslie, Leslie holding Auggie, and for a moment it felt as if we could be lulled into sleep and stay there forever.

"You should know I understand," she said, pressing my hand closer to her chest.

"I know." I tightened my hold on her and let myself relax.

"About your car. I'm sorry I took it without asking." She pushed her backside into me.

"Thank you." I let her snuggle closer.

"I honestly tried to reach you first to get your okay, but when I couldn't, well, I'd already gotten myself into the pickle by offering. I never thought you'd get so mad."

"I'm really sorry about that. I don't know why I'm so—"

"Caryn." She cut me off before I could finish my sentence.

"What's that?"

"Caryn. You're so possessive of the car because it's the last thing you have that you bought with Caryn. Can you imagine my chagrin when I heard her message on the answering machine before I left you mine about the car? But that's not the point, the point is you had every right to be upset. I know how you feel about the car."

"No, no, the point is you let a total stranger drive it, that was what upset me more than anything else. And now that I have you here, why did you let him drive it and what exactly did he do to it?" I was up on one elbow now looking down on her.

She took a deep breath and sat up. "I let him drive it for the same reason I took the fucking thing; I was stupid. I drove all the way out here and did remarkably well, if you ask me, but for some reason he kept making fun of my driving. You should know that it's an incredibly undermining thing to do and it just makes matters worse. So there I am, driving what is essentially a straight line out here, and the way he is teasing me reminds me of you . . . and not a part of you that I love and admire. It made me nervous. Very nervous. So when we left their house—which is an amazing place and I can't wait to get my hands on it—he just walked to the driver's side and said he just wanted to drive to the restaurant." Leslie rubbed Auggie behind the ears and swallowed. "I'm really sorry."

"Thank you. So what did he do to the car?" I asked.

"Well, we went to lunch and in the parking lot he backed into a space not realizing he'd backed the end up over a tree root. When he went to straighten out the car, the bumper was caught on the root and it yanked the fender and the tailpipe right off."

I didn't say anything. I couldn't.

"I know you're mad and you should be. If it was my car I'd be mad, too."

"I keep thinking that my mom always said an accident's an accident because it wasn't meant to happen." I kissed her hand. "I think we'll let this go, but if there's more damage to the car that this mechanic didn't see . . ."

"François said he'll make good. And he will. He was terribly upset about it, not at all the asshole you want to make him out to be. Listen, he's paid for the car, for my rental while I'm here, for this hotel room, for anything I needed to buy while I was here, and, if there is a problem in the future, I can always add it into the decorating costs. He's a very nice, extremely wealthy man who doesn't count pennies. And now he is officially my client."

"So, you got the job just like that?"

"Just like that."

"Well that's nice. But one last thing before we abandon this conversation altogether; why didn't you ask him to leave so you and I could talk?"

"We were in the middle of a business meeting." She pushed her black hair our of her eyes and looked at me as if I had horns. "The man was leaving for France the next day and we were going to take advantage of this impromptu meeting so that by the time they return, they'll have something to return to and not an empty house. I told you I'd call you back, but you were such a jerk." She said this as though a truer word were never spoken. I considered this and decided that perhaps I hadn't been altogether fair.

I shrugged. "So, you wanna kiss and make up?"

"Sure, why not." She moved toward me, but I gently pushed her onto her back and lay on my side next to her.

She held up a finger. "You should know that I'll be spending a lot of time out here as soon as I talk with his wife next week and she signs off on stuff."

"That's pretty amazing, don't you think? I mean you've only been doing this, what? Three years?" When we first met, Leslie was doing a decorating job for her first client— her mother.

"But I'm good." With that, she pulled me out and kissed me. "Really good."

"Don't I know it." I was tempted to replay the morning activities, but knew I had to hit the road. "So what will you do with the rest of your day?" I asked as I rolled away from her and off the bed.

"I guess I'll move these things over to Courtney's. I think I'll stay out here a day or two longer so I can meet with the dealers and contractors, get an idea of the costs out here as opposed to the city. And then I promised Auggie a walk on the beach."

At the mention of the word *beach*, Auggie cocked her head, her black lips pulled back up into a smile, and she started crying happily.

"Is she amazing, or what?" I asked, holding my hands out to the puppy. "This little one understands English." She bounced over the bed and ran right into my hands.

"You sound like you're getting attached to her, Sydney."

We spent the next fifteen minutes saying good-bye and negotiating Auggie's housing arrangements.

As I drove off in the bubble car, waving good-bye to Leslie and Auggie, I decided that my bargaining skills needed improving. I was, however, headed back to the city and would be there before six. With any luck Max and I could compare notes, get to the bottom of things, and set Selma Onderdonk's mind at rest once and for all.

Twenty-four

By the time I dropped off the car it was 5:30 and both Max and Kerry were at the office. I felt as if I'd been gone twelve days rather than twelve hours, give or take a few.

"Where's the puppy?" Kerry stood up excitedly as soon as I walked in. She peered over her desk and scanned the floor for Auggie.

"I left her with Leslie."

"In the Hamptons?" she practically screeched.

"Yes," I said calmly as I considered her half-eaten tuna salad and tomato on a roll. "You look nice, Ker." I admired her ensemble as I took a bite of her lunch. She was in black tights, an oversized shirt depicting what had to be a bad psychedelic trip, huge white plastic earrings, and a necklace that I assumed was made of Ping Pong balls.

"Really?" She sounded surprised. She had piled her wonderful hair high on her head and touched the back of it with her hand.

"Seriously. You look very retro." I asked if she was going to finish her sandwich and then claimed it before she could actually answer. There are no rules when one has an empty stomach. "Max in?" I asked as I headed into my office. Kerry followed and I saw that to complete her outfit she wore bright, orange shoes with two-inch soles that in some cultures might have doubled as furniture.

"Yeah, he's in his office. We've been very busy today." She slapped a stack of messages onto my desk.

Max came in, went directly to the sofa, and flopped down. "You're back sooner than I expected. Where's Auggie?"

"Vacationing on the East End with her new best friend."

"Ah ha! Leslie took a shine, did she?" He hiked his feet onto the coffee table and stretched out. "Do I detect a hint of jealousy?"

"No. What you detect is the fear of being stuck with a full-time pet." This was said with a tone that also implied, "A lot you know, Mr. Detective."

He shook his head smugly and crossed his arms over his chest. "You can lie to yourself, kid, but you can't lie to old Max. You want this puppy and you want to be her top banana, her alpha dog, her big biscuit."

"Well, more than the puppy, I want to find out who killed Jessica Callahan. I know for a certainty it wasn't Michael."

"You found him." Max clicked the toes of his boots together. "Good. Tell us what happened."

Kerry and Max listened as I told them about my trip to Montauk, from arrival to departure, omitting only my time spent with Leslie.

"Wow. That's totally cool. Patrick is working on a mixed-media piece that combines nuns, sex, and Groucho Marx," Kerry said, referring to her artist boyfriend. "Isn't that a coincidence?"

"Really rad, man." Max said.

"Far out, like wow," I concurred.

"Oh fuck off, both of you." Kerry's regal posture made her curse sound like a blessing.

"What did you two come up with?" I asked looking, from one to the other.

"Well, I wasted my time. I traced Mary Grace out to Long Island, but that effort matters about as much as the forty-three hotels I called this morning, looking for Callahan." Kerry said, examining her iridescent green manicure.

"I'm still waiting for a call from Sue at the ME's office regarding Robert Sherman's autopsy. Milt Brown, the physical therapist that Callahan was friendly with? He said he told the police everything he knows but that, between me and him, he thinks Callahan is guilty." Kerry's eyes grew wide. "I fell for it for a minute, too. Not long, but long enough to get pissed when he started laughing. So, it doesn't matter anyway, my work was bullshit, right?"

"Absolutely not," I assured her. "It's all part of the process, you know that."

"Right, look at what I went through today." Max commiserated. "I spent five hours in the filing room at the Treelane and came up empty-handed."

"Were you able to bring back any files with you?" I asked, knowing that three pairs of eyes could cover a lot more area.

"No. Naomi was concerned that her head of security would hit the roof if he found out that I took anything."

"What about tonight? Can we go there?"

Max looked blank. "I don't know. I have a meeting with the managing director at the Madeline Hotel to try and resolve things there. I thought I'd make one last-ditch effort to remedy things with them."

"Excellent." I picked up the phone and as I dialed Naomi's work number, I told Max, "That the Madeline is willing to talk to you in person is a good sign. But I don't have plans for tonight and if it's after hours, chances are that security at the Treelane is just a skeleton staff."

Naomi was there and suggested that we have dinner together and then return to the Treelane, when we could be certain that Von Striker, the head of security, had gone home. I agreed to pick her up at eight o'clock.

"So." I turned back to Max after hanging up. "You didn't get any useful information today?"

"In October of last year, three new people were hired. A dietitian, a physical therapist, and a nurse's aide. No one was fired. One person left for maternity leave. I didn't see

271

any deaths related *to* residents, but one resident—an old guy—died of complications after hernia surgery."

"That's it?"

"That's a lot, given the bulk of information and the time limitation."

"How much insulin was taken?" I asked.

"I don't know. That should be something Naomi can tell you." He refolded the paper and added, "Have you met her head of security yet?"

"Von Striker? No, why?" I glanced through my stack of phone messages.

Max whirled his finger next to his temple. "This is a clear-cut example of a small man who got a little power and it stopped up his brain."

"She said he was a bit much."

"My Uncle Jim is like that," Kerry said. "When he was a bartender, he was the sweetest guy in the world. Then boom, he got an education, went nuts, and now the whole family hates him."

"Why?" Max shifted in his seat and put his head at one end of the sofa and his feet at the other.

"Because he became a lawyer and started suing everyone in the family." Her eyes grew wider as she addressed our skepticism. "It's true, I swear. He even tried to sue my folks once, claiming that after a Thanksgiving dinner at our house he got food poisoning. Personally, I think he's really crazy. Like certifiable."

"Well, this Von Striker's a mental case. We passed him in the hallway and Naomi introduced us." Max tucked his arms under his head and looked quite comfy.

"Don't they have to do some sort of background check on you?" Kerry asked.

"Personnel does, but not security. Anyway, despite his protests, I was put to work today."

"Can you imagine him doing filing?" Kerry poked her thumb in Max's direction. "That must be why you're so exhausted, you did some real work for a change."

"I am a master filer, I'll have you know. Anyway"—he stretched and yawned—"I had only about an hour total to poke into the old October files, otherwise I spent most of the day working with this very nice gal from Brooklyn who's been there for years."

"There's a lot of filing to do there?" I asked, separating my phone messages into three stacks: URGENT, LATER, and WHENEVER.

"Yeah, lots, and they're really backed up. Look, you have a hundred and fifty people needing medical attention every day, and all of that information has to be stored."

"You'd think they'd use computers." The URGENT message pile included calls from Minnie, Enoch Zarlin, and a prospective new client. LATER comprised my sister Nora, three operatives, two clients, and a masseuse I indulge in once a week. Three other messages fell into the WHENEVER pile.

"You busy tonight?" I asked Kerry, hoping she would be able to help me sift through the files at the Treelane.

"Sorry, boss. Patrick and I are going to an opening of a friend's show." She glanced at her watch. "As a matter of fact I was hoping to leave a little early so I could get ready."

Kerry left and Max and I scrambled to finish up last-minute calls and such before taking off for our respective meetings.

In my notebook I found the number Marcy had given me for the Brooklyn precinct handling the investigation. Patrolman Minor wasn't in, but Detective Jake Stavinsky was. As we had talked before, he remembered who I was. I decided that Callahan and Mary Grace could go to the police in their own good time, but I wanted to double-check what the police had found with regard to the three exits.

"As I told you, Miss Sloane, our investigation is only supporting the case against your client." Jake reiterated that the only fingerprints found belonged to the doctor and his wife, and that except for the sliders, all the doors had been securely locked. I didn't know if he was so forthright because he felt so sure of himself with regard to Michael's guilt, or because he was just a generally easygoing guy with nothing to hide from an outside source. When I asked him about the back sliding door, the one they had found open, we discussed the possibility of someone having escaped from the six-foot-walled yard. "It was a definite possibility," he agreed. "But I had my men all over that place and they couldn't find a shred of evidence that anyone other than the dog had been back there. It's purely speculation because the husband won't talk, but given the age of the puppy and the lack of waste in the house, we're assuming that the deceased had left the sliding door open so the dog could do it's business outside."

I thanked Detective Stavinsky for his help and saw that I still had time to make it to Brooklyn Heights before my dinner date with Naomi.

Max and I left the office together, with him headed over to the East Side, promising to leave a message on my machine and let me know what happened at the Madeline. I hopped on the subway and got off in Brooklyn Heights, where I paid an unexpected visit to Rosalynn Hayes-Porter. Her house was swarming with toddlers celebrating her daughter's birthday, so she gave me the keys to the Callahan residence without resistance. Having spoken to Detective Stavinsky I wanted to see the garage again, wanted to see if there was something we were all missing. I let myself in through the house and entered the garage from the door in the kitchen. It was locked securely. The mechanical garage door was also locked securely, and the final door was—as Michael had said—like the door into the house, locking from the inside and out. I walked the circumference of the space several times, not knowing what I was looking for, but everything seemed to be compulsively in order. The doors were locked. Tools were hung in their proper place. Everything had its place and nothing was amiss. There was even a nail by the door leading to the street where a key would normally hang.

I arrived at the Treelane a few minutes early for my meeting and decided to stop in on Selma and see how she was. The residents of her floor were crammed in the dining room for Bingo. I watched from the doorway. Six round tables were crammed into a space just a hair too small. At each table there were five to seven people seated, in chairs or wheelchairs, their cards and chips in front of them. I spotted Selma easily. Beside her sat a bent and arthritic woman, chatting away while Selma rested her fingertips on the edge of the table and nodded silently. I could just see her as a six-year-old waiting patiently for Mom to put dinner on the table. A staff of five went around the room helping the players, while a sixth staff member called out the moves. It was as if the room were filled with kids at a birthday party, and I was an adult interloper. As I stood there, I wondered what it would have been like had my parents lived into old age. I decided that Mom and Dad would have joined a retirement residence where golf and group activities are encouraged (though neither of them ever golfed). They would have had no need for a nursing home. They would have lived active lives and died easily in their sleep.

A frail old woman with skeletal features caught me staring from the doorway. She winked at me, and suddenly, instead of an adult interloper, I felt like the kid caught spying on the adults when I should have been in bed.

Twenty-five

After dinner with Naomi, we went back to a very quiet Treelane. Visiting hours were over and most of the residents had retired to watch television, read, or sleep. Naomi showed me into the windowless filing room, which was beige, with fluorescent overhead lights that look like upside-down ice cube trays. She showed me my starting point, a cabinet in the far corner of the room with files over a year old. The compulsive who headed this part of Treelane's operations deserved a medal. Everything was in order, everything was filed in a way that made sense. I knew that Naomi had to get home to a daughter with flu symptoms, so I shooed her out of there and settled down to work.

When she left, it was ten-fifteen. I stuck with it until near twelve, when I had to stretch my legs. My pincushion behind alternately itched and hurt, and I felt a walk would take my mind off that area.

To explain my presence, Naomi had told her evening security team that I was an old friend and would be in one of the rooms studying for a final at school. The hallway lights had been dimmed and there wasn't a sound on the main floor, where the administration—and filing—offices were situated, behind reception. I knew there was a juice machine on the resident floors, so I assumed there was one on the main floor for the workers. I went in search of an apple juice to wet my whistle, and found the machine in a kitchenette area in the back of the building. I lost two dollars in it before I decided to venture onto a resident floor, as my thirst intensified. This meant, however, braving the world's slowest elevator, as there was, evidently, an alarm system attached to each stairwell door.

I followed the hallway to the only bank of elevators at the front of the building. Thick double doors with smudged, diamond-shaped windows separated the entrance from the back of the building. The windows reminded me of swinging kitchen doors in a restaurant, but they also came in handy. In a restaurant, the purpose of the windows is to see if someone is on the other side and, ergo, prevent collision. In my case, I was glad I looked. Though the lights had been dimmed in the hallway, the reception area was altogether dark. Only the light from the street and a red EXIT sign above the doorway illuminated the area, which was more than enough for me to see the two figures at the front door conducting some sort of transaction.

At first I thought one of the guards had ordered in food, but when he held up a ring in the light for the other person to examine, I knew something wasn't kosher. The second man took the ring and held it as if trying to determine its worth by its weight. This didn't bode well. He then tossed the ring into his other hand, reached into his back pocket, pulled out a wad of bills, peeled off a few, gave them to the guard, pocketed the ring. A few more words were passed between them—none of which I could hear—and then the second man was on his way.

When the guard turned around, all I could see for certain was that his head was way too small for his shoulders. My guess was his suit was about two sizes too big.

I contemplated joining him, as security was aware that I was in the building, but I was curious to see what he would do if he thought he was alone.

He first went to what I assumed was a video camera mounted to a wall, stepped onto a chair positioned just under it, and, with a tool from his pocket, fidgeted with something in the back of the camera and then hopped off the chair. He then shuffled to the elevator, where he happily counted his money as he waited for the sluggish mechanical doors to open.

I waited what felt like a day and a half to see which floor he had gone to. Three. The smell of mothballs and antiseptic in the elevator hadn't faded with the night and I held my breath as the elevator crawled up to the third floor. Naomi had told the guards that I was working in the building, so my presence wouldn't seem so startling if I ran into the guard, but I was hoping to find out whose ring he had been paid for. After all, it might have been his own.

Sure. He had come to work and decided to call the local pawn shop merchant, who just happened to make house calls in the middle of the night.

When I got off the elevator I stood stone-still and listened carefully. Mechanical humming was coming from somewhere in a nearby room. I expect it was either my juice machine or some gizmo meant to keep blood or medicine flowing into frail veins. I turned left and started down the hallway, which seemed almost surreal in the dimmed light. At the end of the hall the nurse's station was brighter, but not by much. I tried to keep myself to the dark edges as I walked the corridor, looking for the little guard. I would have expected any nursing home to be quiet at that hour, but the Treelane was surprisingly noisy. Between the moans, groans, snoring, and a loud nocturnal emission of flatulence from room 368, the place was practically deafening.

As I neared the nurses' station, I saw the guard leaning on the counter, having an animated discussion with a nurse. He moved like a stick figure, four fluid lines branching out from the main stem. Together, he and the nurse were a study in contrasts. She was composed of circles, from her broad belly to her oval bosom to her round cheeks. She patted the counter with her rounded hand, said something to the guard, nodded, and then motioned away from where I stood.

As she waddled down the hall, he moved behind the counter and sat down, leaving only the top of his head visible from my vantage point. He sat there for several seconds, facing the direction the nurse had gone, and then his head alternately disappeared and popped up again, his neck craning in one direction, then the other, as if he were waiting for something. I inched closer to get a better look.

Then, tucked in amid all the other sounds on the floor, was a very distinct jingle of keys. The guard moved like a flash, springing up from his seat, swiveling in all directions to make sure the coast was clear, and finally darting into an area behind the counter, where he was completely out of sight.

I moved quickly toward the station, secure in the feeling that this kid was up to no good. I was surprised that there was no one else behind the nurses' station, but then again it was the graveyard shift, and I didn't know how many people were actually on duty.

I got behind the nurses' counter and walked through the doorway of a small room behind it just in time to see the guard spin around from a cabinet and shove his hand into his jacket pocket. I scared the hell out of the poor guy and I was amazed he didn't let out a scream. Good control.

"Hi," I said, blocking the doorway.

"Who the hell are you?" He spat out his words defensively, and I knew this kid felt trapped, which of course he was.

"Ms. Lewis introduced us before," I said affably. "Don't you remember?"

He paused and I could see him recover, but only slightly. "Oh, right. Well you're not supposed to be here." He brushed his fingers in the air as if he could shoo me away.

"What are you doing?" I asked, not about to budge from my spot.

279

He rolled his shoulders and furrowed his dark brows. "'Scuse me?"

"I said what are you doing?" I nodded to the medicine cabinet behind him.

His upper body moved like electricity, and I knew this young man was one hell of a dancer.

"I don't think that's any of your business. Look, you're not even supposed to be back here, lady. So, let's just move it out. Let's go. Let's go." He started toward me, his eyes shooting nervously behind me and his hands outstretched, directing me away as he approached.

With my hands on the door frame at shoulder level, I planted myself firmly in place. He and I were about eye to eye, which put him at close to five feet, seven inches tall. He clearly weighed less than me but he was also a good twenty years my junior, and—I assumed from the way he moved—in excellent shape under his oversized guard jacket. His hands were small, but a fist is a fist is a fist.

"What would Mr. Von Striker say?" I baited him.

His jaw twitched as he ordered me again to leave. Little devil's advocate, I simply smiled and shook my head no. This didn't sit well.

He shoved his palms at me and caught me hard in the shoulders, but I was able to hold my ground. "I told you to move, lady, now move it." His voice cracked. Up close it was plain to see that he was a quite handsome Latino, no more than twenty-five years old, in a shitload of trouble, and he knew it. He dug his teeth into his lower lip and pressed so hard that the skin around it turned completely white.

"What's in your pocket?" I nodded to his jacket.

He reached out to grab me by the shoulders but I ducked and stepped behind him, placing myself in the middle of the small room. This movement did not make any part of my body feel good; not my scraped elbow or knee, not my shin with the bump, not my backside with the splinters . . . nothing.

He swung around in a crouch, his hands ready for a fight. He was also smiling. "You want to fight, bitch, I'll fight."

Fighting was, of course, the last thing that I wanted, especially given my physical state. It was more than yin and yang, more than youth versus age. It boiled down to the fact that I could probably guarantee that this young man did not have 488 splinter holes healing in his backside, and I did.

"I don't want to fight with you," I said. "I just want to know what you have in your pocket. Or, perhaps, who owned the ring you just sold downstairs? Either piece of information will make me happy." I gave what I thought was a winning smile. However, this last little jibe landed hard and it showed. I was very much aware of the exact moment when my young opponent snapped. It was at that precise moment when his right fist came hurling at my face.

I hate violence. I don't like football, roller derby, or beauty pageants for that very reason, and I find violence directed at me particularly distasteful. I dodged his fist, sidestepped to his right, braced myself against a counter, and kicked him about hip-level as hard as I could, trying to get him off balance.

He was faster than I would have imagined and caught my right foot in his hand, yanked and twisted simultaneously, and pulled me off the counter. I hit the tiled floor like a ton of bricks, but managed to miss banging my head. Controlling pain and focusing it into energy is something they teach you in the martial arts, and in moments like this I always wish I had formal training in that discipline, but I don't. The pain that resulted from my already sore bottom smacking the hard floor was enough to bring tears to my eyes. But it was also enough to make me so angry that I fought back like a tiger, instinctively combining my skills as a boxer and as an instructor of model mugging, a form of self-defense in which one uses one's feet and legs for protection.

In a flash, our simple confrontation escalated into a barroom brawl that rolled us out of the anteroom, into the nurses' station, over the counter and into the hallway. This kid was mad and I was just the one he was going to take it out on. For my part, it really bugged me that this little snot-head thought he could get away with stealing from old people. It was obvious between punches, kicks, pulls, and tumbles that the two of us were exhausted, but neither of us was willing to give up. I was vaguely aware of other bodies around us, voices, and occasionally someone pulling at either me or him, but it was as if we were possessed. At one point I was gliding through the hallway, picking up speed, moving effortlessly through time and space, before I realized that I had fallen onto a wheelchair and he was steering me—high speed—right into a wall. I grabbed the arms of the chair and with all my might twisted the damned thing as hard as I could, swerving the chair onto its side with me in it, as the little guard went soaring overhead.

I lay there on the cold tiled floor in the doorway of a resident's room and saw the guard coming back at me over the side of the disabled wheelchair, reminding me of the cowboy and Indian games we used to play as kids. I was about to be scalped and I just didn't care.

He pulled me up by the collar with his left hand and his right fist was pulled way back over his shoulder. I knew it was headed directly into my face, when an old, veined, knobby hand holding a cane reached out from behind me and walloped the guard's head with several solid hits. I fell back and looked up at my savior, an old lady with practically no hair, no teeth, and no clothes. I shut my eyes and took a deep breath. Saved by a naked octogenarian. Why, this would certainly make me stand out among my peers. How many private investigators did I know could boast of such a thing? Not many. Not many at all.

Twenty-six

Naomi paced back and forth, her hands clenched tightly behind her back, her heels clicking sharply against the tiled floor. The small room, though crowded, was still. I followed Naomi with my right eye as I pressed an ice pack to the left side of my face. Security chief Glenn Von Striker, who had been called in for this, had left the office only moments earlier and Naomi was fuming.

I tried to look around the room without moving my head. Across from me sat my little guard, whose name, I had learned, was Miguel Leigh. He sat low in his seat like a kid waiting for the principal to give a detention verdict. I was glad to see that I wasn't the only one who had been roughed up during our exchange. He had several cuts and bruises, a Band-Aid on his head—which I knew I couldn't take credit for—and his right hand was resting in a bowl of ice water.

Next to him sat the round nurse I had seen earlier, and standing beside her was a beautiful Jamaican woman with the kindest face I have ever seen. Her name was Maudlin and she, too, was a nurse. She had explained repeatedly to Naomi and Von Striker that when the fight had broken out, she had been in with a resident and hadn't seen a thing. Von Striker found this difficult to believe. She had shrugged when he intimated that she was playing stupid. Maudlin was also the one who had tended to our various injuries, supplying ice, aspirin, and bandages, which irritated Von Striker to the point that he began sputtering and finally left the room.

I knew that next to me there were two other guards, both as young as Miguel, but not nearly as cute. Without turning to look, however, I could see only one pair of shoes, black high-top sneakers, that were twitching like crazy.

Naomi continued pacing in her little office, making it a point not to look anyone directly in the eye. After several minutes of this she finally stopped, perched on the front of her desk, and asked everyone except Miguel and me to please leave.

The round nurse shot Miguel a sympathetic look before closing the door behind her. A green sweater swung on the back of the door, its buttons scraping against the wood as it swayed back and forth. The only other sound in the room was the water and ice in the bowl with Miguel's hand, which reminded me that I had never gotten my juice and was still parched.

Naomi took a deep breath and let out an enormous sigh, promptly followed by a yawn. Despite the fact that she had been awakened from—no doubt—a deep sleep to come down here in the middle of the night, she looked pretty damned good. Gone was the business suit, replaced with a loose pair of drawstring pants and an oversized workshirt. I glanced at my watch. It was nearing one-thirty.

When she finally spoke it was with tired, almost parental resignation. "Do you have any idea what you two have done?"

Miguel and I looked at each other blankly, then back at Naomi.

She rubbed the bridge of her nose. "Miguel, I like you. I always have. If your family was having trouble, why didn't you come to me?" She paused. "Do you have any idea how you've screwed things up for yourself? Especially if Glenn has his way?" She shook her head, pushed off from the desk, walked behind it, and sat, maintaining a distance between herself and us.

Miguel looked appropriately ashamed while I considered grabbing his bowl and drinking the contents.

Naomi interrupted this fantasy with her own home-grown reality. "And you." She motioned to me. "What the hell is wrong with you? You call this *circumspect*?" She raised her voice for the first time, paused, and tried to control her anger. "You ought to be ashamed of yourself. This can't be professional behavior. You can't just walk into a nursing home and scare the hell out of everyone in the middle of the night and think you're doing a good, professional job. If I run out of digitoxin tonight it's your fault."

"I didn't plan this," I muttered lamely, my only defense.

"Oh please." She put out a dismissive hand and I felt about three inches tall. "Fortunately no one was hurt tonight except the three of us—"

"You were hurt, Mrs. L.?" Miguel looked genuinely concerned as he pulled his swollen hand out of the ice and patted it on his pants.

"What do you think, Miguel?" She gave him a cold look that had to have hurt. "I thought you and I had a rapport, I thought we could be honest with each other, that we were friends, that we could trust each other. But no. I find out that you're not only stealing *money* from the residents, but now you've started taking what few *possessions* they have left. Did it ever occur to you that the ring you stole from Mrs. Shim had belonged to her mother, and that it was the very last tangible thing she had to remember her by?" Naomi held her hand out in front of her, a painfully empty vessel. "That hurts me, Miguel." She snapped her hand into a fist. "On all sorts of levels. I hurt for Mrs. Shim and her loss. I hurt for your need to do this. I hurt because you betrayed not only the residents here, but me and yourself. I hurt because I still believe in you and I'm going to do whatever I can to see that Glenn doesn't have you arrested, but—and this is a big *but*, my friend—I hurt because you've blown it for the next kid who comes into my office off the street looking to make it 'honest in the real world.' "

I tried to will myself to be invisible. Naomi had tears in her eyes and Miguel was crying. I held my breath and directed my eyes to the floor. I could only imagine what was in store for me.

"The ring was the first thing I ever took, I swear," he mumbled as he wiped his cheek with the back of his uninjured hand.

"And the money?" she said harshly.

"Well, yeah, the money, but the ring tonight was the first time I ever took like, you know, some *thing*. But I can get it back. All I have to do is make a call." He leaned forward and pointed to the phone on her desk.

Just at that moment there was a single rap at the door as it simultaneously snapped open. Glenn Von Striker stepped into the room. Here was a man without humor, a man who had probably been bleak and dark since childhood. His face was a series of hard, straight lines, and I wondered if he had any idea what a belly laugh felt like.

"Naomi, I'm ready to interview the boy now." He was like a soldier forbidden to slouch or make eye contact.

Naomi glanced at Miguel and nodded once. "Miguel, wait outside for Mr. Von Striker, would you, please?"

Miguel slid out of his seat and touched his fingertips to Naomi's desk. "I'm real sorry I hurt you, Mrs. L. You're a good lady." He ignored Von Striker's cynical snort and went out into the hallway.

Von Striker turned to follow Miguel but Naomi stopped him. "Glenn, he's not a bad kid."

"Tell me you believe that crap about his family." He addressed Naomi, but glanced contemptuously down at me.

She seemed impervious to his disdain. "He said he can get Mrs. Shim's ring back, and I want him to make that call. I want him to return her ring personally by morning."

"Yes, well, that's a very Christian way of handling the

286

situation, but first I need to ask him a few questions.''

"I would also prefer that this doesn't go to the police.'' She was perfectly composed.

"Forgive me, ma'am, but if you had your way I'd be rewarding the little bastard with a cookie right about now.''

"Mr. Von Striker, let's get something clear so there's no mistake from this point on. In your position as head of security, you answer to me. Any differences we have can and will be taken to the board, but until then, I am your superior and you will do as I say. Now, I want to get to the bottom of this just as much as you do, but I see no need to play judge and jury in one fell swoop. It is my opinion that Miguel made a serious mistake and that he knows it. He's not a bad kid. If we handle this properly it will make an enormous difference in his life—''

Von Striker interrupted her. "I'd say incarceration or not is a big difference in a scumbag's life. The boy is a thief, plain and simple, Mrs. Lewis. And it's my job, as head of security, to see that the residents and staff of this facility are safe. This is life, not a movie where some dirtbag sees the path he's on and changes with the help of a kindly Samaritan. Kids like Miguel don't fall through the cracks; they ooze, and there's not a chance in hell that your big heart is going to make a flea shit's difference in his life. Now clearly we have a different way of approaching our jobs and, as far as I can tell''—he glanced at me—"your methodology leaves a lot to be desired. I appreciate the fact that you like this kid, but I can't promise that he won't be arrested for his illegal activity. First, I need to ascertain exactly how much he has stolen from the residents. Based on what I learn I will make a decision. It may not reflect what you want, but naturally, as you are my *superior*, I will keep you apprised of the situation.'' Without waiting for her response, Von Striker left the room, closing the door sharply behind him. The sweater hanging on the back of the door swung so hard it fell off the hook and onto the floor.

When I went to retrieve the sweater for Naomi, a key fell from its pocket and bounced on the floor. I slipped the key back in the pocket and hung the cardigan on the hook. This gave her a second or two of limited privacy. Pragmatically, I sat astride a very wide fence, finding merit in both Naomi and Von Striker's arguments. However, from the smug look on Von Striker's face when he left, he clearly thought that he had just publicly humiliated Naomi. The fact is their headbutting only made me respect my friend even more; having to put up with Von Striker's hostility day in and day out couldn't be a pleasant experience.

When I turned around she was staring straight up at me. Her eyes were hard and dark.

"Are you okay?" I asked.

She continued staring at me.

"Naomi, say something." I stood by the door, preferring to face her straight on.

"What should I say, Sydney?" Her voice was cold and flat.

"What are you feeling?" It was a place to start.

"How could you have let this happen?" she asked, not changing her tone of voice.

"Naomi, I observed the boy fencing a ring. I followed him and when I caught up with him, his hand was in the medicine cabinet. I was hired to find out who murdered one—or possibly even more—people associated with the Treelane. In the course of the investigation I learned that the medication used in the most recent killing *might* have been stolen from your supply. Naturally when I found this young security guard in the medicine cabinet, I asked what he was doing. He panicked and started swinging. I had to defend myself. I didn't *let* anything happen."

I didn't like feeling as if I had to defend myself to my friend, yet at the same time I knew that were I in her position, I would be demanding the same explanation. I pressed on without her prompting. "I know that Von Striker isn't aware of the possible connection between Miguel and Jessica Callahan, but we need to question Miguel about it tonight.''

Naomi's brows inched from a furrow into a wide arch. ''You're not suggesting that Miguel killed Jessica, are you?''

''Absolutely. It's a possibility that can't be overlooked.''

''Oh for Christ sake, you can't be serious.'' She slammed an open palm on her desk.

''What is with you?'' I asked, quickly abandoning whatever guilt I had started to accrue. ''I hate to agree with Von Shithead, but the fact is, the kid *is* a thief. He's stolen money, jewelry, and medicine.''

''He didn't steal any medicine. Eve said he could get some aspirin out.''

''And that doesn't concern you?''

''Of course it concerns me!''

''How do you know he only took aspirin? How do you know that in the past he hasn't helped himself to more?''

''What would a kid like that want with Digitoxin or insulin? Use your head.'' Naomi tapped her forehead with her fingertips.

I let the air between us settle before I moved forward. I was calm when I said, ''Chances are you're right, this kid got caught his first time out on the wrong path, but the fact is, he has to be asked these questions in order to exhaust his possible connection to Callahan. Either we ask him or the police will.''

Naomi rested her elbows on her desk and clasped her hands. She then pressed her mouth against her doubled fist and looked at me as if I were a total stranger.

Finally she said, ''You really think that's necessary?''

''I do.''

She shook her head. ''Fine.'' She sighed.

''I'll be able to question him tonight?''

She looked at me with utter disbelief. ''No, Sydney. I honestly think you've done enough damage tonight. I'll talk to him, privately.''

"Naomi—" I started to protest, but she held up her hand and shut her eyes.

"Sydney, I'm sorry I ever confided in you in the first place. But I did, and so I have to accept the responsibility for that action. I do not, however, have to do things your way. This is my job, my problem, and I'll handle it as I see fit. And for starters, you should know that you're banned from the Treelane." She broke eye contact and pretended to look at some paper on her desk.

"Excuse me?"

She paused before looking up again. "I have the welfare of over a hundred people here to think about. I can't worry that you're going to come in here and cause chaos." She leaned back in her chair and crossed her legs, obviously comfortable with her decision. She continued. "So, go do what you have to do and conduct your investigation, but if it brings you back to the Treelane, I suggest you have a warrant or a police escort, or whatever, because you won't be allowed past the front desk without it."

"You can't be serious." I smiled uncomfortably.

"Why? Because we're friends?" When I didn't answer she hurried on. "This isn't about friendship, Sydney. This is about doing a job I normally do well . . ."

"This is about murder, Naomi." My voice was surprisingly high-pitched. "You're right, friendship has nothing to do with it."

"I am perfectly aware that Jessica Callahan died—was murdered—and that she was somehow connected to the Treelane. I am also aware that there has been, in the past, some medication missing from here as well. I don't know that the two are connected, and I certainly don't believe for one minute that Miguel Leigh killed Jessica Callahan, but you have my word that I will check into it and I will let you know exactly what happens. Now if you don't mind, I have more important things than you to deal with right now." She stood up and motioned to the door.

Four thousand retorts and questions flew through my

mind simultaneously, but all I could do was stand there, stunned. Maybe Naomi was right. Maybe I could have handled Miguel in a way that would have avoided a fight, avoided bringing Von Striker into the fray, avoided the grief that was piling up on her doorstep.

But I hadn't. It was after two and she had a long night ahead of her. I left without another word. By three o'clock I was trying to sleep, tossing and turning in bed as best as I could, considering that I now had several more bruises to add to my list of physical complaints. More bruises and a very heavy heart.

Twenty-seven

If I got more than forty minutes worth of solid sleep, it was a lot. Either I was lying on some body part that hurt, or I was thinking about Naomi—having found her after all these years, only to lose her again.

When I finally rolled out of bed I was cranky, depressed, and hungry. Without Leslie's arms in which to find solace, I did the next best thing; I went directly to the kitchen. Here my rummage through the refrigerator unveiled cooked new potatoes, peppers, onions, eggs, cheddar cheese, pickled jalapeño peppers, bialys, fresh thyme, limp chives, and butter—sweet, fresh butter. Coffee first, a strong pot, stronger than usual as I chopped, diced, whisked, and toasted my way into a breakfast befitting a woman preparing to eat her way into old age.

I decided to put the rest of the world on hold as I ate breakfast and took my time reading the *Times*.

By the time I got through the news, I was feeling less agitated. I took the latest *Vanity* magazine with me to read while I brushed my teeth. The game plan was to shower, go to the club and swim, and then deal with work. But first, I needed to chill.

Glancing at the clothing ads I noticed that none of the featured puppies—for there were at least a dozen dogs in various ads—none of them were half as cute as Auggie. That was it. Maybe we could get her to model, make a fortune off the dog and never work again. There was a thought. Never again to deal with a goofy operative who puts the business at risk, never to kiss the buttocks of corporate clients, never to need another tube of Arnica to help heal bruises, never to run the risk of losing an old friend . . . and for what? I still didn't know. Green, green was going to be the new color of the season. I brushed my teeth vigorously as I studied the new fashions, fashions I simply couldn't grasp. The styles seemed to alternate between the *oh too totally cool you have to be fifteen to wear this* to *who would want to wear this dull dull schemata*? Even the Gap was losing my interest. Where were the days when the Gap was reasonably priced and had clothes for everyone? Now, though the jeans and tee-shirts were still safe, the women's sweaters were . . .

Sweaters. Sweaters. Sweaters. I tossed the magazine on the floor as I started running water for the shower. Sweaters. It was as if something was scratching at the back of my brain to be let in. Sweaters. Sweaters. It felt as if I had walked into a room with a purpose and drawn a complete blank upon entry.

I stepped into the shower and let the warm water wash over my body like a salve. I tried to point my mind in other directions, but I kept coming back to the sweater in the ad. Something about it had triggered a memory, but I just couldn't access it. My mother? No. Aprons and culottes reminded me of my mother, not sweaters. A favorite childhood sweater? No. My dad? No, he hated sweaters, said they all made him itch, even through his shirts. Minnie? No. Caryn? No, but I should call Caryn about her upcoming visit. My brother, David? No. Nora? No, my sister only wears angora sweaters or monogrammed numbers. I reached for the baby oil and it hit me like a boulder dropping on Wile E. Coyote. The sweater, of course. I quickly smeared the baby oil on my legs and arms, rinsed it off, and shut off the water.

Why had Naomi reacted the way she had the night before? I understand being protective of her "chickens," but the fact is, she was the one who had alerted me to a possible connection between the Treelane and Jessica Callahan's death. She was the one to open the can of worms in the first place and then got mad at me because I took the lid off. Why was she protecting Miguel? Clearly the kid was a thief, and yet she put herself on the line to see that Von Striker went easy with him. Were they in cahoots? But why? How? What on earth could Naomi gain by murdering the resident's relations?

I put on baggy pants, cowboy boots, and an extra-large pullover sweater, and raked a comb through my hair. Though I had had short hair for the last two years, I was still adjusting to the ease of it all. As I applied makeup and perfume, I called Hannah Miller's Long Island house in an attempt to track down Michael Callahan. Much to my surprise, he was still there. With Hannah. Go figure. After an abbreviated call with him about his garage I shoved my Cubs baseball cap into a leather knapsack along with my gun, wallet, keys and Walkman, and hurried to the subway. It was 9:00, and though Naomi had had a late night, I felt confident she would already be at the Treelane.

The subway was busy, but, unlike me, everyone on board seemed to be in good spirits.

The receptionist with the four-tiered hairdo was off that morning, so I sailed past the new receptionist with a big smile and a wave, mumbling that I was going up to see Naomi.

Naomi's door was wide open. When I stepped over the threshold, she looked up and sputtered. I closed the door behind me and didn't give her a chance to object to my presence.

"Morning, Nai, looks like it was a long night for you."

"What the hell are you doing here?" There were dark circles under her eyes and as she hadn't changed, I assumed she hadn't yet been home.

"What am I doing here?" I slipped her sweater off the

back of the door and tossed it onto her desk. "You tell me what I'm doing here."

"Irritating me," she said without missing a beat. She picked up the sweater and tossed it back at me. "Put that back up there." She motioned to the door.

"Very smooth, Naomi. Even I'm impressed. But now that I know, tell me why."

"What are you talking about? Tell you why what?"

"Why did you kill Jessica Callahan?"

Naomi stared at me wide-eyed for several seconds before bellowing with laughter. This was disconcerting, to say the least, but I pulled up a visitor's chair and eased into it, knowing that the laughter—probably a result of exhaustion more than anything else—would die soon.

"I'm glad you find this amusing," I said when she was winding down.

"I don't find this amusing. I find it absurd. Totally absurd. Almost as absurd as your thinking Miguel was responsible for her death."

"I never said he was responsible, I simply said he needed to be asked a few questions."

"Which he was. He had nothing to do with Ms. Callahan and he gave Mrs. Shim her ring back."

"Well isn't that nice?"

"I thought so. He's also offered to make restitution for everything he's taken."

"Which is?"

"All totaled, about two hundred dollars, give or take. You have to understand, he's a special boy, and the residents here love him, so when they heard he was in trouble, they told Von Striker and me that they would refuse to press charges. The sad thing is Eve, the nurse who gave him the keys to the medicine cabinet. She'll be ousted for this. It was a stupid thing to do.

"Little did the chickens know, but Ms. Big was sitting in the background killing their children and grandchildren." She leveled a look at me that was absolutely sobering. "Tell me why you think I killed Jessica Callahan."

I slid the key out of the cardigan pocket and held it up. "I think you know what door this unlocks."

She stared at me.

"But let's go back, shall we? First of all, you had access to the drugs, and access to the victim."

"Okay. Why did I kill her?" She crossed her arms over her chest.

I studied her face. It was the one question I couldn't answer. The whole ride down on the subway I had considered motive and drawn a blank. I decided to toss out a few loose straws. "Blackmail? She knew something you wanted to keep private? Jealousy? There could be a million and one motives," I said coolly. "But has anyone asked you where you were at the time of her death? A plausible scenario is that you met her here, she drove you to her home, and you struggled in her garage."

"And the key?"

"The key let you out of the Callahan garage. I just got off the phone with Michael Callahan. A nail by the door in his garage is without a key. That key."

"Is that so? How do you know that?"

From my wallet I pulled out the little heart-shaped bronze button I had found in the Callahan garage several days before. I then held up the sweater, matched the buttons, looked for the space where one button was missing, found it, and looked at Naomi as if to say, "I rest my case."

Naomi deflated, and at that instant, my heart felt as if it had shattered. I had been hoping that my old friend would tell me I was wrong, prove that she couldn't possibly have been responsible for Jessica Callahan's death. The thought of Naomi killing anyone was inconceivable, but the burden of proof was before us like the sweater in my hand.

Naomi covered her face with her hands. There was no more laughter. No more questions. I felt my stomach start to knot.

"Why?" I asked softly.

When Naomi finally moved her hands, her face was streaked with tears. She covered her mouth with one hand and shook her head.

I got up, pulled a tissue from the box, and handed it to her. She took it and I placed the sweater on the desk while I leaned down to hold my friend. The wall that had been erected between us from the night before was gone. What remained was the trust and love that time had not sullied. Whatever reasons Naomi had for her actions, she was my friend and I would support her. I let go of her, perched on the desk beside her, and said, "Nai, I'm behind you, no matter what."

A gentle tapping at the door made Naomi blow her nose and take a deep breath. The second knock was louder. I handed Naomi another few tissues and she said, "Come in," loud enough for the visitor to hear through the closed door.

When the door opened Beatrice Carson, my genteel, bright-eyed escort from the other day, stood in the threshold of the doorway and said politely, "I hope I'm not interrupting anything."

Naomi pressed her lips together and shook her head. "No, Bea, not a thing. Why don't you come in? And close the door behind you, would you, please?"

Beatrice did as she was asked. Watching her move, I realized that she reminded me of Minnie, slight in stature, but energetic and vivacious, friendly and warm. I imagined the two of them would get along quite nicely.

"Oh good," Beatrice said as she walked into the room. She reached past the potted plants and papers and lifted the sweater off the desk. "I've been looking all over for that. I'm so glad you found it."

Twenty-eight

When Beatrice Carson confessed in Naomi's little office on that early Friday morning, it felt as if the world had stopped. When she finished I gulped for air like a diver lifted from the sea in a nick of time. Were it not for the streaks of blue mascara washing down Naomi's face, she would have been stark, stark white, her face reflecting the pain that, I too, felt keenly, both for Beatrice and for her final victim—Jessica Callahan—her "mistake," as she put it.

Beatrice was, as it turned out, the geriatric avenger. Not a caped crusader, but a career military nurse well-versed in both common and uncommon poisons. From her account, her death tally registered four; the first taking place in Missouri, the second in Nevada and the last two in New York. She chose as her victims people who had abandoned either a parent or a grandparent to a nursing home, and simply forgot about them.

"Old people become invisible in our society." She sighed. "Old people and especially old women. No one would have suspected me because no one sees me. You didn't, did you?" she had asked me. "It was a fluke, an accident that you found out I was responsible. No one should be invisible."

It had started four years earlier when she was in Missouri and her lifelong companion, Dorothy, had died, abandoned in a nursing home by her only surviving relative, a nephew named Ned, and it ended with Jessica Callahan, an innocent victim who never really knew what hit her. Beatrice had mistakenly believed that Jessica had abandoned Selma the same way Ned had deserted Dorothy and the others their parents. The drugs might have changed, but the scenarios were fairly routine. Beatrice would usually dilute chloral hydrate in a drink, knock out her victims, and then administer the fatal drug (in Ned's case, curare, and in Jessica's, insulin, which might not have caused death, but added to the carbon monoxide from the running car, it was more than sufficent).

"I'm glad you found out." She sighed. "It's been eating me up alive knowing that I'd made such a mistake with this Callahan girl. I was just . . . so . . . protective of Selma, I suppose. Maybe because Selma reminded me an awful lot of Dorothy. I sincerely believed that Jessica had dropped Selma off here and then left the next day."

"She did, but as I understand it, Selma insisted that Jessica take the job in California. Jessica didn't want to leave Selma here all by herself," I said.

Beatrice shrugged her birdlike shoulders. "I chose to listen at the wrong times," she said sadly.

This confused me. Naomi wiped her face and spoke for the first time. "Selma has little slips every now and then," she explained. "Like the other day with you, she slipped back into being a kid with her candy, right?"

I nodded.

"Same thing." Naomi inhaled. To an outsider Naomi might have sounded bored or tired, but I knew it was a deep, incomprehensible, breathless pain she was struggling with. I wanted to reach out a comforting hand to my friend, but found myself glued in place, perched cautiously on a corner of her desk.

Only Beatrice seemed calm as she sat patting her sweater, the evidence. "I'm sorry, Naomi," she said, sounding more like a grandmother than a serial killer. "Sincerely, I never thought a connection would be drawn between my acts and the Treelane, and especially you. I know what a bad position this places you in, dear, and I deeply regret that. I'm very fond of you.''

Naomi turned to me. "What do we do?"

Normally now would be a good time to call the police, I thought, but didn't voice it. I studied my hands and sighed. I did not want to be responsible for arresting a septuagenarian, but by the same token, four people were dead by her delicate hand. I could just picture her in her nineties deciding who should live and who should die, meting out the poison with arthritic, shaky hands, and then accidentally administering it to her dinner guests.

"There is only one thing to do," Beatrice said calmly and logically. "I must turn myself in." When she looked at Naomi, her face melted. "Oh please, dear, you have to realize that prison will be perfect for someone like me. Don't forget, I've spent most of my life in the military, with strict routine and some restrictions. Besides, it's time I was punished for what I've done." Beatrice stood abruptly and slipped her arms into the sweater. "Would it be all right if I went home first and made arrangements for my cat? She'll be lost without me."

I shared a look with Naomi. "I don't think you should go alone," I finally said, needing to clear my throat.

"Jesus Christ, Sydney, it's not like Bea is going to skip town," Naomi defended her elderly pal, not understanding that my concern had nothing to do with her leaving town, but rather leaving life.

Beatrice mumbled a sincere "Oh dear, skip town? No, no. I have no intention of doing that."

A pall of silence fell over the three of us. Naomi pushed back from her desk to get up, Beatrice buttoned up her sweater, and I debated whether to voice my concern. But, of course, I had to.

"I worry about the drugs you might still have at home,

300

Beatrice," I said directly to her, as if Naomi weren't in the room.

It was only a flash, but I saw in her eyes that I had hit the nail directly on the head.

"I'm worried about my cat," she said evenly.

"I'm sure you are. I'm worried about you."

"And I worry about *you*, Sydney, about what happened to your soul after all these years." Naomi pushed past me and slung her bag over her shoulder. "Come on, Bea, I'll help you with the cat."

Naomi stepped past Beatrice to the door and it was at that precise moment Beatrice and I shared a look that confirmed my fears. I had no doubt that while Beatrice and Naomi were tending to the cat in her apartment, Beatrice would slip into the bathroom and take whatever was necessary to end her life. And that pissed me off because it would be my friend Naomi who would have to deal with the aftermath.

"It's not fair to Naomi," was the last thing I said to Beatrice before she turned and moved past Naomi into the hallway.

Naomi's knuckles were white as she squeezed the doorknob. "I have a feeling we won't have much to say to each other in the future. Shut the door when you leave." Her face was hard and cold as she turned away from me, slipped a protective arm through Beatrice's, and proceeded to the elevator.

It wasn't until they were gone that I realized I was clutching the bronze button in my hand, clutching it so hard it had made an impression in my palm. I knew, as sure as I was standing there, that I had just let an old friend and an old lady sail right past me into the end of one life and an endless memory for the other. I tried to reason that we all make choices . . . Beatrice, Naomi . . . but the fact is, I could answer only for my own decision. I hadn't stopped them. I could have. I could have called the police and had her arrested. I could have probably done any number of things to prevent her from making that final trip home, but I didn't. I didn't, though I knew what the outcome would be. So am I any better than a Beatrice Carson who decides who should and should not live? Did I let them go thinking to myself that *I tried*, so I could absolve myself of my responsibility? Did it cross my mind that Beatrice's choice to die was probably better than spending her remaining years behind bars? Was it easier for me to stand back and say nothing? Did I really think for one minute that this wouldn't haunt me for the rest of my life?

Epilogue

It was Beatrice Carson's wish that she be cremated and buried beside her friend Dorothy, in Missouri. As there were no relatives to make the arrangements and see it through, Naomi and I made the trip together. At the cemetery, Naomi and I paid our last respects to a woman whose actions, and whose death, had an impact on my life that will reverberate forever. Beatrice Carson may have been a stranger to me, and she may have felt invisible, but she will never be forgotten. Naomi and I agreed that before running to the police in Missouri and turning Beatrice in as Ned's killer, we would check the status of that investigation.

With regard to nephew Ned, Beatrice Carson had literally gotten away with murder. Because Ned was a severe asthmatic, his death had been listed as natural. Curare, which she had used to kill him, affects the respiratory system. The family had not wanted an autopsy and had had his body cremated. Naomi and I decided that some things are best left undisturbed, and when we returned to New York, this secret was tucked away intact.

Leslie met us at the airport, in the Volvo, with Auggie in tow. Auggie has found her home. With us. When Leslie and pooch returned from Long Island two days after Beatrice died from an overdose of the Haldol she'd stolen a year earlier, I learned two very important things. First, there is nothing like the unconditional love you can get from a puppy, and, second, when a puppy becomes your shadow and dotes on you, as Auggie does me, all the objections of drool and dog hair fall by the wayside. It has been a minor bone of contention in our happy household that Auggie has chosen me, and not Leslie, as her alpha dog, but as always, Leslie is handling the situation with grace and maturity: She is threatening to get a Chihuahua.

Michael Callahan came to my office after my return from Missouri with the intention of making good his promise and reclaiming Auggie. She was dozing under my desk when he arrived, and though she greeted him with the same enthusiasm she shows everyone, there was no question that Auggie was now my dog. His relief was palpable.

During our short visit I learned that Michael was leaving his practice with Dr. Cyclops and planning to open his own office, perhaps out on the Island. He hoped that his future would include Mary Grace—who had left the church—but knew that there were obstacles, not the least of which was her brother Matt. From his candor, I assumed that Michael had few people with whom he could open up, expose himself. He spoke of his guilt, his fears, his hopes. When he mentioned Mary Grace, however, his whole demeanor changed, and I knew that they would be just fine.

When Michael came, he also brought a framed sketch that Jessica had done in California. It was a cartoon of Auggie shaking off a ton of sand on a bed with the words *My Sandbox* written below. I am still debating whether to hang it at home or in my office.

Selma was thrilled when she was told that Michael had been absolved of Jessica's murder, and when her brother, Enoch, asked if she wanted to know who was responsible, she held up her hand and said, "I know." Naturally, this took us both by surprise, and when Enoch asked, "Who?" Selma folded her hands in her lap and said, "God." I watched the elderly brother and sister, the kindness and love that defined their relationship. Enoch nodded slowly, mirrored his sister's posture, and said softly, "That's right, Sel. She's at peace."

When I left Enoch and Selma, I wandered the downtown streets for a while, feeling an emptiness I didn't understand. All the loose ends had been tied up, and—for whatever it was worth—now that the storm had passed, there could be calm. But it didn't make me feel any better. Out on the pier I realized that I was crying. Was I crying for Selma? For Beatrice? For all those lonely, abandoned, invisible people Beatrice wanted to champion? Or was I crying for myself? I missed my mom and dad, and was pissed that they weren't here to grow old, pissed that I'm growing old without them. And though my sister is alive and we have a good relationship, we don't have the intimacy that I had witnessed between Enoch and his sister, Selma. My brother, David, and I had never had a relationship, and now there was no chance. That day on the end of the pier I cried a little for everything, and when I was done, when there were no more tears, I realized that I had become invisible to the kids on Roller-blades, the couples strolling by hand in hand, the guys out to score some smoke or crack or sex.

Beatrice still resides in my head in a daily way. Further investigation into the lives she ended showed that Robert Sherman had been a victim of his father's abuse all his life, which was why he had never visited the now-frail old man. He paid for his father's care, but had no desire to see the man ever again. The female victim in Nevada had stolen her mother's life savings and then dumped her in the cheapest facility in Las Vegas, never once bothering to visit. Beatrice had used the stolen Digitoxin on Sherman. Posing as a potential client, she had spiked his coffee with the drug.

One good thing has come from all this. I have spoken with Sister Janet, and she has made arrangements to start busing city kids out there for overnight stays by the beach.

My car is, much to my surprise, looking and running like a charm. The Frenchman, out of either guilt or ostentation, had the mechanics take out two other dents that had been

305

there for years and also sprang for a complete tune-up. All of this happened just in time for Caryn's upcoming visit. She will not only see her old car in mint condition, but Leslie (not I), invited her to stay with us while she is here. Admittedly, this makes me just a bit uneasy, but then, what can go wrong? Here are two women I love most; either they'll hate each other or love each other. We are all assuming they will become fast friends, but Minnie has offered her guest room in case there's a glitch.

As I write this, I am waiting for Leslie to pick me up and sweep me off to a movie while Uncle Max puppy-sits. Auggie is warming my feet, a rainstorm is pounding the streets below, and Max is in his office, getting to know our new employee, Miguel Leigh, the security guard from the Treelane. Naomi had saved his butt from Von Striker and sent him over to us for new employment. It's going to be a stretch, I know, but the kid has guts, street smarts, strength, and he's dumb enough to be enthusiastic about this job.

"Hey there." Leslie opens the door to my office. She is wearing a black DKNY suit with only a bone-colored camisole peeking out from under the jacket. She looks both professional and sexy. Auggie opens a sleepy eye. Her eyelid must be attached to her tail because the second she cocks her eye, her tail starts wagging a mile a minute. Leslie's appearance, however, has the same effect on me. Auggie goes racing out from under the desk and charges Leslie.

"Oh *mon Dieu*, you look, 'ow do dey say? Superb." I kiss my fingertips and release it into the air. "Who was the lucky client?" I ask, leaning back and resting my heels on my desk. Auggie has been nabbed by Kerry in the outer office for a moment of deep and sincere affection.

"Mr. Frenchie's lovely wife, Mancini, is in from gay Paree." She uses a hard Midwestern accent and crosses the room in her spike heels that, despite being the most uncomfortable article of clothing ever invented, do do wonders for a gal's calves.

"No." I smile at her as she takes a seat on my desk facing me.

"Yes. And if I am not mistaken, Mrs. Frenchie is a member of the club." She pushes her dark hair out of her eyes and winks seductively.

"Really? Competition?" I ask, resting my chin on my hand, and clicking the toes of my sneakers together.

"I think she's more the dominatrix type." She runs a finger under the leg of my jeans.

I consider this for a fleeting moment before asking again, only this time in a perky, young, Sandra Dee kind of way, "Competition?"

Leslie shifts her position, lifting one leg over mine, and straddles my legs. "What do you think?"

"I think a movie is a very bad idea tonight."

"Yes?"

I study her Rosalind Russell legs, sheathed in black silk nylons and disappearing under her black, tight skirt. "Yes." I remove my feet from the desk and push my chair closer to the desk, closer to her.

"And what would you rather do?" She puts the tip of one foot on the edge of my chair between my legs. She then crosses her legs tight, never taking her magnificent blue eyes off me.

At that precise moment Auggie comes bounding in, her black lips curled up into a smile, joins our little tête-à-tête, and barks happily.

"Sydney!" Kerry calls out from the other room. "Are you *ever* going to housebreak that mutt!"

Knowing, as I do, that this is embarrassing for Auggie, I reprimand her gently. I then turn my attention back to Leslie. "Where were we?" I ask, knowing in the back of my mind that our lives have forever been altered by Auggie. Having a dog is like having a two-year-old. All spontaneity comes to a screeching halt.

"You were about to suggest something very intimate, and I was about to acquiesce."

And you know . . . she was absolutely right.

RANDYE LORDON is the author of three other Sydney Sloane mysteries, including the Shamus Award–nominee *Brotherly Love*, *Sister's Keeper*, and *Father Forgive Me*. She lives in Amagansett, New York.

Visit her website at *http://www.barkinfish.com/lordon/*.

The Joanna Brady Mysteries by
National Bestselling Author

An assassin's bullet shattered Joanna Brady's world,
leaving her policeman husband to die in the Arizona
desert. But the young widow fought back the only way
she knew how: by bringing the killers to justice . . . and
winning herself a job as Cochise County Sheriff.

DESERT HEAT
76545-4/$5.99 US/$7.99 Can

TOMBSTONE COURAGE
76546-2/$6.99 US/$8.99 Can

SHOOT/DON'T SHOOT
76548-9/$6.50 US/$8.50 Can

DEAD TO RIGHTS
72432-4/$6.99 US/$8.99 Can

*And the Newest Sheriff Joanna Brady Mystery
Available in Hardcover*

SKELETON CANYON